3-2-15

The
AUTHOR MURDERS

THE AUTHOR MURDERS

Eric Meeks

P.S. I Love Lucy
The Story of Lucille Ball in Palm Springs

Facts & Legends
of the Village of
Palm Springs

ERIC G. MEEKS

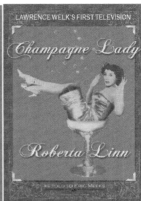

LAWRENCE WELK'S FIRST TELEVISION ...

Champagne Lady

Roberta Linn

AS TOLD TO ERIC MEEKS

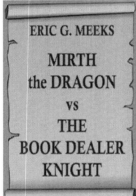

ERIC G. MEEKS

MIRTH
the DRAGON
VS
THE
BOOK DEALER
KNIGHT

Facts and Legends of the Village of Palm Springs

WITCH
of TAHQUITZ

A Historically
Novel Tale of
Western Horror

ERIC G. MEEKS

"The Indians aren't going to like this."
a prediction wishing to remain anonymous

Corporate Wars

APOLLO THORN

Jupiter's
Moons

ERIC G. MEEKS

VAMPIRE

ERIC G.
MEEKS

NIGHTMARE

SELLING
SPACE SHARES

A Short Story

ERIC G. MEEKS

A Brief History of
Copyright Law

Eric G. Meeks

Other Works by Eric G. Meeks

Fiction
The Author Murders
Witch of Tahquitz
Six Stories

Non-Fiction
Lawrence Welk's First Television Champagne Lady: Roberta Linn
Not Now Lord, I've Got Too Much to Do
The History of Copyright Law
Reversing Discrimination

99¢ Short Stories
Apollo Thorn: Moons of Jupiter: Corporate Wars
Mirth the Dragon vs the Book Dealer Knight
Vampire Nightmare
Selling Space Share

Edited by Eric G. Meeks
1853 Cavalry Quest for a Southwest Railroad Route

Websites
https://www.facebook.com/eric.g.meeks
http://ezinearticles.com/?expert=Eric_G._Meeks
http://www.flickr.com/photos/ericgmeeks/
http://www.youtube.com/user/meekseric?ob=0&feature=results_main

The First Xanthe Anthony Mystery

The

Author Murders

Eric G. Meeks

MeeksEric@hotmail.com

Horatio Limburger Oglethorpe, Publisher

The Author Murders
The First Xanthe Anthony Mystery
© 2012 by Horatio Limburger Oglethorpe, Publisher

ISBN-13: 978-1475200348
ISBN-10: 147520034X

Originally published as The Author Murders: A Palm springs Biblio-
Thriller by iUniverse © Copyright 2007

Because of the dynamic nature of the internet, any Web addresses or
links contained in this book may have changed since publication
and/or may no longer be valid.

Cover art by Wes Jenkins.

Printed in the United States of America

For my publisher Horatio,
Who continues to believe in me
again and again

Prologue

THE FIRST AUTHOR TO DIE RAISED NO CONCERNS. Why should it? One of the literati falling prey to a freak pirating incident off the coast of Puerto Vallarta; drinking too much, drifting after dark, alone with a female companion not his wife. There was little cause for alarm and an unspoken understanding amongst the - predominantly male - Mexican authorities. The scenario deduced plausible: a famous married man would not want to be seen in a public place on the off chance a paparazzi or the hired detective of a jealous wife could collect evidence of his adultery. He simply sailed into waters better off left to the privately chartered groups of fishermen or the large tour boats than to challenge them unescorted in such a luxury sailboat. It was an open invitation to the lesser breeds of humanity whose mottos are "Take from the Rich and Keep to Ourselves."

Still, it made headline evening news back home in the states, Well-known author Woodie Stuart found dead with female consort after pirates brutally attack. Film at Eleven.

The wife was the prime suspect, though she had her alibi. Apparently, she too had an affair going on while her husband cavorted around the world. She had been involved with a well to do car salesman in her home town of Walnut Creek, California. Getting caught at a lesser crime almost always negates the conviction of a more serious one. An interesting sidebar that filled the news for an additional two days and then the world moved on.

For a few weeks anyways, until a second author died...

This time it was a female science fiction writer. One who had originally made her mark in society by writing what was modestly called

I

Prologue

Lesbian Sci-Fi. Years ago, she'd busted onto the literary world with a breakout novel whose cover showed breast like white mountaintops behind a snowy wooded clearing in which Little Red Riding Hood embraced Cinderella with a wet lip lock. In the background stood an erect spaceship and nearer the fore a sword stuck out from the carcass of a dead wolf atop rocky ground. The critics called it a 'lightning strike' novel that illuminated all the heart strings of teenage disobedience while simultaneously fulminating America's dark desires. The authoress deservingly had the last name of Cheri.

Cheri had been asleep alone in her mid-west home one night when an intruder sneaked in and slit her throat. The house was left largely undisturbed although there were a few choice items missing, as detailed by Cheri's girlfriend, Desmona, who informed the police that several early First Editions of Cheri's work were gone - especially the ones with dust jackets. These had been in pristine condition and had the wonderful raw watercolor artwork marking Cheri's early career when she was still finding her voice and before she'd gone mainstream. In the year before her death, they'd been estimated at a value of $200-$700 each. Four books were missing in all.

The police were at a loss to figure out the killer. They could see who it wasn't though. It wasn't a local or anyone with close ties to the author. If it had been then the murderer wouldn't have broken a small pane of glass on the back door. The front door was known to be unlocked by everyone from the grocery boy at the local Food King to the water meter reader. Further proof the killer was an outsider included the fact that the dog, an older Irish setter, had been poisoned, although this little tidbit meant the killer had studied the house and been on the property just after dark. The poison had a slow reaction time of 2-3 hours. Still, no fingerprints, shoeprints, or other helpful clues meant the police put on a brave face for the TV crews, who surrounded the house like Santa Ana at the Alamo, but eventually the story petered out.

Except, that is, for one small time cable show which caught a side angle on the two authors deaths: the Internet Crime Division of Court TV came very close to solving the case.

Had they only known how close they'd came.

Prologue

Posthumously, it seemed the two deceased authors had an extremely good run on their collected works over the internet. Specifically on eBay, the internet auction giant, the author's early and signed works peaked with epic proportions of interest. Consumers were swept up in the frenetic tide following the news glut of the murders. People who heretofore had had little interest in the authors now looked upon their works as collectible - notoriety is a far crime from being notable and being notoriously killed is a moniker of infamy. Their untimely deaths thrust their popularity to the forefront of the literary psyche and the result was a spike in prices of their works. Titles which had only days before sold for less than $10 were now selling for $50. $50 books were now selling for hundreds and the exceptionally rare books were scaling higher or being bought off in illegal trade even by eBay standards, like when an auction item is yanked offline by a seller who has a private bidder willing to offer the sky.

Had the detectives in the Cheri case known of the Court TV segment perhaps they would have had a new avenue to follow up on. But the detectives were at a retirement party for a fellow officer and therefore missed the opportunity.

Had the Court TV crew known about Cheri's stolen First Editions they might have found them for sale online and had a real exclusive in solving the case? But the First Editions were withheld from the public as a holdback clue to identify the true killer from the crazies.

There was also an entirely other group of people who had many guesses as to the motivations behind the killings. But these were a loose association of private individuals; mom and pop retailers, and kooky scouts. These people were all book dealers in one form or another. In the year of these murders it was 1995 and their associations were sporadic, but – thanks to the efforts of such ibusinesses as eBay, Amazon and a handful of used book megasites - the world she was a changing.

The internet was changing people's lives, and nowhere was it happening as fast as it was in the book world. Had it been just a few years later the killer would have had a much lesser chance of carrying out his or her deviousness. But that year it just wasn't as tight knit communities as it would one day become.

III

This story began long ago; long before anyone suspected...

First boy, "Hey brother, welcome home, welcome to the house."

Second boy, "Are you my brother?"

First boy, "I am now. What have you got for me?"

Second boy, "What do you mean?"

First boy, "If you want to be a member of this family you have to be willing to help out and share whatever it is you have."

Second boy, "And if I do then you'll love me and let me stay?"

First boy, "Forever and ever."

Second boy, "That's what they said at my last home."

PART I

1
Donlagic Makes His Case

DONLAGIC WASN'T MY KIND OF COP. From the first time I met him he left a bad taste in my mouth. He'd been president of the Police Officers Association. The POA was the political edge of the Police Officers Union and they were backing a different horse. I was running for Palm Springs City Council and knew from the moment I'd met Sergeant Michael Donlagic that I wasn't his man and he wasn't mine. He was the kind of man who could look you in the face and tell you everything was fine while he had a friend burning down your house. I remember a year after the race and he was still two facing me. My dad and his best friend were doing dumpster dives at the back of City Hall and retrieved a document in Donlagic's handwriting. The note read, "Too young, socks don't match, better off not." It was circled with an unhappy face next to it. I never told Donlagic about the note. I didn't need to give him another excuse to lie to me again.

A little more than a year later, after my loss of the race was water under the bridge, and my enemies who'd won settled down to other issues, the Police Chief came to me and asked if I'd serve on an Advisory Committee to the Police Department. I wasn't sure if the Chief was sincere or if it was one of those 'Keep your friends close and your enemies closer' but I couldn't turn it down. I'd openly made bones about my feelings over how I thought things were run in the department and thanked the Chief for allowing me to participate in some way. That and my book business filled my time.

Jill, my assistant, rang me on my cell phone and told me,

"There's a Mr. Donlagic here to see you." and I wished I hadn't picked up. I was sitting at my desk in the backroom of a little bookstore in downtown Palm Springs, my little hideaway from the sun and the fun and the palm trees. I had let myself get distracted from what had grown to be my main focus in life; getting authors off their beaten tracks of Los Angeles, San Diego and San Francisco to come to my little hole in the wall and do some book signings. No easy task. After phone calling up the bibliomaniacal food chain of secretaries, assistants and wannabe's I'd circumnavigate myself to just the right person who could make a decision. And then, every time I eventually got the agent or publicist on the phone to hear my pitch they always asked the same question, "Who else have you had?" My sputtering did not inspire confidence and then they came back with the inevitable, "I'll check with the author and see what they can do." Then they'd politely ask for my number, or not, and never call back.

Today's distraction, which was interrupted by Jill's call about the visiting Donlagic, was trying to adequately describe a copy of Ellery Queens: The Misadventures of Sherlock Holmes, in my database for uploading onto the internet. I was having some problems. Not just because the software was a little new to me. The website, Abebooks.com, provided it for free but gave little tech support or advice on how to improve one's standing in the listings of the books, like when a consumer did a search for a specific title. So, I was left to my own means in trying to describe the book. I was not a total rookie in the art of bibliography but I was far from expert. The book was in rough shape to start with and I don't like to describe in the negative. It was a common joke amongst my employees and me that a description should read, "Chips and tears in the dust jacket, spine cocked, but in really really good shape." Only this one was worse. The cover was completely torn off the spine leaving the pages bound but bare to its glued and threaded binding. Printed by Little, Brown and Company in 1944, it was a plain brown cloth in all its unimpressiveness, but it had one big thing going for it. The two gentlemen who called themselves Ellery Queen had taken the time to sign it. And, as far as I knew, they weren't signing anymore. Death had its restrictions. Plus, it was a first edition. Although

2

you couldn't tell at first glance, there were no markings saying first edition, no numbered sequences to refer too, and no letterings on the back of the title page. Nope, for this one I had to defer to the experts, so I opened my Patricia and Allen Ahearn Guide to Modern Firsts, and looked up the title. The Guide to Modern Firsts is what's called a reference book in the trade. There are lots of them and you seldom need them. But when you do, they're worth the expensive price required to own them. In this case the book paid for its $65 dollar price tag in a single day. The Ahearns confirmed, The Misadventures of Ellery Queen, Little, Brown and Company, 1944, First Edition. Enough said. If Patricia and Allen Ahearn called it a first, then who was I to argue? Their suggested retail price was $500 but my copy of the guide was a few years old. Online there were other copies listed from $800 to $1500 but they were all in Very Good to Fine condition. I decided to set the book aside and talk my bookbinder about what it'd cost to refurbish the book, perhaps even in a fine leather. I made a few notes on a post it and stuck it on the front endpapers. Then I called Jill back and told her Donlagic could come visit.

I put up my defensive walls before he ever opened the door to the back room. When he walked in, I knew I'd made a mistake. I was ready to send him back where he came from like a man shot from cannon. He was thinner than I remembered and now he wore a Hawaiian print. In his uniform, a few years back, he was the spitting image of the cop who'd swallowed a donut factory. Now he was leaner, and probably meaner, his hair had more color than a man his age should still have and I thought he must have a hairdresser and not a barber. He came in with a smile and eyes sizing up the entire room in a quick sweep. I wasn't going to let his pretty face convince me to drop my guard. I was sure he still knew how to fight and he'd already beaten me once in the political arena. Mutual trust was thin.

"Hello, my friend," he smiled, spreading arms in his native Bosnian sign of welcome.

Hello, Mike," I said plainly. "I didn't recognize you without the uniform."

"You like, "he said standing up tall. "My wife says I'm a new man, years younger and a lot more fun."

"You two are still married, huh?" I leaned back in my chair and clasped my hands behind my head.

"Fuck you," he snarled.

"Nice to see you too. You should come back when the library runs out of books."

As if we hadn't just sparred with words, he continued, "There any money in these?" He looked at the stacks and shelves of unpacked merchandise as if they were garbage. And some of it was. There were lots of boxes from purchases I'd made months ago still in piles. Shelves not nice enough for the front room of the store were crammed full, upright and sideways with titles I had either just glanced at or not at all and then there were the free standing stacks of books on the floor so tall you were scared to nudge by them in case you should knock them over. The backroom was packed. Somewhere in the midst of this entire inventory I'd find the few gems that would make the large piles worth going through. It was one of the most fun things about the book business. You never knew where your next diamond was going to come from. It could be the next collection you bought, or an overlooked item from a collection you bought a year ago, or longer.

"There's some," I said, noticing a short pile of unpaid bills under a handful of books. "I'm no Rockefeller, but I'm not living on Top Ramen either. Besides it's not always about the money, you know. It's the glamour too."

"You always were a friggin joke," said Donlagic still trying to cool his head. "I mean joker. You think this Celebrity Bookstore will ever amount to anything?"

I didn't want to talk the book business with Michael Donlagic any more than I wanted to date him. "Sit down Mike and tell me what brings you to the land of literature." I cleared a wooden chair of its few items and he sat.

"Look at you," he said as if he had an invisible friend with him. "No time for small talk. Maybe I just came by to see how you are. Maybe I just came by to invite you on my show, Down Logic with Michael Donlagic. Hell, maybe I'll make another show about you and

4

call it, Collecting Shit with Xanthe Anthony."

I didn't know if he thought he was being cute or if he really was trying to be friends and I didn't really care, so I just stared back at him. The silence hung in the air as the two of us looked into each other's face, sitting in what is affectionately called The Avalanche Room. I hadn't forgotten all the reasons I didn't like Donlagic and he hadn't given me any excuses to start. The thinning hair, the lips that lied whenever they moved, the breath that still smelled of Winchell's - I remembered the final straw on the camel's back of my distaste for the bastard of bosnia. It was when he and a few fellow cops had been caught selling their detective badges online and squeaked out of the spotlight without even a reprimand. At the time, they argued the badges were their property and they could do whatever they wanted with them. No matter what anyone thought, if they were given it, they could sell it. No matter how unethical it sounded. The City Council had been elected with the help of Michael Donlagic and the POA. So, the Council supported them, took the heat from the gadflies who spoke out at public comments, and let the issue fade. A year later, I discovered a similar case where some Oscars were stolen and attempted to be sold. It was illegal because there is an attachment with an Oscar, even though it's personal property. You can only accept them with the condition they are never resold. Only inherited or gifted. But, the argument was 9 months old by then and I didn't want to revisit it.

"Honestly, we never seemed to be on the same side."

"Well, mostly we weren't," he said with the first tone of truth in his voice I'd heard yet. "There were just better pickings at the time. Besides, you have that funny name and that's no good for politics. But who knows, maybe we could work together now."

"On what?"

"A case," he said.

"I thought you retired and moved to the bright lights of Public Access television?" I made sure and let the sarcasm press every word.

"I don't need this shit," he said to his invisible friend and then turned to me. "You .... My shows so hot I got radio stations wanting to syndicate and the local TV stations want to run me on the weekends.

It's still just small time, but all the Rotary clubs, Kiwanis, and Chamber of Commerce's and the like invite me for chicken lunches and steak dinners and all I got to do is give them my opinion on what's happening in the local political scene. A few choice disclosures on old cases and they always invite me back and my ratings grow. Already my schedules so full that my private detective office is getting overlooked but a lot more people want to hire me there too. And that's where you come in Xanthey. I got a case about a book, a rare book, and when I was trying to think about who to pawn this one off on I thought of you. Did I catch your attention yet?"

I hated when he called me Xanthey, but fact was he had, caught my attention that is, although I wouldn't let him know it. Besides, it might still all be a load of crap. "You want me to work for you?"

"Freelance, 1099, consultant, call it what you like." He was leaning forward in his chair now. He thought he had something good. "You make your own hours and use that smart ass brain of yours."

Flattery, I thought. "I'm listening."

"Seems there was an auction on that Ebay sight you raved about at one time. Only this time it had a book on it. It was called "Stephens Dump Truck." I have me a rich client who wanted that book really bad. He's a collector for this Stephen character and apparently there aren't many copies of this book around, so when he saw it at auction he put in a high bid. Only the seller pulled it offline before the auction finished and my client felt cheated. He tried to contact the seller but got no response. He tried talking to eBay but they didn't want to give him the time of day. That's when he came to me and that's why I'm coming to you. This case needs your expertise. You know all about these online book sales and auctions. I thought maybe you'd have the know how to track this thing down. All you have to do is figure out where this book is and put me in touch with the owner and I'll pay you $4,000."

$4,000 was nothing to look away from but working with or for Donlagic was still unappealing. "Tell me more about this book, but don't even start talking until you're willing to pay me $5,000.

Donlagic didn't move for about twenty seconds. When he did, he reached into his shirt pocket and pulled out a pack of Lucky Strikes and matches. He lit his cigarette and waved the match in the air before tossing it on my cement floor. The match flame seemed to dance in front of my books like a stripper enticing conventioneers. "The author of this book was some guy named Stephen Queen or Stephen Duke. Hold on a second I got it right here." He reached into his shirt pocket again and produced a slip of paper. "Stephen Knightly. I think he writes scary books."

"Horror to be exact," I injected. "Yeah, I've heard of him. I'm surprised you haven't. He's only been the biggest thing in books in the last thirty years."

"I knew you were the man for this," he said ignoring my remark.

"But I don't remember him writing anything called Stephens Dump Truck."

"My note says he wrote it in 1969."

"That'd put him in high school or college at the time," I said grabbing my chin and looking at the ceiling.

"Really," Donlagic said as if I'd just given him a pearl. "You see. You will be good on this one Xanthey. I'll tell you what, if you solve this one and like it. Maybe you'll think about coming to work for me full-time. These internet cases are in growing demand. I could use a smart kid like you."

"Right," I replied in my most matter of fact tone. "Tell you what, I'll check into this Dump Truck thing and let you know, but you gotta give me some start-up money. Sometimes there's an expense in checking things out and I don't want to be on the short end of a stick. If this even takes me a couple days work I'm gonna want a thousand dollars just to find out what I can. If I solve it you owe me the whole wad." I was giving him a break he didn't deserve but for some reason I still had my ethics, even if he'd lost his.

He reached into his shirt pocket a third time and tossed me a credit card with his name on it and the American Airlines logo. He'd at least acquire air miles on my expense. He was a smart shopper.

"There's a thousand dollars available on that card," said Donlagic. "You can use it for expenses and draw a little off for yourself at

ATM's. The code is simple 1-2-3-4. I want you to check back with me in a week though, or sooner if you find the answers before. We'll even up at that time."

He got up, dropped his cigarette and squished it into the floor. He left without another word.

Great, I thought. I'd just been played and now I was taking orders from one of my most distrustful acquaintances.

2
Stephen's Dump Truck

I STUFFED DONLAGIC'S NOTE INTO my own shirt pocket and continued on with my duties as proprietor; paying a few of those bills under the short stack, the small ones anyways. I made a call to a publisher to order another two months supply of paperbacks and took a second look at the software for describing books. There was an archaic form of description used to determine a books size. It designated things like a Quarto, meaning a large book and an Octavo, which meant a standard sized book. To think there was a time I used phrases like big book and small book. The book world was one where a little knowledge only gained your interest and then you were in for a lifetime of learning which would always seem as if you were only seeing the tip of the iceberg. And you probably were. No one knew it all and if they tried to tell you they did, they probably only had the grasp of a small segment of a certain subject and the rest of the time they faked it.

It was while I was thinking of other people's specialties that I remembered one of my own favorites. It happened to be Stephen Knightly. As a child, I had started reading his short stories. At the time, it made me feel good to get away from grammar school books centering on fast cars and ponies. In Knightly's stories the pony could run amok and cars were possessed. Nothing like the books I found in my one room Elementary school library. Once, when we were on a family summer trip and I was reading in the back of my parent's car, I scared myself so bad I never forgot. It is still in my memory. It was a short story in his anthology Dark Stint. The story focused on a small Maine town, as a lot of his books do, that had an old church built on top of an ancient burial ground and the demons would come up and try and suck any wandering person into their depths. I don't remember it all, but I do remember how I got so scared that even with my brother and sister in the back seat next to me, and even with Mom and Dad only a foot away in the front seat, I had to put the book down and take a breather, look at the sunshine and convince myself it was only a story. It wasn't easy. I had to do it twice, but eventually I got through the rest of Elohim's Grace. The realism Knightly delivered in that story made me a fan of his for life and ever since, I have been reading his work along with any news articles that pop up on him from time to time.

Pulling the slip of paper from my pocket, I read it again. Stephen's Dump Truck. I didn't remember any book called Stephen's Dump Truck.

What I did remember was his first book was Charlotte, printed in the mid-seventies, a thin novel about a telekinetic girl who gets revenge on some sociable bullies at her high school prom after they make her the butt of a horrible joke. She killed them all and they deserved it. End of story.

His second book was a vampire novel and his third was about ghosts in a big hotel driving the caretaker to kill his family.

The final book marking Knightly's early career was The End, an epic saga whereby the world as we know it comes to its end by unleashing a deadly virus through the inefficiencies of the government, resulting in a showdown of good versus evil in the desert between Las Vegas and Denver. Typical to the Knightly narration, magic plays a significant role in the book combined with technology. Many of Knightly's most well-known characters are in the book in one form or another. This was his landmark novel that set him on the path of becoming the literary giant he so deserved.

Still, with all this in mind, I had no recollection of Stephen's Dump Truck. So I did as I usually do and turned to the computer on my desk. It was an IBM Aptiva, the latest model. I'd bought it at Circuit City by asking the sales clerk, "What's the biggest computer you have in the store." I wasn't sure if my budget would match my desire but in this case I was lucky. The IBM's 400 megahertz processor and six giga-byte memory was available for only $3499 and it came with a large 13 inch color monitor that was only as big as a microwave. I loved it - sleek black and all the bells and whistles; Active desktop, built in phone modem, 80 megabytes of Ram, the works. It was online in just under four minutes with the warm greeting, "You've got mail."

I popped the words Stephen Knightly into the search engine and brought up a page of listings:

Books by Stephen Knightly at Amazon.com

Wanda's Stephen Knightly Fansite   The Official Stephen Knightly Website

Stephen Knightly Official Website

Berts Books

Naughty Knightly Women

Biography.com/Stephen Knightly

StephenKnightlyTrivia.com

We Love Stephen Knightly

Stephen Knightly's Library of Horror

And there were 484 other pages of similar sites. The top ten would be a curious lot if I were not already familiar with the intricacies of the internet. The fact that Amazon pulled the number one spot was no surprise. They either paid a premium to come up first to all the search engines or they could afford the best webmasters to optimize their standings.

Seeing a fan site appear in the number two spot was another natural online. Obviously a fan with way too much time on her hands had learned how to make a website in an effort to attract other horror maniacs so they could get together and live vicariously through the lands and characters of Knighthood. She probably put his name so many times on the web pages and had enough links to other Knightly fan sites that there was no way an indexing spider could give her a lesser position in the rankings.

Seeing two Official websites was another normal happenstance. Most likely, one would be another fan site pretending to be the official and the other would actually be the official one.

Berts Books would be a lucky bookstore who listed a few of Knightly's works on their homepage and the rest of the list I'd just have to click on.

I tried Wanda's Stephen Knightly Fan site first. Its homepage was full of dark colors; red, black, grey and creepy images like a haunted house, bats and skeletons. It read: Stephen Knightly the King of Horror in large letters across the top and greeted me with ghoulish organ music. A nice touch. Down the left hand side was a column of links: Stephen Knightly the Man, Stephen Knightly History, Stephen Knightly Works, Stephen Knightly Characters, Vote For Best Stephen Knightly Story, Stephen Knightly Photos, etc. There were 12 links in all. Her second place listing was confirmed. At least until someone created a page with thirteen.

I clicked on Stephen Knightly the Man. A minute later I was reading fan dribble - America's foremost King of Horror, author of 36 novels and short stories collections, we want to read his mind, oh what a joy to read him, yada yada yada, we love him. The column of links remained on the left so I clicked on Stephen Knightly History. This page was a little more interesting.

Knightly was born in 1947 in Portland Maine. He sold his first stories, which he ran off on a mimeograph, to other kids during elementary school for 5 cents. He graduated from high school in 1966 and then went on to the University of Maine, where he wrote a weekly column for the school paper. He would often submit articles to magazines and created a rejection nail on the wall of his home as a sort of landmark to collect his return letters and this inspired him to write more. His first sales were short stories to men's magazines like Adam, Playboy, and Hustler. In 1971, he married his college sweetheart, Samantha, who he'd met in a poetry club. In 1973, it was the sale of the paperback rights to his first book which allowed him to quit his day job and become a full-time writer. Confirming the message of the sale took a day longer than it otherwise might have because at the time he couldn't afford to keep his phone activated.

All good facts, but, still nothing about Stephen's Dump Truck. I clicked on Stephen Knightly's Work on the left and skimmed the titles.

The Author Murders

No luck. I tried both of the official sites and found they were both just another couple of fan sites that were far superior in layout to Wandas. Go figure.

I looked at the slip of paper again: Stephen's Dump Truck. What could it be? Perhaps something not ordinarily found. One of his magazine articles? Something that was turned down? No that'd be ridiculous. Once you're as big as Knightly anything you've ever written is published, bought and sold. So what could it be?

I typed www.eBay.com into the address box of my web browser and waited two minutes for the page to load. In the eBay search engine I typed Stephens Dump Truck and waited for the list of items. The page came back - No Items Found. I went to the search page and chose More Search Options. Chose Completed Auctions and typed Stephens Dump Truck again. Still No Items Found.

I looked at the slip of paper Donlagic had given me a third time and thought. I knew how the search engines worked. Even a small difference like a simple misspelling would eliminate an item from being turned up in a search, but I had to believe that anyone who wanted to auction off a rarity like this would have taken the extra minute to make sure his spelling was correct. Still, I tried some variations - Stephens Dump. Nothing. Stephens Truck - 36 Listings. Most of which were toy Tonka trucks owned by little boys who thought they were now collectible. One was actually Darin Stephens Truck, a Ford F-150, owned by the actor who had guest starred on the 1970's show Bewitched. Funny, his name was spelled Stevens in the show credits. Still no cigar. So, then I thought, just on the off chance that Donlagic had made a mistake, I tried Knightlys Truck. Nothing. The typo thought recurred in my rock filled head and I typed Stephen's Truck and this is what came up:

A simple apostrophe had done the trick. I read the page and thought about its contents. There was a lot to absorb and my afternoon was slipping away.

13

Item # 1305076
RARE STEPHEN KNIGHTLY BOOK Stephen's Dump Truck 1st

	Books: Antiquarian & Collectible: First Editions: Non-Fiction		
Current bid	US $17648.00 (Reserve not met)	Starting bid	US $1.00
Quantity	1	# of bids	54 Bid history
Time left	Auction Closed	Location	Shreveport, Louisiana
Started	May-28-95 11:28:57 PDT	Ended	May-31-95 21:37:22 PDT

Seller (rating)   CrandallPhlag11265 (-036) (Read all reviews)

View seller's other items   Ask seller a question

High bidder   FloridaDr49@aol.com

Description
The RAREST STEPHEN KNIGHTLY BOOK in existence. This is a compilation of Knightly articles that have never before been seen. It is a First Edition because it is the ONLY edition. If you have to ask what it's about then you probably don't deserve this. The 8-1/2x11 pages are reproductions of the original articles finely bound in red leather with gold gilt scrollwork to the cover and ribbed binding. Marbled end-papers decorate the front and back. The book was hand bound in the late 1980's and I prefer not to sell it but alas times force me to commit this heinous act. My loss is your gain. If you win this you will be the Stephen Knightly admirer holding the Holy Grail of Knightly memorabilia.

On May-31-95 at 21:29:43 PDT, seller added the following information
I apologize to all the Knightly fans out there who have shown an interest in this item. I no longer am in the dire straits I was and therefore will not be selling this item.

x
Image no longer available

43261 *Number of hits*

With work still to do and a dinner appointment for the evening, I printed out the page for future reference and went to Amazon. Using its search engine for books, I punched Stephen Knightly into the title slot and found a few biographies. There were two I thought might help my search. I still didn't know exactly what Stephen's Dump Truck was and I needed help. The Stephen Knightly Story: A literary Profile by Barry Green and The Shorter Works of Stephen Knightly by Collin Michaels. Neither of which I would probably ever want to read for pleasure, but they could serve a dual purpose of helping me solve this case and going onto my burgeoning shelf of reference books. I jotted down a few quick notes and then opened a second browser window, went to Abebooks.com and bought the two books. They were considerably less in price since I could get them direct from the dealers.

Death of an Author

TODAY HIS NAME WAS CLYDE BARSTOW. These days, he always had a new identity when performing the duties of his job.

And, his job was collecting books: first editions, early works, unique printings, and the rarer the better. He'd save them up, collecting them over weeks, months and years, and then when the opportunity came along he'd get them autographed to increase their value. At first that was enough, the mere autographing on the title page by a best-selling author to drive up the value. A simple stroke of a pen by the hand of a bard upon his work, turning the book into something more like a paper brick of gold to be traded amongst dealers and collectors as if its possession somehow transformed the bearer into a likeness of its creator.

But then one day, the man who called himself Clyde Barstow discovered an even greater method of increasing the value of the books he collected. He found that if the author died the significance of the autographed item increased demonstrably. Originally, this was a chance occurrence. But after that initial happenstance of luck, he devised a method to ensure his own fortune as a book dealer. Now, he went to book signings of famous authors and after getting his books signed, he killed the author. After his first investment, he even made a game of it whereby he'd assume a name similar to the author he was going to kill. Today he was Clyde Barstow.

His namesake was a famous horror writer who had penned more than twenty books. Clyde's favorite was Magicka, but The Devils Cube had been a good short one that made an even better movie. He had others too: The Damned Nation, Tapestry Planet and The Crook

15

of Never. All great works, all worthy of the fame heaped upon their composer. He'd watched and read in envy as this writer climbed the best seller lists in the last twenty years.

Clyde always wanted to be a writer himself. Even gaining some notoriety in his own hometown with some local magazine articles, but never achieving the national spotlight, never successfully accomplishing what it is all writers crave - a real breakthrough novel. One that actually made the publishers return phone calls. One that made the agents scramble for his signature on a contract. But that dream never came true.

What did come true was a failed first marriage, a bankrupt business venture (his first bookstore), and a drunken night of debauchery ending in a first class felony hit and run, complete with a police escort to the pokey when he was finally caught. The worst night of his life. The low point. Rock bottom. Or at least, his first Rock Bottom. If you live long enough, you can hit Rock Bottom over and over and over.

After that, or should we say, after the court case, the plea bargain, community service, a divorce, and the closing of the store, the man who today called himself Clyde Barstow began to rebuild his life in a better way. He began to actually have some good luck.

The Internet was growing up and while his store had closed down, he retained most of the merchandise. Albeit stacked in boxes on the back porch of his bug infested apartment, they were still his best chance for income without going out and becoming a laborer. Plus, as he listed them online they actually sold and at a premium. Collectors around the globe were becoming fascinated with this new marketplace of websites and internet auction houses. The income was good and it allowed Clyde Barstow to rebuild his life.

When he listed his first autographed book, the price it drew was worthy of note, so he listed more. But soon, he ran low of good stock and needed more signed books. So, he started going to book signings around Southern California, in the Los Angeles area.

In the meantime he'd met another woman, Tracey. After their courtship had culminated in a second marriage she'd confided in him that she'd thought him a liar at first. What with his grandiose tales of

The Author Murders

being an internet book dealer, bent on getting his book 'Atlas' published (A story using Greek mythical heroes and the land of Atlantis as the causation of the Flood via a nuclear holocaust), she'd thought him just another semi-drunk male who wanted to get into her pants. That's why she'd evaded him after letting him buy her a drink and then chewing on her ear. When he went to get a pen, she'd slipped out. He returned to find his dance partners chair empty. But a month later she was available still and went to see if this book dealer was for real. When she saw him in his blue jeans and cowboy boots, making deals by the minute and handling a wad of cash, her libido kicked in and she formally entered his life.

She'd been the real reason he'd achieved so much at first. It was her faith that inspired him to be a better man. All fine and well until the checkbook began to run dry. What worked for a while became a barren river bed and even Tracey jumped ship when it ran aground. A two time loser has to look extra hard to keep his spirits up.

We owe, we owe, so off to work we go. Today he was going to work as Clyde Barstow..

It was nearly a two hour drive to the bookstore where the author would be signing, a big fancy privately owned independent bookstore in Pasadena. The last of its kind. The book world seemed dominated by major chains these days, making it hard for the little guy to earn a living. But for those with the motivation there was always a way.   Clyde knew the way. The way got him to the store 3 hours early. He wanted to make sure his car would be in a premium spot. Easy in. Easy out. The first spot nearest the exit so there wouldn't be any problem leaving in a hurry. He was familiar with book signings at this store because he'd been here often for signings in the past. Some of his favorites had come to this store; Dean Koontz, Mary Higgins Clark, Robert Parker and lots of others. His prize signing though came the time he convinced Lawrence Block to sign 53 books. That was a real haul.

Tonight he had thirteen books to get signed. There was usually a limit to the number you could get signed at one time. Three was the normal max. So, it would take several times through the line to get them

17

all autographed. No problem. All part of the job.

He wandered some of the nearby stores and bought another three books. Then he roamed around the store where the signing was to happen. He always thought it good practice to buy a few of the author's newest book at the store holding the signing. Kind of a way of paying homage to the people who put on the event. Plus it made the author more agreeable if you had a stack of his newest book, rather than just older titles. Tonight's book was Malabat. A funky name. The book didn't even look that interesting. It was just a bunch of childish poetry with a few pencil drawings thrown in for measure. Malabat was a lead character in one of the longer poems and probably recurring throughout the book. But what did it matter, Ma and Pa Kettle, or little Jimmy or Sally Mid-west who was going to buy this book was more interested in having the authors signature than what the book was about. Truth be known, the people who lived in parts of the world where authors didn't roam were always star struck by the thought of running into their favorite writer. To the man who tonight called himself Clyde Barstow it was all part of the job.

Now with a total of nineteen books and an hour and a half until show time, he placed himself in line. There were already a few people ahead. He'd be about twentieth from the front but that was good placement. The first person was easily remembered and given a difficult time. Further down the line the fans were given more flexibility as to how many books could be signed. Plus, their faces were just a blur to the author and staff. By the twentieth person, everyone was just a blur of thank you's, questions, and adoration. By the time the author sat down to sign there was over two hundred people in line.

Clyde saw the author and his assistant walk in through the front door. A spot on the street had been reserved with a city barricade so the author could access the store with ease. After a quick parade of royal waves to the line, the author sat and motioned the first people forward. The assistant, a young neatly dressed gal in her early twenties, helped the fans open their books to the correct page. As the authors first stroke caressed the title page, in what is known as the sweet spot, a thrill rippled down the line. The time had arrived. Surrounding the man who called himself Clyde was a bevy of dealers and serious collectors. Staff was adamant about the three book rule and that was all anyone got.

Clyde got his three signed, walked out front to see what kind of car the author had taken to the event; a small dark blue Porsche Boxster. The barricade used to save its parking spot leaned up against a No Parking sign. That alone was enough to make a person want to kill him. Anyone who got to break the law simply because he was a celebrity deserved to die. Clyde got back in line and prepared for a long wait. There were some 150 people ahead of him this time through.

The wait took an hour and Fifteen minutes, before he was near the front again. Several people around him this time helped to get the books signed if they only had one or two. This time through he'd got 11 signed. He got back in line for the third pass. With only five books to go, Clyde was positive this would be his last pass in line. It was. The author signed all the books without having to ask any others in line to help. There were about a dozen people behind Clyde waiting for the author to sign their books too. Clyde carried his books to his car and gingerly placed them into boxes to hold them straight up and down. A bent spine or torn dust jacket would only decrease the night's earnings. Then he started his car, repositioned his parking spot to the corner nearest the little blue Boxster and waited. Over half an hour later it sped past. Clyde started his silver Eagle Premier and followed.

Driving the streets of Pasadena was easy. He had a pretty good idea of where the author would be heading. He lived in Beverly Hills and the freeways were a safe bet for the route. With only minor reckless driving procedures, Clyde was able to not get caught at the wrong end of a stop light and turn onto the freeway behind the author. Then the Boxster really throttled and the chase was on.

Clyde wondered briefly if the author knew he was being followed. Then he decided that was impossible. This type of killing was new to the business. So long as he wasn't overly anxious, didn't stay too close to the Porsche, there was no way for the author to know. Other cars sped along the freeway too. Clyde would just hang back far enough - several lanes to the left, a few cars back – and wait, until the right time.

The time came when the author veered off the interstate into an industrial area of the City of Commerce, pulling into a commercial office complex and parked in a secluded spot next to a landscaped planter with several bushes and trees, partially obstructing his car from view.

Clyde drove past the parking lot and parked across the street, reached into his glove box and pulled out a 9MM pistol. He checked the ammunition to make sure the clip was full. It was. Then he reached into the glove box a second time, retrieved a silencer, and screwed it onto the barrel. A flicker of memory danced in his head of when he'd won the gun; in a poker game with a drug dealer with whom he'd had previous business dealings - back in the old days of being a restaurant cook and a semi-serious cocaine user. Clyde had had a more leisurely lifestyle back then, back when the most dangerous things he did was lie to women, buy them drinks, and invite them to after hour parties so he could screw'em. The good ol' days.

Today, the man who called himself Clyde Barstow, a bastardization of the name of one of his favorite authors, a favorite author who was about to die, today, or should we say tonight, because the sun had set several hours ago, he was going to work in his current profession. So, he put the car in drive and creeped with his lights off toward the parked car.

The street lights couldn't find the Porsche in its spot next to the landscaped divider. The seclusion would make the job so much easier. Clyde reduced his speed even further so he could roll up on the author without being noticed. Parking directly behind the Porsche he got out of his car, leaving the door open so as to not make any unsuspecting noises and walked up to the driver's window.

The Porsche had its targa top removed, making visibility into the car easy. As Clyde Barstow walked up he saw the head of the young female assistant lifting from the lap of the author, obviously just finishing with her more elite services. The author meanwhile had his head craned back with his eyed closed on the high bucket seats of the Porsche. Clyde reached over the window of the car and pushed the nose of his pistol into the forehead of the author, whose eyes opened instantly. Clyde raised a shushed finger to his lips. The assistant was adjusting her visor mirror to aid in her application of new lipstick. Clyde leaned on the top edge of the window, being careful not to touch it with his hand.

"I haven't read your latest book," said Clyde. "What's it about."

The author didn't speak. The assistant turned her head quickly, instantly drawing a red line across one cheek. Clyde raised a finger to his lips again and motioned for the assistant to continue.

The assistant didn't understand, was afraid and reeled back in her seat begging, "Oh my god, oh my god, what do you want?"

"Not you," said Clyde disappointed in her behavior. He parted her brown hair with a bullet and she immediately slumped in her seat. He turned back to the author, "I'm sorry. We were interrupted. What's your book about?"

"Poetry. Poetry that t-tells a story about a young boy on an adventure."

"I'm not much for poetry," said Clyde. "Do you have anything else coming out soon?"

"Yeah. Yeah." The author saw a ray of hope. "I've got a third book in the Devils Cube trilogy coming out. There's an advance copy in the trunk."

"Really," said Clyde growing interested. "I love that story, especially the first one. Man, when I saw that movie I was so scared. I remember going to the bathroom and thinking there was something alive in the mirrors."

"You can have it if you want," offered the author. "Just please don't kill me."

"That'd be great. Pop the trunk. And do me a favor."

"What's that?" asked the author, relief filling his tone.

"Toss your cell phone over in the bushes." A twirling motion with the barrel of the gun showed him where.

The author tossed the phone, reached into his glove box, and a click was heard in the rear of the Porsche. Clyde went to the trunk, pulled a handkerchief from his pocket to cover his hand and lifted the lid. There was a briefcase inside. Using the handkerchief, he grabbed the case and carried it to the front of the car. He handed it to the author, who laid it across the center console and opened it, the lid leaning against his dead assistant. In the case was a non-impressive red paperback book with the title "Squaresville" typed on the cover.

Clyde recognized it for an advanced reading copy of the book. This one would probably even have typos, grammatical and spelling mistakes, still to be corrected by editors, with final approval left to the author.

"You can have it," squeaked the author, his throat running dry.

"Wow, that's awesome. Would you sign it for me?"

"Sure," said the author, reaching into the briefcase again and pulling out a sharpie pen. "Who should I sign it to?"

Clyde lowered his voice, "Just your name please."

"Here you go."

"Thanks," said Clyde growing tired of the conversation. "Are there any other copies of this around?"

"Only a couple hundred. Marketing has already begun to most of the major bookstores."

Have you signed any others?" asked Clyde.

"Just a few."

"Good."

4
Daily Hunt

DETECETIVE TREY HUNT HAD BEEN ON SHIFT for eleven and a half hours when he caught the call. Working one of the new 12 hour shifts was no piece of cake. The plan was supposed to reduce overtime. But the next shift was still in briefing and his four decades on the force had taught him rudimentary diligence so he picked up the receiver on the second ring. Better to take the work now before the Upper Brass gets the swing of the new scheduling.

The call was from the duty Sergeant at the front desk. Apparently, a security guard at the Brooksline Industrial park had found two bodies with bullet wounds to the head in a parked car. Hunt scratched the address down in his flip pad and hung up. He gave his partner the heads up and they drove to the scene.

Hunts partner was Susan Daily, a rookie detective recently promoted after five years on the job. Only seven months ago she was riding bikes around Santa Monica pier. In the locker room, she was unofficially voted most eligible for a Police woman's layout in a men's magazine. Hunt had gotten used to the wisecracks of working with a female officer half his age and eventually the other officers backed off after she proved herself during a shootout her fifth week in the field.

Daily was handling a call of her own, a personal one. It wasn't pretty. Her voice was trying hard to remain a whisper and failing. "Don't give me that It's not you it's me crap. Is this really what's necessary right now? Fine. Fine. FINE. No. I don't need anything from your place and get your stuff out of my apartment before my shifts up." She hung up the phone and sniffled back a tear, wiped her eyes with a fist and looked up to find her partner staring at her.

"Bad day," he said.

"Yeah."

"Well, we can either talk about it or not," Hunt offered. "I can offer you a shoulder to cry on or we could go check out this murder scene and you could sink your frustrations into a case. Your choice."

Sometimes, Daily really appreciated having an older partner who could cut through the BS. She decided, "Let's roll."

Arriving at the scene, Hunt navigated through a throng of reporters encamped on the barricade line created by the police tape and defended by two uniforms. Detective Daily went to interview the Security guards, while Hunt proceeded to the crime scene. Upon reaching the kill point, Susan found both a man and a woman hunched over themselves in the front seat of a dark blue Porsche Boxster with neat wounds to the head, indicating a small caliber weapon had been used. They were both well dressed and in good shape. The passenger had a section of her scalp dangling from her head like a taco shell gone soft. Blood had pooled into the lap of her business suit and spilled onto the floor around her expensive shoes. There was spit caked part ways around the corners of her mouth and her lipstick streak on one cheek reminded Daily of Indian war paint. The driver was shot almost straight into the top of his head, leaving no visible exit wound. His pants were undone and pushed down onto his hips. There was a briefcase open between the two of them. The most visible evidence was written across the windshield of the car with the females lipstick. The word ASS-HOLE had been scrawled in big childish letters with a black fine tipped marking pen. A police photographer was busily snapping photos of the victims.

While Hunt was making notes and directing the crime photographer on certain necessary angles, Detective Daily came along side and peered into the Boxster. "Couple of lovers get caught with their pants down?"

"What'd the security guard say?" Hunt asked, ignoring her comment and reaching in with a pen to inspect the pockets of the briefcase.

"The bodies were found about an hour ago. Security called the station without touching anything. Said he knew he wasn't supposed to because he's tested for a department in Northern California. Thinks there might have been more to it than a lovers spat because of who the victim is."

"Who is he?" asked Hunt pulling a business card from the briefcase. It read Carol Denkins, Agent, and gave her phone number and address.

"One of the top horror writers in the country," said Daily. "Scary."

Later that day Susan Daily made a call to Carol Denkins. A secretary at first claimed Miss Denkins was busy, but when Susan identified herself as the detective handling the Clyde Barstow case Miss Denkins schedule was miraculously cleared. After a brief introduction of names and titles the conversation began.

"Do you know of anyone that would want to kill Clyde Barstow?"

"Not really. He was well liked in the writing field and was one of my best clients. I wish I had another twelve like him."

"Had he made anyone angry recently?"

"Not that I can think of. We were business colleagues, not best friends. He had several lovers but no one that he spoke of directly."

"What was his family like?"

"He had, oh gods I can't believe I'm talking about him in the past tense. He had two kids living in a boarding school upstate. His mom lives in Georgia in one of those assisted living centers. He visits her about every other month. His ex and he didn't communicate although he paid her alimony like clockwork. I know, I had to divide his royalty checks into separate accounts and then direct deposit her share. It was in our contract. There was no hate there. He just didn't want the memories revisited every month."

"In looking at his possessions we couldn't find any books. Is it common for an author to travel without any copies of his own stuff?"

"The bookstores carry his merchandise. All he had to do was show up. Sometimes he'll carry one or two copies of something as a gift if he's staying with a friend but he has his own house in Beverly Hills. The most he would have had on him was the advance copy of his newest book. He was supposed to be proofing it."

"Proofing it?" Daily didn't recognize the term.

"Checking it for errors in punctuation and spelling. He hated doing it. Usually he could get one of the assistants to do it for him. They love that sort of thing, makes them feel close to him, like he let them into his world."

"Where would he keep it?"

"On him, or near him. If he did the work himself he could skip into it at anytime. I'd check his briefcase. Once I got so mad at him over this. He was always putting it off or trying to escape his responsibility. Felt that he wrote it in the first place and didn't need to recheck his own work. His actions almost lost him a publisher."

"What did he do?"

"He sold the bloody thing on eBay."

The next day, while watching the news, Hunt found out two things related to the murder:

First of all, the security guard must have carried a video camera and done some shooting before he called the station because there was practically a full length movie running on CNN of the crime scene, giving every armchair detective a chance to second guess the investigation before Hunt and Daily had even been on the case for six hours.

Second, the price of autographed copies of the authors books were soaring at bookstores and auction houses all across the country, especially online at eBay.

Asking the local used bookstore for advice, Hunt and Daily made a list of book dealer websites and scoured the net for the missing book. There were two online, neither of which was at auction. Each detective took one of the books and called the selling dealer. Both books were already sold and each copy was traceable to the publisher through legitimate means. The killer had not been stupid enough to list the book for sale yet.

Autographed titles of the authors work numbered in the thousands of copies and were virtually untraceable. As the days turned into weeks, the detectives found no new leads and the case slid to the back of their duties.

Detective Daily relied on her partner's experience and expertise. Under his supervision they followed every lead down to its brass tack. The family members were all confirmed out of the loop. His Ex was easily alibied and despondent over the loss of her income. Apparently her money train was only going to deliver while he was alive. The alimony ended with his death. His other lovers were nowhere near the scene. Only one lived in the city and she had been getting ready for a late night rendezvous with him. She knew her role in his life and was comfortable with it. Apparently more people were going to be hurt by his death than helped from it. The case slowly came to a crawl.

Even the press slowed down after several critical reviews of the PD; the case and the author, slid into obscurity.

5
Book Dealer Dinner

OVER IN RANCHO MIRAGE, a group of five book dealers were gathering for a quarterly dinner. With the world changing so fast in the industry, there was a small contingent of proprietors who embraced the technological revolution and shirked the attitude of competing commercialism in favor of sharing ideas; what's working and what's not, as a way of minimizing mistakes, learning how to maximum knowledge, and gaining an edge towards an ever increasing body of people who thought buying a few books at a garage sale and listing them online entitled them to the moniker book dealer.

I was one of the dinner guests and navigated some of the best landscaped streets in the world to get to the party. The roads in the desert are a truly amazing feat. One has to wonder where all the flora comes from. The Coachella Valley, a misnomer in itself, was so called because in the days of California's oldest founding father – Father Juniper Sierra, a Spanish monk who had misinterpreted the Indians naming of the desert Conchella shells as Coachella. Under the desert landscape is the remains of an ancient ocean. Only 400-500 years ago the Pacific ocean is said to have reached its beach head at the base of Mount San Jacinto which juts up out of the sands Palm Springs to a height of more than 10,000 feet; a landmark which dominates the landscape for hundreds of miles and is the steepest face in north America. Over the centuries, as the oceanic waters receded, they left behind a harsh basin of sandy debris, including conch shells. Underneath this Arabaic pasture is a water table so vast it is claimed to be virtually bottomless. In the latter half of the twentieth century this aquifer was tapped and the advent of the modern condominium country club was born. Today there's little but golf courses, condos and meandering sidewalks so crooked a drunk could walk home blindfolded lining every street.

After passing my tenth or fifteenth pink and tan basilica to the lesser gods of the PGA, I made it to my destination. It was Justin Blake's, of Word Merchant Enterprises, turn to host. We took turns at hosting the dinner as a way to share the burden and add to the variety.

Justin's house was a nice three bedroom with a Spanish style roof and the modern stucco finish, located in a neighborhood of unique homes, not one of the planned communities where each house looked exactly like the one next door, or at least like the one three houses away. No, Justin's home sat between an east coast Victorian and a Mid-century modern. Even the front lawns were a mixture of cool grassy knolls, desert landscapes and the occasional over cemented driveway. The only thing they all had in common was each of them being well maintained. As the sun set behind the high face of Mount San Jacinto, I parked my car at the end of the cul-de-sac under a large shade tree and walked up his driveway onto the Spanish pavers that designated his front porch and pushed the doorbell.

After only a few seconds I heard the phrase, "I'll get it," and my friend Sal Moor, of Sunshine Books, opened the door. "Well come on in. Tonight we're only accepting bibliophiles." His face was succumbing to wrinkles but was dominated by a warm smile and a large pair of glasses that was to be the traditional fate of anyone who spent a lifetime reading books. In his earlier life, he had been the head of Eisenhower Medical Center, but after retirement let the number two love of his life (the first being his wife) move from a part-time hobby to a full-time occupation. He easily had the nicest inventory amongst us, having had the advantage of a well-paying job to jump-start his collection.

"Then I qualify," I responded. "Thank you," and I walked inside where the pavers became highly polished and cascaded around the corner into the hall, down the steps into a sunken living room and to the left into the kitchen, from where I heard, "Who is it?"

"It's me Justin," I said.

"Hey Xanthe," he shouted. "Come on in and get a drink. Cold beers and soft drinks in the fridge. Whatever you want. I'll be done in a minute."

Sal waved a hand in the direction of the kitchen and did a half-hearted courtly bow. I followed his gesture and found Justin chopping vegetables in a kitchen immersed in the smell of steaks simmering in the oven. I pulled a Corona from the fridge and offered one to Justin by pointing the label at him. He turned me down by tapping a glass with some dark liquid in it with his knife. I found the opener on the counter then followed the pavers back into the living room and plopped myself onto the couch.

Sal was looking at Justin's bookshelves which lined every available wall space in the house. Keeping his back to me he said, "Any good buys lately?"

I had known Sal only a few years at this time, but I knew him enough that if he was asking about good buys then he must have come across one himself. He played facts close to the vest and seldom gave up specifics. "One or two picked up a few items this week. How about you?"

"I saw one collection this week I'm hoping to grab."

A couple days earlier I had been invited to make an offer on one of the nicest Western Americana libraries I'd seen in a long time. There'd been several works of early California History. Lots of the sets had unique bindings; there were several omnibuses of cartography, a few Audubon tomes and things even rarer. The whole selection was kept under the protective glass doors of specially made oak shelves. A person who took the time to collect such artifacts of literature surely could afford a few extra dollars to beautify the room they were stored in. I had done my best and offered $1800 for all four shelving units. It was a far stretch for me but I got the itch and did everything short of knocking out the owner and his wife, to take the items home with me. I failed. They thanked me for my offer and let me leave hat in hand.

"There was this one collection of Western Americana. Did you get a call on it?"

"Uh-huh," said Sal.

"Did you buy it?"

"Uh-uh."

"Me neither," I said. "I made an offer but I guess it was too low. After I made it, he told me he was waiting for a couple of other offers too."

"I think he was just fishing," said Al. "He didn't really want to sell. He just wanted to feel good about what he has." This was a common occurrence in the business. Somebody had a great collection and a free way to get an appraisal was to bring in a couple of book dealers and let them make offers. If any of them would make it in writing, it could be used for insurance purposes.

At that moment, a toilet flushed down the hall and after running the sink water a few seconds Brad appeared. "Were you two talking about those beautiful Californiana books?" Sal and I both confirmed. "Oh they were gorgeous. I just wish I could have afforded them. Wow, what a collection." Brad Confer, of Bloomsbury Books, was Justin's former business partner and lover. He stood on the steps leading down into the sunken living room making his six-foot tall frame loom even larger over me before accusing, "You didn't try and steal them did you?"

"Who me?" I was often the butt of jokes when it came to low-balling sellers and deservedly so. I was saved by the doorbell ringing.

Sal, still nearest the door reached over and opened it. The final guest had arrived, the biggest pessimist in the group, Gary Craig, of G. William Craig Rare Books. Never one to talk about good business. All days were slow days with Gary. It was a wonder he had the longest surviving store in the desert with over ten years under his belt. "Gary," we all chorused. Gary dropped his cigarette into the planter out front and walked on in just as Justin came out from the kitchen, wiping his hands on a towel and stated, "Dinner is served."

Dinner was a sweet ensemble of southern cooking. Lamb chops smothered in mustard gravy, yams instead of potatoes, black eyed peas saturated in butter and good old fashioned macaroni and cheese. The table was large enough to fit us all around although Justin took a three legged stool since chairs were in short supply. I had always wondered why Justin and Brad broke up. For myself, I prefer the company of women and had enough failed relationships in my past to prove the point. But Justin and Brad seemed a good mix of similarities and opposites. They were both tall and in their mid-forties, yet looked younger. Both were educated men having graduated with at least four year degrees. Brad had gone on to serve in the planning department of a city hall and Justin had a short writing career in Hollywood. Still, you never know what makes or breaks a relationship unless you're one of the participants. After Brad moved to and opened his store in Palm Springs, Justin had followed him out and temporarily worked alongside him so each could have a day or two off a week. But that lasted less than a year and then they separated. Now Justin had another man in his life.

"Where's Leonard?" I asked.

"He's finishing up some errands," Justin said. "He was gone visiting his mom in the mid-west recently and came home to catch up on life's little duties."

"I can see you did the cooking," said Sal holding up a clump of macaroni on his fork.

Gentle laughs rocked the room and Justin took it fairly. The night slipped by with lots of ribbing and reminiscences of our best buys and worst customers. Much the same conversations we'd had over dinners in the past.

"I had a customer today who just wouldn't let go of my ear until he told me the whole tale of how his grandmother used to read him this one story over and over again. I thought he was going to tell me the story itself until the phone rang. Luckily it was a telemarketer and I could excuse myself."

"Have you noticed how thin AB Bookmans Weekly has gotten? I think the magazine is soon to die off. It used to be the only way to sell but these days the internet gets all the attention."

"If I get another person with a box of book clubs who thinks they're valuable I'm going to strangle them."

"That's not as bad as the person who tells you they have all the latest titles and authors in great condition who brings in 10 year old books without dust jackets."

Justin asked me about my longtime endeavor, "Any luck on getting authors to sign at your store?"

"Not yet. I call all the publishers but none of them seem to want to be the first. They all want to know how my other signings have gone and until I get the first one in I have no track record. I could probably just write a best seller myself before I could attract a real author at this rate." It had always been my dark little secret to become an author but the lack of confidence in my abilities prevented me from really attempting it.

"That's a hell of a catch 22," said Sal, wiping the corners of his mouth with his napkin. "Ever think of just making it up? Creative license." he chuckled. "We are selling fiction aren't we?"

Unsure of being the brunt of a joke, I asked, "Make up a track record or make up a novel?"

My being unsure of the direction of the comments made my friend's center on me a bit longer than I'd liked. But it was my turn to sit in the sarcasm chair. I got a good round of laughs at the table and a few jests of "Is it a True Crime?" and, "The Plot Thickens."

"Speaking of book signings," began Gary, "Didn't you go to a Cliff Barkley book signing the other day?"

"Yeah," I responded. "Got a lot of stuff signed. I even got an advanced reading copy of his newest book."

"Did you hear about his drive home?"

"No. Why?"

"He was killed," said Brad jumping in.

"Get out of here," I said. "I didn't know."

"Yep, murdered in a parking lot in the City of Commerce," agreed Justin.

"Not much news on what he was doing in that location," inserted Sal. "Could have been forced off the road, although unlikely. The news said he had his assistant with him, who was also shot."

"His sales have picked up," said Gary between bites of lamb. "I've sold all three of my signed copies of his books."

"People are probably buying them off you to list on eBay," said Brad. "I've pulled all of mine off Abe and Bibliofind. Gotta go where the money is."

"You mean there's room between my list price and what they sell for on eBay for someone else to make a profit?" asked Gary incredulously.

"In the short run there is," answered Brad. "Things are doubling in price pretty quick."

"It'll be like that until the hype is over," said Sal. "I've listed a few."

If Sal had done it, then we all knew we should too. He could squeeze the leather off a pig and still have the livestock for a second a season.

The conversation shifted to complaints about the selection at the local thrift shops and aggressiveness in pricing at the library sales. It was agreed that even the volunteers in the non-profits we all bought from were trying to squeeze every dollar from us. As dealers, they gave us little sympathy. The volunteers thought we could either afford their raised prices and if not, another dealer would come in and take our place. In the end, there's no loyalty amongst merchants. Soon all the libraries would have full-time staffs and never closing book stores right inside their buildings.

The night grew darker and so did the stories. Complaints rose about the available collections. It seemed more and more people were checking the value of their books online, making it impossible for an honest book dealer to make a living without having to pay a considerable amount for low grade inventory, or what is commonly called - store stock, because it sits in the store forever. Everybody and their Uncle was a book expert these days. It was too easy for a person to go online, check the price and then undercut the market just enough for a fast sale but not low enough for a dealer to buy and make a profit.

The Author Murders

At one point, my interest became peaked as we were talking about computer systems and their growing complexity coinciding with higher technician fees should a system have a problem and need repair.

"I'm lucky," said Sal. "I have a team of people who can handle the problem at anytime. I've even started hosting websites and doing database work on a consulting basis."

"Well good for you," said Justin. "I have to pay through the nose every time a real problem occurs. So far I've been fortunate. As long as I can hold down three different keys, wiggle one ear and bite my tongue I've been fine. Restarting or rebooting or whatever is about as far my comprehension goes."

Most everyone agreed with Justin. The problems of finding a good techie were paramount to being able to solve anyone's problems. It was similar to finding a mechanic you can trust to fix your car. They had you by the balls. If they said it was a major problem you simply had to trust them and get out your checkbook, but you never really knew. It could be just a simple loose wire but you still had to pay.

It made me think though of a way to get a better handle on Donlagic's case. I chalked the thought into my memory banks and enjoyed the rest of the evening.

6
Milo

THE NEXT DAY I SET TWO BALLS IN MOTION.

First, I gave my assistant, Jill, a stack of autographed books and a short lesson in how to list items on eBay. She was thrilled with the opportunity to learn a new system and spent most of the morning putting books up for auction. We laughed that it was like running our own personal stock market and made a few special notes of the books we thought would go up the highest in price.

Second, I gave my computer guru a call. His name was Shane and if I could count the number of times he'd saved my butt from total ruin I'd owe him a car. I'd probably paid him enough in the past to buy one. In the internet book business, if you can't fire up your IBM or your Compaq, or heaven forbid, your Apple, you were offline. It was like having your mothers nipple ripped away from your mouth. The minutes of being down turned into hours, the hours offline seemed like days, and the days seemed like hell. The world was passing you buy and you knew it. The wondering about unanswered emails, orders left unfulfilled, who were probably within minutes buying elsewhere, mounted in your mind like a Jenga game. When you finally got back online, sometimes days later, the amount of emails that were now wasted efforts was boggling because the buyers had bought elsewhere. I don' think there's anything worse than answering a buyers request and hearing or reading, 'Well, you didn't get back to me so I went to the next dealer down the list.' For Christ's sake, I was only offline four hours! And on top of all that, you knew there was a big bill coming from Shane or whatever else little Quasit of a devil had crawled out from his own personal trash can, to wreak revenge upon society now that the nerds had triumphed into careers of their own.

I was lucky. Shane had come to me as a personal referral from a friendly Real Estate Broker who had an extensive computer network. The first day Shane walked into my apartment - because that's where I sold books from at that time - he fixed my problems in just under three hours and charged me $200. He told me he wanted to give me a break because I was going to be a future reference for him as he got business through me. Not sure where the truth lay, I simply paid him and thanked him.

The message center picked up Shane's call and I left my request for him to call me after the beep. I was surprised when only a few minutes later he called back.

"Sorry, I missed your call Xanthe," he said. "What's up?"

"I need some advice," I said. "I need someone who can track down an eBay listing."

"Can't you do that yourself?"

"Not this time. The lister has disappeared from the net, or he's changed his email. The account he used gets the mailer daemon if I try and send him something."

Shane cut to the quick, "So what's so important about this listing?"

I told him what I knew of the Stephen Knightly book and how I was hired to find it. I shared what Donlagic had told me and briefly detailed how rare the item was. Shane listened with only the occasional uh-huh so I could tell he was paying attention. When I had shot my wad he interrupted, "What you need is a hacker."

"No, I don't think so. Just someone a little better at this than me I figure. Can't you do this?" I pinned all my hopes on Shane.

"It's out of my data bracket," he said. My hopes deflated. Shane was my best guess for someone who could dissect the net. "The information you want is all encrypted, fire walled and password protected. I do some reprogramming, downloading of games and software and stuff. I can rewrite a few programs, delete a few expiration dates on 30-

day trial offers for software, but that's about it. For the really hard stuff I have to get help."

"Where do you get help like this?" I asked seeing hope rekindled.

"I go to Milo."

"Who's Milo?"

Before Shane could answer the front door of my store opened, letting in a bit of Palm Springs most precious commodity – warm sunshine – and a slender man of undiscerning age walked in; too old to still be called a kid but with the confidence and experience of one who's mastered his craft. He wore plain Levi's with an open collar faded red golf shirt and had a backpack slung over his shoulder. He had to be at least forty but his brown hair was sheared into a youthful crew cut. He sported square rimmed tortoise shell glasses and had a spring in his step that bounced him up to my front counter.

"Hello," he whispered, seeing me with the phone to my ear. "Is the owner here?"

I stuck a thumb in my chest. "Shane, I'll call you back. Someone just came in." I gave my attention to the man in front of me who continued talking as soon as the phone touched its cradle.

"I was wondering if we could talk about my doing a book event, perhaps a signing of some sort." He looked me in the eye and smiled.

"Maybe." I'd been down this road before. No reason to get my hopes up. "What do you write?"

"Mysteries."

A little better, I thought. "How many have you written?"

"Three so far. But I've got a fourth one in production that'll be out later this year."

The big question, "Who's your publisher?"

"Putnam," he replied.

Bingo. "Let me introduce myself. I'm Xanthe Anthony. Welcome to Celebrity Books." We shook hands.

"I'm Thom Racina." He slid the backpack off his shoulder, unzipped the main pouch, pulled out a couple of glossy paperbacks and asked, "Could you fit a few of these in your window?"

7
Daily eBay Sales

DETECTIVE SUSAN DAILY STUCK WITH THE BARSTOW CASE and buried thoughts of her ex-boyfriend in police work. Between her other duties she was comparing lists of dealers currently offering the deceased authors' work available online or having sold copies in the last two weeks since his death. This was one of those times. She was particularly interested in cross referencing dealers who had items listed on multiple book dealer websites; Abebooks, Bibliofind, and Interloc that had mysteriously come up with more autographed titles by the victim and then subsequently listed them on Ebay. Between the four sites she had over 4,500 dealers to check. It was a daunting task. One that her partner, Trey Hunt had deemed a worthless pile of hay dung.

"Still looking for the proverbial needle?" He sauntered over to her side of the desk and peered over her shoulder at the computer screen. Lists of names and addresses scrolling forever.

"I started with 985 possibles and eliminated over 350 with phone calls already." She talked while she read with barely a blip in her information absorption.

"What's your strategy?" Hunt had been her mentor since taking her on as partner. Daily was smart but she needed someone to help her implement details on a street level.

She rattled off a stream of particulars, "Some dealers weren't physically close enough to rate. If the killer had to drive more than a day to kill the author and get back to work without being missed then

I took them off my radar. I'm down to just over 600 left."

"You know your treading in a new direction. Not a lot of track records to ask for advice on this one." Hunt himself had never been comfortable online. Until this past Christmas he had sworn off the thought of ever learning a computer but when his son had shown him how he could talk to his granddaughter in Vegas without paying for a phone call he was hooked. Now his favorite thing to do was fire up his home computer as soon as he walked in the door and listen for those magic words, "You Got Mail." More than that though and he was lost online.

"Yeah, just getting the information has been difficult," Daily admitted. "Online entrepreneurs are a highly unregulated bunch of cowboys. The federal government has forbidden the taxing of internet sales meaning every government agency has a 'hands off' policy towards the internet."

Daily discussed her task with her partner but expected no help. Detective Hunt was so long in the tooth that she figured there was no way he could be of help in an internet crime. Each time she mentioned it he furled his wrinkles into a patchwork of creases, shaking his head side to side till the dandruff sprinkled from his gray hair. When her frustration reached its zenith, much to her surprise Trey offered to untie her Gordian knot.

"Preaching to the choir partner," Hunt chimed in falling into the padded overstuffed chair on his side of the desk, "Only the FBI has any real capabilities online and their forces are few. Like me, most detectives and agents are limited in the knowledge required to even buy an item off Amazon, so how could your average badge be expected to lead an investigation into that ghostly world of the net? Most of the best crime stoppers were former internet criminals themselves, hackers. Several convicted web pirates turned state's evidence. Then they get relocated through the witness protection program, and are now probably working in some dark and dirty little hole in the basement of a Washington building, catching their former friends."

"Why Detective Hunt, have you been catching up on some reading lately," Daily batted her eyes at the senior officer, "Or are you just trying to sweet talk me?"

"Maybe I can offer a hand."

"You? How?"

"I have a friend with the bureau. He might be inclined to let me cash in a chip." Detective Hunt picked up the phone. He still owned one where you stuck your finger in the hole and turned the dial. He paused as the phone made its connection and then spoke to an operator, "Agent Henry, please."

Another pause, then "Patrick? Trey Hunt here. How ya doin?" Pause. "The missus is fine. But say Pat. I've got a case involving this internet thing. Have you got someone who can give me a hand with it?" He gave thumbs up to Daily. "Here do me a favor and let me have you talk to my partner."

Hunt handed Daily the phone who was anxiously waiting like a small town baker at the Betty Crocker cook off. "Just tell the man what you need."

8
A Hacker

GETTING IN TOUCH WITH MILO WAS NO EASY TASK. Shane had been reluctant to tell me how to contact him at first. He said Milo was a bit quirky about who knew him. Shane wouldn't even confirm if Milo was his real name. In the end, he told me he'd have to get back to me. He needed permission to allow me to contact Milo.

Permission came three days later. Shane rang me up from a payphone. He wouldn't even use his cell or his home phone to tell me how to contact. I was not to state anything of importance when I made first contact - no mention of who he was, no description of what I wanted him to do, do not use any foul language and no jokes. Just tell him you need his help, and don't mention Shane's name. He'll know who I am and was expecting me. Milo would direct me from there. I thought Shane was being ridiculous. But who was I to complain? He gave me an email address: fgetboutit@aol.com. Great, I'm dealing with the nerd mafia.

I sent the email immediately after Shane hung up. On just the off chance I checked my email ten minutes later. There was already a response. It read: Starbucks, downtown, 9:30PM, tomorrow. Fast service. I liked Milo already.

The next night was Thom Racina's first book signing at Celebrity Books. It was also a Thursday night; the night of the weekly street fair in Palm Springs. Only Palm Springs is too hoity toity to have a street fair so they call it Villagefest instead. It's a nice way to encourage traffic downtown on a pre-weekend basis. Lots of music, lots of food and limited retail fill the streets, which are closed to driving traffic for six blocks. Retailers are limited on their ability to participate to Hand-crafted and Collectible merchandise because the store owners were too narrow minded to participate and they feared that a successful vendor could pay a fraction of their rent and steal all their business. Never mind that for a decimal of their rent they could increase sales ten-fold.

I, on the other hand, was an active participant in the street fair; having grown my store out of selling books and comics in front of the downtown library. It was a natural success. When the library got jealous of my sales and the customers obvious misconception that I had some-thing to do with the library behind my booth I was asked to move across the street. I begrudgingly obliged and within a year after moving a Starbucks opened in the empty store front behind my booth. Within two years I opened Celebrity Books and never looked back.

I set Thom up at the corner of my booth with a stack of books in front of him and Jill working the cash register inside. Over the years I'd hired two or three teenagers a season to help at the booth. I set one up as Thom's personal assistant and told him to do whatever Thom asked. The moment he sat down he began to pitch his books to the crowd. This looked promising.

The night was good all the way around. Sales were brisk. We were in high season and the crowd was thick with snow birds, shopping bags and accents of a non-California nature. I was knee deep in a river of fun. It was what I liked best about my business. Meeting people from faraway places and talking to them about stories and history and life. One thing about book people I love is you don't have to twist their arms to meet them. Every one of them has a story to tell or a thing they want to know more about. The night flew by like a flock of seag-ulls with the wind beneath their wings.

I slid to the back of the booth and went to Starbucks at about 9PM to order a medium light coffee with a slice of carrot cake. The impish girl behind the counter corrected my order out loud with the phrase "Vente mild coffee," over her shoulder to the college kid work-ing the syrup bar. He moved over to the machine with a magnetic clock affixed to its front and dispensed my coffee. My impish order corrector got me my carrot cake and $6.92 later I found myself seated on their umbrella patio sipping a hot drink and unwrapping my plastic fork and napkin from its cellophane.

Looking around the patio, I sized up the other patrons. Half the tables were full. There was the romantic couple sitting in the corner, a couple of lone business types wearing a suit far too late into the evening. One had his tie off. They were probably both conventioneers. Two separate tables of high school kids from different clicks that don't mix sat at opposite ends of the patio and smack dab in the middle, practically blocking the front door, sat a small group of thugs. Twenty years ago you'd call them punk rockers. These days they were just punks. The spiked green and purple hair, the ragged Levi's jackets and pants with the worn out knees. I had to wonder where they got all the leather braces and gloves. Although, I had to admit, I liked some of their boots. They'd be cool with the right black leather jacket. Which, by the way, the one or two of them which had'em were probably rich kids just playing punk. Mommy and daddy's little boy and girl who didn't know how to pay respect but made darn sure they swallowed their pride and rode with the trash. I had had to fight that trash to get inside Starbucks when I arrived and on my way onto the patio. How come a group like that could make a nuisance of themselves just by showing up? I'd have to remember to cancel my subscription to the ACLU newsletter.

9:30PM came and went and so did most of the patrons. The streetfair was winding down and soon I'd have to close up. One set of lovebirds left and were replaced by another. The conventioneer with his tie still on left and was replaced by a couple of Stevie Nicks wannabees. I thought that dress style had already passed for women but apparently there were still a couple of Fleetwood Mac fans in the world.

One set of the high school kids had left and the other was starting to break up. As they passed the punk rockers a skinny kid got pushed by one of his friends into the table and it looked for a few seconds that a fight was about to break out. All the boys stood up and clenched their fists. The girls scooted to the back of the pack and those

---

closest to each other on the opposing sides began a shouting match that drew a security guard from inside. His presence was felt immediately and the high school kids walked away. The security guard went back inside, but not before one final coffee cup was thrown from a punk rocker at the girl in the rear.

The two groups rushed at each other and fists flew. It was the preppies versus Sid Vicious. The preppies did well too. The tallest punk, a skinny tall kid who had a large Adams apple and a multi-colored Mohawk making him look like a starved rooster, was slammed onto the ground by a letterman who must have earned his jacket on the wrestling team. A small punker cleaned the clock of a same sized preppie with a quick 1-2-3 punch set that landed the prep on his butt. Then the security guard was back outside blowing a whistle and yelling. The kids divided themselves into two huddles and resumed the screaming match which the security guard eventually won. The preppies were told to walk away first, when they hesitated the guard said, "If you stay I'm calling your parents," and he pointed at the wrestler, who must have had this done before because he didn't argue again, turned on his heels and the rest of the preppies followed his lead.

Then the security guard turned to the punkers and in a less confident voice told them they had worn out their welcome for the night. The punkers argued with lots of curse words highlighting their speech. Not the debate team, I thought. It almost grew to the pitch of another fight with the security guard outnumbered six to one. But, the security guard pulled a smart move. He raised his voice and said, "If anyone here wants to stand up for this bunch of loudmouths let them speak." All the patrons had seen the fracas and no one spoke up. To take on the entire crowd on the patio was a bit too much for the punkers and with a few final words of "This is bullshit," they moved on.

I looked at my watch. It was 9:55PM and I figured Milo was a no show. From my point on the patio I could watch my book booth. The kids who worked it had already started their pre-packing sequences in preparation for a complete breakdown. I remembered once I had read an Amy Vanderbilt Book of Etiquette which stated a person should only have to wait fifteen minutes past the appointed time to be polite. I had given Milo 25 and I figured another five wouldn't hurt. At 9:59 one of the punkers came walking towards me on the outside of the bushes and trendy grill work marking the boundary between sidewalk and patio. He was the tall skinny kid, rooster boy, who had fallen first in the fight. I watched him from the corner of my eye so as not to stare. He was angling himself as close to my table as he could while smoking his cigarette and blowing towards the street. As he passed me, he flipped a folded piece of paper onto my table and kept walking another twenty feet then propped a heavy booted foot against a palm tree, leaned back against it, and did his best James Dean.

I unfolded the paper and found a badly written note that read - Meet me at Peabody's. I turned and looked at the kid. In the lamplight he made a dark Rock and Roll silhouette with a burning ember sticking from his lip and shading his face in a red glow. When our eyes met he turned away and crossed the street, heading towards another coffee bar not as trendy as Starbucks and with some bad music droning from inside.

I tossed my trash and headed across the street. The main drag downtown Palm Springs is a wide thoroughfare called Palm Canyon Drive. You only have to look one direction to make a safe crossing on it since it's a one way street. Whenever I see someone doing the traditional look back, up and back to ensure there is no cross traffic I think, Hey you idiot. What are you doing? You only have to look one way. I never even wait for the cross walks to turn green. So long as there's not a cop around I just cross.

Peabody's was doing a karaoke night which explained the bad music. There was a fat dyke who had a remarkable resemblance to Chris Farley belting out Donna Summer's On The Radio at the top of her lungs. I'm sure somewhere there was a female John Belushi who was going to get lucky.

Rooster boy was sitting under one of the green umbrella tables on Peabody's sidewalk smoking his cigarette down to the filter. I walked over and sat down.

"Milo?" I said trying not to make it a question.

"I hear you're looking for a book." He said.

"Yeah, can you help me?"

"Tell me what you got."

I told him about the Stephen Knightly book and the history of its origin as far as I knew. Milo was a horror fan and had read a lot of Knightly's work. No surprise. Being a punker didn't necessarily qualify you as an illiterate, just a rebel. But at least I didn't have to go through elementary education to bring him up to speed. I showed him the print-out of the eBay page and he asked me a few standard questions.

"Did you try and email the seller?"

"Of course," I said. "The email was returned via mailer daemon."

"Has he ever listed any other items?"

Good question. "I'm not sure."

"There's no image available?"

"Not when I went to the page." I said. Then I asked, "Is that a problem?"

"No, not really," he said. "Just curious. How much?"

"How much what?"

"How much are you going to pay me?" Milo was sticking his goblet neck in my direction. Apparently payment had been a problem for him before.

"How much do you want?" I hadn't thought about payment until this point.

"I'm going to want a hundred just to get out of this chair. If I bring you what you want, I want $500. Even if I come up dry, my time still costs $200." He tried to stare me down with an unblinking stance, his neck wobbling in the wind.

"I'll do the $500 if you bring me something good," I said. "But today, all I've got is $20. That should buy you a coffee, dinner, whatever. Agreed?"

"Yeah, OK," he slunk in his chair.

"Hey Milo," I tried to restore his confidence. "Bring me whatever you find and I'll be fair with you. Contact me at my store alright."

"Sure." He said. "It'll take me a couple of days though."

"Not a problem. And uh, thanks."

He gave me one of those head nods where you look up the nostrils of the cool guy, and then he reached into his pocket for another cigarette. I was going home and Milo's night was just starting.

When I got back to the booth the kids were nearly done packing things up. I loaded the last few boxes onto the cart with them and we rolled our goods back to the store where Jill was ringing up the nightly sales all alone.

"How'd it go?" I asked.

"Went great!" Thom was stoked about it. He said he sold 68 copies. That guy can sell. He's in the bathroom right now." She was thrilled about having a really good author night. I know from firsthand experience it's no fun to hang out with an author wanting to sign books and nobody shows up. It's like a party where you're the only guest and you barely know the host. To have a successful night like this could mark the beginning of something. When Thom came back up front he looked like a kid who'd gotten his first kiss and wanted to know if he could come back next week.

"Sure you can Thom. You can come every week if you want." This had the feeling of a beautiful relationship. I couldn't wait to make some phone calls to the publishers.

9
Another One Bites the Dust

TODAY HIS NAME WAS STEELE DANIELS. Knocking off little old ladies was not in his usual job description, but killing America's top romance writer was an opportunity he couldn't resist. She seldom came out from her Bay area mansion these days and seeing her on a book tour was a rare treat. Sometimes you had to strike while the iron was hot.

His job of collecting books, autographed books, had grown till it was all he knew. These days he wouldn't survive if he didn't get out and make the rounds. His sales strategy was like feeding a monster. If there was no fuel for the fire then the flames died and Steele Daniels would be left holding the bag, bill and checkbook with no cash left in it. What do you mean there's no money left in the account? There are plenty of checks left in the book. But that joke only got you so far and he didn't want another call from a District Attorney's office like the one he had five years ago. "Excuse me sir, but I'm from the County District Attorney's Office Department of Fraudulent Checks Division. Could I have a moment of your time?" No, not again.

So, today he'd rather kill a nice old lady who'd earned the title of Best Selling Diva and the Queen of Romance. That was a more palatable future than accepting a bad phone call.

If only he wasn't so damn late. He usually arrived at least an hour early. With this author, he'd have been best off if he'd arrived three hours before the signing. Now it was fifteen minutes to starting time and he was just pulling into the parking garage. He pulled his tab from the automated arm control booth, drove up three floors of parking and found a spot in the corner squeezed between a monster truck and a Ford Expedition, barely leaving room to open his car doors. If he wasn't driving a compact vehicle he would have never fit.

Popping open the back hatch, he grabbed two backpacks full of books. The Romance Queen had been writing so long her books were in great abundance at every bookstore, thrift shop, library sale and garage sale. This would be a real haul even if he missed his chance to snuff her. Her signature would guarantee a spike in price at the minimum of $50 per book and inside the two backpacks were no less than 28 trashy novels waiting to be turned into bricks of gold. That made his haul today worth at least $1400 and possibly more. He had a first printing of her second book, Love's Liability, in mint condition. It could easily bring $500 by itself. With the packs on his back and the promise of a profitable day ahead, he headed off at a full sprint. Not waiting for the elevators, he took the escalator steps three at a time, sliding past other riders without even an excuse me.

The Barnes and Noble hosting the book signing was in a new center called The Grove, just west of downtown Los Angeles. It was a stylish shopping complex with a plethora of the most fashionable stores. It didn't matter if you were shopping furniture (Crate & Barrel), cell phones (ATT Phone Center) or clothing (Nordstrom), The Grove had all the latest chic styles and a few newer cutting edge ones that hadn't made the magazines yet. The architects who designed the center created the feel of an old fashioned main street complete with a trolley car traveling its entire two block length.

Reaching the glass doors of the Book store, the man who today called himself Steele Daniels entered one of the finest displays of literary merchandise on the planet. The books were elegantly arranged on finely polished lacquered tables and shelves. Only the most decorated covers showed forth. Stacks of Best Sellers were all about. The Authoress of the day had her own table with a mass assortment of hardbacks and paperbacks befitting an icon of her stature directly in the path of all who walked in.. He grabbed up six copies of her newest book, paid for them at the front counter and then bounded up the interior store escalators towards the third floor where her signing was to take place.

The line was monstrous. He couldn't even follow it through the shelves. It wound this way and that through the stacks. He began to follow it away from the direction of where the signings and readings traditionally took place. To ensure he was headed the right way, he asked an unimposing girl with her nose buried in a copy of the new release. She confirmed the way to the back of the line with a soft jerk of her thumb. He kept moving, losing count of how many people were in line. He only hoped that the authoress would not tire early and call it a day before signing at least something for everyone.

Michael Crichton had done that to him twice before. The first time Crichton had signed at the Festival of Books at UCLA he had cut short his signing time after only an hour or two. People were infuriated. Steel Daniels had at the time wished Crichton many ill thoughts. But what could he do? He simply packed up and left. The next year Crichton was there again and even though Steel had gotten in the line hours earlier, Crichton still left before he got to the front. Steel still wouldn't read any Michael Crichton books to this day, although he had no compunction about killing him should the opportunity arise. He'd probably do it for free and not even worry about getting anything autographed. Finding the back of the line, he planted his backpacks on the floor and sat down. He was in for a long wait.

While he waited, he went over his action plan for the afternoon. Parked close the front of the store, on the side access road, was a new black Lincoln Limousine. It's only plausible explanation was for it to be the Diva's. Steele Daniels would have to make it back to his own car in time to place his vehicle in a tail position. Being at the end of the line with so many books to be signed weakened his chances of making the day as profitable as possible. It also increased his chances of being remembered, which was not good. It looked like today was going to be a shoot from the hip kind of day. Like when Sundance had asked his employer if he could move while he shot. The boss man was a little surprised because Sundance couldn't hit the coin in the road while standing still and carefully aiming, but the boss man said, 'Sure.' Sundance drew his gun, quick draw, and bounced to the left and right while fanning his trigger. The coin danced in the street as it flipped over and over as it was hit again and again. Sundance had said, 'It helps when I move.' Steel Daniels liked to think of himself as a sort of gunslinger. It helps when I move.

Moving was slow in the line, progressing at a snail's pace. Steel had time to sip a coffee, eat a sandwich, go the bathroom and even lie down before the line made its first lurch forward. All of five feet. A half hour later it moved again, and then it started picking up speed. It took over three hours to get up to the front of the line. When he was fifty people away, standing on tiptoes, peeking over a shelf of children's books, he got his first look at ground zero of the book signing. The line stretched along the right hand side of a seating area comprised of a mixture of folding chairs and padded wooden benches. In the back were a couple of couches that had been scooted to the rear to make room for the audience. There were still a couple of stragglers and weary participants who chose to relax rather than lug their signed novels, standing three-to-ten in a stack by the side of the fan, who was carefully readjusting dust jackets and placing them in bags for the journey back to the car. At the head of all the excitement was a schoolteachers type wooden desk, with a wall of Romance novels filling in the background, in front of which sat the authoress, occasionally lifting her head in a plaintive smile and a polite nod of her head as she accepted the congratulations of whatever devotee was filling her ear with their praise or request. She must have already had enough of the exalted glorification, because she was looking up less and less, and letting the small entourage of staff members slide stacks of books in front of her prepared for her signature by pre-opening them to the title page, sometimes five or six on top of each other.

Standing to the back of her left shoulder was a warm surprise. In the past few years, it had been rumored in the entertainment talk shows that the authoress and a certain aging handsome male actor had been engaged in a romance of their own. It made for good news blurbs about the two as a way of keeping their careers in the public eye at a time when their stars should have been eclipsed by a new brat pack of stars and starlets. He had made himself most famous when, in the 1980's, he had played a Vampire with a comic sense of humor and devilishly good looks combined into a hit summer movie that parlayed his presence to the forefront of a new age of cinemagoers. One movie had led to another and before a five year span of popularity faded into the next genre, he had become America's, and his authoresses, favorite hunk. Now, here he was as living proof that all the news footage had been sincere and so was their desire for one another. Although it was kind of like thinking of your grandparents making love, Steel Daniels was glad for the aging couple to have one more fling before the end of their days, which could come as soon as today.

Steele Daniels had a special way he'd like to kill the Romance Queen if chances allowed. His hometown had a very common poison which grew in nearly everyone's yard. It was Oleander and its power had matured to that of Urban Legend to the locals. Back in his school days there was almost yearly warnings to kids not to chew on the leaves and there was always a tale of a friend of a friend who had died from swallowing some of the bush. Steele carried a small packet of the bush dried and ground to a fine powder. If there was an unwatched moment he could slip a little into her glass and let nature take its path. Of course, he wasn't sure exactly how much a person needed to be killed but he hoped for the best or worst as it were.

The line moved forward and Steele Daniels was grateful in one way for what he was seeing, but in another way he was let down. The authoress was signing any and all books laid before her, even if the stacks were in the tens. Yet, there were far too many people around to slip anything into her drink. Sighing dejection, he got out all of his books and prepared for the moment. Behind him the line had grown to another 75 people whose schedules were even worse than his. His time in the warmth of her glow came and went with little fanfare. Not wanting to draw attention to himself, he laid his books on the table and when the staff member said, "Quite a collection you've got. You must be a big fan," he just smiled and said, "Yes, he was." The Romance Diva, whose hair was thinning and dyed red, her hands frail and only slightly shaking, did jerk her head up when she saw such a pristine copy of her second book and remarked to her aging boyfriend, "This should fetch a pretty penny on the net." Steele only smiled and said, "I hope not before I get to enjoy it a while." Then her staff whisked him off and he joined the ranks of those readjusting their packs in the sea of chairs where the audience once sat.

His packs adjusted, he headed for the car with only a casual backwards glance. He left his victim to be with what would probably be her final moment in the sun. Outside the real sun was setting and the shadows engulfed the entirety of the parking garage. The monster truck had left its space allowing Steele easy access to his vehicle. Carefully, placing the backpacks into the hatch area so as not to twist a spine, he climbed into the front seat, started the car, and drove towards the exit. It was blocked by a long line of cars with the one at the front having its hood raised. Quickly, Steele tried to back up and go out another exit. But before he could, the monster truck pulled up behind him, blocking him in. "What the..?" He swore under his breath and thought of ways to blow up the truck. Twisting the steering wheel in his grip was his only recourse though and he waited. Thank goodness, a moment later some maintenance staff arrived and pushed the car off to the side allowing those waiting to leave. Exiting the garage and driving around the block he was able to position his car downstream from the flow of traffic and wait for the authoress to depart. Ahead of him waited the limousine, catching some movement in his right-hand mirror; he saw a meter maid cart sidle up alongside. The matron pulled up so she could talk through his window at him, "You have to move your car sir," she said.

"I'm waiting for someone," Steel replied. "She'll only be a minute."

"You can't wait here; you're in a red zone."

In his haste to make it around the block, he must have missed that simple fact. Thinking fast he lied, "She's pregnant. I'm sure she won't be long."

"I'm sorry. I don't make the rules," responded the meter-maid from behind her Aviator glasses. "You'll have to motor about and keep rechecking this spot. You can't stay here." She stared at him like a rock.

"Crap," said Steele under his breath. If only I could take out the people I want instead of the ones I have to. He started his car and pulled away from the curb. As he passed the limo he saw his victim walking down the block with a few lingerers flocking her.

"Oh no," he muttered. The meter-maid passed him on the left as he slowed his car to a crawl. When the matron turned the corner to the right he pulled on the side of the road and pretended to fumble with his glove box. Cars passed him with drivers passing out dirty looks and one yelling, "Find a parking place you idiot." The limousine passed him and he allowed one car to get between them, then he followed.

They turned right onto Fairfax heading south and proceeded to Sunset and turned left About 5 miles down and the black Lincoln limousine turned into to The Beverly Hills Hotel, a beautiful towering pink mission style colonial building overlooking Will Rogers Park at the base of the Los Angeles foothills. It had a long driveway and lots of bellmen to help the guests. This presented a problem. It was a very busy place, too busy for someone to slip in unnoticed. Maybe today wasn't his day. What are you thinking? Come on Sundance: shoot from the hip.

On the way to the hotel, Steele Daniels noticed two shops that could be of use; a flower shop and a costume shop. He went to the costume shop first and asked if they had any delivery boy costumes for rent. The older lady working the counter replied, "No, I'm sorry were temporarily out. If you'd like to wait till after the weekend..."

That wouldn't do. "How about a bellman uniform?"
No again. "But, I've got an idea," she said. "It's a little showier, but it works real well if you want to impress someone with a delivery."

Steele Daniels soon found himself dressed in a blue and gold High School Marching uniform, complete with the white gloves and a tall hat. He told the lady the hat was a bit much. Could we do something else? She replaced it with a policeman's dark blue dress hat. Perfect. She needed a credit card to rent the clothes and he supplied her with one from his last victim. All paid for and accounted, he left and went to the flower shop where $75 bought a grand bouquet with a vase and he headed back for the hotel.

He parked at the end of a long line of cars so as not to get out directly in front of the main doors thereby minimizing any memory of his vehicle. He salted the bouquet with Oleander dust, saving half for another time, placed his silencer revolver in the back waist of his trousers. He used the flowers to block his face as often as possible and went to the front desk of the hotel. There a smartly dressed college aged girl asked what he needed. He requested the room number of the Diva. The clerk informed him she could not divulge that information but if he would leave the flowers here she would have one of their service people deliver them. That simply wouldn't do, he thought. But what were his choices? Shoot from the hip. "That's OK with me," he said. "They're not for her anyways and I'm sure there won't be any tip."

"Excuse me," she said holding up her hand to stop him from placing the flowers on the counter. "What do you mean?"

"Well, they aren't for her. They're for the man she's been with. But, just between you and me," he whispered. "They're from another lady. I think there's another chicken in the fox house. If you know what I mean."

"Why don't you just bring them up yourself? She's in room 314."

She pointed to the elevators and Steel Daniels willingly obliged. On the third floor he got off and followed the numbers to her door. He rang it and waited. In what seemed like a rudely long time the door was answered by the Diva herself. She was dressed in a bathrobe and carried a paperback of Silence of the Lambs in her hand. Upon seeing the flowers she said, "Oh, put them over there with the others," and pointed to a table covered in dozens of assortments of roses, daises, petunias, and other flowers. "Wait a second," she said and came over and took a big sniff of the bunch, breathing in several lungs full of the intoxicating flora. "They are so lovely when they're fresh," she said. Then she walked over to a narrow table under a mirror, pulled a twenty from her purse and laid it on the counter. "Help yourself to this and then show yourself out." She turned and walked from the room.

Steel couldn't believe his luck. She had breathed deeply from the flowers. She hadn't fallen, but she could hardly have taken in a better gulp of the potent poison if she'd used a straw. He noticed a silver tray on a coffee table loaded with tea and cookies. She wasn't around and he needed to make sure she died. He walked over to the tray, looking towards the doorway through which she'd walked. He lifted the top of the tea pot and poured in the rest of the Oleander, quietly shut the lid, grabbed the twenty dollars and left.

Not too long after that, a very good looking gentleman who had once starred in the movies, exited the hotel room bathroom and saw his venerable beloved sprawled a kilter on the floor, her bathrobe open and her arms spread. He didn't even notice the new flowers on the table along with all the rest and cried while calling the front desk to get security and an ambulance up to room 314. He was still shaking when he hung up and had to sit down. Then to help calm his nerves he poured himself a cup of tea.

10
Daily's New Lead

AUTHORESS AND ACTOR DIE IN MURDER-SUICIDE

BEVERLY HILLS - Best Selling Authoress Danny Stole and Legendary Actor Georgeham Milton was found dead in their hotel room in what appears to be a murder-suicide.Shortly after 5pm Thursday night Milton called the front desk to report Stole laying unconscious on the floor of their Beverly Hills hotel suite When paramedicsarrived Milton was also dead. Both had consumed poison.The famous couple began dating a few years ago when.....

Detective Trey Hunt put down his copy of the Times and took a sip of coffee. He drank it black, liked things simple and usually thought the most direct path was the correct one. He was also good at reading between the lines and this one had a lot of white space. The article mentioned poison but not a type. It also said Milton had called the front desk for help and this fact made little sense if he had already poisoned his girlfriend. Why would the old man reach out after being guilty of murder?

Another thing hung on Hunts conscious. His partner, Susan Daily had been doing massive amounts of legwork on the author murder in their district. He knew she was trying to get beyond some romantic emotional problems, but for all her effort she was covering some good ground. So long as she didn't let the murders become her own blueprint for revenge everything would be fine. Daily didn't seem imbalanced and he didn't seriously think she would become a liability in the force. Although he'd seen good cops go bad in the past. He mostly felt his partner just needed a new love interest in her life, mostly. But for all his concerns, he couldn't deny her the fruits of her labor. Could there be a string of murders happening? He picked up the phone and called a friend on the Beverly Hills Detective bureau, Oscar Layton. Layton had been partnered with Hunt in their early years at the LAPD. Layton picked up and rather than play a long winded game of catch up, "How's the wife and kids?" Hunt went into why he was calling as soon as he identified himself. Layton didn't mind. Hunt had had the same personality as long as they'd known each other.

Layton only knew the edges of the case. It had been assigned to another detective named Craig Prater. Without any further small talk, Layton gave Hunt the correct extension and transferred him with an insincere, "Keep in touch."

Prater wasn't in, but he called Hunt back before the end of the day. The two seasoned police veterans were reluctant to share notes at first but after a few sample exchanges they talked openly without fear of jurisdiction. Prater used a term called, "Splitting the hog." Their cases were on similar paths. Prater let the papers run with the murder-suicide story to throw the public and the murderer on the wrong track, leaving the investigation unhindered. Stole and Milton were not killed in a murder-suicide, they were plainly murdered. The poison was an inhalant that the boys in the lab would diagnose in the next few days. The culprit was a white male in his mid-thirties, slight of build with blonde hair. A desk clerk had identified him after he made a delivery of flowers. Prater and his partner were sweeping flower shops and uniform rentals in the area, hopeful to come up with more leads.

Hunt was betting heavily both the murdered authors were killed by the same perpetrator; Milton was just a crime of convenience. The detectives agreed to keep in touch. A few days later Prater and Hunt talked again. The shop was found where the flowers were purchased. Unfortunately, false Id and a stolen credit card were used for the transaction leaving no trail. The flower shop and the hotel desk clerks both had similar descriptions of the suspect. They were put to work with a police artist to develop a sketch.

Artists sketched wouldn't do any good without something to compare it against. Hunt made two phone calls; one back to Layton to get a copy of the video tapes from the bookstore Danny Stole had been signing at that afternoon and the other to his own evidence department to get copies of the tapes from the store where Clyde Barstow had done his signing. Fans who loved both authors would be few but dealers attending the events should be abundant. Either way it was a starting point for the way Detective Hunt knew how to police. It was unfortunate but solving a crime sometimes took more than one incident to recognize a pattern. Finally something to sink his teeth into other than computer work and he could do all his detecting from his nice comfortable chair.

In the meantime, Hunt kept his mouth shut to his partner about his worries over her romantic life and instead told Detective Susan Daily about his conversation with Prater at Beverly Hills and the soon to be arriving tapes. With the new information of a physical description, Daily decided to redirect her attentions and begin whittling again. She reviewed her narrowing list of possible bookstores. A week later, armed with the sketch, over five dozen grainy video pictures and a list of only 128 possible book dealers, she was ready to do some store to store shopping.

11
Milo's Discoveries

MILO SAT ON A PLAIN WOODEN CHAIR working late into the night with his computer tucked into the closet of his small apartment in the low rent district of a neighborhood inappropriately called the Dream Homes. The only comfort he had was a hand-made pillow from his mom to sit on. The runners of the sliding doors caught from time to time on the legs of the chair until he accepted the distance from which he had to sit from the screen. He was uneasy with leaving the computer visibly exposed in the main room. Anyone who happened to come by or glanced in the window would see it and Milo felt it wouldn't stay around for long. Someone would walk off with it and none of the other renters would see anything.

His right hand gripped the mouse delicately, like an artist holding a brush. His canvas was the net and his colors the script of various programming languages; HTML, Java, PERL, C++ and many others. His strategy: knowing where to look and what to insert. The primer was the document Xanthe had given him: a printed page from eBay titled Stephen's Dump Truck and it stood to his left on a stand made for just such an occasion.

Milo leaned back in his chair until it was balanced on two legs and looked at the paper. A few things caught his attention right away. The seller had used the name CrandallPhlag11265. Crandall Phlag was a character in several of Knightly's books, namely The End, The Desperado Series, and The Orbs of The Wyrm. In all of these, Phlag was at least an evil wizard and occasionally a demon. The seller had to be amused at his selection for an eBay name. One thing about the name created further consideration. The number 11265 at the end was too long to be a recommended suffix by eBay. Could it be a birthday? If so, it meant the seller was 30 years old.

The seller was 10 years older than Milo. Milo wondered where he'd be in another ten years. Far from here, he thought. Life was a struggle. He'd moved away - thrown out was a more truthful wording - from his parents Baltimore row house when he was sixteen. "Get out you little Rat Bastard," was his step dad's final farewell. Hopping over the crack whores passed out on the curb and fleeing to the safety of Fort McHenry Park was his first stop on a cross country joy ride that nearly landed him in a New Mexico jail. But due to the favors of a truck stop owner's daughter, he was instead ferried off to the California desert in the passenger seat of an 18-wheeler. Four years later, he was a community college drop-out hanging out with high school kids and plying his burglary skills on the internet. He had to stifle a sniffle as he thought of the situation he'd left his mom and baby sister in back on the east coast.

Milo clicked on the -36 feedback rating and read a few reviews on the seller. They were all negative. Seller should have never listed the item. Seller doesn't return emails. Seller is a BIG FAT ASS for teasing SK fans, and so on and so forth. There were thirty six negative comments in all. The only fact Milo could discern from this was that the seller had never listed other products before. This had been his or her first and last.

He took a look at the bid history and for the most part this was another waste. But there were some interesting facts. First off, the bulk of the bidders were names that meant nothing to Milo. He printed the list and made some notes on it. Reading down the list went:

FloridaDr49@aol.com (High Bidder)(Florida Doctor?)
SKFan1
DwarvenHo
KnightRidder@netzero.com
BaughmannBooks (Bookdealer)
HorrorScope

The Author Murders

Darwinistic
BertBooks (Bookdealer)
Queerdini
Latinlady836
Brahmstein
Sankyu15@hotmail.com
CanadianIce123
HermitageBooks (Bookdealer)
Hoser4Life
8ntIgr8
Bidnezman
etc.

Cross referencing the bidding list against the list of negative feedback resulted in almost everyone who was a top bidder relieving their frustration, except FloridaDr49@aol.com. A statistic worth noting. The bidder was probably a Florida doctor who could afford the high price of the book but wouldn't take his time to complain.

Keeping a personal profile was something most idiots did on the internet. In truth, this habit was more a liability than an asset. The good luck stories mainly culminated around adopted children finding lost parents or siblings. Or, it could reunite long lost high school friends from distant parts of the country. Still, thinking with a criminal mind, Milo realized profiles were the perfect hotbed of information waiting for someone seeking to assume a new identity. Innocent people were lining up to be victims of identity theft by criminals far less scrupulous than Milo. The identity thieves would take unwarranted advantage of anyone willing to list everything from marital information to business leads to educational history on their profile or personal website.

Milo checked AOL to see if FloridaDr49 kept a personal profile on file. No such luck. Milo thought of trying to hack into a customer account but there were a few places he felt better left alone and AOL was one of them, eBay was another. These companies could afford the very best in security and anti-piracy technology. Sure, there were individuals who had hacked these systems but generally they got caught or if they succeeded their tactics were to simply barrage the systems until they eventually buckled under the workload. Neither strategy would deliver the desired result in this instance. He had to find a strand of information leading to the weak link.

Looking at the bottom of the page, Milo saw an X above a sentence which read, "Image No Longer Available." He right clicked on the X and clicked properties. There was a destination listed through an image source code. It read:

<img src="http://www.imagesexpress.com/CrandallPhlagg11265.jpg">.

This was what Milo had hoped for. Here was a little website most likely lacking in funds and security. He put his mom out of his mind and went to work.

12
Donlagic's Return

IT WAS THURSDAY NIGHT AGAIN. But I couldn't be at the street fair. Thom Racina was doing his second book signing at Villagefest and I was going to have to get a report on it later.

It was time for some community service. I had my monthly Police Advisory Committee. It was held in the community service room of the Palm Springs Police Department headquarters, a large rectangular room with folding tables and chairs drawn in a square. We were a loose assortment of known and unknown names in town. A full third of the members had been recommended to the committee by me. Almost everyone had been outspoken on one issue or another in the last few years. Most had an axe to grind, an agenda of their own, and to me that was a good thing.

A small audience sat in tonight for what seemed to be our most important meeting to date. I was sure nearly all of the two dozen or so members of the public were waiting for item number two. Two uniformed officers sat in the chairs closest to the doors.

Lying in front of me was a sheet of paper with tonight's agenda on it. I lifted it and read:

PALM SPRINGS POLICE ADVISORY COMMITTEE
AGENDA
1) APPROVAL OF BY-LAWS
2) HIGH SCHOOL RACIAL INCIDENT
3) INDIAN TRIBAL POLICE AUTHORITY
4) SELECTION OF OFFICERS/BOARD OF DIRECTORS

The meeting was run by Allen Baumgartner, a graying man of some girth, who seemed to fit the image needed to get the meetings going originally but had grown a reputation for being short of patience with anyone who disagreed with him. He ran the meeting with an iron fist, demanding short sentences from those who opposed his views and pontificated when he deemed it necessary. I hated him in that he was an unfair man.

The first item of the night was APPROVAL OF THE BY-LAWS. A boring discussion if there ever was one. The By-Laws passed with only one or two minor modifications.

The door opened to the room and two people entered. The first was one of my placements on the committee, Keith Winters, a notoriously tardy member for nearly every meeting so far and the other was my nemesis and employer, Detective Michael Donlagic, wearing a fresh Hawaiian print shirt. He shook the hands of the two officers sitting near the door and sat next to them.

Appropriate timing, I thought. Donlagic had been the lead investigator in the High School Racial Incident, a crime which reignited tensions in Palm Springs buried for over thirty years. In our audience tonight was over 10 black leaders in the community who were furious over the lack of investigation, after more than eight white students were caught after hours vandalizing the High School, writing racial slurs about the new black principal on the windows, painting a swastika on the doorways and the hanging of a dead cat. A few of the kids were caught red-handed on High School grounds. The remainders were scooped up nearby in a parent's garage and all of them were merely taken home to their parents or released on their own recognizance rather than booked into juvenile hall.

The uniformed officers were brought up to the table, bracing themselves for the derisive barrage of Public Comments. They refused to answer questions which only infuriated the crowd more. The pitch and tone of the room climbed to a crescendo of hatred which was not abated by the officer's stoniness.

Nearly an hour later, public speaking was done. The Chairman called for a ten minute break against several members' objections. He claimed to need a bathroom break and thought some people might need refreshments. He banged his gavel and declared to reconvene in ten.

Taking my leave, I also headed out to go the bathroom. The outdoor corridors are dark around the Police station, making me wonder about safety in an area where criminals were known to frequent. The lamps used to light the area were either burnt out or dimly lit. I figured it had to be because there were several apartment complexes nearby and Palm Springs has this odd argument arising anytime a new development tries to put in street lighting or outdoor lamps because it obstructs the view of the stars.

So, I walked in the darkness until I came to the poorly lit area of the bathrooms around the corner of the building. Chairman Baumgartner was in the stall and as I waited my turn I attempted to strike a conversation, but Allen saw me first and cut me off before I could start.

"They don't have to do the police's job," Baumgartner shot at me as he zipped up his pants. "It's easy to kibbitz from the sidelines."

"You don't think they're justified?" I asked.

"I think it's an issue for the school board," he said, quickly washing his hands and shouldering past me, out of the bathroom.

This was his way of throwing the police out of the spotlight, trying to make it seem like it was another governments jurisdiction, a path I had already heard from others who wanted to soften the blow on the police and a path I didn't care to venture. I changed my tact. Call a spade a spade and let the chips fall where they may.

"I think the police cut the kids a break they didn't deserve." I shouted after him.

"You're screwed in the head," he threw his comments back at me, getting in the last word before the door swung shut.

I washed my hands in the same sink. When I lifted my head I saw someone standing in the mirror that I didn't hear come in, Michael Donlagic.

"Hey Xanthey," he said, a smile widening on his face and his arms spreading. "Got anything for me."

"Hey Mike." I turned around and pulled a few towels from the machine to wipe my hands. "Not yet. But I got some things working. They should bear fruit soon."

"You wouldn't be holding out on me would you?" He stood in my way of the door.

"What? No." Why would he think that? "Listen, I've got someone tracking down the seller right now. He's been on it all week. I'm gonna owe him a little money any way about it. But I think he'll come through." I tried to sidestep Donlagic and he moved in my way a second time.

"Do you mind," I said staring into his black eyes.

Wham. He knuckle punched me in the gut. "Don't think I can't see what you're doing Xanthey. You will bring me whatever you find."

I doubled over in pain. It was like a sack of bricks had launched into my gut without someone first yelling 'Catch'. I couldn't believe he'd just punched me. He stepped past me and looked in the mirror leaving me with one hand on the wall tiles to hold myself up. They were cold on my hand, just like Mike.

"When you work for me, you keep in touch," he was smoothing his hair with a little water. "It's been too long since you called. I thought I better stop by and remind you who the boss is. I'm sure it was just an oversight."

He pushed past me, throwing a fake punch to my stomach, just stopping short of connecting. I doubled over a second time in expectation of the pain. Instead he thrust a business card into my shirt pocket and chuckled, "Maybe you just forgot the number," and walked out the door with parting words: "Book dealer pussy." I slid down the wall onto my haunches until I caught my breath. Then I crawled to the sink, hoisted myself up, splashed some water onto my face and walked back into the meeting.

He was still sitting in the audience, laughing and joking with his fellow officers as if nothing had just happened. I walked straight backed to my seat, still in a daze over what had just happened and not wanting to show any signs.

Chairman Baumgartner banged his gavel to call the meeting back to order. The majority of the spectators had remained to see if the police were questioned. They were not disappointed. Several of the committee members chastised the officers for their lack of enforcement. The crowd applauded every time a point was scored. The officers again shifted in their seats uncomfortably. Committee members were relentless in their criticism, resounding many of the same notes heralded earlier in public comments.

There was a point in the evening when I thought they would turn over their shoulder and ask a question of their former lead detective, Michael Donlagic, yet instead they held, "That information is confidential to the investigation." I had to respect that attitude even though it was the same attitude I had collided with in the past and would again many times in the future.

Near the end of the discussion I put in my two cents. "I believe this incident requires a return to statements I have made earlier. I believe the city needs a full fledged Police Commission with capabilities to investigate Internal Affairs of the department or else when incidents like this arise we shall never know the full extent of what is fair." The room went quiet. While every member I had brought onto the committee knew, and shared the feeling that this was the direction the committee should grow, they were scared of how to proceed. Their silence indicated to me they were unwilling to follow yet, even though this abuse of authority over a racial incident could be just what was needed to pull the city in the right direction. The silence lingered for nearly 30 seconds and then a lone audience member, a black man who must have been 20 years past retirement began clapping his hands. He clapped alone until the Chairman decided to break the spell with yet another pounding of his gavel. I hate that gavel.

"Next item on the agenda," he declared loudly, raising his voice to a near shout in an effort to regain control, "Tribal Police Authority. Do we have a report?"

"Ahem," said Captain Danielson, clearing his throat to gain notice.

"The Chair recognizes our Advisor, Captain Gary Danielson."

"Yes, well," Captain Danielson began, a bit befuddled, "It seems that this item may as well be skipped or postponed. The Indian Tribe had been asking for permission to address the committee on the issue of extending Tribal Police authority off the reservation because of the unique situation here in Palm Springs. You are all familiar with the checkerboard layout throughout town. One square mile of which is reservation land and the next is fee simple standard public domain land, with a hybrid of these properties culminating in the mixture of land that makes up Palm Springs. It is a very unique situation and the only one in the country. While this normally doesn't interfere with ordinary police work, the growth of Indian casinos has formulated scenarios heretofore unconsidered in Tribal Sovereignty. For example, should someone shoplift from the Casino or hotel gift shop, which should arrest and prosecute?"

Keith Winters asked the obvious question, "You mean they want arrest authority off of reservation land? Where would they bring the alleged criminals? Here?"

"No," said Captain Danielson. "It is assumed that Tribal Police with roaming capabilities would house their own suspects in Indian Jails and prosecute the offenders in Indian Courts."

Uproar burst upon the room. Comments of, "They could come knocking on just anyone's door and arrest?" and "Looks like it's time to circle the wagons," emanated from all over.

"Now, now," interrupted the Captain. "Let me be clear. I am not advocating this. I am merely repeating a statement put forth by the tribe. But, as I look about the room, I do not see a tribal representative present and I suggest we table this discussion until further notice."

"Ahem," came loudly from the back of the audience. "I was sent here tonight on the Tribe's behalf. Mr. Chairman I have a letter for you." Michael Donlagic stood and held out his hand in which was an envelope.

At the Chairman's direction, Captain Danielson stepped forward and retrieved the letter, handing it back to the Chairman. Allen looked at its face and recognizing the seal of the Tribe opened it. The room fell silent as he read it, low grumblings bubbling up as he took more than a moment. Finally, Allen made an announcement.

"It seems we are invited to select a sub-committee of five members who will participate in a public forum to explore the possibilities of a Tribal Police Force."

"A debate?" asked one of our junior members.

"No, not really," said Donlagic, cutting in. "See it more as a discussion of equal parts. I even thought we'd do it on my radio program so the public can listen in."

"I'll put it on the agenda for our next meeting," said Allen.

"The Tribe was hoping for an answer tonight," insisted Donlagic.

"Next item on the agenda," shouted the Chairman, forcing Donlagic to sit down, "Selection of Board of Directors." Apparently, Allen had been waiting for this item all evening. He quickly pulled a sheaf of papers from his folder and asked the Secretary to pass them out. "These are my recommendations for Board members. While anyone may nominate anyone, I would appreciate consideration for a Board capable of functioning fluidly with one another."

That was another way of his saying, 'Give me only people who will do as I tell them.' I read down the list and noticed my name was omitted. I can't say I didn't expect this but I had hoped he would see me as an active participant. I had served on several sub-committees beyond the By-Laws, such as the Racial Incident sub-committee which had produced tonight's most active meeting and I was the largest procurer of new members - qualities which meant nothing to Allen.

"Is there anyone who would like to nominate," Allen said, allowing his tone to linger on the last word, "Anyone, anyone... well if not."

A hand raised in the corner of the table. A small lady named Yolanda Valenzuela who ran the Boys and Girls Club. "Yes, I'd like to nominate."

"O-Oh, Ok," stuttered the Chairman, lowering his chin and staring at her hard, "Who would you like to nominate?"

"I'd like to nominate Xanthe," she said, "For Vice-Chairman."

"Hmmph," said Allen, "Alright then. A nomination needs a second. Will anyone second the nomination?"

Seconds ticked away, then... "I'll second that," said Keith Winters.

"Will Mr. Anthony accept the nomination?" reluctantly asked Chairman Baumgartner.

Jake was Allen's recommendation for Vice-President. Jake was a good man. I liked him plenty, but who was I to argue with the motion. Plus, if successful, I would be in a better position to push the concept of becoming a real Police Commission.

"I accept."

Several more nominations came forward after that. Allen's attempt at railroading the elections had been derailed. When the vote came, I won. The meeting ended with Allen turning his back away from me in an early departure. I didn't mind. Other members were coming forward and shaking my hand, offering support and congratulations.

* * *

When I finally broke away from the crowd I made my way back to the store. The street fair had ended and the kids were packing the books from the booth into boxes. Thom caught my eye as he was putting his pen to the last book for a customer who was leaving with three titles. When the customer left Thom burst out, "Wow, what a night!"

"How'd we do?" I asked.

"A new record, I think we sold about 150," he smiled a grin so big he looked like the Cheshire cat.

I joined him in smiling. "That's awesome. You coming back next week?" As if I didn't know.

"You bet," he said. "I think we got a date every Thursday from now on. I've got other big news too."

"What's up?" I could tell he was excited.

"I got a new agent," he said eagerly. "And this gal's motivated. She thinks she can convince the publisher to push hardbacks and give me a marketing budget."

"That sounds great," his excitement was infectious.

"Yeah, I might even get a shot at the New York Times Book review section.

13
A Day at CelebrityBooks.com

THE NEXT DAY I AWOKE FEELING as if my encounter with Donlagic had all been a bad dream. Through my bedroom window the sky was Palm Springs perfect, a bright blue with wispy clouds visible. Palm trees framed the view like goal posts and I could even hear a few birds chirping. I tried to roll out of bed until a sore stomach reawakened the reality of what had happened the night before.

Maybe that was his point. Donlagic was anxious for information and I was his informant. Never mind that I was a shopkeeper and he'd been a police officer or the mere fact that his very existence was an affront to everything I considered decent and pure. As far as he was concerned I owed him big. I made a mental note to stop by an ATM on the way to work and draw out $300. If I was going to get punched I was going to get paid for it.

I drove downtown to the bookstore in my Jeep Wrangler, a car that I loved from an earlier career as a car salesman. In the past, it had taken me out to abandoned gold and silver mines in the middle of the desert and I only hoped I wasn't mining for fool's gold now. Four days had passed since Milo had taken on the job of finding information for me about the whereabouts of the Stephen's Dump Truck seller. I needed the information now but I had neglected to get his phone number from him. I would have to send an email and wait for a reply.

I parked in behind the store and walked around to the front. The beautiful Palm Springs morning had followed me to work. Hair thin clouds flew out from the looming mountain of San Jacinto like white lace. It was just another day in paradise.

Waiting outside the store, on the public bench off to one side, was an attractive lady in faded snug blue jeans and a white collared shirt. She was staring down the block in the other direction, allowing me a moment to capture a full view. She had longer than shoulder length blonde hair that sparkled in the morning sunshine. She was slightly younger than me, most likely in her late twenties and had an athletic yet not over emphasized physique lending to a naturally healthy glow. She turned to me as I walked past and I got a glimpse of a thin nose and high cheeks. I had to pull my eyes away so as not to stare.

She called at me as I put my key in the door, "Opening up?"

"Yep," I said. "Just give me a minute to turn off the alarm."

She waited outside on the bench as I scurried inside to turn the alarm off and the lights on. There was more to the opening procedure but I didn't want to make her wait. I leaned back out the front door, "You can come in now if you'd like."

She stood up and walked past me into the front of the store, stopping just a few feet inside and looking around.

Celebrity Books.com is an old-fashioned little mom and pop operation that had made the transition to the internet age. The front counter was covered in stacks of books and papers broken up by the two massive computer screens dominating the service area. Nothing fancy but functional, its shelves are mostly 1x8 inch pine boards nailed together and stained to give them a bit of style. Most of the shelves are uniform in size. But there are a few of oddball dimensions built for specific spaces from previous locations to round out a corner or fill in a gap created by forcing them into places they weren't originally de-signed. The overall effect was a bookstore blended with symmetry and unusualness into a unique display. Even the floor had a sort of mystical appeal, bricks painted yellow, as if leading to the Land of Oz.

My early morning customer took all this in with a sweep of her saffron hair and then asked the obvious question, "Why are you called Celebrity Books?"

"We, I, specialize in celebrity biographies and autographed books. The whole left wall is biographies," I spoke pointing down a stretch with signs up high listing: Authors Bio's, Royal Bio's, Sports Bio's, Celebrity Bio's, Political Bio's, etc. "And on this side," I continued, directing towards the right hand side of the skinny store, "is the Autographed books." Motioning to the shelves at the end of the counter, there were three large shelving units full of signed books. Many of the giants of modern literature were shown on display. Often there were 5, 10 or twenty copies of the same titles available for perusing. The result was an overwhelming stock of signed books. She looked at the books for a lengthy browse, standing out against the books like a chestnut. I excused myself, "I've got a little more to do with opening up. Would you be alright for a few minutes as I finish?"

"Sure," she nodded and I rushed off to start the back computers, turn on the bathroom lights and perform the rest of the tasks necessary to opening up the store. When I returned she had some more questions for me.

"How do you get so many signed books?" she wondered.

"A couple different ways," I said. "Out here in Palm Springs, it seems that in almost every collection I buy there's one or two signed books in them. Also, I go to a lot of book signings and meet the authors and get their books signed. Finally, I entice the publishers to send the authors out here to my store." Although so far my success in that field has been limited.

"How do you do that?"

I knew what she was thinking. Why would the authors come out to this store? I'd seen the look before in the faces of customers and authors. The look that said, 'This store isn't nice enough to bring out the top-notch authors.'

The answer to my beautiful customers question hung in the air and it must have been her influence on me which made me think of the reply. It was a lie but over the next few weeks it would begin to dawn on me the eloquence of my response. "I intend to use a very ancient secret I hardly ever share."

She opened her already dangerously inviting green eyes a little wider and looked square into my face with anticipation.

"I send flowers to the publishers when I make my request."

"You send flowers?" she blinked, not quite understanding.

"That's right," I said, emboldened by her interest. "It's the old tricks that work best and I find if I take the time to send flowers with my request I always get an answer." This was all conjecture on a plan I was formulating as I spoke. "Even if it doesn't work on this tour the publisher never forgets me and I'll break through to them eventually. It probably helps that most of the publishers are women. If I sent them to a male publisher it would have a kind of queer feeling to it. If you know what I mean."

She laughed a warm pleasant giggle causing the sun shine to brighten and I was tempted to ask her to come back for lunch. Before I could though she had another question, "Did you have Danny Stole in for a book signing?"

"No, (I wish) I had to go see her up in the Los Angeles area."

"How about Cliff Barkley?"

"I've tried several times. But I never seem to get him out here. I ran into him up in Pasadena recently. Shame what happened to them both."

"Yeah," she said without pause. "You don't have any advanced reading copies of either of them do you?"

"I had a Cliff Barkley," I said. "But, I sold it on Ebay. Caught the whole death wave that followed his demise. Couldn't pass it up, I'm sorry to say."

She shrugged her shoulders as if to say, 'That's life,' then asked, "Are you going to any other signings soon?"

"I'm going to a Jay Landsbury signing next week. I wish he would come out here for me. But his publicist said he got sick this year and isn't traveling as much. Funny how often some of these authors get sick. I hear that one a lot."

Turning back to the shelves of signed stock she asked, "You don't have any signed or rare Stephen Knightly do you?"

My job for Donlagic swept past my mind. This cool breath of fresh air couldn't be a set-up could she? "No, not right now. I come across him sometimes, but he's a bit pricey, as you probably know. If you want to put your name and number on my want list I'll keep an eye out for you." I figured it was a great way to secure her information. Both for the Knightly case and personal reasons.

"No, that's OK thanks. I've got to run," and she swept herself back out the front door, swinging the back of her blue jeans onto the street. I was left in a slight daze until the door reopened two blinks of an eye later with another customer who asked, "Do you carry the New York Times?" and my day began.

* * *

Detective Trey Hunt had his morning coffee and donut disturbed by the phone ringing. He picked it up, "Hello, can I help you?" He never liked identifying himself or the precinct in case it was one of his criminal informants or an old trap laid long ago and forgotten about. Not to his surprise, it was his partner.

"Trey? Susan. I've got a lead and I need some advice."

"What have you got partner?" Detective Hunt put down his coffee while sitting up and splashed some of the mocha on the hash marks s on his sleeve. It made him grumpy. Some officers prided themselves on their rank. Trey Hunt preferred longevity of service. Each small stripe, or Hash mark represented five years on the force. So far he had six of them. He didn't think he'd be around long enough to earn another. He picked up a pencil and swung his attention back to the phone.

Why are all the good ones taken and the handsome ones crooks? "I just met a suspect I like for the author murders. Lot of circumstantial so far, but it just feels right. Trouble is I'm a long way from home and I don't have any friends here." It was at times like this she depended upon her senior partner's expertise and contacts.

"Where are you at?"

"Palm Springs."

"OK. I've got a friend there. I knew him from the academy a long long time ago. If he's still on the job he should be a lieutenant by now. His names Mike McCray. If he doesn't remember me at first remind him about the incident at the at the USC football game. He'll remember real quick or my names not Hunt."

With a chuckle in her voice, "You gonna tell me about what happened at the game or what?"

"Maybe another time partner, I don't want to end up in an HR lawsuit this close to retirement." Hunt knew he'd tell her sometime, but not today. Let her earn her own Hash marks. "When you talk to McCray he should assign you one or two uniforms to assist in the arrest. They may or may not allow you to just cart the guy back her to our pokey. That's their choice. If they're hesitant at all then do the interview there. Now tell me what you got and where you're going just in case I need to follow-up on you."

Susan liked the fact that that Hunt cared enough about her to take notes. Not an annoyance of someone looking over her shoulder. Instead the two had good symmetry. He offered back-up even when he was hours away. She spilled her guts and he listened and wrote.

* * *

Over the course of the next couple hours, I managed to answer all my emails. Twenty-two books in all were ordered and placed on the To Be Shipped shelf in the second room, awaiting my high school staff of shippers on Friday. I also sent an outgoing email to Milo although I didn't expect a response until the next day.

In between my normal clerk duties I took the time to fulfill one of my most successful strategies in life. It was the secret to my triumphs in another arena – dating. Anytime I met a woman I found intriguing I made notes on her so if I ran into her on another occasion I could review my findings. It's worked for me many times. I'd meet a lovely damsel at a bar or in the store or the supermarket or wherever and when I was back at my desk I'd jot down a few things: hair color, height, job, kids, parents, pets , anything at all so upon our next visit or phone call I could make a remark like, "How's your mother doing? Is she still sore from her Rheumatism?" or "I'm sorry about your cat last week going astray. Did you find him?" In this way I could break down the girl's defenses about me being a guy just wanting to get in her pants.

The Author Murders

I pulled out my blue spiral notebook which served as my little black book and made a few notes; Blonde hair, five foot four, nice build, almost thirty, likes Stephen Knightly. I wish I had a phone number and address to go along with the info but no such luck. Maybe she'd come in again. This same game plan had me dating up to thirty women at times. It wasn't like it always got me laid but it did allow me never to go dancing without a partner if I wanted one. It seemed to make the women think, 'Even though he's not that handsome, at least he LISTENED to me.' After all isn't that what any of us wants deep down inside – to be heard.

Jill came into work about 11 am. She was unusually happy. Her husband had just received a line of work on an upcoming cable network series. He was to do the sound for a show called JAG. It had something to do with military lawyers and if the pilot episode was successful it would become steady work, something that would greatly improve their quality of life. I congratulated her and she dreamed openly a few moments before I informed her of her duties for the day. There were two stacks of books with her name on them, one was to be put away on the shelves and the other was to be data-inputted into the Abebooks database. She put a post-it note on top of each pile in case she couldn't remember which was which.

Our camaraderie was broken as the front door opened and my early morning blonde haired customer walked back into the store. Only this time she was flagged by two officers from the Palm Springs Police Department. There was no warm smile on her face, she still wore the same clothes although this time there was a distinctive difference in her stance and she had a badge fixed to her belt. She was a police officer.

Her introduction began, "Xanthe Anthony, You are herby under arrest for the murders of Cliff Barkley, Danny Stole and George-ham Milton. You have the right to remain silent. Anything you say can and will be used against you in a court of law. You have the right to an attorney. If you cannot afford an attorney one will be appointed for you by a court of law." I was spun around, handcuffed and walked out the front door.

As I was being walked out, I yelled, "Jill, close up for me."

Eric G. Meeks

14
At the Police Station

I WAS STILL HANDCUFFED as I waited in a sparsely decorated square box of a room with a plain table and the reflective side of
a two-way mirror on the wall staring back at me. I knew this to be an
Interview room. The ride to the station had been silent. The two officers who'd accompanied the female detective were friends of mine, or
so I thought, Detectives Donald Craft and Brian Andrews. They must
have been at a celebration of some sort. They normally don't wear their
dress blues anymore.

I wasn't entirely sure how I was connected to the murders and
I wasn't going to open my mouth until I knew more. Not sure I would
have been told anything helpful, but I couldn't ask the detectives anyway
in the presence of Detective Susan Daily. At least I'd learned her name
on the drive. I sat in the interview room for what seemed like a long
time. When the door opened, Detective Daily walked in, escorted by
Detective Andrews. Andrews sat opposite me at the table.

Detective Andrews was a tall fit man in his mid-forties, well sun
tanned with hair graying at the temples. He'd been on the PSPD for
nearly all of his twenty something years of service and as far as I knew
he'd worked his way up the chain of command honorably. The only
vice I was aware of was his drinking, which usually started in the morning before he even had a bowl of cereal. He was stone cold sober now
as he looked across at me.

Detective Daily sat next to him. I still found her pretty. She was
going to take a run at me.

80

"Xanthe. Xanthe Anthony. Is that your name?" She was cold. The term ice bitch floated in my mind.

"Yes," I said remembering to keep my answers simple.

"What kind of a name is that?" She opened a folder in front of her and read down the list of information. I didn't realize the department kept a folder on me. It wasn't as if I didn't have a past. I just didn't think they'd have a hand written anything on me. All my offenses were petty and obscure distant infractions, mainly from my childhood. They were supposed to be sealed. I'd had the question of my name come up plenty of times till I'd finally honed a pat answer.

"Just the one my parents gave me."

"Hmpf." She read a few more lines in the folder and then she snapped it shut. "I'm not going to lie to you," unblinking, she held my gaze, "You're in deep. You want to get ahead of the curve on this one."

She paused. I sat there returning her stare. I hadn't heard a question and doubted if I would have answered it even if I did.

"You fit the description of the suspect I'm looking for. You fit the profile and the modus operandi and you've been at the last known whereabouts of the murdered authors. How do you explain yourself?" I sensed she didn't want to come right out and say I was a murderer. I glanced at my would be friend next to her. Detective Andrews sat stolid in his chair, his face impassive. If he had any misgivings he hid them well. Hell, it's what we pay and train them for. I wasn't going to make it any easier for either of them. It was impossible for me to be pegged as the murderer.

Daily spoke up. "Where were you on the night Cliff Barkley was killed?"

"How would I know? Probably in my car driving home."

I turned my gaze on her. She was angry. Her Mona Lisa was replaced with a nasty snarl but the thin nose and high cheeks stayed with her.

"Where were you a week ago when Danny Stole was killed?"

"OK, OK you got me. I'll talk. I'll talk." Andrews face picked up and Daily leaned forward onto the table, placing her hands evenly on its surface as she leaned in.

"I've been,... wanting to talk. I can't stand it anymore," I said drawing them in – pausing for dramatic effect, "I want to talk...to my lawyer. His name is Joe Romero. Get him in here and we'll talk."

Disgusted, Daily tossed her arms in exasperation; Andrews dipped his chin and said, "You're going in."

I was scared. I'd never spent more than six hours in jail before, and that was for a DUI on a night of poor reflection after my first marriage. I wasn't sure what going in meant. But, I knew that if it was just a procedure Andrews would have looked me in the eye.

Two other uniformed officers, lesser ranks, entered the room and I was led out. The cell I was tossed into was even barer than the interview room. Standard prison issue quarters. Three cement walls, bars of steel, a cot bolted to the wall and a stainless steel toilet with no seat looking like it hadn't been cleaned in a week. I'd say a month but evidently Palm Springs has standards.

* * *

Somewhere in the precinct Detective Daily was having an argument over procedures with Craft, Andrews and Detective Hunt's friend Lieutenant McCray.

"He's my prisoner," she was shouting. "I want him back in the City of Industry!"

Craft turned to his superior, "Lou I know this guy. He's got a good rep. He's a member of the Advisory Committee."

Daily cut in, "He wouldn't be the first crooked politician."

"Where are you on this?" McCray asked Andrews.

"I'm in the middle boss. The pieces kinda fit like Detective Daily says, but it's not perfect by any degree."

Daily was madder than a cat with her whiskers cut. She didn't expect a tussle over jurisdiction and these three men were staring down at her in more ways than one. In frustration she made a leaping comment, "There may come a day one of you needs something from Industry."

The Lieutenant wasn't one to get his hairs crossed without reason. Daily's comment was cutting but painless. Still he had to make a decision. "Anthony's lawyered up already and he isn't going anywhere tonight. Get me some evidence of his crime Detective and I'll hand him over to you tomorrow."

"You know I can't do that right now. My partners gone home for the day and it'll take at least till tomorrow afternoon before someone can drive out the tapes and the internet logs."

McCray steamrolled on undaunted, "Just because he's getting a lawyer doesn't mean he's getting out. I can hold him for 24 hours to facilitate questioning. If we need more time we can still have him booked and then he'll have to sit in somebody's jail until Monday when he can be arraigned. He's not going anywhere for now. We'll hold him for you till you're ready for him."

"I'm ready for him now," and she spun on her heels. Bastards.

* * *

The wait in the interview room was miniscule compared to what was in store for me now. I waited so long I fell asleep. When I awoke, I wasn't sure of the time and briefly wondered as to what day. My watch and all possessions had been confiscated before my being placed in the cell. Even my shoes must have been considered a dangerous weapon, because the cops took them too. I lay awake and contemplated my predicament.

As far as Detective Daily was concerned I had murdered two of America's top authors. Cliff Barkley and his assistant almost a month ago. They were definitely shot to death in what had been fixed to seem a crime of passion. Then, Danny Stole and Georgeham Milton just a week back - although, if I remembered correctly, it was a poisonous murder-suicide. The papers must have lied. So what else is new?

There was at least one problem with all this. I hadn't done any of it. I could see how I would be a suspect, especially if I fit the physical description of the killer. I tried to place myself on each of the murders. I was in the vicinity of the crime. I had gone to both book signings and had no alibi as to my time of departure from the event. I had traveled alone and stopped at fast food on the way home. Fast food. I stopped for something to eat on the way home from Danny Stole. I had thrown the receipt in the bag given to me at Del Taco and tossed the bag into the back of my Jeep with my usual carelessness. It had to still be there. I was notorious for being a mess monster and just about always threw trash over my shoulder into the back seat of my car. If I could just get my car looked at and make sure - I'd have a provable alibi.

My own situation resolved, I decided to pit my brain on the subject of reviewing the rest of the facts of the case. If the murderer was not me, and I was pretty confident it wasn't, yet I fit the profile of the killer, then who looked like me and was in this same business? Who indeed. I thought of all my friends in the business and while many of them would share the same motive as I, namely PROFIT, there wasn't anyone who looked enough like me to cause a case of mistaken identity.

But then again, profit couldn't be the only motive could it? I mean how much could a person make off selling their books online? Even with the rise in values due to the death a person would have to have a mountain of books to make enough money to make it worth it. And then wouldn't that person be easy to find? Books take up space, a lot of space, both in real life and online. Even if they had all the books they'd be so obvious online they'd stand out like an albatross in a gaggle of geese. Most people believe the internet is an endless stream of money once you have a business online. The truth is a little more realistic. It takes a lot of work and effort, blood and sweat, just like anything else worthwhile to make it function. One person can't do it all.

If the motive wasn't just the money from the sale of signed books then that had to be secondary operation. The primary reason had to be more selective, perhaps even more personal. I wished I had a notepad. This could mark the beginnings of a real story line. If I could collect enough information maybe I would get to write a book. With nothing else to do, I spent my time organizing the info I had in my head.

Detective Craft appeared outside my cell. He was six feet of lean muscle, sporting a Barney Miller mustache and wearing a crisp uniform, creased as if he'd just stepped away from the iron. I first met him when once I helped foil a burglary ring by pretending to be a fence for some stolen books. We'd created a bond at the time and he told me it was the easiest bust he'd ever been on. We'd further cemented that bond another time when he let me play the cop at a Citizens Police Academy lesson on how to arrest an unwilling suspect. He played the crook. I surprised him with a quick trip maneuver and flipped him on his back to cuff him. It was a lucky move on my part and one that'd never get by him twice. I didn't let it go to my head. The next day I went out of my way to hunt him up and tell Don he was the toughest guy I'd ever fought. He welcomed the compliment and ever since we'd been friends. He sometimes brought his wife's books to me to buy as an excuse to talk over city issues. He was standing outside my cell now looking from side to side.

"Is my lawyer here yet?" I asked.

"It's 9 at night."

"Can I get a room with cable?"

Don stood outside wearing the look of a pall bearer. He stared back towards the entrance of the cell block, not wanting to look directly at me. "Do you want to tell me anything?"

"Not really. Do you want to tell me anything?"

"Did you do it?" he asked. Police are trained to not answer questions yet keep asking them.

I was lying flat on my back staring up at the ceiling. I lifted my head to look him in the eye. "No."

"Can you prove it?"

"I'm working on it."

"I can't help you on this," he said. "Not yet anyways. If you can really get yourself more in the clear, I'll be there for you."

"I understand Don," I said. "Maybe tomorrow though, when my lawyer finally gets here, if you'll be available I may need a witness."

Don took a deep breath and nodded, "You betcha."

I rolled over onto my side and Don walked away. It was a long time before I fell asleep again, but eventually I was mugged by exhaustion.

The next morning, I was given a hearty breakfast of a sandwich sealed in plastic with the flavor of a baseball. It was supposed to be ham and cheese but the preservatives were losing the war on sustenance. I ate it like I hadn't had anything in 36 hours, which I hadn't.

Shortly thereafter, I was put in a lineup. Me and four other guys all bearing the same general description; blonde hair, early thirties, five and a half to six feet tall and we were all wearing some sort of band uniform. At one point I was asked to step forward and say, "That's OK. There's probably not a tip in it anyways." Two of the other guys were asked to repeat the words also. I wasn't told the results but was placed back in my cell.

My lawyer showed up before lunch. Joe Romero is a tall pale drink of vodka, laced with black hair, who carries himself like he's one of the Rat Pack. Dean Martin must have been his role model. His suits were impeccable. He sauntered up to my cell like he'd just stepped off-stage. A uniformed officer stepped in front of him and unlocked the door. Joe stepped in and the guard swung it shut, then left.

Joe had been out of town yesterday and hadn't got my message until this morning. A court appearance had delayed him till now. He apologized for the delay and I accepted his reasons for the slow arrival.

He didn't think the police had much to go on. So far it was all circumstantial evidence. The lineup had been unsuccessful. No one was fingered. I had been in all the wrong places at the right times but I couldn't be positively placed at the scenes of the crimes.

Joe asked where I'd gotten my advanced reading copy of the Cliff Barkley book and I told him it came directly from the publisher. Was that verifiable? Yes. There had to be a record of it somewhere with my sales agent. I gave Joe her name and told him the number was in my rolodex back at the store. Furthermore, I told him about the fast food receipt I supposed was still in a bag in the back seat of my car. I told him to bring Detective Craft with him when he retrieved it. He agreed this was a good idea.

"You know this might take a while," said Joe. "Even if all the information and the receipt checks out this Detective Daily doesn't

The Author Murders

want to let it go."

"Daily. Yeah she's got a hard-on for me." The visual would have been funny except for the fact I was sitting in jail.

"I could have my secretary bring you over some reading material."

"How about a copy of Helter Skelter?"

By four o'clock that afternoon I was a free man again. When the police released me there was no fanfare. No one came and apologized. The uniformed officer who had let Joe Romero into my cell merely tapped on the bars with his night stick and said, "You can go." The formalities of signing out for my possessions took about ten minutes and I was shown the door leading to a side exit from the station. It was late in the day and warm. No summertime temperature, but the sun felt good – a traditional Palm Springs welcoming.

At first, I wasn't sure what to do but decided to head to the store. The local public transportation, SunBus, ran a straight line down Tahquitz Canyon Way to downtown and I could walk the final block or two. The bus ran right past the Indian casino, the only Indian casino in the heart of a downtown in the entire country. There was a new garish sign going up. It had what looked like a thousand lights, a large message board and was painted bright green and purple. It was the Indians answer to Vegas. They were putting up a new tent also. An easy construction job to expand their business and business must be good. I remembered how they originally got the slot machines onto their property. They'd smuggled them in during the middle of the night using produce trucks. And these folks want their own Police department.

The whole concept of Indian Gaming was a hot issue and not yet approved by California voters. It was divisive. The opponents claiming it would bring a dark element of crime and misfortune to the valley. I agreed with them, but it was an argument destined to lose. The prospect of jobs and new big money for a people who were wronged by my great-great grandfather had convinced the majority to roll the dice in favor of Gaming. A misnomer if I ever heard one: Gaming was a Monopoly. Gaming was what kids did to pass the afternoon. Gambling: Gambling was BlackJack, Roulette, Poker, and Slot Machines. The closest thing the Indians offered to Gaming was Free Parking. My bus stopped, I got off and walked down the sidewalk to my store.

Jill greeted me with a giggle, "How's your cellmate?"

I didn't think the situation a joke. But I knew my own whacky sense of humor had earned this comment sometime in the past. "Really nice, but somehow I think he'll forget about me. I didn't even get a goodbye kiss. How's business been?"

"Good," she said. "Do you need to clear out the register for bail money?"

"No," I snarled. "Look, can I get a break here? I was just in jail accused of murder."

"Oh, all right," she muttered. "Are you OK?"

"Yes, thanks," I wheezed while squeezing by her to the number one spot behind the counter and logged onto my email account. "Any messages for me?"

"Your dad called, a couple of publishers, one I think was from the billing department. Oh, and some guy named Milo."

I almost fell off my stool turning around to her. "What'd he say?"

"He said he'd be at Starbucks tonight. I thought he was one of your five dollar customers."

15
Shortsighted

DETECTIVE SUSAN DAILY WAS PISSED. After she tried to go around McCray, she'd spent the better part of the day getting her butt chewed out first by her own Lieutenant and then by the Chief of Palm Springs Police Department. Every superior all the way down the chain of command to the bailiff at the jail asked her, "Got anyone else you want us to put up for the night?"

Her instincts for Xanthe Anthony being the killer were strong. He was more than a mere person of interest. At this point he was her only suspect, her only lead, and here she was two hours away from a home field advantage. Like a dog with a bone, she didn't want to let go. But Andrews and Craft didn't think Anthony was her guy. The PSPD hadn't fought her on the arrest but they hadn't allowed her to run the interrogation either. The detectives had gone easy on Anthony, letting him lawyer up before the questioning had even commenced. In her opinion, they had given him a break because he was part of a second rate Advisory committee that didn't even warrant any policy making decisions. Daily was familiar with committees and commissions. LAPD and Los Angeles City Hall was full of them; a bunch of no good week-end warriors and citizen wannabes that get in the way of honest police work. The whole arrest, interview and incarceration were a joke. She had the right person and the local cops let him go.

Still,..the back of her mind tugged at her: What if she were wrong?

She needed to vent and gave her partner a call. Detective Hunt didn't give her much consolation. "Flat out, the bust was bad," he said. "You lacked hard evidence." He sided with the locals although he was at least sympathetic. It had been her first unilateral action and she had blown it. "But, all is not lost," he said. "If you really feel strong about this Xanthe character, why don't you take a couple vacation days and spend some time in the desert. It'll clear your conscience and the warm sun will do you some good." He went on to offer to file the paperwork for her and Daily agreed. She had to play this out. She needed answers and info. If Anthony was the prime suspect then she would find out. If not, she'd cross that bridge when she got to it.

"We have had one bit of news on our case partner," Hunt interjected, adding a spark to the conversation. "Beverly Hills PD have ascertained the payment method on the band uniform rental. The perp used Cliff Barkleys credit card. The cases are tied at the hip."

"You think each murder is a chapter in some book?" asked Daily.

"No," said Hunt. "I think the motive is money, pure and simple. Each author was killed after a book signing. Our man is a bibliophile. A manic book lover. Although there could be more than one motive."

She hung up the phone and looked for a place to stay. The only hotel offering a view of Celebrity Books.com was the Hyatt, a little more expensive than Daily wanted to step. Yet, if her hunch played out, she'd get reimbursed by the department. If not she was in for a real nice vacation.

16
Milo's Info

JILL'S USE OF THE PHRASE: a five dollar customer - was an old cliche around the store. It had started a few years back when a former employee named Steve had been cornered by a raving Star Trek fan into more discussion than Steve relished. It happens sometimes. A customer has a certain topic which totally thrills them and we, as book aficionados and employees, feel obligated to join the discussion as an attempt to make a sale while just being friendly. But then the customer keeps going, they're eyes start bulging with excitement, their speech speeds up and they begin moving in for the time of their life. They'll pull up chairs, put their elbows on the counter and really open up. This had happened to Steve and despite his best efforts to politely excuse himself; Excuse me, but I have to take care of this other person; Oh, yeah, that's interesting but I can't sit here and talk about Star Trek all day, heh, heh; I know what you mean, but I think that lady is about to need help delivering a baby - the customer wouldn't let him go. This particular customer could've kept this discussion going all by himself and most likely did. After what must have been more than twenty minutes Steve finally extricated himself from the situation and said to me, "If I ever have to talk to another person like that, you owe me an extra five bucks." Hence the phrase five dollar customer was born.

Milo could easily be mistaken for a five dollar customer, but I had higher hopes for him. I was sitting outside on the patio of Starbucks again, waiting to meet him for the second time in a week. The tables were littered with coffee drinkers much as they had been on my first visit, except there was only one high school group and none of them looked familiar. I sipped my mocha frappucino and didn't have to wait long.

Milo meandered onto the patio with a freshly painted neon hairdo and wearing the same holy Levis and leather jacket except now his black t-shirt was adorned with Barney sporting an eye patch and toting a gun in one hand and a bottle of Jack Daniels in the other. He let me look up his nose again as a warm greeting and sat down across from me.

"Sup," he said.

"What've you got?" I asked.

"Man, that Ebay listing was hot. I've never seen so many people interested in a book before."

"Were you able to locate the seller?"

"Well, it's like this see," he began, pulling some crumpled notes from inside his jacket. "The guy who listed it isn't far from here."

"Really." I was astonished. This was good, better than expected. "What'd you find?" I set my drink aside and sat up straight.

"Well, I couldn't check out his email address because he's with AOL and while they're internet for beginners, they're also the big boys of the net and they have the best security systems. I'm not done with them yet, but I had to find another source for info on the lister. Luckily, he used a second rate image hosting site for his photo of the book and I was able to get him that way."

"Wow, you're good," I said, inflating his ego. "Now I see why Shane recommended you."

"Here's the address," and he slid the crumpled paper towards me. I reached for it. "But first," he injected, pulling back the paper away from my fingertips, "We've a little matter to settle concerning finances."

"I said I'd be fair with you and I will."

"Could you be a little more specific?" He was toying with the paper, pushing it forward and pulling it back.

I had gone to the ATM as I'd promised myself and pulled out the maximum of $300. "I've got $200 earmarked for you in my pocket. Is that fair?"

Milo slid the paper across to me and I unfolded it. He was right;

the address wasn't too far away: Joshua Tree.

"But before we're done," he interrupted my train of thought. "You should see what I've made of the list of bidders."

This was an aspect I hadn't anticipated. I thought the bidders would just be a bunch of nobodies, miscellaneous dealers, collectors and wealthy fans. "What about the bidders?"

"Mostly they were just a bunch of dealers and people I couldn't care less about. But one of them was a local." Milo had caught me by the huevos and he knew it. I must have shown my emotions on my shirtsleeve. "And it'll cost you extra."

"You mean one of them was from Palm Springs?"

"Yep," and he pulled a second piece of crumpled paper from his jacket. "Wanna see it?"

"I've only got $100 more to work with right now." I knew saying 'right now' was a mistake as soon as it left my lips. Milo jumped on it.

"That's alright," he said. "I'll just have to trust you for the second hundred." He was twirling it in his fingers. "You're in the store tomorrow aren'tcha."

"Yes," and I motioned with my fingers for him to give it to me. If I don't get thrown back in jail. I doubted Detective Daily would give up on me. I looked at the piece of paper and read. Babsplum@netfree.com/Barbara   Plumley/760-949-2126/Palm Springs. When I looked back up at Milo he was smiling. "What do you do for real work?" I asked.

"Odd jobs, this and that," he replied.

"Why don't you come by and see me at the bookstore?" I said. "It's not as glamorous as hacking but I could use someone who knew his way around the internet."

"What would I do?"

"You'd start with taking off that eyeliner and letting your hair go natural." It was the wrong thing to say. He threw his hands up in a defensive gesture.

"Whoa man, do I tell you how to live?"

"Just think about it. We could put your talents to honest work and like I've said before, I'm real fair about the pay."

I went back home and hunted up the business card Donlagic had stuck in my pocket the other night when he so gingerly asked about the information. One thing on it caught my attention real fast and I had to pull out Milo's paper on Barbara Plumley to confirm what I was seeing. Donlagic Security company phone number and Barbara Plumley's was the same.

17
Antiques & Collectibles

68902 Highway 62 #6
Joshua Tree, CA

THE CRUMPLED PIECE OF PAPER with the sellers address would lead me farther out into the desert to Joshua Tree, a small town 45 minutes to the Northeast. Heading out of Palm Springs on highway 62 took me past one of the windmill capitols of the world, the windiest stretch of the United States, nestled between two of the largest mountains in Southern California; Mount San Jacinto and San Gorgonio. The area has over 2,000 modern windmills scattered over 10 square miles and was a hallmark of the energy conservation plans of the Jimmy Carter era, although Ronald Reagan got the credit since they were built during his tenure.

Once past this arsenal of airstreams, the highway wends its way through a small cleft in the hills on the far side of the valley, seeking higher ground, past squatter shacks and the occasional house scattered in the foothills of Morongo valley. Then the road becomes a long straight ascent capable of rupturing many a radiator until an area called the high desert is reached and a city named after the cook (Joshua) of the great adventurer and surveyor of the 1800's, Colonel John Charles Fremont. Story has it that after a lengthy summer desert crossing, the cook came down with an incurable disease and died just as the party reached a small oasis in the vicinity of a land snickered with the ugliest bunch of cactus malformations ever to be sighted by man. No leaves, but more of a frond, and a trunk covered in sticklers with just enough branches to make it resemble a man with up stretched arms. The town is riddled with them and there are few other places in the world they grow. So Fremont, who had never seen them before, named them after his deceased and beloved cook and the name stuck.

Over the final crest, a string of freestanding mercantile buildings dot the sides of the road. Buildings that would be torn down in more active cities are good usable real estate in Joshua Tree. I drove past one windswept, sun dried and decaying strip mall after another until I came to the corner of Highway 62 and Old Woman Springs Road, then the numbers made a match; but not at any apartment complex or condominium group as I thought. The address drew me to a little antique shop called Pete's Collectibles. I knew I was in the right place when I saw a sign in one corner of the window which hadn't been cleaned since the trees were named. There was a small piece of dirty cardboard with a few faded paintbrush strokes reading: BOOKS.

I parked in front and walked inside. Pete liked western motifs. The decoration was a page out of the annals of the OK Corral. Rough wood floors led to plank walls and an open beam ceiling. There was no need for sawdust on the floor because it had never been swept free of dirt. Wagon wheels made of chandeliers hung from the ceiling, old license plates and poorly painted western scenes dotted the walls. There was the occasional worn and empty holster and even a pair of wooly chaps, meant to keep a rider warm in winter, an item speciously out of place in the desert. The counters were glass cases streaked with years of filth and grime. Located within were what's often referred to as one man's treasures and another man's trash; Lone Ranger comics, rusty Sheriff's star badges, matchbooks from forgotten dance halls and old medicine bottle boxes from the days when snake oil was a common remedy. Behind it all sat an overweight clerk dressed in a cowboy hat and flannel shirt, wearing Mork and Mindy rainbow suspenders, who was picking the seat of his crotch, smelling his fingers and needed as much cleaning as the place he kept. Pete I presumed.

I gave him a nod to say hello as I checked out the premises and pretended not to notice his bad habits. He nodded back and mumbled,

The Author Murders

"Howdy." The front room was his, with its odd assortment of wall hangings and dirty glass cases. A doorway with swinging saloon doors held back by straps of leather lead into a second room with stalls separated by walls of chicken wire and two by fours. Each stall had its own distinctive display. They'd been rented to individuals, each offering their own selection of collectibles. I gave Pete a choked "Hello" in return and walked back.

In the first stall was a nice collection of salt and pepper shakers, china dolls, and porcelain figurines. As its centerpiece: a full-size Howdy Doody puppet still in its box. It'd be worth much more than the $175 asking price if the box wasn't so heavily taped together and one leg hadn't fallen off the doll inside.

The second stall was a Life Magazine empire in the making. The chicken wire walls had massive paper clips attached to show off all the best covers; Roy Rogers and Hopalong Cassidy, Baseball legends Willie Mays and Willie Stargell, The Jackson Five, John Wayne, Gary Cooper, Clark Gable and Vivien Leigh, it was a smorgasbord of Hollywood yesteryears wrapped in plastic sleeves. I had to pull myself away. My own bookstore deals in the same merchandise and when I see a good presentation I am awed by the creativity of the competition. But, at present I was not prospecting product.

The next booth clobbered me. It was what I'd come for. I knew it the moment I saw it. Bookshelves filled the stall and books filled the shelves. Nothing fancy it seemed at first glance but I had to inspect closer to be sure, assorted hardbacks on every subject. No order raked the ledges. Books of every size and condition were found aplenty, some with dust jackets and some without. Harold Robbins, Edna Ferber, Tom Wolfe, Danny Stole; college text books, Readers Digest condensed, and harlequin romances. I took a look. The Danny Stole was one of her later novels in poor condition. The front endpaper was torn out and on its spine the distinctive marking of a library book sale leftover. The shelves were filled with crap. Nothing worth more than the two bucks they were each marked and even that was too much for most. The quality was lacking but there was plenty of it. Usually in a pile like this I could pull out something worth at least 10 or 20 dollars but here there wasn't anything worthwhile. I was looking at somebody's pile of excrement. The formation of a book dealer who thought by leaving a hoard of debris another unhappy scrounger would muddle up a gaffe and pay for it with cash.

As I ended my perusal, I backed up to take it all in. The shelves were of lesser quality than my own. Scrap wood and cinder blocks, they were filled with books worth less than the shelves. The floor was covered in a threadbare rug meant to give the stall a bit of homespun and the bottom of one of the shelving units had a paisley handkerchief hanging over it like a doily. That was an odd place for a decoration. I bent over and picked up the front of the handkerchief and saw the bottom shelf had been removed. In its place was a large wooden box with a padlock; an old gun box made of wood gone warped with age. The clasp was antique iron, but the lock was new.

I looked back down the hall towards the front of the store. Pete was perched on his stool, hidden behind his copy of the Hi-Desert Gazette, squeaking out a left cheek sneak and shifting his massive buttocks back and forth like a mother hen settling on her eggs.

The hair on the back of my neck stood at attention. This had to be the stall of the Stephen Knightly seller. A refuge for his refuse. A place to sell his junk that wouldn't sell fast enough at a yard sale. Plus, there wasn't a single Stephen Knightly or horror novel in the lot. Sometimes it's not what you see, but what isn't there that adds understanding.

Pulling my pocket knife out, I checked the lock in greater detail. I would have no luck with it, I was no lock pick and it was new, solid and secure. But the clasp, in all its wrought antiqueness was retrofitted with new screws painted black to blend in and hopefully thereby diminishing their detection. With little effort I was able to unscrew the clasp and flip the lock up onto the lid. Slowly opening the crate I peered into a mass of straw filler. I pushed it aside and found an assortment of odds and ends wrapped in plastic; glassware, forks, knives, sunglasses and beer bottles. The plastic was a waste. Nothing here was a collectible. The dishware was cheap stainless steel and the beer bottle was too new. There was also an envelope which, with a second glance towards Pete,

I opened. Inside was a sheet of paper with monetary values on it. The numbers started off big and decreased after each one above it was crossed out, starting with $49,283 and ending with $26,721. Somebody owed some money. The seller was in debt, but to whom?

A loan shark or the mob quickly entered my head. Some wise guy with wide lapels and a red shirt was shaking down the seller and wanted a payoff. Probably a bit melodramatic, but it made sense. That'd be why the number was listed and then reduced. The seller had a problem he was trying to fix. He'd found a way but still had some distance to go. The Stephen Knightly book would have cleared out most if not all of the debt. Whatever other path he'd found to eliminate the balance was working, but I had to wonder if it would be fast enough for the bill collectors. At times, their patience could wear thin.

I put the box back together as if I'd never been there, placed it back at the bottom of the shelf and covered it under the paisley handkerchief.

On my way out of Pete's I feigned interest in the Lone Ranger comic in the glass case, but when Pete only paused briefly from his nail biting to look over the top of his newspaper I walked out.

I sat in my car collecting my thoughts. The only thing I was immediately sure of was I was due a payday. Across the street was a bank and I used its drive thru ATM to collect a second $300. Then I spied a payphone in the parking lot and decided it was time to call Donlagic.

I pulled his card out of my pocket and dialed the number. Barbara Plums name popped up in my memory. Why had she made a bid on the book? It could be basically because Donlagic's customer wanted it and Donlagic had spotted it for a rarity online. For all his bullish stupidity, he could spot a winner. The number rang twice and then it was picked up by a woman with a nasally voice, "Hello Palm Springs Indian Casino. How may I help you?"

"I'm sorry. I've dialed a wrong number." I hung up and dialed again.

The same woman whined her welcome to me. "Hello Palm Springs Indian Casino. How may I help you?"

"I'm sorry. I dialed a wrong number again."

"Who were you trying to reach, sir?" The sound of smacking gum filled in any silences.

"A Mr. Michael Donlagic"

"Let me check," smack, smack, "One moment please."

"There's a Mr. Donlagic who runs the Security and Collections part of the premises Sir. Which would you prefer I connect you to?"

"Uh, that's OK. Something has come up. I'll call back later." Donlagic wasn't just offering to host a debate on Indian Sovereignty out of the goodness of his heart. So what else is new?

I do my best thinking when I'm browsing books. I'd spent way too much time in the thrift stores around Palm Springs and decided to take my time going back home. There were lots of little stores in the upper desert I could while away my afternoon in. I had some thinking to do and why spoil a good afternoon rushing back to talk to someone I didn't like? Besides, there just might be a little brick of gold wrapped in a dust jacket up here.

18
Back at Pete's

PETE'S DOOR SWUNG OPEN A SECOND TIME. A good looking blonde lady wearing snug levis walked to the counter and presented her badge. "Do you have a minute?"

"I'd have a minute for you even without that," said Pete, smiling to show a yellowed tooth in a mouthful of bad hygiene and putting down his magazine. He'd switched from the Hi-Desert News to Gun and Ammo. He stood up from his stool, tugged his belt up over his behemoth navel and brushed away imaginary crumbs from his shirt.

Detective Daily was unfazed by his comment, his belly and his tooth. Pete wasn't the first smug face she'd encountered during her tenure on the force. Not that she'd ever been tempted, or even caved in to a witness, informant or even a fellow officer for that matter, but Pete wasn't in the running. The fish she caught weren't judged by weight. They needed something Pete didn't have; looks, intelligence, charisma. Pete was three in the hole.

"That man who was in here a little while ago," she said snapping her badge back in its case and clipping it to her belt, "what'd he want?"

"He just looked around," said Pete. "Why?"

"Was he looking at anything particular?"

"He kinda had an interest in this here comic book," Pete said pointing to the one in the case. "But, I didn't figure him for a real buyer."

The Lone Ranger comic book looked in fair condition, Silver stood on two legs with the masked man riding high in the stirrups and waving his white hat in one hand, but Daily's intuition told her the comic wasn't worth an hours drive. "Anything else?"

"He spent some time in the second room." Pete jerked a thumb over his shoulder towards the saloon doors. "Was looking at the book booth down on the left."

Daily looked into Pete's face to try and discern if a follow-up question was needed. All she got was a feeling that the farther out in the desert you go the farther men stand from the razor in the morning. "Thanks," she said and went to the booth.

She noticed the Howdy Doody doll and the Life magazines in the first two booths, and then stopped in front the booth loaded with books. Lots of them, she thought at first glance. Folding her arms and peering a little more in depth. OK Xanthe, what brought you way up here?

The books didn't look overly impressive. Daily was no expert, but she did have a fondness for certain horror writers. She'd known who Cliff Barkley was without having to be told and if a Stephen Knightly book were to be turned up in this pile, she'd probably buy it just on speculation. As far as she could discern these books were nothing to write home about. Not a single early printing was to be found and even the quality of the authors was a little lacking. Ratty covers made the whole booth unappealing. Maybe something was inside one of the books.. She pulled one down and fanned through the pages. Nothing caught her eye. She tried another. Yellow highlighting and underlining, a destructive habit that ruined the value. She tried a third, nothing. There were too many to continue at this pace. Checking each one would take all day and even then she might not recognize a note if it was written in a code. Chances were this wouldn't be the source of motive anyways. Why come all the way up to Joshua Tree and look in this booth? She tried looking behind the books and still came up wondering.

Detective Susan Daily was not one to give up without a fight. To get promoted from the bicycle tourist squad of Santa Monica pier, she'd had to do more than put in her time. She had to prove she had what it takes to solve serious crime and she'd won over her contemporaries and superiors by catching a would be thief who was robbing un-suspecting joggers. The thief had earned the name of 'The Hooded Bandit' because he wore a hooded sweat shirt whenever committing his crime. Daily had caught him by waiting him out and putting on a wig. She'd followed his modus operandi and scoped out his crime area until she knew how often he struck and where. Then by changing her appearance enough and jogging the scene with just enough jewelry to entice, she'd finally caught the eye of the bandit. When he finally struck, she was ready with a small can of mace and she had the guy in cuffs before the cavalry arrived.

Today she was on her own in a little sagebrush town putting together the trail of a biblio-murderer. The books were inconsequential. They had no significance and no value. So why would a person keep such an unworthy heap? She wandered back up to talk to Pete, who had a finger stuck in his nose and his nose buried in the Gun and Ammo magazine.

"Excuse me," Daily began, "What's a booth like that cost a month to rent?"

"Seventy-five dollars a month and 15% of sales," said Pete, wiping his finger on his jeans.

"Does that booth make you any money?"

"Naw, not really," shucked Pete. "If better merchandise would come along, I'd get rid of it to tell the truth."

"So why keep it?" asked Daily. "Couldn't you just put some of your own stuff in there?" She looked around and motioned with her hands at all the stuff in the front room.

"Sure. But the guy pays his rent several months in advance and I never see him. Well, almost never. Unless he gets some mail or some-thing."

"He gets mail here?" This just might be the reason. "When did he pick up last?"

"Just a day ago. Had a real mess of mail from all over the coun-try. Goes in spurts. Sometimes nothing for weeks or months and then gets a whole mess of it all at one time." Pete finished with wiping his mouth with the same finger that had moments ago been up his nose.

"The guy who came in here earlier, he ever been in here before?"

"Nope. Never seen him before today."

"Who rents the booth?"

"Feller by the name of Leonard something. I can check my records to be more exact if you'd like." Pete might not be clean but he was polite and resourceful.

Daily got out her notepad, "That'd be a big help Pete. Thank you."

"You're welcome little lady. But, name's not Pete. It was just on the building when I took over. Mines Cletis, not that I reckon it matters much," he said, flashing her his yellow tooth.

It didn't, but Daily thanked him again just the same.

Pete's Collectibles had one more visitor that day worth mentioning. He came in just before closing and had a bad fashion sense. As soon as Cletis saw the Hawaiian print shirt he knew he didn't like the guy. When he flashed a badge an inward groan escaped his lips. He was has hard to understand with a thick Eastern accent. When Cletis tried to say he'd already answered all the questions for another officer the guy broke the glass of the counter just over the Lone Ranger comic. After that Cletis told him whatever he wanted.

The Author Murders

The two boys meet again, only now they are young men…

First young man, "Hello brother, you did good."
Second young man, "You said we'd be together forever."
First young man, "We will, when the timing is right."
Second young man, "Didn't things work out like you said? I gave you my all."
First young man, "They're working. But I need more. What else have you got for me?"
Second young man, "Whatever you want. And then you'll love me?"
First young man, "Like I said, forever and ever."
Second young man, "Yes, then I'll do it one more time."

PART II

19
Leonard's gut

LEONARD WAS WORRIED.

He sat on the edge of his bed, swinging his legs back and forth like a kid waiting to get a spanking from his dad. He'd settle for a spanking about now, if that would settle matters. Although he knew, for what he'd done, no mere spanking would suffice.

His room was in the same sad state of affairs as his life. His bed sat on a platform of drawers, two of which had lost their handles and sat askew in their sliders. The carpeting was strewn with clothes both dirty and clean, making it hard to tell which was which. And the shelves lining the walls were a collision of books tossed into place as if by a hurricane.

Sitting on his rumpled covers, Leonard rummaged through a shoebox filled with driver's licenses, credit cards, and other forms of identification he had pilfered from the victims of his own personal crime spree. They were a telling of how he'd become who he was.

He picked up a license of a Latino male in his late forties. The name was unimportant. What was important was that this was the first step down a very dark path for Leonard. He'd met the man outside the bathroom of a public park. The man had cruised up in his late model American sedan, gave a heads up sign and flashed a bill between his fingers. Leonard was smoking a cigarette and leaning against the wall with one leg tucked up like a flamingo as he recognized the glance. The man parked and walked up the sidewalk jiggling his keys in his pocket, briefly looking into Leonard's face, before sauntering into the last stall and waiting.

The bathroom smelt of urine, disinfectant and dirt. The walls were covered in graffiti and broken tiles. The mirrors had been badly scratched with rocks and pen knives. Most of the lights were either burnt out or broken in their sockets making the room a discourse in light and shadow. The floors were bare cement. No comfort for the knees.

Leonard tossed the last bite of his cigarette on the ground and snuffed it with his high top. Taking one last sweep of the park, he saw the children playing on the playground. A little boy in blue coveralls was chasing a girl in a pink frilly dress across the jungle gym rope bridge as if it were a pirate ship, or a castle, their arms flailing wildly in their excitement. She was screaming joyfully; no terror, just the warm knowledge that someone wanted her, wanted to play.

Real life was no playground.

Leonard walked up to the last stall and took the twenty dollar bill sitting atop the crusty toilet paper dispenser. The man loosened his pants and tilted his head back awaiting service. Leonard was the service and he worked hard for his money. He could tell by the moans of the Latino man. He bobbed and sucked and licked and when the man put his hands on the back of his head, Leonard worked harder.

It was disgusting work.

How far had he fallen? How much farther was there left to fall? Or could he return?

Leonard looked again at the license in his hand. This had been the turning point, the low point, the point of no return. He'd told himself that day in the bathroom this was rock bottom and from that day forward he'd become a smarter criminal, further onto the dark path. Afterward, as he spat the man's glue into the sink, staring at his sweat soaked face and wet lips in the cracked and scratched mirror, he decided - no more.

He'd taken a trophy from the man, the first victim of his new spree. While down on his knees, working for a Thomas Jefferson, Leonard lifted the Latino man's wallet; its brown imitation leather worn at the corners and shaped with a soft curve from long wear in the back pocket. Back in his car, he went through it to find a drivers license and credit cards marking a new step in Leonard's future. He realized he hadn't been aiming high enough.

The road of his discontent had begun two years earlier. His problems had become undeniable with the financial defeat of his divorce, landing him $2500 a month in alimony payments. At that time, he'd lost his second bookstore and his promises of "Don't worry honey, one day the store'll make enough money to clear away the clouds and life will be better," had dried up. His wife of six years, Tracey, had waited patiently through most of their marriage for the sun to shine. But the clouds never cleared. By the time their marriage was in its final year, they'd been to see two different counselors and a priest in hopes of a turnaround, or at the very least - an extension on feelings. In the last six months, they used four letter words in their conversations so much sometimes days began with, "Good Morning," and jumped directly to, "Fuck You." The shine was off the apple and nobody wanted a second bite.

When the split came, Leonard left in a storm of curse words. Tracey had been out partying with her girlfriends till late and in her drunkenness had exclaimed how little of a man Leonard was and how little his manhood meant to her. Leonard lost his drive to rekindle. Grabbing a few blankets and a change of clothes, he spent the next two nights sleeping on the floor of his soon to close store. The next day, after cooling off, he returned home one last time to see if there was any chance of salvaging the marriage. When he arrived, he found the locks changed and she never let him back in.

What she did do, was hire the best divorce lawyer in the area and kick his butt in court. The alimony was ridiculous considering she knew Leonard wasn't earning a thing and he was losing his business. Besides, all the money they had was hers. She'd come into the marriage with an inheritance of 1.7 million dollars in a trust, and although she'd spent $100,000 a year on their lives, he'd spent much of the marriage trying to talk her out of the spending. The cruises, the big wedding and honeymoon, the large house; he'd wanted her to keep their expenses down and instead she'd demanded a better quality of life. Now he was footing the bill for the life he'd tried to steer her away from. He'd gone with the only attorney he could afford, a pre-paid paralegal service and he'd lost every battle in the courtroom.

When the bills started coming in, Leonard was astounded. The alimony was just the beginning. Then there were the attorney's bills, his and hers: a matching set. Then there was the $48,000 owed in unpaid balances resulting in the closing of the bookstore. Add to that the personal debts of another $22,000 on miscellaneous credit cards and $15,000 on his car and he had accrued a total of $139,764 in obligations, with interest every month. Soon the notices were printed in larger ink, then in red, and finally being sent UPS or certified mail.

The creditors were calling at all times of the day and night. He'd tried to work with them at first, but it didn't take long before he realized there was no acceptable plan he could offer and he couldn't file bankruptcy because he'd done that seven years ago when he closed his first bookstore. So, he did what any red-blooded American would. With his last few credit cards, a credit report that didn't yet show the dings of his misfortune and the rewards of some simple crimes like pet hostage, panhandling with a deaf-mute act and selling forged concert tickets, Leonard frequented the Coachella Valley Indian casinos.

His first two passes netted him a very lucky $18,000 in winnings. But rather than take the cash, he allowed a credit line to be set up. His timing couldn't have been worse. Immediately his luck dampened and before he realized what had happened his debt had climbed to $362,000.

With his last $100, he moved his few belongings into a storage unit, drove his car in and shut the door behind himself. Sleeping as much as he could, he'd awake when his growling stomach forced him to go foraging in the trashcans of downtown near the store he once owned. Within days, his clothes were dirty enough to warrant a homeless look. It was then he went to his former drug dealer and asked for a shower and a job.

The dealer obliged. Leonard could be a runner, bringing baggies to buyers. It kept him busy, put gas in his car, afforded him showers to keep himself clean and let him stop by the park occasionally to make some extra twenty. It was his first leg up. He'd hidden himself from creditors by moving into the storage unit, he'd made himself presentable again, protected his assets by finding an untraceable job, but he'd also cut himself off from decent society by going underground. And it was on the morning of meeting this Latino man that Leonard decided to go even further into the murky depths of dishonest society.

At night, he'd put himself to sleep by reading motivational books under the light of a single bare bulb on the wall of his storage unit. His books were one of his possessions he would never get rid of. A book which impacted him greatly was, Seven Habits of Highly Successful People by Stephen Covey. It outlined in great detail the structure of many unbeaten and triumphant individuals who had taken paths to improve their lives. Leonard wished he was one of those individuals and treated the book as if it were his bible. It instructed him to write a plan outlining his strategy to succeed. At this point in his life, Leonard's resources were few, so he listed what he had to work with: car, computer, books, drug dealer job, small scams, gay hooking. It wasn't enough, but it was a start.

He made an effort to broaden his opportunities. By asking his dealer friend for advice he was able to move one connection up the drug chain and become a dealer himself. The promotion required Leonard to go to the sources place of business and meet the man. The connection was a biker in a motorcycle gang called the Devils, his name was Snakebite. Snakebite hung out at the clubhouse. It was a hole in the wall in a rough section of one of the highest crime ridden cities in the desert: Desert Hot Springs. To get to it, he had to go down a potholed street in a residential neighborhood made of small houses badly in need of paint jobs with front yards consisting of dead lawns and chain link fences. At the end of the block, he turned off the pavement onto a dirt road running along the backs of houses like a one-sided alley until he came to the clubhouse on the right. It was actually a house behind a house. Leonard suspected the leader of the gang lived in the house and the rest of the bikers just lounged around drinking beer and working on their bikes everywhere else; the yard, the garage, the patio, the living room, wherever there was room for a milk crate and a bike.

Beer cans and bottles were tossed about like ticket stubs at a carnival, turning the floor into a potpourri of aluminum and glass.

Snakebite was a war veteran turned delinquent. He talked about the Gulf War like it was a vacation spot and he was there on Spring Break. His arms were strong and muscular with a tattoo of a coiled cobra on one side and his Semper Fi on the other. His face was pockmarked, and his hair long, black and curly. He wore a Levis jacket with the arms cut off to make a vest and somehow he'd earned his colors on his back: a bastardization of the American Eagle. This one had its wing spread, in one claw was a bottle of XXX Spirits and in the other was a smoking pistol. Its head was replaced with a devils skull.

Leonard was woefully out of his element. The living room had two bikes in different states of disassembling scattered about. Snakebite sat at a cheap round laminated dinner table with two spindly chairs fallen over where the last guests had stood up. The walls hadn't been painted in twenty years and some holes had been punched in the plaster for ventilation. As Leonard walked in with his drug dealer escort, the smile dropped from Snakebites face, "Who's the pussy?"

"A friend of mine," said Leonard's dealer.

"I thought I told you never to bring anyone here?" said Snakebite.

"You said, 'Don't ever bring anyone here who's not a part of the program," said the dealer. "He wants a job."

Snakebite questioned Leonard more after that. Wanted to know his history and seemed to take particular pleasure in Leonard's bad divorce and how he was screwed over with alimony payments. Before an hour was up, Leonard was given a sales district of his own and a couple of contacts for users who wanted pot and speed. Crystal Meth was where all the action was, according to Snakebite. Lots of teenagers were using it and needed refills constantly. Leonard was loaded up on what was to be a week's supply and told to call first before coming over, ever. Snakebite told him, "You don't want to be here in case there's some undesirables around." Leonard couldn't think of what it would take for Snakebite to consider someone an undesirable, so he just shook his head, said, "OK," and left with the paraphernalia of his new job in a grocery bag.

His new job would be higher paying than the park, maybe $300 to $500 a week if he didn't use any of the products himself. Shouldn't be problem, he thought. Still, it would take a week before he had any money in his pocket. He better not quit his day job.

That's when he met the Latino man whose wallet he lifted and a light went on in his head. Some of the kids he sold to were in college and under 21. They all talked about how they wanted to go to clubs and which ones had easy access or didn't check ID's.

What if Leonard sold them ID's?

When Leonard went back to the Devil's clubhouse he brought the subject up with Snakebite. At first, Snakebite was a little slow on the uptake and didn't see the picture but two weeks later when Leonard went for his bi-monthly fill up, the Devil's had found him a brand new high quality printer, scanner and laminating machine. Leonard was stoked. They also had some samples of licenses and showed him how other states like, Arizona and Utah had a simple design easily reproducible using just a photo from an instamatic camera. California was harder because they used a license with a magnetic strip. But the bars would accept any state ID. Leonard was in business.

He took his profits from drug sales and rented some cheap office space over the top of an industrial park. Still no shower, but a lot better than living inside a storage shed. At least there was a restroom down the hall. He moved in his clothes using file boxes so no one would notice his suite was his domicile. It was a great place to set up his computer system too, since he could have a phone. He got a gym membership to give himself a place to shower and embarked on a workout regimen in the mornings.

Selling fake ID's wasn't the only idea he got from his Latin lover though. He also spent a few hours a week pilfering mailboxes and stealing mail. He liked the ones with their flags up and the flip down lids in a residential neighborhood he could drive through. Usually he just came across utility bills, personal letters and junk mail, but sometimes there was useful information. Bank statements, credit card applications and the occasional approved credit card were all good stuff. These trinkets of prosperity combined with his ability to produce a driver's license could open up a shopping spree. Then he could either keep the items he bought or return them a week later in a different town for cash. At the very least he could pawn merchandise, converting booty into loot.

Within a few more weeks his business was thriving. He was bringing in $1800 a month on drug sales, $1200 a month on fake ID's, $600 a month on returning or pawning merchandise, and another $300 a month with his infrequent pet hostage or part-time blow job. Nearly $4,000 living under the radar; much better than when he was a legitimate businessman, but still not enough.

His next breakthrough was a combination of events he could never have foreseen. With the money he was making, he started going out at night, prowling the bars, looking for love. But he was a known entity and after one conversation with another businessman who wanted to know the usual, "What do you do now?" Leonard avoided the nightspots of San Bernardino and switched to the clubs in Palm Springs. He was already in the neighborhood when he went to visit the Devil's and at least he wouldn't run into anyone he knew. The only thing was, most of the Palm Springs clubs were gay friendly. He told himself he wasn't gay. What he'd done in the park was merely a performance to help him through a tight pinch. He'd been married to two beautiful women. But, eventually he got worn down emotionally and the settings he was in became comfortable. Before too long he was dancing, then came the buying of drinks, next thing he was kissing and going to their apartments. Soon, he was a swinger. This lasted for little more than a month and then he met Justin.

Justin was another book dealer and they had loads in common. Together they talked the high points of literature and collecting. Faulkner, Hemingway, Steinbeck were their compatriots. Houghton Mifflin and Simon & Schuster were there friends. Stories read and re-membered from all their lives were shared freely. It was a wildly romantic time for Leonard. Justin was handsome and fun. Sleeping with him was a welcome reprieve. Leonard was surprised at how willing he was to embrace and copulate. Together their days and nights seemed to stretch far beyond the night clubs and walls of their bedrooms. They especially enjoyed going to book signings together and meeting authors. It gave them a reason to go out of town and inspired Leonard to reenter the world of legitimate business.

Leonard was listing books for sale online with the auction site eBay. The autographed ones were selling at a premium. $15 to $30 each for books that cost him $2 to $10 plus it gave him a reason to spend an afternoon with Justin meeting the authors. Then one day an even more miraculous thing happened. Woodie Stuart was killed on his boat down in Puerto Vallarta and Leonard's book sales spiked in price like gasoline during an energy crisis.

The Woodie Stuart books went for quintupled their normal price. That week his online sales went from $300 a week to $1700. He happened to have several Woodie Stuarts online and he'd made more money that week than he did from his criminal activities. He was hooked. He quickly listed every autographed book he had but was disappointed when the living authors didn't bring him the same kind of money and he was wiped out of the autographed book market temporarily.

One thing about the book market is it's very easy to get back in. Hitting the thrift stores, library book sales and garage sales, Leonard bought up more copies of the author's books like Cliff Barkley, Danny Stole, Jay Landsbury and many others. At one garage sale he came across a collection of J. C. Cheri and he had an epiphany. Cheri lived only a few towns away from his mother's house in Oklahoma. He bought the collection and planned a trip. Killing her was considerably easier than he would of first thought. It was merely a matter of a little stalking, waiting for the opportune moment, not hesitating and making a quick getaway. Using a pillow simplified matters more since he didn't have to watch her face while he slit her throat.

The results were a second windfall on eBay with more to come.

In the meantime, his relationship with Justin had grown to the point of him moving in. It was a little difficult to hide his income source, but he told Justin he worked for a small telemarketing firm in Victorville. It was a boring enough position, just far enough away, that Justin never cared to visit him at work and he could always pretend his pocket full of money was the result of reaching some performance bonus. To add to the cover-up, he put a phone machine in his office with a phony message adding to the illusion of a real company. The make believe commute he was committing to with the move helped mask his daily routine and explained the mileage on his car. It was a convenient masquerade that fit comfortably over the dregs of his real life.

In this entire charade, he was succeeding against his bills. Even with the fun he and Justin were having he was making much more money than he was spending. If he continued on the road he was on, he could see the possibility of eventually paying off the most devastating of his debts. Unfortunately, as is the case with most people who never learn to handle their finance, he was also getting urges to splurge on himself with bigger and fancier toys and trips. He was feeling cozy with his underground life and was considering less and less paying off his bills at all. The thought of disappearing completely from society was becoming a romantic notion. His most major concern was, if he let his mind wander this way, how to bring Justin into his confidence? Or should he?

After all, it's not as if he was always monogamous. He had other boyfriends. Leonard was one who always liked more than one out. But lately he'd wanted more than just a short-term relationship. Promises. Promises. His other friend was gaining ground in his job, getting more stable and he'd never have gotten to where he was without the love of a good man. Neither a borrower nor a lender be and Leonard was both. He was owed. At times, he just wanted to cash in all his chips.

Well, Rome wasn't built in a day. It was done one brick at a time. It was time to go work. Leonard had accumulated a fantastic collection of Jay Landsbury books, with one real diamond, a first edition of his masterpiece, Celsius 232.777.

Leonard tossed the licenses back in the box, hid them behind one of the broken drawers under his bed and grabbed a backpack for his books.

20
Milo Looks Further

NESTLED INTO THE CONFINES OF HIS CLOSET, his chair half sticking out into a less than tidy bedroom, Milo settled in for a night of hacking. Milo was a computer geek mercenary. Simply put; a hacker for hire.

Tonight's mission, should he choose to accept it (which of course he already had), was to identify the last few missing high bidders. If he should fail in his objectives or be caught in an illegal activity there would be no one to save him, no one to stand up for him and no one to post bail. Like there really is an internet police anyways.

He figured to start easy, with requesting eBay profiles on all bidders. He turned up some information on everyone. Names and mailing addresses, but this didn't really tell him who they were, or if their information was legit. It was pretty easy to create a profile on the site. All you had to do was input the correct data on enrollment and application to be a bidder or seller. But, once approved, a person could revisit their information and make alterations. Still, it was a beginning.

After culling everything he could from eBay, Milo began cross-referencing what he could from the major search engines of AOL, Yahoo, Alta Vista, Excite, and Lycos. He gleaned more information from these databases by either visiting their profile databases or just putting the eBay Identification into the search engine itself and seeing what he got back. Many times he was brought to a website where the name matched an email address and then it was a process of reading the website and seeing what person the address related to.

People were funny. They must be lonely, he deduced. They posted personal information on themselves in hopes of meeting someone. There are online dating services whereby individuals posted desires and requests in anticipation of meeting Mr. or Mrs. Right. Usually all they got was a Mr. or Mrs. Right Now, or some false response by a character trying to lure them into sex. It was also a great place to find someone willing to allow the instigator to behave in a way he or she might otherwise be afraid of if they had to meet casually through normal channels; like employment, mutual friends or church. What a sad state of affairs. But, it made Milo's work easy.

After harvesting all he could from these sites, he revisited the list of bidders to see what he'd completed:

FloridaDr49@Aol.com – Probably a 49 year old Florida Doctor, unconfirmed

SKFan1- Eugene McIntyre, 12 year old kid most likely bidding over his allowance. eBay info

DwarvenHo – Agelina Cunari, Dwarven fighter for the Society for Creative Anachronism living in Phoenix, Yahoo Dating Services

KnightRidder@netzero.com – Darrell Thompson, columnist for the Chicago Tribune. eBay info, netzero profile

BaughmannBooks – Major New York Book Dealer, Excite search engine

HorrorScope – Dan Kantz, Fellow Horror Writer and Newport Beach, CA resident, AOL profiles

Darwinistic – Michelle Pratt, English Teacher at Stanford University, eBay info

BertBooks – Stephen Knightly's Local Bangor, Maine Book Dealer. AOL search

Queerdini – Charles Lubbock, Dallas Texas business owner with strange sex tastes, Excite Dating Club/search engine

LatinLady – Barbara Plumley, Mother of 2 and an adopted child herself uses her work phone number as her primary. Palm Springs, CA. AdoptionResources.com., Alta Vista search engine.

Brahmstein – MIT College Kid, from Boston, real name is Michael Kennedy (The Kennedys?), eBay info

The Author Murders

Sankyu15@hotmail – Adam DeSanto, High School Student Body President, Portland, Oregon. eBay info, Hotmail profile.

CanadianIce123 – Pattison International Acquisitions. Canadian firm. Vancouver, B.C. Lycos search engine.

HermitageBooks – Major So. Cal Book Dealer, Alta Vista search engine.

Hoser4Life – James Cain, surfer dude, Maui hotel manager, eBay info, AOL profile.

8ntIgr8 – David Robbins, Jet Propulsion Laboratories, Los Alamos, New Mexico, eBay info, Lycos Personality Matching Services

Bidnezman – W. Gretzky, Los Angeles, Cal. Hockey fan, Memorabilia Collector. eBay info, Excite search engine, Yahoo search engine.

Milo had found enough information to identify every bidder save the top one. Enough for polite inquisitions, it was time to play hardball. He opened several browser windows so he could watch a couple sites at a time. He set his windows on chat rooms and typed a false receipt in document format. This game, which he thought of as fishing, would require waiting and relying on a little chance. He would have to instigate conversations with individuals on false pretenses.

He didn't really mind though, not in this instance. He was on the side of the white, the good and justice. He hoped. Xanthe was a Police committee member, and Milo would have to trust Xanthe wouldn't drag him through the mud for less than noble reasons.

Opening multiple chat rooms at one time, Milo created several threads on the same subject. In book review sites, he stated "Stephen Knightly eBay book fraudulently Resold," in another site - America's Top Authors - he avowed, "Knightly Book taken off eBay was Sold Under Our Noses," in Scary Writings and Readers he wrote "eBay Auction case of Fraud for Knightly Fans" and so on and so on. He made fourteen threads in all and for each he ran what was supposed to be a news article he had worked on for an obscure website, just getting off the ground. He even prepared a phony site under a web server providing free service and filled the simplistic news letter rag with stories about top writers in a less than honorable, and truthful, fashion.

Then he did the kicker. He produced a link on each of the chat room threads allowing the readers to download an image scan of what was supposed to be the credit card receipt for the fraudulently sold Stephen Knightly book. Only buried within the image was a bit of code, which created a cookie, permitting Milo to visit any of the computers that downloaded the image. It was his aspiration to hack into the computer of FloridaDr49@aol.com.

This wasn't something Milo did lightly. He had respect for people in general and the internet in particular. As a matter of fact, this would be a first for him to perform this feat for money. In the past, he'd done this as a joke amongst his high school friends, leaving them special pop-up windows or forcing porn sites to come up as their homepage. A trick that caused several parents to be severely concerned about their kids web surfing habits even though it was always done in the name of fun. And there was that one jock that he'd avenged himself on with this ploy after the Starbucks fight. But tonight was different.

The whole set-up took Milo till well into the night. It wasn't an easy project. By the time he felt his eyes closing, Dave Letterman was roasting America's elite in his pre-show monologue with a classis top ten list. He drifted asleep.

An alarm jerked Milo awake in his computer chair. It wasn't the first time he'd fallen asleep at his desk so far laid back his nose was like the Statue of Liberty's torch and he knew his faults. His wake up call was ringing like a firehouse. He leaned forward and swirled his mouse around to activate the screen. The Chat rooms were still open and a lot of people had visited his threads, his newsletter site and downloaded the receipt. He clicked off the alarm.

He scanned down the list of viewers until he found what he wanted. FloridaDr49@AOL.com had taken the bait. Opening a program he saved for just this particular capability, a capability that would scare the Pentagon, Milo found the link enabling him to connect with the computer housing his cookie. With a few clicks of his mouse, he found himself trespassing in the good doctor's personal files.

"Wow," exhaled Milo aloud when he discovered who FloridaDr49 was and he certainly wasn't a doctor.

21
Daily and Xanthe Meet Again

CLUB 285 WAS A WARM PLACE TO EAT and drink up the afternoon sunshine. It's a breezy outdoor cafe under the shady palms of Palm Canyon Drive, where patrons can order fancy beverages and simple fares with extravagant names. Its patrons favored pastime is watching shoppers bustle up and down the sidewalks of downtown Palm Springs. It's also the place where I became reacquainted with Detective Daily.

She was sitting at the bar, watching a TV with enough glare on its screen to light a high school football stadium, trying to listen to CNN giving details of another Presidential scandal. This one had the heading of Whitewater, a Special Prosecutor named Ken Starr was giving an interview. It was of as little interest to me as a sporting event, which was of no interest at all. I thought sports were the result of an overly aggressive educational society putting its ideals into the hands of parents whose children were sold on brawns instead of brains. The ironic side of this argument was the American public had bought into the notion; ever the easy path instead of the more sure slow growth. There was a silver cloud in this lining though, the Baseball players were talking about the possibility of a strike and the opinion of average citizen Joe Six-pack was the Rounders were getting too greedy for their own good. If there wasn't even the appearance of playing for the love of the game, then the fans wouldn't exactly be thrilled enough to watch. Even famed sportscaster Howard Cosell had made a remark as such before he died during Spring training earlier in the year.

When she caught my eye Detective Daily was wearing a scrunchy pink tube top and short blue shorts, her blonde hair wreathed by a white tennis visor. If she was trying to be inconspicuous then she'd failed miserably. She didn't look like a cop but she was just my cut of cake and she blinded me with beauty. She became the epicenter of my vision and the rest of my world went black for moment. In my dalliance, I nearly stepped off the curb into the wake of oncoming traffic. I caught myself as I realized who I was staring at. I weaved my way around the shrubbery and watercourse serving as a railing between sidewalk and patio to reach her and tapped her on the shoulder.

"Hello officer," I said. "Aren't you facing the wrong way? My store's behind you." I would have thought she'd have left town by now. But, I was glad she hadn't even though I could be angry at her for the arrest. Seeing her here in the shade of the palm fronded bar, basking in the warmth of the day like any other tourist, I was smitten. I could even forgive her if she'd offer an apology. She gave no hint of remorse over her mistake.

"Xanthe, Xanthe, Xanthe. You were proved innocent. I'm just taking a few days off work." She shook her head back and forth and continued eating her Caesar salad. "Killed any good books lately?"

I played along. "Not lately. But I did mug an English teacher just to stay in practice and on the way over here to throw you a compliment, I knocked down a little old lady. You may want to radio the paramedics." I figured I had nothing to lose. I didn't know if her comment was meant to scare me off or if she naturally took an offensive role when men came up to her. I decided humor was my best defense. It worked.

She chuckled. "Oh, attacking the blue hairs are we? You have to watch out. From what I've seen, if you don't knock them all the way down, they may hook you with their cane. It's an old vaudeville trick."

Her grin spread into a smile. I was caught between her rosy lips and wavy hair. I stood there as if waiting for a poke from a pin, unsure of what to do next.

She broke the ice by showing me some white teeth. "Did you

say something about a compliment?"

"Yeah," I said. "I think I did." The moment hung in the air.

"Well."

"OK, OK. But before I give the compliment can I offer some help detective?"

"On what?" She turned back towards the bar. The epitome of the cold shoulder.

"Your case. I want to help you solve the Biblio-Murders." I pulled a stool out next to her and sat myself down. Waving to the bartender, I ordered an ice tea.

"The Biblio-Murders?" she said. "Where'd you come up with that name?"

Trying to look casual, I shrugged, "It fits. There's a string of murders, all well known authors and the book world is rocking over it. Four authors dead in the last year. That's no coincidence."

She paused as if doing calculations, "Four murders? How do you count four?"

"Ticking them off on my fingers, I ran down the list, "Woodie Stuart, J.C. Cheri, Cliff Barkley and Danny Stole. All four major authors and all four dead."

Daily moved her mouth to the side as she pondered my words. It was what poker players called A Tell and it showed I'd said something that gave her thoughts. She followed it by tilting her head to one side, "Four, huh. I'd only thought about Cliff Barkley and Danny Stole. But you forgot Georgeham Milton?"

"As far as I can tell, he was just a coincidence; wrong place at the wrong time. The motive doesn't seem to fit." I picked up my ice tea and took a sip. If we'd been playing chess, I would have just swept one of her bishops.

"What do you know about motive?" she asked.

"Isn't it obvious?" I said, expecting the question, cops are good at questions. "The killer is a fan, or more likely a book dealer down on his luck. It's a great way to increase the value of some otherwise only slightly valuable merchandise. It's the talk of every dealer in the country. I've even thought about starting a Dead Pool except I didn't want to appear to be romanticizing the deaths. Some people already have a hard time with what drives my business and it could be like throwing gasoline on a campfire."

"You're motive sounds like a fair enough assumption," Daily said. "But, what the heck is a Dead Pool and what's this about gasoline?"

"A Dead Pool is like a lottery where everyone throws in a guess for what famous person is going to die next. I won one in the early 1980's when I picked Russian President Yuri Andropov. I didn't really have any insight into his health or anything. I just figured Soviet leaders don't last very long and they all drink way too much. So, I..."

"Tossed his name into the hat," she finished for me. "Probably not too bad of a guess."

"Well, yeah. That's what I figured. I mean, he hadn't been in the news much at the time, which to me was a sign he was hiding some condition."

"I see it. Good guess." She took another bite of her salad. "Now what do you mean about gasoline on the campfire."

"Well, the best example of that is when Jackie Kennedy died last year. She was my first major celebrity to die where I made a window display of her photos and books. I went ahead and framed the photos with some of my old frames that were still in good shape and of course everything was clearly priced."

"Kind of made a little shrine to her," suggested Daily.

"That's right," I agreed, motioning palms. "Only some people didn't like it. They felt it was making money off somebody else's ill fortune. They considered it grisly and in poor taste. I had more than one person walk into the store and give me a hard time over the window display."

"So, did you take it down?" she asked.

"No way. I sold everything in the window. It was one of my best days at the time." My ice tea was getting down to the ice. "Most people realize that's the business I'm in and accept it. But, for those wackos who have to butt into everyone else's business, I'd rather not give them an excuse to tirade into my store. A Dead Pool would bring out the worst in'em. And, it wouldn't be fair to Jill to entice those kinds of people to come in."

"Jill?" She was quizzical. She really needed to do more homework.

"My assistant at the store"

"Oh, yeah." she nodded, remembering. "Ok. I get it. Can I ask you a question about somebody else though?"

"Sure," I said, the sun felling a little warmer.

"Who's Leonard?"

"Leonard?" The name threw me for a loop. The question seemed from left field.

"Leonard Beschloss. You drove to see a booth of his up in Joshua Tree the other day. Who is he?" She stared at me waiting for an answer, her face blank and unwavering. It was another long pause in our conversation.

I was slow in realizing what this question meant. Then it dawned on me. She was a cop again, her tourist persona gone. She'd been following me. She'd tailed me up to the high desert and therefore I was still a suspect in the murders, at least in her mind. "Is that whose booth that was?"

"Come now Xanthe," she said, angrily wiping the corners of her mouth with her napkin. "You can do better than that."

"I do know a Leonard, but I don't know his last name." I wasn't convincing her. She'd lowered her gaze and was staring up at me as if ready to challenge. "Really, and I wasn't up there for anything to do with this author murderer."

"Biblio-murderer," she reminded me in a mocking tone. The conversation had gotten much too serious. Her smile was gone, her eyes took a skeptical tone and she put one hand up on the bar, as if she were ready to block my exit. The other she put down low on her hip, ready to strike. I was glad she didn't have a gun on her. "So, what were you there for? There are a lot better books much closer to home if you were looking for merchandise."

I decided to play it straight, nearly. Once again, I knew I had nothing to lose. I was not mixed up in anything illegal. "What do you know about horror novels?" I told her why I was up there. I told her about the case I was on. The Stephen Knightly book. The chest under the bandana, nearly everything. Well, almost everything. I didn't tell her about Milo. I mean, what was it to her? I also left out the regards to my feelings towards Donlagic and his act of barbarism in the bathroom. I wrapped up with, "I hope you now see why I was up there."

She wasn't convinced. "The only thing you haven't told me is who Leonard is."

"I'm not sure he's the person you think he is. I find that hard to believe." I folded my arms in front of me in subconscious defiance. "But, the Leonard I know is a boyfriend of a friend. He lives with my friend...in Rancho Mirage."

"I'd like to meet him." She hadn't blinked once since she'd brought up the subject.

"I'll give him a call," I offered reluctantly.

"I'd prefer to surprise him," she said. "Alone."

"No way. You busted me on circumstantial evidence and there's no way I'm sicking you on my friends."

"I thought he was a friend of a friend," she wiggled her pretty head as if to add, 'Isn't that so?'

"I'll take you to him," I offered.

"Today."

"Right Now." I figured that'd be the final word.

"Good," she waved for the bill. "Come with me while I get my stuff."

Can cops play me or what?

22
Leonard's House

DAILY FORCED ME TO FOLLOW HER up to her hotel room. The thought of going to her room had crossed my mind. It wasn't on the terms I'd prefer but it'd do under the circumstances. Apparently, she didn't trust me on my own to stick around or make some effort to warn Leonard even though it was the furthest thing from my mind. I was confident events would play out favorably.

Being up in her room was slightly awkward, especially waiting for her to change clothes. I stood in the little hallway just inside the door as she picked through her suitcase getting some long pants and a nicer blouse. As she bent over to grab her clothes, I got a full view of her derriere in the short shorts and was reminded yet again what a lovely woman she was. She turned around quickly and startled me. I'm sure she saw me staring. Our eyes met and she pushed me into the bathroom so she could change. A minute later she released me from the confines of the lavatory while pulling her hair out of the collar of her blouse and we left. I never saw her grab her gun, her clothes seemed too tight to have it hidden on her, but she had a large black Gore-Tex fanny pack with more than enough room for her policewoman apparatus.

Leonard lived in a room at Justin Blake's house. I had a secret I kept to myself. It was a dichotomy of two parallel thoughts that perplexed me constantly. One of the thoughts went like this: Homosexuals are deviants and ethically perverse. They have a mental disorder forcing them to choose the most obnoxious social pattern they can. It isn't a popular secret but there it is. The other thought went like this: If angels were physical beings then homosexuality would be a natural extension. Love is love regardless of physical form. If two beings can share a bliss that is more than purely physical but satisfies a base urge and need, one of security and acceptance not of lust, then homosexuality is just a name placed upon that love by hard hearted outsiders. These two thoughts clashed persistently in my thoughts. Even if Leonard was the killer, was it because of a mental breakdown from his gayness? Or was it just because he was sick and subject to the same bad choices any other criminal made? After all, not all convicts are gay.

And on top of all this, I have several friends that are gay and I sincerely like them.

These thoughts swirled in my head like a dust devil as Detective Daily and I drove the twenty minutes to Rancho Mirage. The ride was largely in silence; only occasionally did we talk beyond giving directions. The streets to Rancho Mirage took us out of downtown Palm Springs along Highway 111, the main thoroughfare through the desert cities. It's a stoplight filled drive skirting by strip malls and condominium projects in front of finger upon fingers of rugged foothills. Through most of it there's winding sidewalks mixed with grass and the newest trend in landscape, called desertscape, as a way to conserve water. I think it's just a way of making more money. Turn desert into yards and then charge the residents to make it look like desert.

Between Palm Springs and Rancho Mirage is Cathedral City, named for the towering rocky hills ringing the center of its growth now filled with rundown trailerparks, fast food restaurants and badly painted businesses. Its nickname was Cat City and its furthest edge is marked by the largest Ford dealership in the valley, guarding the entrance into Rancho Mirage, the Playground of Presidents. We turned left onto Frank Sinatra Drive to emerge into a realm of stuccoed walls hiding some of the nicest country club homes and golf courses in the desert. I tried to move the conversation along.

"I hope my willingness to cooperate proves to you I'm not involved," I said.

"You could just be appearing to cooperate," she returned. "Lots of criminals do things to throw the police off their scent."

"Perhaps I'm telling the truth."

"Maybe. Maybe not."

"How about trying this on for size," I ventured. "You think the killer's motive is making all sorts of money online selling the books he or she just got autographed, correct?"

"That's right," she confirmed.

"How many books do you figure a single person can get signed?" I wanted to work this through with her. See if she'd done her math.

"Twenty or thirty, I guess. I've seen people at the signings empty out entire backpacks and go up to authors with armfuls."

"True. I've done that myself. I've even gone through the line two or three times like that. Especially if I'm working alone as I think the killer must be."

"Why do you think that?" Ah, a speed bump in her thoughts.

"Because you arrested me and never asked me who I was working with."

"Oh."

I'd played her back one of her cards. "Sometimes in negotiations I find it's best not to pay attention to what you're being asked or shown but more important to hear what the other person is not saying. It's the areas they hide where the truest answer lies." This was a little holdover from my earlier days of selling cars but I found it worked itself into many other areas of my life. "You might know the same sentiment from another famous detective."

"And who might that be?" she asked.

"My dear Watson, when scrutinizing the facts of any case," I prophesized, "one must simply eliminate all the possibilities and then whatever is left, no matter how improbable, has to be the answer we seek."

"Brilliant Sherlock. So how does this case add up?"

"Well, I figure a single person can get as many books signed as you. But let's say thirty for the sake of argument. I've done as many as fifty-five a couple times in my life: the last was with Mary Higgins Clark. But those were exceptions."

"Fifty-five books!" she exclaimed.

"Don't stop me I'm on a roll. Yes, let's average about thirty. How much do you figure each book is worth?"

She bit her lip and calculated in her head. This was the tricky part. Most people thought the internet a fathomless sea of money. But if you took the time to really add up the time and money factors you ended up with a lot less.

"About a hundred bucks?" I know she'd done this math already but there was no way to force her into a conversation without covering familiar ground first.

Try about $25. But let's split it down the middle at $50 because the author did just die so the prices are going at a premium. Even so that only adds up to about $1,500. Would the killer really risk capture, imprisonment, even possible death of themselves for that?"

"People have killed for a lot less." She was wrenching both hands on the wheel, trying to strangle it as my deductions settled.

I opened my mouth to speak, thought again and snapped it shut. Every minute we drove the tension rose in the car till the silence was thicker than snow on a polar bear's butt. When we pulled up in front of Justin's house, I put my hand on the door handle and froze.

Daily got out of the car and spoke to me through her open door. "You aren't chickening out, are you Xanthe?"

"No," I said getting out. "But, if my friends had nothing to do with this then I'll be putting them through an ordeal they don't deserve."

"I'll be gentle," she promised.

"I hope so. My friends mean a lot to me." We paused, staring at each other. "You know," I said preparing a nice line, "We could be friends. More than friends, if we'd met under different circumstances. You're very pretty." She didn't even flinch. If she had feelings under her cop persona she'd learn long ago not to show them. "Come on let's get his over with." We walked up the driveway, rang the bell and waited on the Spanish pavers of the entryway.

There was no answer. We rang again. We were about ready to go when we heard the clip-clop of hard soled shoes on the other side of the door and it swung open. Justin was pulling a white terry cloth bathrobe around him and making the last twirl of tying the belt. His feet were clad in black leather loafers making his stark white ankles stand out like Popsicle sticks.

"Hey Xanthe," Justin said hiding around the corner of the door.

"Hey Justin," I replied. "Sleeping in till the crack of noon these days?"

"I was… taking a shower," his voice quavered.

"Hum."

I heard a door shut down the hall. A second later, Brad erupted from the bookshelves lining the hall, tucking his shirt into his shorts. Our eyes connected and he strained to retain eye contact. "Hello Xanthe." His eyes darted from me to Daily to Justin and back to me. He'd been caught.

"Hello Brad."

Justin tried to break up the tension with a joke. "Well, isn't this a precious moment." He opened the door a little further as if hiding was no longer necessary, which wasn't particularly true. He and Brad had broken up more than a year ago. Justin now lived with Leonard. The promiscuity of homosexuality is a myth often fomented amongst the breeders. That's what gays call straight people with kids: Breeders. It's an unquantifiable claim that being homosexual is all about sex; kind of an oxymoron that's more fiction than fact. Heterosexuals don't have to go around flaunting the fact they have sex with people of the opposite gender. Yet gays often have to emote the verity of their private lives as a way of sanctioning their behavior to the legal and legislative world, not to mention the emotional assertions of the hetero community.

The whole issue reminded me of a female City Hall worker who complained once in a private conversation that gays were allowed to share health insurance with significant others, yet she wasn't allowed to share her insurance with a girlfriend, who was just a girl who happened to be friend. The friend was in dire straits financially and had high probability of further complications, possibly death. In the female City workers distress, she rhetorically remarked, quite vocally, 'I'll screw her if I have to, I just want to help my friend.'

I pulled myself back to the issue at hand. "Where's Leonard?"

"He left a little while ago," Justin confessed unknowingly. "Why, what's up?" His eyes fell upon Detective Daily, who until now had been quiet.

She spoke up. "I'm Detective Susan Daily Mr. Blake. Can we come inside and ask you a few questions?"

Stillness swarmed. Background noise filled the void; a few birds chirped, a lawnmower thrummed in the distance and a slight wind pushed the leaves in a circle at our feet.

"Sure, come on in." Justin stepped back from the entrance making the sunken in living room the obvious destination. "Have a seat. Do you mind if I put on some clothes?"

"Not at all," said Daily. "We'll wait."

Justin disappeared back down the hall and Brad took over as the host. "Can I get you anything to drink?"

I accepted. Daily declined. Brad went into the kitchen to get me some water. He returned with two glasses filled with ice. "I was always taught to bring one for guests anyways," Brad explained, handing one to both the detective and myself. "Most people decline just to be polite."

"Thank you," Daily said accepting the glass and setting it down on the table without partaking.

Justin came back in wearing a fresh t-shirt and a pair of blue jeans taking the love seat caddy-corner to the couch. Brad sprawled across the back of the loveseat, resting on its ridge. One arm spread across the back of Justin. The two were much more a couple than they'd previously let on.

I couldn't resist. "You two back together?"

"Not officially," Brad answered.

Justin gave him a quizzical look. "What he means, is that we're not living together or anything and we were trying to keep this our little secret."

"What about Leonard?" I questioned.

"Yes. What about Leonard?" forced Detective Daily.

"Honestly, he hasn't been around much lately," defended Justin.

"The past few months he seems to be more and more into his work than anything else. I hardly ever see him."

"His work," repeated the detective. "What does Mr. Beschloss do?"

At the mention of Leonard's last name Justin's voice went uncomfortably up an octave. "He works for a telemarketing firm near San Bernardino." He coughed to clear his throat and his voice returned to a normal tone. "He does pretty well too. But more and more it's all he thinks about. It must be pretty fulfilling because he works all the time."

"All the time," Daily was pulling out her notebook to jot things down. "How often does he come home?"

"A couple times a week," Justin said, sitting up at attention, then as an afterthought, "Not enough to base a relationship on." He turned to Brad and they shared confirmations. Brad rubbed one of Justin's shoulders.

"He's making pretty good money though," established Brad.

"Why do you say that?"

"He pays cash for everything," Justin said. He looked at Brad a second time and Brad nodded for him to go on. "Rent, utilities, dinner, everything. Once I saw him fork out $400 for a television and then pay $175 shipping for overnight express. He didn't even need that TV."

"That was when their relationship hit the skids," Brad whispered over Justin's head. Now it was Justin's turn to nod. He placed his head in his hands and then wrung the sadness away with a downward wipe.

Justin and Brad took turns telling the tale of the past few months with Leonard. He had become more and more aloof. Leonard had lost weight and dyed his hair blonde. This made Daily and Xanthe exchange a glance. Xanthe was a natural blonde. Leonard's personality had changed too. His demeanor had developed into a nasty temperament. He talked with a trashy mouth and no amount of loving or compassion could quench his distemper. There'd even been a bit of a fight when the TV was bought. Justin didn't understand why Leonard was so adamant about it and when Leonard was questioned he'd nearly gone to blows rather than answer what he called, 'The Inquisition.' Only later did Justin find out Leonard had mailed it to his ex-wife.

"His ex-wife?" Daily was thrown for a loop. "I thought he was gay?"

"He was, is," dignified Justin. "What do you think; everyone is born with the Gay gene? He was straight when he was married. But when he separated he came out of the closet. He'd been gay for months by the time I met him. Then after he starting making money again, he tried recontacting his ex-bitch. They exchanged a few letters and before I knew what was happening he was drifting back." Justin paused.

Brad finished for him by wagging a finger between himself and Justin. "That's when we reconnected. Only Leonard didn't like that either. The little receptacle. That's the way it is with most bottoms."

"Bottoms?" I said. "What's a bottom?" As I was looking at Justin and Brad I got an image in my head. "Oh crap, never mind. You don't have to explain."

Daily didn't get it. "Wait. What's a bottom?"

"You are honey," said Brad, pointing a finger at her. "In sex, you're the receiver right. Well, with men they're called bottoms. Get it?"

"Oh," she said. Then even bigger, "Ooooh. Yeah. Got it."

Daily took a second to recompose herself by looking at her notes. Her cheeks turned red. She shifted in her seat and pulled at the top button of her blouse to let a little air in. Placing three fingers against her forehead helped her recompose her thoughts. "You mentioned letters from his ex-wife?"

"Yeah," said Justin.

"Are there any of those around?" She looked up and tilted her head sideways. Her tell that she'd hit an important clue.

"They're probably in his room. Wanna take a look?" Justin offered as he rose.

"I'd love to. But it would probably get thrown out of court if I did." Daily was covering her back, crossing the t's and dotting the i's. "I've already made one bad bust on this case and I don't want to do it again. Now, if the door was already open and I just had to walk by, anything in plain view would be safe. It's procedure Mr. Blake and it's important." She capped her pen and slid it back into the spiral binding of her small notebook.

"I'll check and see if he left it open. But, may I ask you a question detective?" Justin requested before he stood up.

"Go ahead," said Daily.

"What is it that Leonard's supposed to have done?"

"Murder, Mr. Blake." The words hung in the air like a twitching hangman's noose.

When Justin spoke, the words came as if from inside a dry and crackling paper bag again. "Let me check his room." He thrust his hand against his chest and coughed once; carefully placing a hand on the arm of the sofa, then rose one more time and strode down the hall. Apparently stress affects us all in different ways.

If Justin helped the door open we didn't hear it. He was gone only a few seconds. When he returned his face had lost some of its color. "Come on back."

I started to rise but Daily showed me the flat of her palm. She wanted me to stay and I obliged her. She was the detective and I, just a civilian. By the time she was out of sight down the hall I had ants in my pants. Brad brought me back to the moment with a question.

"Is this all for real?"

I nodded my head up and down, "Yes."

Daily stood on the threshold of a killer. She couldn't confirm her feeling with emotions but sometimes instinct kicks in. The room had the messiness of a mind left to wander in darkness. The floor was covered in clothes and the bed was unmade. Shelves were a scattering of literature with no accounting for style. Bad housekeeping did not a killer make, after all Jeffrey Dahlmer had been a neat freak and Ted Bundy was meticulous, yet still...all the pieces seemed to fit like when you finally pick up the right jigsaw puzzle piece and you know it's going to be the critical step in completion of the picture. There was just the right amount of color on all the corners.

There was one problem she had to overcome - she had no warrant. Her questioning of Xanthe had been a mistake. She hadn't identified herself and when she finally did she'd screwed the whole thing bad enough so even if he had been the right suspect a good lawyer could have gotten him off. Xanthe,..her thoughts about him floated in a new direction. He wasn't bad looking; intelligent too. Later.

Looking at the room was like trying to count the stars in a clear night sky. Where did she start and how could she find something significant enough to garner a warrant without blowing her hand.

Leonard collected books. Most of these were not impressive but some of them were very nice. She wasn't a serious collector but she knew the most valuable ones were probably the least impressive. It stood to reason when an author began his craft the publisher put the least into the presentation. A first run hardback by a virtual unknown author could easily have a plain dust jacket if it had a dust jacket at all. Often times authors first books were a trade paperback. John Grisham had first written A Time To Kill in the mid seventies and had self-published the book. It was a plain yellow large paperback book worthy of insignificance. If he hadn't been so damned fantastic at his craft no one would have paid it a second glance. But, once a reader was involved in the work there was no putting it down. Grisham had made 1,000 copies of the book and most of them ended up as gifts pawned off on friends. Very few of them actually sold. By the time he'd written The Firm, and especially after it was produced as a film starring Tom Cruise, collectors were searching attics all over Mississippi for the lost copies. These days they went for at least a grand.

The room reminded Daily of herself as a girl. She'd been a collector of porcelain dogs and they'd lined the shelves in her room much as the books did here: Great Danes, dachshunds, collies, Dalmatians. Her favorite one was the least expensive of the bunch. It was a small unpolished English Cocker Spaniel made of white and brown caresses of flowing paint, textured just enough to give it a sense of realness. She'd named it Lady Dog. If either of her brothers had come into her room and moved it as they sometimes did when they wanted to give their G.I Joes a pet, her eyes could scan the shelves and find it in an instant. If it wasn't there she'd go hunt them down and holler till they gave it back. Looking at the room also reminded her of her favorite place to hide things.

The Author Murders

She didn't want to disturb the crime scene if this room was going to be the subject of an official search but she did need some hard evidence to justify the warrant to a judge.

The way to find a needle in a haystack was to sit down on it. She carefully stepped her way into the room without mussing up the clothes on the floor and sat on the bed. It was soft, just like hers was as a child.

Her dad had been a man of great significance. Johnathan Gaylon Daily had served as a Los Angeles assistant prosecutor to one of the best, Vincent Bugliosi, and he'd learned the trade well. A.D.A. Daily had been support staff on the Manson murder trial. Daily's understanding of justice had grown during a time of stark differences in people's perceptions as to what was fair play and appropriate procedures. Hippies were marching on one end of the country and blacks were marching on the other. The country was finding itself and Manson had brought about the end of free love and the sixties. After the conviction, A.D.A. Daily got a promotion to the job of Federal Prosecutor. From that time on, Detective Daily's dad had been but a glimpse in her life. There was an incident with the daughter of a very wealthy man that took up his time, one Patty Hearst, and dad just didn't have the time anymore for his little girl and her mother.

Daily leaned back and watched the sunlight fall through the half drawn curtains until it touched the pillow at the top of the bed like it was marking a holy site. With her left hand she stretched under the pillow, startling only a little as she felt a piece of paper. Grasping it in her fingers she withdrew it from its hiding place. It had the fragmented torn edge of a page ripped from a large notebook. Clean smooth blue ink lined its yellowed breadth in the handwriting of a woman. It read:

Leonard -

Please don't write me anymore. Any hope for us is long gone. As a matter of fact, I'm surprised I'm even responding to your last query. I moved on emotionally a long time ago and suggest you do the same.

The actions you allude to are revolting. I quit wanting you when you were an honest yet incapable husband. Why would I ever want you as a dishonest, yet productive man of lesser qualities? Your delinquency is repulsive. What you have become only proves I made the right choice in leaving you. I will never ever love you again. Never.

You still owe me a great sum of money. Please repay it, but only with honestly earned currency. I returned the television for cash. If you have to resort to criminal acts, I prefer you let my attorney escort you to the courthouse or the nuthouse, whichever you choose.

Never yours again,

Tracey

Detective Daily emerged from the hallway, stopping just before the steps into the sunken living area. "Mr. Blake I need to ask you a few more questions."

I couldn't contain myself. "Did he do it?"

She ignored me and again pulled her little notepad out of her fanny pack, slipping the pen from its spirals.

I hated being ignored. I asked her again, but she was already into her questioning with Justin. I blurted a different question. "Did you see it?"

"See what?" She stopped writing long enough to look at me.

"The book. THE BOOK." I was frantic. She had her case and I had mine. It was the intersection of two divergent courses and I wanted to know if I too was on the correct path. I felt as if I could see a finish line.

"That's not important at this time," she stated as if discussing a dead issue.

"Like hell," I said jumping up from the couch. I darted past her towards Leonard's room.

"Don't go in there," she yelled at me. "It's a crime scene."

I stood in the doorway peering at the shelves looking into the mess Daily had already summed up and others would shortly pilfer through, visually scanning the shelves I was forbidden to touch. I saw many great books of modern fiction: Pat Conroy's -The Prince of Tides, Tom Clancy's - The Hunt for Red October, Kurt Vonnegut's - The Sirens of Titan, Philip Roth's - The Human Stain, John F. Kennedy's - Profiles in Courage. Could that be a first? I ran my eyes more rapidly over the spines. Many books were in excellent condition. Few were book clubs. Some were limited printings of Easton and

Franklin Mint presses, but only a few and Heritage press, although their value was well known to be diminished compared to the earlier publishers. I also saw quite a few advanced reading copies, but the titles were unknown to me. ARC's only printed their titles on the cover; their spines were plain wrappings of yellow, blue and tan. This was a collection of someone with an astute eye for modern Literature. It wasn't the best collection I could ever hope to attain, but it was something of a piece of art unto itself. It was definitely leagues above any collection I'd been asked to bid on recently.

Wait. My eyes caught something on the far side of the bed lodged into the shelf above the table lamp. A red spine with ribbed edges and light gold scrollwork ran upwards nearly a foot in length, wedged between something old; a G. H. Henty book of children's adventure from the early 20th century and papers stuffed into a green essay folder. It was taller than most other books - taller than the standard height of a bestselling book. The binding was leather, a handmade job of excellent quality. There was no writing on the spine but there was the gold stamp of a vehicle, a dump truck. It was there. It existed. And I was forbidden to enter and retrieve it. I stared at it as if it would evaporate before my eyes. I was still standing there frozen when Detective Daily came up and placed a hand on my shoulders.

"Is it there?" she asked.

I nodded it was.

"It'll still be there when I get the warrant." She led me from the house with Justin and Brad wagging at our tails. They wanted to know what book had grabbed me hard enough to shake my senses. They hounded us and Daily turned on them.

"Mr. Blake, Mr. Conniber. There is a specific book in that room which I inform you will be the key to discerning if anything has been disturbed before I return. That room is now a crime scene and you are forbidden from entering it. Should you decide to disobey my order then you shall be arrested for interfering with an investigation. Do not enter that room."

I got in the passenger side of Daily's car and we drove away. Brad and Justin went back inside. After we turned the corner, a heretofore hunkered down head popped up in a gray Lincoln Town Car. He had been easy to miss. His car was inconsequential and was perfect for hiding in plain sight. The driver wore a Hawaiian print shirt and dark sunglasses. He lit up a cigarette and watched the street for the length of time it took to smoke. Then he moved his car down the block towards Justin Blake's house, parked in front of the mailbox and got out.

23
The Book Disappears

THE DOORBELL RANG.

"They must have forgotten something," Brad said, swinging the door open. When he had pulled it all the way free, he remarked, "Who are you?" Not his normal introduction.

"Where's Leonard?" demanded the man in the doorway. He wore a Hawaiian print shirt, had dark hair and reeked of cigarettes, one of which dangled from his mouth as he spoke in a thick Eastern European accent hard for Brad to understand.

"You can answer my questions first buddy," defied Brad. This stranger had an unwelcome attitude and if he didn't start explaining himself soon he was going to get a door slammed in his face, "Or you can just get off the porch."

"This looks like the right kind of place," spoke the man in Hawaiian print, eyeballing all the books lining the shelves of the house. He tossed his cigarette on the ground, mashed it with his foot and put his other over the threshold, preparing to walk inside.

"Hey." Brad placed his hand on the chest pocket of the Hawaiian shirt, crumpling the pack of cigarettes, stopping the man from entering.

There's a maneuver known in police work used to control an unruly individual. It's called a come-along. It's as effective as a Vulcan nerve pinch and as simple as twisting someone's fingers. That's what the man in the doorway did to Brad. He reached up and grabbed Brads hand from his chest did a little under arm promenade that ended up twisting Brads hand and fingers into a very painful and precarious position lifting Brad up onto his tippy toes in an effort to minimize the pain. Come along and walk with me.

From ringing the doorbell to the finger dance took only a matter of seconds. Justin had been sitting on the couch trying to gather his thoughts as to Xanthe and Detective Daily's revelations uncovered only minutes before. Seeing Brad get swung into a chicken wing hobble lifted Justin from the couch. He stammered, "What the,..."

From beneath the flowered shirt, the intruder pulled a fiendishly large pistol. "Stay where you are fairy boy. I want what I want. Where is it?"

Justin stopped in his tracks. Seeing a gun pointed at him had turned his feet to mud. He dared not step again.

"I don't know what you want," objected Justin.

Brads fingers were twisted a little tighter forcing him onto the balls of his feet. The gun was thrust under his chin making him look like a marionette on a stick. His face was panicked like Porky Pig's when he wore the cursed shoes that wouldn't stop dancing and in less time than it takes to change the channel the pistol pushed Brads chin to the furthest reaches of his neck.

"The book, THE BOOK, The fucking Stephen Knightly book! Leonard owes me much more. But right now, I'll settle for the book. Get it now!"

The door was still open behind Brad and the gun toting luau. A shadow stepped up to the rear of them and cracked a fistful of metal against the intruders head. The Hawaiian print shirt and its wearer crumpled to the floor like a fallen palm tree. Brad took a deep breath as he collapsed against the wall gasping for air, untwisting his fingers and rubbing his arm with his other hand.

Leonard brandished his own revolver. He stood angry and sweating over the trespasser, who was lying on the floor in a groaning mass. As the man on the ground moaned and lifted a hand to his hair, Leonard dropped to his knees and struck him once, twice and a third time again. The man quit making any noise or movement. Blood trickled from his scalp.

"God," whispered Justin. "What are you doing?"

"I'm protecting you," snarled Leonard. His hair was a dyed blonde and he wore frumpy cloths over an otherwise athletic build. He was of average height but pummeling the stranger the way he was, he appeared a giant.

"From who," said Brad shaking the soreness from his hand? "Who is he?"

"Michael Donlagic. He's a police officer. Well, former police officer. Now, he's in charge of security for the casino."

"Security? What could you owe a casino security guard? Is it money? Do you owe him enough money to make him come here like this?" Justin asked finally getting his shock under control.

Leonard didn't answer. When Justin stepped forward to check Brad's arm Leonard lifted the gun and pointed it at him to stop his progress.

"You going to shoot me now?" asked Justin.

"I should. I should waste you both for what you've been doing behind my back." Leonard lifted the gun till he was looking down the barrel at Justin's head. "Get in the bathroom. Get you're boyfriend and get into the bathroom." With a wave of the muzzle Justin and Brad stepped into the hall and entered the first door. Leonard shut it on his former boyfriend and his lover despite their protests and claims that he was in way over his head.

"I learned from the best," shouted Justin back at him.

"Lock it," Leonard yelled. Then to frighten them even more, "And I'll shoot the first person to come through that door."

The knob jostled with a click. Satisfied, Leonard walked into the kitchen, grabbed a knife and went back into the foyer towards Donlagic. He grabbed the mini blinds around the sliding door leading to the back yard and cut the strings controlling the blinds. With the thin rope he bound Donlagic's feet and hands together as if he tied hogs for a living. When he was done, standing over him, letting his hatred swell, he aimed his pistol at Donlagic's head.

Leonard had killed plenty. One more death would mean little on the life sentences he'd receive should he ever face trial for all his crimes. This one would be a cop. He'd be a hero in prison - one of the cellmates to be looked up to. The other prisoners would welcome him with an honor guard. But then who wants to live life in prison. If he killed Donlagic now, like this, the police would haunt him till the ends of the Earth. There'd be a vengeance inflicted on him till his dying days and no amount of distance would lessen their determination. Better to leave Donlagic alive.

He put the gun back in the waist of his pants and took another three whacks at the dastardly Bosnian. Good things come in threes he figured; whack - bloody nose, whack - swollen eye, whack - cracked ribs. After the first strike, Donlagic passed the point of complaining.

24
United We Stand

RIDING BACK TO THE STORE in the passenger seat of Detective Daily's car, I went over the facts of the case as I knew them. Leonard was not only the seller of the Stephen Knightly book I was searching for, he was also the killer of the Biblio-Murders. He'd killed several authors to increase the value in their collected autographed books which he would then sell online. But that wasn't the only reason. There had to be another.

Donlagic entered a wild card factor necessitating careful evaluation. As Security for the Indian tribe, his role would most likely be seeking a debt collection. But to warrant his interference rather than some under lackey the amount would have to be staggering. And from what I knew about gamblers habits, having served on a sub-committee investigating the social impacts of a casino on the community, Leonard had to have gone through a period of escalating mega-failures culminating in a desperate attempt at redemption. The patterns had been established long ago, but viewing them first hand was another matter entirely. The scrap of paper from the Yucca Valley store and his relative aloofness to Justin reconfirmed all this in my mind.

"So Detective," I asked, turning in my seat to face Daily "What do we do now?"

Daily didn't answer right away. For all my efforts to establish some understanding of the other sex, they are often still a mystery. I thought she was choosing her words carefully. Instead, she pulled over to the side of the road and once parked, turned to face me and leaned closer. I was surprised but let gravity take over. We embraced and kissed. The feelings I had for her when we first met and she was just a lovely lady browsing my store returned. I smelled her hair: delicious; felt her curves; sensational; and I pushed myself against her, instantly getting hard.

She pushed me away. "We," she spat out as if she'd just bitten into an apple and found a brown spot, "aren't doing anything. I'll start with checking out some of the new leads from Mr. Blake's house. You will be going back to your bookstore," she gripped the steering wheel and twisted her hands as if needing to reaffirm her grip, then finished, "in a while."

This was incredulous. "What! Wait a second. This morning I was a suspect to you, even after going through an interrogation, a line-up and a stakeout. All of which proved me innocent. Yet, you still put me under surveillance. Don't tell me you just happened to be sitting at the cafe across from my store." I tried my best to stare her down. She refused to turn her pretty head towards me as if catching my gaze would turn her to stone. "And then you KISS me?" After a minute of waiting for her to reply and getting no response I chose a different tact. "Well. If you won't listen to reason, then I'll just have to use my ace in the hole." Now it was my turn to stare out the windshield.

"And what's that?" she retorted.

"Detective Daily," I stated as if I were a cross examiner and she a hostile witness. "Did you or did you not wrongfully arrest said book dealer, forcing him into confinement, after questioning him without first reading him his Miranda rights?" I folded my arms.

"You were a suspect!" she blurted out. "You can't be serious?"

"At what point was I a suspect? Was it when you collected enough evidence to justify driving two hours from your home department to ask questions? Or do you commonly conduct an investigation so far away from home? Perhaps you had already financially obligated your department with or without the knowledge of your superiors? Purchasing gasoline, hotels rooms, and meals? These are all expenses that would have to be reported, would they not?" I was building a case against her she knew would stand up in court. My time with the Palm

The Author Murders

Springs Police Department had alerted me to the sensitivity of budgeting investigations for overtime and other expenses. I couldn't be sure I had hit every nail on the head, but I was reasonably sure she understood how far a good attorney could take this line of analysis to justify a false imprisonment lawsuit.

"You should be locked up for thinking like that," she spat furiously." I can't believe you consider yourself an asset to the force. You're on the Police committee. You know what it takes to do our job? How can... Why...I don't believe..." She continued to mouth more infractions at me like a Texas teenager; some of them seeming to linger on four letter words. Eventually she ran out of breath. There are times in life when it's all about the leverage. Courtesy can go take a flying leap. It was time for me to lead the discussion.

"So tell me what you got out of Leonard's room?"

She sat and sat, finally she spoke. "You go ahead and do whatever you want Mr. Anthony, I am a detective with the City of Industry solving a crime of murder. You can shove all your threats up your ace hole." She was still a cop and had to play it close to the vest.

For more than a mile we rode in silence. I couldn't quit thinking about the book. Also I couldn't quit thinking about kissing her.

I was mad as hell and she'd gotten me horny as hell, but as far as the investigation went, I was pretty sure what her next steps would entail. She was going to alert her partner to the new course of the investigation and ask the San Bernardino authorities to set up camp on Leonard's work place. The local cops would watch for Leonard to reappear at Justin's house. Most likely this would be assigned back to Detectives Craft and Andrews since they already had some involvement on the case. In the meantime she'd go back up to Pete's Collectibles and check out the hidden chest. I had to wonder though what she'd found in Leonard's room. Even with her recent mistakes, she must be pretty sharp overall. Departments don't promote just anyone to Detective.

Furthermore, I made a gut check as to my own motive in persuading her to divulge information. I wasn't vindictive and I wasn't wicked. I genuinely wanted to solve the murders and get the Knightly book. This was shaping into a case I could sink my teeth into and I couldn't forget about the kiss. Women.

I decided to break the ice by pretending to accept her judgment. "And one more things Detective: What are your intentions about seeing more of me?"

"Well, I wasn't lying to you when earlier I had said I was here on vacation?" She reached over and gave my hand a squeeze, then placed a palm on my leg, her fingers dangerously high on my thigh. "OK. But I'm not committing to stay out of the case, no matter how much you torture me?"

She slid her hand higher, touching the swell in my pants. "Oh, is this torture?"

"Not really. Kinda. Just drive faster. Don't you have a siren on this thing?"

We went back to her hotel, walked through the lobby while trying to be respectable. In the elevator we digressed to a couple of star struck lovers. By the time we groped our way into her room we were ripping each other's shirts off. Women are still a curiosity to me. Yesterday I was her number one suspect. Today I was her number one in another way. My mind kept going to Harlequin romance and I wanted to make sure she got the best of her weekend away. I didn't know if tomorrow I'd be just another chapter in her diary. Today I didn't care. One thing for sure: I really liked the way she whispered my name and how her lips formed a silent O while she gave me her most intimate embrace.

25
A Sidekick

LATER, WHEN I ENTERED THE STORE, Jill greeted me with a warm smile as did the shelves full of spines and covers. The whole world seems to shine brighter after sex and there's something about walking into the store and seeing all those books that brings good feelings to me. It's my happy place.

Jill caught my attention. "You have a visitor," she said. "And there's a message for you. Which do you want first?"

"Who's here?" I asked.

"Give me five dollars," she said extending her hand.

"Can I have a hint first? One of our regulars? An old friend? Politics? A family member?" It could be anyone. A lot of people I knew fit into the five dollar customer category.

She kept her hand out. When I didn't fill it she said, "He's in the second room. 'Said something about the computers and you'd be OK with it. I didn't feel like challenging him on it."

I knew who it was. "Who called?"

"The Chief," she said.

"Thanks," I said. It must be serious. The Chief almost never called me. Still, I put off calling him for a few minutes and went to the back of the store. When I swung the door open, I saw a gangly young man with slicked black hair perched at the terminal with one leg tucked underneath him in an awkward position. He wore an oversized suit older than he was. Once upon a time I thought he'd looked like a chicken. Now I thought of Elmer Gantry with less scruples.

"Milo," I exalted, startling him from his seat.

"I'm sorry," he said, looking like a kid caught with his hand in the cookie jar.

"For what?" I shrugged. I was happy to see him. This was turning into a great day.

"For going on the computer. I didn't know what to do or how long you'd be and hanging out in the front of the store just didn't feel right." He pushed away from the keyboard as if anxious to run. I got a better look at him and noticed he'd cut his hair and dyed it to remove any of the other colors that had been there on our last meeting. He'd shaved too and taken a bath. Out of his leather jacket and Levi's he looked presentable.

"You're taking me up on my offer?" This probably didn't need to be said, but I needed an opening if he was to come to work for me.

"Do you still want me?" He stood nervously, shifting from foot to foot and stuffing his hands in his pockets then immediately pulling them out again.

"Sure I do," I said and he relaxed, letting the air slip out of himself in a heavy breath. I hadn't even noticed he'd been holding it, "But two things first."

He drew in a breath again.

"First off, you look great, all cleaned up and all. But we don't wear suits to work here. Slacks and a collared shirt are the rule."

"Slacks and shirt, no suit," Milo repeated. "And…?"

"And, tonight we don't work. We're going to a signing. Can you ride with me into Los Angeles?"

"Yeah," he said brightening. "Who's signing?"

"Jay Landsbury," I explained heading back to the front of the store. "Just give me a few minutes will you." I had to make some pillow talk notes in my little blue book about a certain female detective and then place a phone call.

I dialed the PSPD and asked for the chief. His secretary put me on hold and I sweated the thirty seconds it took for him to pick up. He spoke first.

"Xanthe," he said, "I need you to do something I know you won't like."

"What's that Chief." Keep a stiff upper lip. What could he ask?

"I need you to step down from the committee until this Author investigation comes to a close."

Sounds of silence filled the chasm of my thoughts.

"Are you asking me or telling me?" He couldn't force me off it without a fight, if that's what I wanted to do. I was asking more to garner time to think than being sure I wanted to challenge him.

"Right now I'm asking you," He paused for dramatic effect. "But if you want I could go in front of the committee myself and make this a formal request. The committee could even vote on it if you like. Although you're a popular guy, I'm not sure which way this'll go. You want to see?"

"Not really," I caved in. "Is this permanent? I thought I was cleared?"

"You're still a person of interest."

In more ways than you know. "And that's enough?"

"Just till this blows over. Right now you're still too close to this case. Some people doing the investigating still think you're even connected to it."

"And you?" I asked.

"Jury's still out. I like you but I still think you care too much about what you got to risk it all."

What'd he mean by that? Sometimes his answers weren't really answers at all. That must be how he rose to become Chief.

"So, after this all clears over I can come back?" Better to press him now on this point.

"This case moves far enough away from Palm Springs again and I'll make it clear to the board I want you back myself."

Who could ask for more? I reluctantly agreed to my suspension pending the investigation, stupidly adding the words, Thanks for calling," out of respect for his position.

I didn't have time to contemplate all the implications of what I knew, guessed and needed to do in regards to the case. There was store business to attend to and I had a new employee waiting to be orientated and we had a long drive ahead of us. When one door closes…

On the way into LA Milo and I got to know each other in greater detail. Milo told me of his situation back in Baltimore and why he'd come out West. When he spoke of his mom his voice would crack and his lip would quiver. He spoke of love and a desire to get her out of the inner harbor as if it were a piece of purgatory and he her guardian angel. She deserved better. A concept I understood. Any person with strong feelings for another would want a better life for the ones they loved.

It was a lot to find out in one sitting. Long ago I'd determined if someone had too much to divulge there was probably more to the story than I was hearing. Yet, something about this lanky kid rang true. I listened and responded with the appropriate Uh-huh when it was fitting. When he paused, I sat silent to let him catch his breath and then nudged him further with a question or gentle reminder of where he left off. Before he was done I was complimenting him on the attributes I respected; his ability to learn a trade like computers, his courage to leave, his resolve to make his own life better and his ability to stand up for himself.

"Stand up for myself? What do you mean? I ran out on everyone back home."

"You stood up to that jock at Starbucks last week," I corrected.

"I lost," Milo said dejected, then slyly "on purpose."

"Yeah right," I chuckled.

"You doubt me?"

"Yeah-huh."

"Before I forget," he said, "Pay me my other $100 and then I'll tell you a secret."

"Oh cripes, I forgot. "I dug into my pocket through the seatbelt while trying not to accidentally change lanes. I came up with my money clip and peeled off five twenties. "So, what's the secret?"

"I really could have kicked that jocks ass, I mean butt if I wanted. I know karate. But if I had then the whole scene would've been much more involved, maybe even the police would've been called and you and I would've had a much harder time making our first meet."

"So you threw the fight to get rid of all the preps and your friends?" My admiration grew. The phrase dumb like a fox came to mind.

"It seemed like the best way," he tucked the money into his shirt pocket and patted it flat. I snuck a glance at him out of the corner of my eye. He was looking at the mountaintops as if contemplating climbing them in a few quick strides. Turning back to me he said, "I cracked AOL too and found one more thing about the bidders you may find interesting."

"And going and going and going..." This kid seemed to get better and better.

"One of the highest bidders was the author."

"What author?"

"Stephen Knightly."

I didn't know what to make of that. Why would Stephen Knightly bid on his own book? The biography I'd ordered, The Stephen Knightly Story by Green, had come in two days ago. I would have to make some time to read it. Perhaps the answer would be in there.

We went on to the Jay Landsbury signing. It was held at the nicest privately owned bookstore in Southern California: Vroman's of Pasadena. I liked Vroman's a lot. In the world of booksellers it was a hard row to hoe when competing with the majors of Barnes and Noble, Brentano's and Crown Books. Yet, in spite of the pitfalls of the major players, they're buying power with the publishers and subsequent discounting, Vroman's had succeeded in a significant city market. The store was a showpiece of high ceilings and shelves. They pulled in the best authors on tour. Anne Rice, T. Jefferson Parker, Joseph Wambaugh, Terry Brooks; they all paid homage to Vroman's. It was a book lover's book store and I was one of their fans.

We arrived early enough to buy a few extra hardbacks and get a good place in line. With Milo along with me there was even a good chance we'd only have to go through the line once. We had 12 books in all. Not my largest haul, but once these puppies were signed they'd be worth substantially more and well worth the two hour trek to Pasadena.

The line was brimming with anticipation from an eclectic array of Landsbury worshippers ranging from high school students with baggy clothes and nerdy expressions to senior citizens needing to find an iron. There were even multi-generational families of aficionados whereby mothers had brought their kids who didn't even realize the import of the personage they were about to meet. I had first read Landsbury in Junior High school, adoring his short stories from 'S is for Spaceship' and 'The November Land' before moving onto his longer works like 'Something Cruel This Way Cometh.' He was a master. And more than that, by viewing the crowd around me, their enthusiasm to see him sometimes for the third and fourth time made me feel Landsbury was a man who at a ripe old age in his life was reaping the rewards of working hard and long at a single career. He fully deserved the homage he was about to receive at this presentation of prose.

The line began to move. The event had begun. The author had arrived. Anticipation swelled. People fidgeted with their books opening them to their favorite pages for a signature and I was no different. I showed Milo the Sweet Spot for signatures and he quickly prepared the books in his hands. As we got within view of the signing area, we saw Landsbury was dashing his pen across as many copies of whatever the people had brought. No limit. Landsbury was quick, polite and gracious. He loved his fans and they loved him.

Milo and I stepped up to the desk where the novelist was holding court and slid our books in front of him. He was a man whose age could no longer be denied. Well past the age of retirement for most jobs, a writer's life was one whereby a man could remain active at his craft for decades beyond most others and Jay was taking full advantage. His hair was long gray strands hanging loose from his scalp in clutches. His skin was pale and botched with spots. Hard of hearing as he was, I found I had to nearly shout at him even as he turned his good ear towards me to increase reception.

"Nice to meet you sir," I barked. "I was wondering..."

The Author Murders

"Eh," he returned.

"I was wondering if you'd come out to Palm Springs and do a book signing for me?" I had leaned over the table considerably to aim my voice at his ear.

"What kind of event would you be doing?" he asked.

"A book signing," I declared. "At my book store in the downtown area there. But let's do a Thursday night at Villagefest, the streetfair, and we'll have a great showing."

"I have a house in Palm Springs," he said.

He was getting it. "I know."

"Fax an invitation to this number," he said and he wrote a phone number under his signature in one of the books I'd laid before him. "And don't lose that book." Then he waved for the people behind me to step forward and Milo and I were ushered off.

We drove back to the desert like Cortez returning the spoils of the New World to Spain. Twelve books had increased in value over 5 times their present worth. They'd make a great display and I'd print out a fresh place card to emphasize the fact they were now autographed. Letting our triumph go to my head, I divulged some information to Milo I hadn't expected to share.

"I wish I knew how to fight better," I confessed.

"Why's that?" Milo wondered aloud.

"There's this guy I know who deserves a six-pack of whoop ass opened up on him," I confessed, "and I'd like to have a can opener with me the next time we meet."

I told Milo about Donlagic and how he surprised me in the bathroom.

"Wow," Milo agreed. "That's harsh. Sure I could show you. But, I gotta warn you. The only way to learn to kick ass is to get yours kicked a few times. I hope you don't have anywhere important to go in the near future because I might just be messing up that pretty face of yours. Well, I guess it's not that big a loss."

"Thanks."

26
The Alibi

THE NEXT MORNING was a Monday, I opened the store as I had a thousand other times. When I got to checking the phone for messages I found I had one.

It went, "Xanthe, this is detective Daily. I need to talk to you right away. There's been another incident. Call me at the City of Commerce Police department. Here's my number..."

Great, I thought and dialed the phone. On the second ring it was picked up.

"Daily."

"Detective Daily. This is Xanthe in Palm Springs. You called."

"Yes. Where were you last night?" She was curt and to the point. No time for foolishness. I could hear a typewriter in the background.

"Why, what's happened?"

"Just answer the question Xanthe." She raised her voice to a command level.

It worked. I answered, "I went to the Jay Landsbury book signing up in Pasadena. Why?"

"What about afterwards?" The typing stopped.

"I came straight home."

"Can anyone verify your story?"

"Yes. I had an employee with me. A new kid named Milo. He was with me all the way there and back. Then I worked the store till closing, pricing the books I got signed. A few customers came in. One or two regulars. Not that I'd know how to get hold of them. But, they can't be impossible to track down for a detective like you. I closed up around nine and then went home and watched an episode of ER and Friends and called it a night. Are you going to tell me what happened or come and arrest me? Because if it's the latter I want to call my attorney right now."

She breathed heavily into the phone while thinking. Some other time I might have enjoyed the husky sounds. Finally she spoke. "Alright, I believe you. I knew it couldn't be you, but I had to ask. There've been a couple of incidents and I had to check your whereabouts. Before we go further I have to warn you there may be other departments at this very moment looking for you and you better keep my number on hand just in case you need me to stand up for you. If you get arrested call your attorney first and me second. Do not call this character Milo because if your phone is traced it'll look suspicious even if you only talk about the weather."

I was stunned. My head was racing with a dozen thoughts. Most paramount was what seemed inevitable. She said it before I could ask.

"Jay Landsbury is dead."

"No way."

"Can you explain how your fingerprints got on a broken bottle in front of his house?"

'No way' couldn't even leave my lips. My mouth went dry. My head spun. I fell forward onto the check stand and had to hold myself up with two elbows and my face cradled in the palms of my hands. I shifted one hand to my forehead before I pushed myself back up to a standing position.

"No, wait, Yes. Leonard must have gotten it from one of my book dealer dinners and saved it up at Pete's. He had a beer bottle wrapped in a plastic baggie. I thought it looked too new to be a collectible, but at the time I didn't pay it any attention. There's a trunk hidden under all his junk up there. If he hasn't cleaned it out there'll be other things in it too." This was absurd. How far would Leonard play this charade? When I thought it was just a case of mistaken identity I was upset yet understanding. But now, he was making a hard effort to portray me as the killer. The guy was relentless in his setting me up.

"Wait a sec. Let me check my notes." I could hear drawers opening and then the flipping of pages. "Nope. No bottle in a doggie bag. No bottle at all in the chest. Maybe I should take a second look at it. Do you remember any other items in the chest that could be important?" Good, she'd already been there and could at least verify he kept a stash of similar things.

"A deck of cards, some wine glasses, silverware. Now that you mention it - none of that stuff had any apparent value to it."

"Let's not get ahead of ourselves. I'll need you to take a look at an inventory list and see if you can spot any other irregularities." Daily was taking control but my mind was racing ahead.

"Have you put out an APB on Leonard?" I asked

"Don't worry." I was already getting crossed wires from her; typical cop or consoling lover? She had to really know I wasn't involved or she wouldn't have gotten with me, I'm sure. "We missed him at your friend's house yesterday. But we'll get him." She was confident, efficient, and capable.

"Missed him how?" I said returning to the subject. I slipped a finger into my mouth and caught the edge of a nail in my teeth.

"A former Palm Springs Police Officer was assaulted last night at Mr. Blake's house."

"Detective Donlagic?" I wasn't sure whether to be hopeful or not.

Her confidence slipped. "How'd you know?"

Since I'd lost my wind with the Chief, I spilled my beans and told her of my history with Donlagic, about how he was collecting on debts for the casino, about how he'd hired me to find the Stephen Knightly book and how he'd socked me in my gut in the men's room at the Police department meeting. I finished it off with, "It couldn't have happened to a nicer guy."

"He's in the hospital with broken ribs and a fractured arm." Daily stopped talking and I didn't jump in. She broke the silence first. "You sure you're not involved with this? You have enough motives to convince a jury of Catholics their priests are pedophiles. You're at or near every scene of the crime and you're a personal friend of the number one suspect. You could be a co-conspirator. If I didn't know better I'd say you should be locked up."

"You already did that remember?" She had gotten my dander and I wasn't pleased. "Unless you've forgotten we've been down this road already?"

"Yeah, well the road less traveled sometimes has to be repaved more than once."

"Are you done?"

"I'm done."

27
Tracey

I COULDN'T SIT STILL DESPITE DAILY'S WARNINGS. I called Milo first and asked him if he could watch eBay for Landsbury books listed by someone reasonably close to or in the desert. It would be a large cache of books and there'd be at least one ringer in the bunch, a real homerun copy.

Then I called Justin Blake to check on the status of Leonard's room and the book.

"Justin, this is Xanthe. Tell me what's happened?"

"It's my house. The police kicked me out. Apparently it's a crime scene and they don't want me in it until it's been thoroughly picked over."

What? How?" I was nonplussed.

"A Detective Craft from Palm Springs showed up today with a county Sheriff. They had a warrant to secure the premises and they escorted me off my property! They came in and watched me while I packed a bag to make sure I didn't take anything important. I can't do business like this! I'm losing money every minute that I can't access my listings online!" He was despondent and angry. Like most of us who do businesses online, once you get disconnected from the net you feel helpless. And to think only five years ago the fax machine was considered modern. In another five years we'll probably all need cell phones glued to our heads.

"Justin, Justin," I interrupted. "Here's what you do. Are you at Brad's now?" No assumptive leap.

"Yeah," I'm there now." His bearings were lost, but I could ground him.

"And you know your password for Abebooks right?"

"Yeah?" he was coming closer to home.

"Go onto the dealer link and log on to your account. You can access your database and download a copy for adjusting inventory. You can access your emails from anywhere by just going to AOL.com. You still use AOL right?" Internet for beginners.

"Yeah, but I don't know what you're talking about with the database. I'll screw that up for sure." Anxiety rising.

Funny how some of us online really have no clue how all the nuts and bolts fit together. His situation wasn't entirely my fault either. It was his ex-boyfriend who'd committed the crimes. Still, we were friends and I didn't want to make his situation worse that it had to be.

"I'll help you out Justin. But I can't do it myself. I've got my own problems with Leonard I'm trying to clear up? I can send a guy to show you how to access what you need. It'll cost you a couple hundred bucks but at least you'll be operational again. His name's Shane," and I gave him the number.

"Thanks Xanthe," and he started to hang up.

"Wait!" I shouted.

"What?"

"I need help too. I need something on Leonard to help clear my name. Your problems are small compared to mine. The police think I'm connected with Leonard in the killings. Have you got anything on him that I could use?" Now it was my turn to be desperate.

"Other than his absences lately I don't have much. He's been disappearing from me more and more the past few months. I guess that's why Brad and I have got back together. He's a got an ex-wife that might know more. He cried about her when we first got together."

It was something.

I got the address and phone number of Leonard's ex, Tracey Beschloss. She lived up at Newport Beach, in an area called the Peninsula. I knew it well. It was my dream neighborhood. One that I briefly got to live in when I was selling cars in the 1980's. Well, not exactly in,

I lived on 48th street at River Avenue, across the street from the Jack in the Box and Tracey resided on Miramar Drive down at the tip, only a stone's throw away from one of the hardest surf spots in California, called the Wedge.

The Peninsula was filled with million dollar homes even if they only looked like a weather beaten cottage. Most of the domiciles in the vicinity were three story square blocks that filled all but a thin sidewalk between the buildings by owners who had learned the best use of land was to maximize square footage and face the beach with huge plate glass windows. In between these mastodon dwellings was the occasional leftover of a forgotten era, when a home was merely an affordable plank beach house of meager standings. These holdovers from the time when Korean War veterans were enticed to purchase housing in the middle of a man made sandbar surrounded by oil derricks were out of place in modern times. Often as a distant reminder of way back when that foolishly encouraged tourists to think there was still a chance an average Joe could own a piece of heaven.

As I cruised down the stretch of road onto the Peninsula past the Lucky's supermarket, the Fun Zone and into Tracey's environs, I remembered my misspent youth; the days of riding my motorcycle from pub to pub along the sandy parking lots facing the beach, drinking until well past midnight and if I couldn't drag anyone home with me catching a late night presentation of the Rocky Horror Picture Show at the Harbor Theatre. Whew, what a time.

I drove near the end of Miramar before I found the right address. There was an available spot in front of the house, a rare occurrence in this neighborhood where parking spots are reminiscent of snipe hunting. I knew Tracey would be home because I'd asked her number from the Verizon operator and then called first. She'd agreed to see me on the premise of me being an old friend of Leonard's and a book dealer wanting to discuss a few items in his collection. She'd wanted to talk on the phone but I put her off saying I was busy at the moment but would be in her vicinity that afternoon and would rather discuss this more in private. She agreed and set a time. I felt I'd get more mileage out of her responses if I could look her in the eye when asking questions.

I parked my Jeep and took measure of the house. It was a post-war clapboard with a shingled roof and all the gingerbread. She kept the paint up and it was one of those quaint little bungalows that could easily have originated on either coast of America. A soft yellow with white trim, a painted red porch and walkway leading up to it with a grass lawn kept neat but long; humble surroundings in an otherwise elegant setting.

I walked up to the front door and rapped twice on the wood framed screen. The real front door was open behind the screen exposing a plush living room with a gray and white Berber carpet underneath flowered green paisley couches and antique looking lamps. If there was a television it was hidden in the large stained wood armoire against the long wall stretching towards the back of the house from where I could smell something baking. I knocked again as a woman my own age appeared from what must have been the kitchen.

She was wiping her hands on the apron she wore, a neat tan with red fringes covering her purple and yellow speckled dress. Did she always dress for cooking? Her hair was long and blonde. She wasn't the tiniest girl in the world. Other words come to mind; voluptuous, curvy, Loni Anderson or Delta Burke at her best.

I called from the porch, "Tracey, Tracey Beschloss?"

"Yes," she said, letting her apron drop from her now clean hands.

"I'm Xanthe Anthony. I called you earlier."

She was now at the door and scanned me with her eyes as if she could confirm I was who I said I was.

"Come in," she said feeling satisfied, swinging her door open and causing me to step backwards before I entered. "You're right on time. I was just baking some brownies to eat while we talked. Do you prefer coffee or tea?"

I didn't normally have either in the afternoon but I found myself saying, "Tea please." She pointed to the small sofa and I gently rested as she returned back to the kitchen, A few moments later she reappeared with a woven bamboo tray laden with the wares she'd promised. I took my own plate and cup. She poured the tea. As I bit into the brownies and enjoyed their warm delicate flavor, I looked around the room. Stained wood trim etched every angle, floor board and doorway. It also separated the painted lower walls from the wainscoting papered upper. The papering was of worldly diagrams, maps of ancient ages, and mariner's symbols. There were bookshelves also. Many more than necessary and they had few books on them. The knick knacks seemed spread thin to cover so much space.

"This is a nice place you have Miss Beschloss."

"Please call me Tracey and Thank you. It was left to me by my parents."

"Wow, Lucky you," I said. Instinctively she flinched and I realized my mistake. "And unlucky too, I mean." Trying to recover, I continued, "I don't see many books though. The way you wanted to talk on the phone when I said I was a dealer, I thought there'd be a lot more. Do you have a library here too?"

"No," she sipped her tea and set her cup down before saying more. "I thought you'd be helping me with that. Regrettably, I can tell by your statement you do not know of my loss."

"I'm sorry," I said. "I'm a friend of Leonard's and he's in some trouble. I thought you might be able to help me."

"And you, I," she said. "I thought you were coming to tell me of the whereabouts of my missing books."

"Missing books?" She'd peaked my interest.

"My husband, or should I say soon to be former husband, is always in some sort of trouble. It's the reason we're no longer together. What's he done now?" She leaned back on the couch in preparation for my telling as if she'd been through this discussion many times in the past and there was no need to hurry.

"He's killing people as far as I can tell," I said. I thought this would jerk her back upright but she continued to sip her tea.

"And...?" she queried nonplussed as if there was more to the story.

"Miss Beschloss, I mean Tracey. He's killing authors. He's murdering them and then selling their books online to maximize his profits." I was surprised by her lack of concern.

"It was only a matter of time," she set her cup down on the coffee table and wrapped her hands around one knee to balance her as she rocked. "He always was a celebrophile; wanting autographs, signed photos, and such. I introduced him to books as collectibles and now he's using what I taught him to create a market capable of disposing his debts. He does have debts doesn't he? He always does."

"Yes, he has debts; massive ones to be exact. They go far beyond what he owes you. But what's that mean - celebrophile?"

"Somebody who's almost a stalker. Someone who's so intent on meeting celebrities, he thinks by circling their world he becomes one himself. He showed his first signs of being one when we used to play games at being different celebrities. It started off innocent enough, Rhett Butler and Scarlett O'Hara, Bogart and Hepburn, but when he wanted to pretend to be more recent ones, Arnold Schwarzennegger and Maria Shriver or Alec Baldwin and Kim Basinger, I began to wonder."

"What kind of games are you referring to?" I asked.

She blushed and looked into her tea, "Oh, the kinds that husbands and wives play to make their evenings more exciting. Our counselor had a more derogatory term for it." Reducing her voice to whisper she said, "She called him a Star Fucker."

"Star F..," I stopped myself from repeating it in her presence. Even though she'd said it first I didn't want to be vulgar. When she said it was surprising. If I repeated it would be like leaving a turd in a swimming pool.

Raising her whisper only slightly, like a teacher prompting a student she remarked, "Someone who wants to have sex with celebrities, or fantasize about having sex with them."

Again, I noticed Tracey's hair, sculpted to perfection. It was blonde with darker streaks underneath as if the sun had warmed its overlays. If I'd met her under different circumstances I'd most likely have started with a compliment on her hair. She sat with the confidence of someone who knew they were good looking and couldn't change a thing. Even if she'd worn a trash bag there'd be no concealing her sexuality. She quit her rocking and tucked her legs up underneath herself on the couch, causing her bare calves to be exposed.

"He seems to have changed fantasies. Now he's killing them," I continued.

"I think he's just surviving with the knowledge he has," she said reaching into the depths of their past. "When we first met he was an autograph hound with the dream of becoming a script writer. He'd go get their signature on a photo and then try and plug his latest screenplay. They'd placate him at first but if they saw him a second time they'd get ruder."

"Sure, he was bothering them. They must get that a lot; people pushing their ideas on them." I finished my brownies and tea. When I set my cup down it clanked noisily.

"Would you like some more?" she offered.

"No," I said, and then corrected myself as she stared directly into my eyes. I could swim in those eyes. "I mean, Yes."

She poured me the rest of the tea, grasped the tray and went back into the kitchen. The vacuum left by her walk away caused a cold sensation I couldn't place. She'd made me feel warmer in her presence than I'd anticipated. When she returned, so did the heat. Watching how she filled her blouse and how it moved with her step made me blush.

I grabbed two brownies and transferred them to my plate, not allowing my head to rise until my emotions were under control. I changed the subject again.

"You mentioned some books you were missing?"

"After Leonard and I broke up he came back and broke into the house. At one time, I had a really fantastic collection of Easton Press Science Fiction. Many of them were the rare Signed Firsts. Leonard helped himself to them while I was off to the market. When I returned, he'd left me a note claiming they were half his. Yet, he took them all." She'd tensed up as she spoke. "Plus I'd had many early copies of the giants of Sci-Fi; Isaac Asimov, L. Ron Hubbard, Jack Chalker, Philip K. Dick. They were pristine copies and irreplaceable. That's why my shelves are still so bare."

I thought of Leonard's room back at Justin's. There'd been lots of modern firsts, a few of the Easton Press, but nothing resembling the collected works she'd described.

"There were a few Easton Press books in his room. But they wouldn't fill these shelves. I did see one book in his room that I wanted to ask you about," I mentioned with a nod of my head. "A Stephen Knightly book called Stephen's Dump Truck."

"You saw it?" she whispered, her throat gone dry. "And you didn't take it right then?"

I gulped my tea, "I couldn't. It was out of reach within a police protected crime scene. But God, that book practically called to me from the shelf. It was like seeing the fabled tomb of Tutankhamen opened for the first time, like seeing the Sun stone of the Aztecs unearthed."

"It was my gem. My most coveted piece. I'd had it for years and when he took it, even I almost lowered myself to hire a private detective or a hit man to recover it." She'd moved to the edge of the sofa closest to me and lowered her voice to share a confidence. Her eyes were even wider than when I first peered into them, their greenness engulfing my world.

"How did you come by it?" I asked. "If you don't mind telling, of course." Sometimes in the book world a collector does not divulge his provenance because of the fear of another person stealing their secret, like a path to a lost treasure.

Before I tell you that, I'll need to know a little more about you Xanthe."

"What would you like to know?"

She asked me all sorts of things and I didn't mind telling. It gave us a chance to just get to know each other. I told her about the store and my great employees. I told her about the Police Advisory Committee and my desires for it to become a full fledged Police Commission. I down played the parts of my life that paralleled Leonard's. I was aware of the similarities and wanted to widen the gap between ourselves. I had dual motives. I didn't want Tracey considering me a threat, like Leonard was, and furthermore I wanted her to think of me as a potential mate.

We shared stories of our pasts, mine as a car salesman who'd gotten his tail tucked between his legs and returned home to enter the book world with a few comic books and she as a college student who chose to go as far from home as she could in pursuit of finding herself.

That was how she'd happened upon the Stephen Knightly writings, as she worked as a volunteer in the University of Maine's library. Stephen Knightly was a former college professor turned famous author and his earlier writings as a student on the school newspaper were archived in the basement of the library. It was only too easy to convey them to the photocopy machine and run off a complete set of his college work. Years later she'd paid a book binder to create the book I'd seen on the shelf at Justin's house.

"Do you think it's still there?" she asked.

"It's possible," I said. "Although, he did return to the scene of the crime and take some items."

28
On the Road

THE BOOK LAY ON THE PASSENGER SEAT OF THE CAR as it sped across the mountainous desert of the southern tip of Nevada. Leonard hadn't slept since he'd left Palm Springs the day before.

After assaulting Donlagic, Leonard had grabbed anything of importance to make a quick departure, including Donlagic's Chrysler. He'd been prepared to leave anyways. He'd ridden the bus home earlier in the day, thinking it was time to steal a car. His own would be too easy to trace. A feeling had crept over him in the days before concluding his time here was running short. His efforts to frame someone had come up short and running seemed the most sensible option.

He'd headed for his San Bernardino office, but by the time he was within a block of it, the police were already stationed in an unmarked car. He was lucky and spotted an officer in civilian clothes climbing into the Chevy Caprice with sandwiches and drinks down the block from his rented place of pseudo work. Realizing that the police were already hot on his movement, he turned away from the building and headed east.

There was still one more job to be done with the biggest payoff to date. After that he could go anywhere he wanted. He passed a sign reading Welcome to Arizona and zoomed out of Nevada. Interstate 15 barely caught the Northwest corner of Arizona and less than an hour later he was greeted by the Utah Welcomes You sign. He was careful to not speed too fast and alert attention to himself, better to fly just under the radar and not catch the eye of a highway patrolman. A license plates check or a warrant search could spell the end of his getaway.

The Desert Mountains transformed into canyons of colorful reds and browns. This was a unique place on Earth: Virgin Canyon. An oasis in the middle of nowhere made of rock formations, waterfalls and geological wonders. Years ago, as a much younger man, he'd traversed this countryside several times making trips back and forth across the continent. This time his trip was one way.

In Utah, Leonard felt he could relax a little. He was three states away. Computers weren't linked effectively enough to create immediate concern. A man could still get lost in the wilds of America.

He had to change cars though. Spotting a dirt road he pulled off and drove more than a mile until finding a second and even less used path to hide the car on. He loaded the few items he really cared about into the backpack he'd brought for just such an occasion and started walking back to the main road.

As he walked, he remembered a story he'd read somewhere, sometime in his life and never forgotten.

It went like this: At the beginning of the last century, there was a man named Mr. Johnson who had a son. Mr. Johnson was a man of meager means and did his best to bring his son up well. One day his son disappointed him when he and a friend stole their father's car, robbed a local liquor store and escaped west to California before finally getting caught and extradited back to Texas, where dad and the authorities were waiting. The sons name was Lyndon, and years later when he was President of the United States, Lyndon Baines Johnson remarked how fortunate he was to be raised in an era before computers. Because, had he been a young man born much later in history then his past indiscretions would have been duly logged and filed into a system that never forgets and he would never have been allowed to become the man of greatness he was destined to be later in life.

Leonard recalled this story with the hope his life had not ended yet. There was still a chance for him to redeem himself and rise to greatness.

He patted his pants pocket and the two pockets on the backpack to assure himself he would not run short of resources. Then he pulled a .38 caliber pistol out of his upper inside jacket pocket, flipped out the chamber, saw it was fully loaded and placed it back inside his jacket. He shifted the backpack on his hips and set his sights back up the dirt road towards the highway.

29
Hells Book Angels

IT WAS LATE IN THE AFTERNOON by the time I got back to the store. As usual Jill was running the front desk. She jerked a thumb over her shoulder towards the back and said, "Milo's here."

"Really?" My frustration evaporated and I did an I Love Lucy hop, skip and a jump towards the rear of the stacks as my spirits lifted. This wasn't his normal day to work. He must have found out something worth trekking down to the store.

I cracked the door to the back room open just enough to see him sitting at the terminal. His most comfortable spot. Typing away at the keyboard, pounding at the keys was more like it, he was an inferno of work. He barely glanced at his hands. Mostly he kept his head up, nose just inches from the monitor, scanning at bits of information like a master quilter inspecting his work. It was a pleasure to watch him taking pride in his craft. In such a short time he'd already shown great promise of lifting himself up from the dregs I'd found him in.

"Heh-hem," I cleared my throat.

He didn't notice.

"A-heh-heh-hem," I coughed a second time.

He stirred in his seat but didn't turn my way, "Xanthe, that you?" He was still pounding keys, doing a thing I'd only heard about, called crunching. Crunching is what the kids call typing into the computer so fast they don't even seem to be paying attention to what they're doing. But they are.

"Yeah it's me. What's up?" I sauntered up next to him to see what he was working on. He had the book database open in a spreadsheet and was making changes, massive changes. "What are you doing?"

"I'm doing mark-downs. Jill told me there was a bunch of old books that had been in the database for a long time and she wished there was a way to easily find them and lower their prices without having to touch each one. So, I shot the inventory into Excel, sorted it by date and then changed the price of the books in bulk giving the biggest reductions to the oldest stock. I hope you don't mind." He said all this as if it'd be obvious to me, as if I'd already asked for this at some time in the past.

Truth was, I'd mentioned to Jill often how I'd like to do price changes but the process of going through each book had always been too cumbersome. The job was way too huge to tackle and therefore never happened. Milo had single-handedly performed the most desired task I ever wanted and never could achieve on my own. I liked this kid more each time I met him.

"You mean you couldn't just defrag and maximize the system?" I said in a half joke. It was another thing I'd been meaning to do and mentioned to Jill.

"Done."

"How about setting up the hard drives for sharing through a network?"

"I did that first, it made the clean wipes of the C drives easier to handle because I could move the data storage from computer to computer without having to format disks and waste time downloading info."

"Well, excuuuuse me. It seems the only thing you haven't done is find out who's selling the Landsbury books." I folded my arms and waited.

"It's someone in Desert Hot Springs on Peach Street, near the corner of Poplar." He paused long enough to crack me a smile.

"You son of a..," I chuckled. "I love you."

"Hey, that's sexual harassment." A paper started to squark out of the printer. "There's the exact address," he said.

I reached for it, read it and folded it into my shirt pocket, then paused to reflect on my day so far. No amount of frustration or anger should guide my actions on the next move. This was critical mass as far as solving both the murders and finding the Stephen's Dump Truck book. I had to be careful and there was the possibility on the other side of whatever door I knocked danger could be waiting.

"You want to come with?" I asked.

"Sure," Milo said. "You think there might be trouble?"

"It's a distinct possibility."

"Righteous," He said. "What's our cover?"

"Cover?" I hadn't thought of that.

"We need to have a reason for going over. What were you going to do, just walk up and ask them if they've got this rare book? Killed anybody lately?" He tapped his chin with his fingers three times, then said, "Don't you have a religious section here?"

I kept a sports coat in the back of the store and we stopped at Milo's place and he put back on the Elmer Gantry suit. Most of his chicken boy qualities had washed away with the sprucing up he'd gone through to work at the bookstore. Now, he reminded me more of an old Looney Tunes cartoon, where the rooster dressed up as a door to door salesman.

Desert Hot Springs lies across the railroad tracks from Palm Springs. There's a big windy section of desert and then the leftovers from polite society had set up a town where they could live against the distant hills of the Little San Bernardino mountains. It was rumored a big portion of DHS's population were criminals forced to live more than 100 miles from Los Angeles under court order when released from prison. I don't know for sure whether that's true or not, but looking at the average citizen walking around the sloping business district I could believe it. We exited the main drag by turning left past a pawn shop and were cruising down Peach Street looking for the address Milo had gleaned from the net. It was at the very end of the pot holed pavement, just before the street changed into a tire tracked dirt road.

The Author Murders

The house at the end was a flea-pit mansion. The 1960's stucco had fallen off decades ago to be replaced with cardboard beer signs or left barren, exposing the insulation behind. The roof had lost enough tiles that if it were the space shuttle it'd be permanently grounded or refused reentry. Windows were either cracked or covered in aluminum foil or both. The sure sign of poor white trash trying to hide from the sun. The grass was long dead, leaving behind a sparse yellow patchy weed lawn interspersed with dog crap landmines surrounded by a short chain link fence so overgrown with cactus it resembled a Mexican farm boundary. We stopped two houses short of our destination and got out of the car, grabbed the few books we'd brought, straightened our ties and pushed open the rusted gate to gain entry to the yard and porch.

The doorbell didn't work so we knocked on the thick wooden door that seemed in remarkably solid condition considering the property. The sounds of Def Leppard emanated from within, a song I remembered from my high school years called Pyromania, and after waiting a few minutes we increased our knocking to a pounding.

The music dimmed and moments later a small 4x4 inch window opened showing me the eyeball quarter of a ladies head through the crosshairs of iron barring.

"Yeah," she said. A warm greeting if I'd ever heard one.

"Hello," I began, "I'm Peter Decker from Palm Springs Kingdom Hall and my friend and I were servicing door to door. Have you ever considered the future of our world?"

I could see strands of black hair sparsed with gray. Her face was craggy and pointed as if life hadn't been generous to her. Her eyes, or should I say eye, was black with a thin brow. "You ain't been on our street before," she accused.

"No ma'm," I continued. "This neighborhood is new to me. Although Jehovah is welcome in all places."

Milo chimed in opening a bible, "Perhaps a verse is more to your liking." He flipped through the bible in his hands until his eyes fell upon a passage. "In Proverbs 15 verse 5 it is read 'A fool despiseth his father's instruction; but he that regardeth reproof is prudent.'"

I wanted to slap my hand to my forehead. Use of the word fool was not going to gain us any ground here. "Try again brother," I urged.

Milo flipped through more pages and then said, "Deuteronomy 4, verse 27, 'And the Lord shall scatter you among the nations, and you shall be left few in number among the heathen, wither the Lord shall lead you." He lifted his head with a feeble smile almost begging me not to make him read again.

"Don't you mean Jehovah?" The woman said shifting her eye to Milo.

"Huh?' he said.

"Jehovah," she repeated. "Don't you mean Jehovah instead of the Lord?"

"Of course." I tried to smooth it over. "Brother Winters is new to pioneering. He only recently joined our Hall."

"So what you want? I ain't got all day to chat up the porch." She'd grown impatient and I wasn't surprised. There was a shuffle and creak from behind her. She shifted her gaze, glanced over her shoulder so we couldn't see her face and then returned her eye to us through the peephole.

Our plan hadn't come close to hitting the target or even the broad side of a barn for that matter. I decided it was time to make a hasty retreat. "Would you like us to leave some literature with you? You look like a literate lady." I was rambling. "This copy of the Watchtower tells of the story of Abraham. His was a life filled with hardship but in the end he begat the promised people who now fill the Earth." I held the magazine in front of me as if I was extending a hive of bees.

"Don't you want anything for that?" The black eye said from behind her cross bar.

"No, no," I said. "Your willingness to read the truth is enough."

Milo was backing his way off the front steps. I was following in a like manner till he tapped me on the back with the palm of his hand. As I turned to see what he wanted, I spotted three thugs in biker clad coming around the corner of the house. I heard a gate swing open from the other side of the house and we were surrounded by a gang of men who didn't appear to care one bit about who's on the bestsellers list. The biggest one on each side stepped forward allowing his not so much smaller compatriots to flank. Milo put his back to mine and said, "I got these three you with me?"

I had only gotten out, "What are you talking...?" When I was grabbed up and swatted around like a mouse by a bull dog. Over the sound of my own skull being knocked around I could hear a more raucous chorus behind me. I blacked out seconds after I hit the ground as I was being kicked in the ribs.

* * *

Detective Daily had returned to Palm Springs to more thoroughly search Leonard's room and had stopped by Xanthe's store to see him when he and Milo had come out with the books and wearing a sport coat. Out of curiosity she ahd followed them only to become more intrigued when Milo had donned his Elmer gantry suit. Now, she found herself coasting her sedan up to the corner of a disgusting neighborhood, easing past the pawn shop and peeking down Poplar Street. At the far end was Xanthe's Wrangler, parked in front of a rusty short chain linked fence protecting a yard more practical as a waste disposal site than a habitat. No one was in the yard or at the front door, which was surprising. As she was scouting out the location, three scraggly men in ragged blue jeans vests and bearing tattoos came out. One jumped in the drivers' seat of my Jeep and the other two got behind it to push. They glanced down the street towards Daily. She leaned over to the glove box, pulled out a map and spread it across her dash.

"This doesn't look good," she said to no one in particular. She checked her bearing of where she was at. There was a payphone on the corner across the street in front of an Italian restaurant that may or may not have still been an operable business. She got out of her car, darted across the street and called 911.

An efficient female voice picked up the phone, "911 operator. Desert Hot Springs Police department. What's your emergency?"

"This is Detective Daily of the City of Industry, in the county of Los Angeles and I'm at the corner of Poplar and Palm in Desert Hot Springs. I need assistance. Can you transfer me to your desk Sergeant?"

"One moment please." Without hesitation the operator transferred the call, squeezing in a few words to her commanding officer, "Dick, we have a request from another department operating within our jurisdiction. You need to get this."

"Commander Dick Baird here. How may I be of service?"

Daily identified herself and gave the man a rundown of her situation. He was polite and to the point, not deviating from the necessary facts and understanding the situation entirely.

"Detective Daily, your friend is most likely in some serious trouble. My officers won't go to that house to answer a noise complaint without at least four men and permission to use deadly force. We'll get you a couple of squad cars out there pronto. Hold on and for Christ's sake, don't go in their alone. I'll roll my men now but it'll take them five minutes to get there. We'll do this silently. No Alarms. Once we're onsite we'll decide how to attack this situation. It won't be easy. If these guys are taking hostages there's something serious afoot. They're a nasty biker gang with ties to all sorts of criminal activity."

"Thanks Commander. Daily out."

The 911 officer turned to Commander Baird, "Dick, did that go like it sounded?"

"Yeah, round up the boys and send them on over to the Devils clubhouse. You know the one." Betsy operated the phone for the department. It was a small one, with no more than 8 officers on duty at any time. She was both secretary and 911 operator and she had a nose for when something big was gonna go down. This smelled ripe.

Commander Baird had grown up in the desert and was well aware of its lower parasitic residents. He'd grown up on the outskirts of the finer establishments and refused to become one of the leeches himself. He looked down at the four hash marks on his sleeves as he made up his mind about what to do for this officer in distress.

He picked up the phone and got a dead line. "Betsy, there's something wrong with my phone. Help me place a call to the Riverside County Sheriff's. I think we're going to need more back-up on this one."

The Author Murders

"They're on 2 Dick, beat you to it."

* * *

The fog lifted from my head leaving one hell of a headache in its absence. I tried to lift my hands to massage the pain but couldn't. They were restrained at the wrists, taped down to the spindly legs of a vinyl dining chair. I tried to open my eyes and quickly shut them. Two of the bikers were scrounging around for something. I got a flash of someone crumpled on the floor before me.

I peered through my lids just enough to skin some sight through my lashes. The bikers were outside the room and I could hear them shouting at each other.

"How can we be out of duct tape?"

"I had to use it to fix my gas tank."

"Your gas tank? You ever hear of liquid metal?"

"They use duct tape to fix stuff at NASA. That's good enough for me."

"Did you have to use so much though? What are we going to use to tie up the other guy?"

"I don't know. Keep looking."

I could see Milo on the floor in a crumpled heap. I whispered at him, "Psst. Milo. Milo. Can you hear me?"

He lifted his head and looked at me. One eye was already severely blackened and his cheeks were bruised. A fat lip whispered back, "Yeah. Don't worry. I've got a plan."

From the other room, "Hey, this'll work."

"Yeah."

Two bruisers in tattered Levi's vests came into the room. One of them, a scraggly man with an eye patch and a hat that made him look like he'd just left the Pirates of the Caribbean crew, held what looked like a phone cord. The other, a clean shaven man similar to the evil android from the Terminator sequel, grabbed Milo and tossed him into another cheap dining room chair. Milo's hands fell behind his back and they were quickly laced together by the pirate. Milo's head lolled

181

and he slumped in the chair. The Clean Terminator biker pulled him up by the shoulders as the pirate wound the cord around Milo's waist attaching him to the back of the chair. Then they bound his feet to the legs and let him slump again.

Seeing this, I tried my own legs and felt that one of them was free. That must have been the point they ran out of duct tape.

"Hey," the pirate said, "The book guy's awake."

"I'll grab the boss," declared the Terminator and he left the room.

'Great,' I thought. They know who I am. What had happened to my nice day job at the bookstore? Footsteps came into the room and I opened my eyes in time to see a hand come slapping across my face. The hand was attached to the woman I'd seen through the peephole. At full view she was even more hideous than when I'd got a peep through the door hatch. She was amazingly thin, as if she'd spent a previous lifetime doing Sally Struthers commercials in Africa. I now saw both her eyes were black, reflecting a non-committal attraction to the human race. She hit me again, "Wake up."

"I'm awake. I'm awake dammit," I barked before she could slap me a third time. No more hiding my eyes. I looked directly in hers. As far as bosses went, I'd thought these bikers would've needed someone bigger to answer to. A toilet flushed from a distant part of the house. Seconds later I got the role model I was seeking. A man large enough to curl a Harley in each arm came out. Age had seasoned him to a type of beef jerky skin laced with scars and tattoos. His hair was totally gone. Leaving a heavily tanned head polished to the color of lacquered wood. His face had the look of a righteous Republican. That is if you can call G. Gordon Liddy righteous, complete with the moustache.

The muscle bound G. Gordon stepped up to my chair, wiping his hands on a towel he tossed back on the floor in the hall when he'd done with it. I figured if that towel was as scared as I was it'd go hang itself back on the rack rather than face this monster.

With my one free leg I went up on my toes of that foot. My heart raced. He walked up to my chair and said to the others, "This here the one?"

They all nodded yes. The woman sneered at me and pointed her finger, "That's him alright Bazal."

He turned around and slapped her hard across the cheek, causing her to spin backwards and slam into the wall. "No names bitch." Momentarily, I felt a bit of chagrin at the thought of him giving her one for the Gipper. Then he returned his attention to me and I thought better.

He was a beast. He was huge. I reformed my impression of him into G. Gordon the Barbarian Biker from Hell. But it was no time for poetics. Bazal, she'd said his name was. Bazal. I remembered a book I'd perused once that had given me nightmares called the Necronomicom, "Bazal. Short for Beezelbub right?"

He leaned down on me until I could smell his stinky breath and look down his open leather vest at his enormous stomach rippling into huge pecks. "You say something wormy?"

His dominions laughed. A retinue of demons bearing homage to their overlord.

"Bazal. It's short for Beezelbub. A Philistine devil. Lord of the Flies. But he's not the boss. There's someone higher than you isn't there? Where's Asmodeus?" It was a reach but it was the only thought crossing my mind and I went with it.

I caught him off guard and his eyes lost their vigor. He paused and I knew I'd said something he hadn't expected. In that instant I had him. This overgrown gladiator was reduced to an errand boy. The gang behind him became a flock of gawkers. Silence swept the room. He sensed this too and stood straight. Swiftly he swung his foot up between my legs and caught the edge of my seat flipping me onto my back as the chair carried me with it. My head thunked the ground as it connected with the bare floor.

"You don't deserve the Dark Lord. He wouldn't waste the gas on you," he roared. "Let me introduce you to one of my little demons, Snakebite."

A new man entered the room from a doorway leading to what must have been the backyard. He was tall, lean and muscular with a face full of pockmarks and flowing brown hair filling his shoulders like a

183

mane. "We got his car in the garage. It looks like we're all clear."

My heart sank. They were thorough. I suddenly felt as though I was going to die in this dirty shit hole of a house. My blood would spill onto this threadbare carpet and then they'd roll me up in it and bury me out in the desert. Even though Jill knew the address Milo and I had come to investigate, by the time anyone arrived it'd be too late.

Snakebite reached to his belt and unsheathed his buck knife. With a flick of his wrist it extended to an obscene blade length fit for carving. It was thick enough to break bone and shiny enough to use as a mirror. Snakebite loved his weapons like a trophy and I was to be its prize.

"So, tell us bookworm," Snakebite said, "what brings you here? And don't give us any bullshit about Jehovah."

He stood before me twirling the knife around his hand like a magician spinning coins on his knuckles.

I tried to stall, "How do you know we're not Witnesses? This could be a bad case of mistaken identity."

"Wilma," Snakebite said.

The witch who answered the door stepped forward and recited, "Deuteronomy 4, verse 27 in the New World Translation reads, 'And Jehovah will certainly scatter you among the peoples, and You will indeed be let remain few in number among the nations to which Jehovah will drive you away.' You didn't even read it from the right bible. Plus Witnesses make you pay for literature. They'll accept almost any contribution, but they don't give it away for free."

Gulp. Time to leave the sinking ship. "Did I say we were Witnesses? I meant Mormons. What does it matter? You already know who I am anyways."

"Xanthe Anthony. Bookstore owner and former City Council candidate. What, you think just because we're a couple of lug heads we don't watch the news or read the papers? Or maybe you don't think we read at all? How about this punk?" He yanked up Milo's head, who still appeared dazed, "Does he read?"

Snakebite waved the knife in front of Milo's face. Spinning behind onto one knee he seized Milo's head in a full Nelson and pointed the tip at Milo's jaw.

"You're here about the books? Aren'tcha, what'd ya call him Bazal? Wormy? I preferred the Croat's nickname Xanthey."

The Croat? Donlagic had given us up to these goons? He was in deeper than we knew. I needed more and I needed to survive. When all else fails, go with the truth.

"Yeah, I'm here about the books. The Jay Landsbury books. I want them. I want them all and I'll pay. I know where you got them and I want to find Leonard too." I was breathing hard enough to bust a gut. I was in deeper than a nerd on rope climb day in gym class and I wanted to call in the coach to spank the football team for snapping me with a wet towel. Only there was no coach to call and a snap with a wet towel would be a welcome relief. Milo was about to go through serious reconstructive surgery and there was no amount of part-time work or mentoring capable of making up for the change in his life about to happen.

From outside the house a bullhorn sounded, "This is the police. Michael Deavers, Jesse Stone, Agatha Christianson. We know you're in there. Open now and we won't have to use force."

There was a unanimous expression of "Shit" from all the bikers, Bazal included.

A loud rap on the front door was followed by "Open up." Then a battering ram struck but the door held.

Milo's eyes flew open and in a transient moment of dexterity grabbed Snakebites knife hand and pushed it through the bikers other forearm between the split bones of the fibula, just above the wrist.

Snakebite howled. Canisters crashed through the already broken windows and began to leak a noxious gas into the room blinding us all. Seconds later the front door burst open with a battering ram and black clad officers in flak vests bearing yellow titles on their backs spilled into the room.

The bikers ran in different directions. The Pirate and the Terminator ran out the back door, G. Gordon and the witch ran down the hall and Snakebite fell to the ground holding his forearm.

Milo crawled to me. He pushed me onto my side and untied

my hands, setting me free.

Together we crawled to the front door. Before we got there, Police officers in face masks were scooping us up, raising our faces above knee level, into the fumes, and causing us both to choke and gag.

Behind us, gunshots rang out.

30
Over Hill and Dale

LEONARD WAS PICKED UO WHILE HITCH-HIKING only a half hour after he first stuck his thumb out. A retired Christian couple, who thought he looked like a nice boy, pulled onto the shoulder of the road in their late 80's blue Honda Accord and a short jog later Leonard was at their window.

"Where you going son?"

"To visit my mom in Iowa."

"Hop on in."

As Leonard hopped, the wife, a Mrs. Diane Hansen, who wasn't apprehensive about the idea of picking up a single man on the highway, said to her husband Dale, "See I told you he was a nice boy?"

Dale wasn't yet convinced.

Leonard made small talk with Diane. He found out she had a son in Laramie who was a Pharmacist. He'd decided to stay there after getting his education in the Northern Midwest cowboy town because it was cheaper to live and a lot easier to pass the State Pharmacy exam in Wyoming than in California. She and Dale were both proud of their son and mentioned how his distant home gave them a good reason to get out of their LA suburb, of Downey, at least once a year - twice if you include Christmas to visit the grandkids.

Meanwhile, Leonard had shared some truths about his life. His mom lived in Creston, Iowa, just a short drive out of Des Moines. She'd been a grocery store clerk most of her life but in the recent past had gone into management to increase her retirement. Diane noticed the way he lugged such a heavy pack and he responded that travelling would be easier if he didn't have to bring his library with him. His backpack would be a lot lighter if he wasn't carrying a few of his favorites with him, but it was a burden worth enduring for the love of a good book.

"So what do you do for a living son?" Dale asked.

"I sell things on the internet," Leonard admitted.

"Oh yeah, what sort of things?" asked Diane, turning around in her seat.

"Books, of course."

They drove onward, heading North on Interstate 15 passing several small towns, letting the hours pass, talking about books, the state of the country and the internet. What a wonderful thing the journey was turning out to be. It was pleasant small talk for all three of them. Leonard was just another young man finding himself in a brave new world turning a corner in history and the Hansen's got to enjoy his company and experience the views of someone who was living on the cutting edge of a new technology. It would make great fodder for table discussions when they got to Laramie.

When the 15 crossed Interstate 70 in central Utah, they took it heading East and refilled the gas tank at the first truck stop they encountered, a Flying J with a large number of pumps, two fast food restaurants and a mini-mart.

Leonard attempted to use his last stolen credit card and it refused him any money from the ATM. He didn't exactly need the cash. He had two pockets full, but he wanted to stretch his money as far as it would go. There was no new money coming, not from his alter identities anyways. But the fact of the card being rejected made him wonder if it was already being traced.

He got back in the car and offered the Hansen's a twenty towards his share of fuel. They refused it and said they couldn't take money from him on a path they were already traveling. Besides, they could only take him as far as Denver. From there, they were heading north and he'd have to find another ride.

"You could catch a bus," Dale offered.

"That's alright," he refused. "I'll find a way. I always do."

The Author Murders

There's a Scenic Point at the state line where Utah meets Colorado on Interstate 70. It's a majestic view at the foot of the Rockies looking over a series of plateaus as you gaze back west. At sunset it's even more spectacular, watching the fading sun paint the hillocks and mountaintops swathes of purple, ochre and sage; a breathtaking observation on the effects of solar infusion combined with geological splendor.

The Hansen's were well familiar with this spot, as was Leonard. All had traveled this way many times in the past visiting loved ones. They each looked forward to pulling off to the side, stretching their legs and taking a roadside break.

Diane had warmed to Leonard considerably. Even Dale had started to feel Leonard was just another good ole boy, a regular chip off the old block. He could, with no trouble of the imagination, have been the son of a friend.

The Rest Stop serving as the Scenic Point was empty of any other visitors. The Hansen's were comfortable enough with their passenger to let him lead them to a higher point offering just a little better view. They never noticed how much quieter the place became as a rise in the ground created a natural barrier preventing noise from carrying to or from the road. They didn't even see the perilous cliff yawning into a void of incredible depths into which their bodies would fall.

Only Dale had the opportunity to think, as he first saw his beloved high school bride of 47 years fall off the edge she shared alongside him, watching the end of the day wash across the horizon. He thought, 'Oh Dear God, she must have tripped,' and then with the gentlest of nudges by his hitchhiking companion, as he inadvertently reached out to save her, he seemed to trip himself.

Back in the car, Leonard turned on the radio and switched stations from the Country Western songs the Hansen's had enjoyed. He found a megawatt classic Rock Station out of Salt Lake. It was playing a song by the Police strumming a melody about how easy it was to become a murderer, as easy as learning you're A, B, C's.

He listened as he continued east, till the Rockies ate up the airwaves leaving only crackle and hiss.

31
Debriefing

MILO AND I WERE LOADED INTO AN AMBULANCE
from the Devil's clubhouse, to have our injuries checked at Desert Hospital. I tried to refuse, but then Milo protested going also and I gave up fighting so as to guarantee his wounds could be attended to.

Daily got in the back with us. Though we were hurt, it wasn't an emergency, so with a little pleading we convinced the driver to turn off the siren allowing the three of us space to talk.

I was laying on my gurney, loosely strapped in. The day had been a catastrophe. Milo was severely beaten and had still done a miraculous job of defending himself. The boy's stamina had remarkable vigor even though now, he apparently had relaxed enough to lie unconscious.

Daily spoke first, "You didn't have to go do what you did. I can't believe you went in there and tried to solve this yourself."

"And if a few good men did nothing?" I was still in a state of disbelief as to what had transpired. The day seemed more a page out of a Bruce Willis movie than 6 hours of my life.

"Don't give me anecdotal quotes. You're not the only one in this van who's read a book." Daily was sitting on a small folding stool attached to the back door.

"How did you know we were there?" It was a question I'd thought since I first heard the bullhorn alert us to the police presence.

"Easy," she said. "I followed you."

"You followed us?"

"I'd come out to search Leonard's room and inspect the items the PSPD had already obtained. I knew you'd nhold out on me. Not that I blame you." She threw in this latter statement as an afterthought. As if she was giving herself an excuse to justify her attendance at the raid. "All I had to do was switch cars and follow you. Once I saw Milo in your Jeep I figured we had a pretty good chance of finding the source of Leonard's drug ring, even if it didn't trace to the murders. Yet."

"Drug ring?" Why was I surprised? Leonard was a murderer, a book scout, a homosexual, and now he was a drug dealer too.

"San Bernardino County Sheriffs set up surveillance on Leonard's workplace. It was nothing more than rented office space. There was no telemarketing job. When, after a few days, he didn't show up, the locals got a warrant and searched. They turned up a combination of marijuana and meth amphetamines. Not a lot, but enough so when combined with his scales and other paraphernalia we could make a possession with intent to sell charge stick. Similar contraband was discovered upon a more thorough search of his room in Rancho Mirage."

She hadn't entirely answered my question. "I still don't understand how you knew to follow me."

"Leonard used a sub-machine gun when he murdered Landsbury. That's not an easy weapon to acquire. There had to be a more significant player involved somewhere. You'd made the leap of deduction in the past to put together his role in the other author murders. I figured Leonard, at this point in his criminal career, wouldn't want to part with cash or it might jeopardize his opportunity for flight. His dealer wouldn't need drugs. So what did he have to barter with? The answer was his signed Landsbury books."

"If you figured that much out, why didn't you just go ahead and search online for the dealer the same way you originally found me?" The bruises under my shirt and on my face were starting to blacken up. I could feel'em hardening.

"Time," she stated flatly. "I could have done the grunt work to find the seller but it would've taken more time than I preferred. It was easier just to follow you."

"You risked my life to save yourself a little paperwork and web browsing?" The anger was finding its way into my voice. The tension

was subsiding from the heat of the moment also. Weariness was engulfing me.

"I didn't plan on this happening Xanthe. When I saw where
you'd gone to, I called in for back-up immediately. I had to go back to
the Pawn shop to do so because staying on the block left me vulnerable
to their look outs. When I returned on foot and saw your car was gone
I knew you were in trouble. Luckily, S.W.A.T. was able to make a direct
response."

My eyes were fighting to stay open and shock was wearing my
nerves thin. "You were vulnerable..?" I tried to protest. I was very tired.

Daily threw me a hug and a kiss. It hurt, "I'm sorry," she said.

"What about Leonard?" My last words before slipping off to
sleep.

"We can't find him," she said.

Prior to the emergency police rescue of Milo and I, Daily's partner, Detective Trey Hunt, had been pursuing the Biblio-murderer file
from his desk station. Not one to chase down the bad guys on foot
anymore, he'd learned to use his head and the phones as his key tools
in crime solving. Certain facts had come to light.

Following the path of Leonard's route to the Beverly Hills hotel
originally discovered when the flower shop surfaced as the point of
purchase and mechanism of delivery for the poison on Danny Stole
and Georgeham Milton, Detective Craig Prater of Beverly Hills was
able to locate the rental business where the marching uniform was acquired. Fortunately, the uniform hadn't been dry-cleaned. As a matter
of disgust, it hadn't been cleaned for a considerable time prior to the
murder either. Seventeen hairs total were found on the uniform. Four
of them were blonde. One of the blonde hairs was bleached.

The hat was unable to be of use. It had been tossed into a bin
of hats of various styles. Mixed casually with fireman hats, baseball
caps, medieval masks, top hats, safari hats, cowboy hats and 9 other police hats, the merchant was unsure which hat had been rented.

Palm Springs Detectives Brian Andrews and Donald Craft had

completed the search of Leonard's room at Justin Blake's house in Rancho Mirage. Photos of the room were taken from twelve different angles before the search began so as to establish the foundation of the crime scene in advance of it being torn asunder.

Under one of the bed's drawers, a box of ID's and credit cards was found. Two of the cards bore names remarkably similar to the authors who were killed: Clyde Barstow and Steele Daniels. Hair follicles from a brush directly matched the bleached hair found on the rented marching band uniform.

The killer had been made. His name was Leonard Gaylon Beschloss. Now it was just a matter of finding him.

The beer bottle had come from the book dealer dinner party. Justin confirmed Leonard had access to the trash and knew the night's guests were fellow book dealers and likely suspects to throw the police off his trail. The rest of the bagged items in the trunk up in Joshua Tree at Pete's Collectibles proved to be kitchen ware from Justin's house.

The poison in the Danny Stole murders was Oleander bush. A deadly natural toxin easily made from simply crushing dried leaves of a very common plant. The Beverly Hills police department had one of the best crime labs in the Los Angeles basin. Those skills coupled with the efforts of the Los Angeles morgue, an agency that'd had many dealings with celebrity deaths, determined the poison in quick time

Upon learning the identities of the corpses needing service, Chief Coroner, Dr. Miles Dietrich, had rushed down to the morgue and performed the autopsy himself in order to make substantial notes, including the fact Danny Stole had recently had sex with Mr. Milton. A forensic sidebar to log into his memoirs, which he hoped one day, would elevate himself to the rank of his hero and forbearer, a man who'd held the Chief Coroner position through many unusual and elegant deaths, Dr. Thomas Noguchi.

Noguchi had written two books. His first and most significant had been Coroner at Large detailing the deaths of such renowned personalities as Marilyn Monroe, John Belushi, Robert Kennedy and Natalie Wood.

Dr. Dietrich longed for such opportunities as the death of

Danny Stole brought.

Coincidentally, Noguchi's second book Unnatural Causes had been co written by a Palm Springs City Councilman and mystery writer, Arthur Lyons, who had beat Xanthe in his attempt to win a seat on the Council.

The list of Drivers licenses and credit cards were faxed over to Detective Hunt who photocopied them and passed copies on to Detective Prater. Hunt cross checked the names against eBay account listings and found matching names on several collections of both Danny Stole and Cliff Barkeley works.

Prater did similar research to uncover rental car locations in Banning, San Bernardino, Redlands, and Ontario correlating to the timeframes of the murders. Likewise, he searched for places where computer terminals could be utilized, namely Public libraries, and found each of the four rental car ID's had matching library card accounts. This was an unsettling fact for Detective Prater. To date, he'd thought there were only two murders he was attempting to solve.

Snakebite, Bazal and the other Devils made plea bargain deals with the Riverside County District Attorney's office in exchange for information regarding Leonard's drug dealing. These confessions set off a chain of events, sending repercussions throughout the drug denizens of the lesser Palm Springs area.

In the desert, there's multi-jurisdictional squads comprised of police officers from all the different departments of the Coachella Valley because drug runners and other criminals do not respect city boundaries. The one who got the biggest bang for their snitch dollars was the NTF, Narcotics Task Force, also known by the moniker they had emblazoned on their black shirt sleeves, the Scorpions.

The Scorpions were a bunch of hard-nosed young men who'd rather accost than arrest. Their favorite game was knock-knock. They loved to knock on doors of known drug felons, search warrant in hand, and before anyone inside had the ability to respond they'd kick the door in. Hut-Hut; guns a blazing for anyone who didn't lie down with their hands behind their heads at first warning. The Scorpions were a sting operation in waiting and a heavy handed financial stream for their respective departments.

Drug Seizure and property confiscation laws had been passed in the early 90's. The courts had ruled in favor of the police in every instance and police departments all over America had grown accustomed to the rewards of seizing cars, big screen TV's, boats and even houses. Police auctions had grown far removed from just the simple stolen bicycles and the annual revenues had reached climactic proportions capable of funding entire divisions.

Attorneys had taken to calling the officers jack-booted thugs and they weren't far off. The Scorpions, like many of their counterparts across the state, wore military style night raid clothing complete with black multi-pocketed pants tucked into their shiny black army boots.

Snakebite and the rest of the Devils had made deals to protect themselves, all the while selling out their distribution networks and the Scorpions responded effectively. Hundreds of thousands of dollars in drugs and merchandise were brought in over the next couple weeks with a ripple affect that would rock the desert's drug cartels for years.

Unfortunately for Snakebite and his biker friends, they thought the whole affair was over drug business and they made their deal too soon. When a second District Attorney came after them for conspiracy to commit murder they had nothing left to bargain with. On their property in Desert Hot Springs was found a multitude of signed Jay Landsbury books. Their computer had eBay listings electronically tied to it with cookies giving a direct link to evidence associated with the killing, and Leonard's fingerprints were found on the computer. On top of that, semi-automatic shells were found in a lock-box under the floorboards of Snakebites room of the exact caliber of weapon used by Leonard in the murder of Jay Landsbury. There was a second round of charges filed connecting the household with the author murders and the gang had no more bargaining chips. That's where the rubber met the road for Snakebite. His hog had checked out leaving him a face full of dirt and the rocks were flying.

32
The Cowboy Bookman

I DIDN'T KNOW WHAT TO DO that first night out of the hospital. I wandered around downtown as if in a fugue. The stores all looked run down. I noticed every crack in the sidewalk, every chip of paint on the store fronts and all the signs seemed to have at least one bulb burnt out. After more than an hour of walking up and down the strip called downtown Palm Springs I ended up back at the place I first met Milo.

Starbucks.

The smell of coffee welcomed me like a mothers embrace. I went in and ordered a cup of their strongest brew. It was bitter – the perfect match for my feeling towards all that had happened since my taking on the Stephen's Dump Truck case. The table where Milo had first tossed me a note was open. I took it and sipped my cup.

The end of my rope seemed to be the bottom of my cup. I didn't want to reach it so I took small sips and thought: How could I let this happen? Why didn't I do things differently? I wasn't as smart as I thought I was. Where could I turn? How could I make things right for Milo? What would Milo do at a time like this?

What would Milo do at a time like this?

He'd turn to the Internet, that's what he'd do. Turn to the Net, but how? The net was a big place and I was on unfamiliar ground except for the places I did business: Abebooks.com, Bibliofind.com and Interloc.com. All they were was a loose network of dealers wanting to sell their merchandise online to the highest bidder. They listed their books through a series of uploads, continually modifying their databases. They didn't communicate with each other unless one was buying or selling a book.

Or did they?

I got out of my seat and started walking the two blocks back to the store; each step increasing my pace. By the time I was a block away I was in a full on sprint. I reached the front door of the store out of breath, breathing like a man missing his respirator. In my excitement the keys struggled to get it in the lock. My hands shook so badly I finally had to put two fingers on each side of the lock to act as a guide. I swung the door open and relocked it behind me then headed to my desk in the back.

My computer was waiting for me and I slid in behind the keyboard. A deep breath slowly calmed my nerves as I punched in Interloc.com into the web browser and started scanning the website for the link I knew would lead to my absolution. And there it was - my light of Apollo, like a beacon shining the way on a dark channel, my ship had found its harbor. I clicked on the link titled DEALER NETWORK. A few seconds later a list of dealer names, addresses and best of all - email addresses ran the length of my monitor and beyond.

I opened my version of Microsoft Word, not the newest version but it would do and wrote a letter:

Attention Book Dealers,

I need your help solving a crime. I am a book dealer from Southern California and there is a murderer ruining our good names. He has some books with him and will most likely come into your store wanting to sell them to get some cash. His name is Leonard Beschloss. He is about 5 feet 8 inches tall, slight build, and as of today he had blonde hair although that could change. The books he'll most likely try and sell are autographed science fiction and mystery and will be quite nice, possibly even Easton Press.

Whether or not you buy his books I warn you – HE IS A MURDERER! He has killed many people already and he will do so again. He is on the run now from the law in California. Please alert the police as soon as you see him and please let me know so I can

tell the local authorities.
   Thank you for your assistance,
   Xanthe Anthony
   Owner@CelebrityBooks.com

Fine. It'd do the job. I opened another window on my screen, this one for emailing and prepared to multi-task. Looking at the Interloc dealer network I copied the first email and pasted it into my email Send column. Then I copied the letter from Microsoft Word into the body of my email and I clicked send. The first one was off. It felt good. It felt as if I had helped. No better way to catch a book thief than seek the help of every book dealer in the country.

I stared to click on the next email address from Interloc and had a second thought. I opened a second Word document and pasted the email onto the blank page. No sense wasting all this effort on a single shot. Who knows I might just want to do this again sometime and having a list of Internet book dealers may just come in handy. Settling into a stream of work I found comfort in my efforts to help solve the case. It was like fishing. I cast out my line and wait for a tug.

Copy. Paste. Copy. Paste. Copy. Paste. Send.
Copy. Paste. Copy. Paste. Copy. Paste. Send.
Copy. Paste. Copy. Paste. Copy. Paste. Send.
I had a long night ahead.

The next morning, about 1250 miles east in Aardvark, Texas, Larry McMurphy was opening his store on the corner of Main Street and Ranger Way; a slightly run down heart of a small town once upon a time left to the dregs of hookers and truck drivers. It was making a sort of renaissance comeback since one of its local boys made good, after his well received run as a western writer, took advantage of the cheap real estate and began setting his shingles on the block. This morning he had three doors to unlock on each of his three stores, the first being his main store, where he worked pricing books he bought from other dealers going out of business by the truckload. On his others stores, he'd hang a sign on their dusty front panes reading "We'd be obliged if you'd carry your merchandise down to the corner store for purchase."

The streets were now mostly empty, their sidewalks strewn with loose litter from an evening of wind. McMurphy kicked a crumpled paper bag out of his entry way, walked under his wooden shingle declaring Lonesome Covers to all of no one passing by, unlocked his door and went inside. He went through the mundane morning ritual merchants all over the country go through to make their establishment welcoming. Within a short time, he found himself sitting at his counter and flipped on his computer, during its warm-up sequence he read the Dallas Morning News and found the airport expansion was running into cost over runs again and the sports section confirmed his favorite teams were losing pretty much universally.

The misery of the world consumed and put aside, he returned to his computer to check his email and found a desperate plea for help from a Palm Springs book dealer seeking to solve a murder mystery that had been the subject of many a biblio chat room and coffee klatch in the book world. Larry McMurphy thought it was time to exercise his mind on books. His store needed running but he found the email from Palm Springs to be intriguing, when a few seconds later he heard his door bell, an old fashioned servant's bell neatly taped to his door handle. It started clanging and he lifted his head to say hello to his first customer of the day; his hair stood on end.

A blonde haired young man of slight build carrying a backpack over his shoulder walked into his store wearing a thin smile. "Pardon me," he asked. "Are you buying any books today?"

Without missing a beat, his intuitions kicked into overdrive, McMurphy replied, "Could be. What have you got?" He cleared away his paper from the counter and nonchalantly steered the screen of his computer away from the young man's sight.

Unzipping his backpack on the counter he produced three books: The Foundation Trilogy by Isaac Asimov, Lord Valentine's Castle by Robert Silverberg, and The Belgariad by David Eddings. All were neatly bound in leather by Easton Press. "They're signed," offered the young man.

McMurphy gave a knowing nod, as if to say Thanks for sharing, lifted the Asimov book and checked it on each side for bumps, scratches or other flaws. There were none. The leather was perfect and the gilded edges still shined with the luster of its print day. He carefully turned the first few pages and saw it was signed on a special front end-paper specifically laid in by the publisher to highlight the signature in bold blue ink right on the sweet spot. He checked the other two books in silence, casting glances at the young man as he browsed the shelves around the front of the store.

This had to be the same person who'd committed the crimes in California. He fit the description, he had the merchandise, he must need some money to extend his getaway or maybe he just had the illness. Bibliosomnia – the inability to live without handling books. It was a disease that once infected seemed to never find a cure. Already Mc-Murphy had met at least two people who'd died from it. When he'd first given up being a cop a few years ago he thought he'd find a better crowd of people than the hoodlums, druggies and prostitutes that being on job introduced him to and most of the time he was right. People who loved books were educated and made interesting friends, they were generally of a better stock and many of them had money. But there was also another class of booklover who used them to fill the voids of their lives as if there was nothing else in the world worth living for and although McMurphy knew the feelings that drove these sentiments like a vintage Camaro going off a high cliff, he also knew how to put on the brakes. This kid was apparently on cruise control to the deep end of the ocean.

"What's your name," McMurphy asked as way of starting the negotiations.

"Paxton. Bill Paxton," said the young man. First Lie.

Most people can't help but letting you know when they're lying. Their eyes warble or look away, even slightly. When they tilt their head searching their brain for thought they do it differently than when they're telling the truth. Body language, subtle hints, sweating, facial ticks, they all want the world to know what they're doing unless they've been lying for a long time or they've been trained to mislead. But most people just can't help themselves.

The Author Murders

"Mine's Larry," McMurphy said extending his hand. And breaking a habit he'd learned to maximize years ago from a friend of his who was a police officer in his day. Cops don't shake hands. Criminals who shake your hand as a police officer are usually trying to get you off balance or take away one of your attacks. As a book dealer, Larry McMurphy used the handshake to size up his opponent for the inevitable tug of war that comes when trying to get the other man's treasures at the lowest possible price. The young man calling himself Bill Paxton had a firm grip. He was strong and at least thirty years younger. He worked out and he held his gaze steady as they shook. "Like the actor?" McMurphy added.

"Yeah," the young man lied for the second time, his eyes flickering. "I get that a lot."

"I bet."

Paxton waited for the bookman to start. Someone was going to have to name a price. Best to let the give and take begin from behind the counter.

"I like your books. They're nice copies. Where'd you get them?"

"I got them in a divorce." This was the truth.

"Your wife know about these?"

"Sure." It was a truth but not the whole truth.

"How much you want for them?"

"How much you want to give?" Right back at ya.

"Well, like I said, I like them. But I also got to consider my overhead and how long it'll take for them to sell. As you can see I don't get a lot of traffic out here."

Bill Paxton didn't budge.

Time to start, "How about $125."

Paxton considered this then said, "I think it's a little low. The Asimov book alone should be worth that much. But I'll make you a deal. How about $200."

The kid does know his books. This was going to hurt. How come I always get caught up in the illegal deals and then have to play straight arrow. They weren't just nice books. They were great books. Priced right he'd turn $200 into $500 in two weeks or less. Deals like that don't just come around every day. But sometimes being scrupulous had its downside.

"How about $150."

Paxton gave this pause. He was obviously near his acceptance point. "Make it $175 and you got a deal."

"Nope son. I'm trying to be fair with you but there's got to be enough butter on the bread to make it work for me if you know what I'm saying." It was time to play hardball. Playing the Sheriff and doing the right thing was all fine and dandy but he was also still a bookman. "I'll tell you what. I'll give you a check right now for $160 and you can walk it down the street to the bank and have the cash before you can say Jake's my uncle. Sound fair?"

Paxton backed down, "How about $150 cash."

The bookman looked pitifully at the killer like a dad getting ready to tell his son he was doing something stupid. But there was no time to be fatherly. "I have to get it from the back," the writer lied. "I haven't got all my cash in the drawer yet. It'll take a few minutes."

Paxton shrugged acceptance and McMurphy hiked to the back of the store. It's messy leaving the front unguarded for a moment because the stacks blocked the view of the back room.

The young man quickly scanned the shelves around the front a second time then tipping up onto his toes tried to look around the shelves to the back from his point in the front. He couldn't see anything. As far as he could tell the shelves went all the way to Shangri-la. He took a step towards the back of the counter acting as if he were trying to read the spines of the books in some glass cases alongside the register. Carefully pivoting around the cases so as to act nonchalant should the dealer come back Paxton got a full view of the bookman's workspace. Messy lower shelves filled with boxes, papers in disarray and jacket mylars were at knee level. On top of the counter were pens, pencils, erasers, a squirt bottle filled with glue remover and a computer monitor on screensaver. Pin-up magazines from the 1940's and 50's were flashing on the screen every few seconds. He grabbed the mouse and gave it a swirl. On the screen appeared a letter from Celebrity Books just as the sound of feet began padding back towards the front of the store. He swiftly returned to the proper side of the counter and waited.

Larry McMurphy had a plan. He'd give the money to the man claiming to be Bill Paxton and then he'd grab the pistol he kept hidden behind the register and arrest him. Counting the twenties as he walked back up front loudly so as to act natural he made his play. He kept his piece velcroed against the bottom of the counter within easy reach. He almost went for it while negotiating but decided he didn't know if the kid had one in the back of his waistband and he sure didn't want a shootout in the store. Merchandise might get damaged. It'd be easier and neater to just wait until the kid stepped towards the exit and then catch him off guard. He wasn't going to get the chance.

The kid had jumped away from the glass cases near the register like a stir crazy rabbit and McMurphy saw the computer had the letter open on it. He ran forward like a bullet but the kid did a dirty thing. Paxton shoved hard on the glass case full of his best book stock, knocking it off the counter and into his path. McMurphy made a grab for it and had to go down on one knee to prevent it from breaking. Without hesitation the kid gave him a roundhouse in the jaw. The case fell to the floor and shattered, spilling thousands of dollars in books into the glass shards. The bookman had a secret of his own to help save him. In his younger days he'd been a medium weight boxer and when he was the same age as the killer he'd been state champ. If he'd just been a soft book dealer he'd been down for the count. As it was he took the blow hard and it sent him down but he was far from out. The kid started kicking him in the ribs while he was bent down on all fours. Two fast kicks were strong enough to blast the wind from his lungs but the third kick was caught under McMurphy's arm and he flipped his opponent to the floor. Scrambling on top of him it was time to return the favor. Smashing his fist into the kids' nose brought up blood by the second hit. A third blow dazed his eyes. A fourth to the solar lexes knocked the fight right out of the kid. The bookman stood up and dragged the kid over behind the counter. The phone was smashed when the book case had been tossed.

Under the counter, in his toolbox, McMurphy kept some wire

ties. They weren't quite as secure as handcuffs but they were handy in a pinch. He happened to have them on hand to help with wiring his computer cables. He grabbed Leonard - now confirmed to not be Bill Paxton - and dragged him over to a book shelf. Binding one hand first, he used a second tie to lace through the shelving and then bound him one hand on each side of the shelf, immobilizing the kid. He had to go to the back of the store to make the call to the Police. He could just drive the kid in. But, what the heck, that's what the cops were for. The kids' nose was clotting already and he was still loopy from the fight.

McMurphy pulled his head back by the scruff of his hair and determined he had more than a few minutes before Bill Paxton the murderer would come around. He hastened to the back of the store where he kept his own little private office amidst boxes and stacks of books to call 911.

He dialed the phone.

"911 operator,..."

"Yes, I have an emergency at..."

"...if this an emergency please hold. All operators are currently busy and we'll be with you in moments."

"Christ," swore McMurphy. Never one when you need'em.

He looked at his watch. A minute later he looked at it again. He was still on hold.

A loud crash came from the front of the store. He dropped the phone and ran, letting it dangle on its cord. The shelving unit Bill Paxton hand been bound to lay ripped apart, the side beam pulled away from the shelves. Books and shelves splayed across McMurphy's path blocking his access to the front of the store. Through the mess he could see the back of the kid stuffing his books and the money into his backpack.

"Hey, you better stay where you are! I've got a gun." It was a lie but what the hell.

Bill Paxton turned, a .38 revolver in his hand. He plunked off two shots, forcing McMurphy back into his hole of a back room. A second later the familiar tinkle of the doorbell sounded and the kid was gone.

"…Marshall's Office. Hello. Hello. Call again if you can."

"NO," shouted the bookman. He dove for the phone but by the time he placed it against his ear all he got was dial tone.

He dialed 911 again.

"911 operator. If this is an emergency please hold. All operators are currently busy and we'll be with you in moments."

"Christ. Not again." Dejected he let his back fall against a shelf and slunk down to the floor.

33
Visiting Hours

MILO LAY IN HIS HOSPITAL BED in a drug induced slumber. His injuries weren't life threatening but he was pretty beat up and the doctors thought it best he be watched overnight. He'd had trouble sleeping after the action at the Devil's clubhouse and so the nurses shot him a sedative.

Late that night he had a visitor slip into his room and closes the door behind him. The room was poorly lit with just a dim glow cast by a streetlight through the narrow window. The visitor gave Milo a nudge. But he couldn't wrest the thick blanket of slumber he was wrapped in. He nudged again, this time hard enough to knock Milo into the side rails of his hospice bed.

"Snn...Huh?" snored Milo.

"Kid. We need to talk."

"What's up?" Fighting off the sleep was hard. The drugs were deep in his system. He pulled a hand up and tried to wipe his eyes. His hands were knocked away.

"Don't worry about that. I don't want you looking around anyways. Do you know what this is?"

Cold steel touched the side of Milo's head. It felt like a lead pipe but it had the smell of oil and ash. He had a pretty good guess what it was. "Uh huh," he slurred, waking up fast. He tried to look out of the corner of his eye to see who it was. All he could make out was a stocky shadow with short hair.

"Don't even try looking over here," said the shadow pushing

the metal and forcing Milo's head to turn away. "Good boy. Stay just like that."

Milo had a view of the television set. There was faint reflection on the dead screen showing his room and its intruder. The reflection was thick in several ways. His body was tone yet weighty. His haircut was crisp almost militarist style. He wore an orderly outfit but the collar sticking out was bright and multi-colored. He also spoke with an east European accent. The shadow pulled the pillow from under his head and placed it against his temple and adjusted his gun on its backside still pointed at Milo's head.

"Now, we're just going to talk for a few minutes and if you tell truth you will go back to sleep and tomorrow wake up feeling fine. If you lie then you go to sleep and no wake up. Ready to talk?"

Slowly, Milo moved his head up and down.

"Tell me 'bout what you know about the book?"

Milo wanted to resist. Every fiber of him told him to lie or not talk. He'd told himself many times in his life what he'd do if faced with an impossible situation and every one of his make-believe scenarios had him doing some heroic action lightning fast reflex maneuver that incapacitated his foe and ended with him in a godly light then kissing a beautiful girl. But in the cold recesses of night, lying half-drugged in his bed, sleeping in a gown with no butt and opposed by an unknown assailant he caved. He talked and told the interrogator whatever he wanted to know. He told about his findings online, of the bidders, of the author, of the history of the book, all he'd found on the seller of everything he could. It didn't take long. When his questions started repeating the same answers or ending with "I don't know," the questions came more forcefully until Milo started to cry.

The gun gave a slight pause and then Milo felt a prick on his arm near the same spot as his first earlier that evening. After that his eyes grew heavy again.

34
The Patriot

36 hours later I was waiting for Milo to awake. The doctors had kept a constant vigil and death was not imminent although a contusion induced coma seemed to have escalated his status to critical care. I was at his bedside two mornings after his arrival at Desert Hospital when he finally came to. He was groggy and climbed from his sleep as if he'd walked up a long staircase with lead ankle weights. A small sweat had gathered on his face during his last few hours of slumber and a cold sore had broken out on his dry cracked lips. Earlier in the day the nurses had begun feeding him a steady diet of proteins and vitamins intravenously.

Unknowingly, his eyes slid open while I was watching a morning episode of The Price is Right and he caught me off guard.

"$1.59," he said.

"What?" I turned to him.

"The dishwasher detergent is $1.59," he repeated.

Bob Barker agreed with him, "It's $1.59 and you'll be a Final Showcase contestant." A heavy set African American woman was jumping up and down, hugging Bob like a long lost relative returned from the Titanic.

"Welcome back. I was worried." I placed a hand on his arm. "How you feeling?"

"I've got a headache. But Xanthe...," his head lifted to look me in the eye. I could see there was more troubling him than his head.

"I had a visitor last night."

"Are you sure you mean last night?" Did he know how long he'd been unconscious?

"What do you mean?" Milo asked.

"You've been asleep almost two days."

"Oh man no. He's got a head start on us." He squirmed to sit up more in bed shaking both the sleep and his feelings from his mind. "Who?"

"Donlagic. He visited me while I was asleep here my first night, whenever that was, and forced me to tell him what I knew about the book. I'm sorry. I couldn't help it." The kid was frightened and sorry. His Adams apple bobbed up and down fiercely as he swallowed his pride and told me all about it. I couldn't blame him. Anyone would have done the same under the circumstances. I comforted him, told I him it was alright and then after a few minutes made my departure saying there was work waiting for me back at the store.

Once I was secure in the avalanche room in the back of the store I called Detective Daily and told her what Milo had told me. Her response made me furious.

"I'll pass the word on this one Xanthe to the local authorities. But from what you've told me about Detective Donlagic he'll be prepared for the accusation. I'm sure he'll have an alibi."

"We can't just let him get away with this!" I yelled. How dare she?

"Xanthe. When you run with horse thieves somebody's going to get hanged," she replied coolly. And before I could counter against her again, she went on, "Xanthe there's something else. There's a police officer who'll be down to get you soon and please don't run. As a matter of fact you'd do better to go down to the station now on your own."

I waited a couple of hours out of shear frustration over Milo's affair. But it was unwarranted. That afternoon Milo recovered quickly and against my better judgment he returned to the bookstore computers in the back room of leaning book towers. Thom Racina showed up early prepared for another successful Villagefest. I finally got a few minutes to talk to Thom.

"Thom, tell me. How'd you get your start in writing?"

"I did a lot in Hollywood when I was younger, writing things behind the scenes. I wrote the book adaptation of the movie Nine to Five."

"You mean the one where Dolly Parton and those other gals tie up their boss and hold him hostage?"

"That's the one." Then he whispered under his breath. "Don't let Jill read it. She might think it an instructional manual."

We both laughed. "Yeah but there must have been some point when you didn't have any resume and you had to get your first deal. How'd you do that?" He'd probably answered this question a hundred times. It was the one everybody wanted to know about any author.

"My first book is called the Devil's Apprentice. It didn't sell a whole lot but it did catch the eye of a real publisher. After that I got an agent and things got a little easier but it was still a lot of work." He was unpacking his own box of books, so I knew he was still schlepping his own bags so to speak. But he also had built up an impressive and growing body of work.

I was intrigued. "What was it about?"

"It was about a guy who kept getting the short end of the stick in life. He keeps trying to improve himself, seeking love, a career, whatever, but all he gets is a kick in the ass. He finally makes a pact with the devil and it becomes his job to lure others to the dark side."

"Kind of gloomy isn't it?"

"Yeah, but reviewers all over the country loved my depiction of the main character. They called it surreal."

"Wow," I was soaking it all in. "And from there?"

"My next big break was writing on the script for the biggest wedding of the century."

"You mean Prince Charles and Princess Di?" I asked.

"Bigger," he said. "Luke and Laura."

"From General Hospital?"

"That's the one. After that I could get a job just about anywhere even if I do have to unpack my own books."

We both laughed again and I left him to his preparations.

Jill poked her head out the front door of the store.

"You got a phone call," she yelled.

It was Detective Donald Craft, one of Palm Springs finest, asking me to come see him down at the station.

He was waiting for me in the reception area when I arrived, a room almost made entirely of glass. The public thinks this is so the police give the appearance of being open to scrutiny but in reality it gives the police a clear view of everyone who enters the station. Detective Craft came out to greet me, then led me to his car and asked me to get in. "We've had some developments," he told me, "and we could use your expertise."

"How so?" I wondered.

"You'll have to wait on that." He fired up his Ford LTD and proceeded to drive down valley.

We ended up at Justin Blake's house. There were strands of yellow police tape directing access.

"Why are you showing me this?" I asked.

"We've hit a snag in the investigation," Craft said as we walked up the driveway. "We need to know the whereabouts of Leonard. Quite frankly, we're at a dead end and were hoping you could help."

"How would I know where he is?"

"You were in this room before it was even searched by me and Detective Andrews. You're a book dealer and you may notice something we might have missed." Detective Craft was playing to my expertise; a kind of flattery claiming I might be able to look at a crime scene and glean more information from it than a biblio novice. I was willing to help but as always I wanted be on the inside tract and able to make use of other information.

"You said WE a couple times there Don. Are you now working with Detective Daily on some sort of cooperative investigation? I wouldn't want to jeopardize or minimize her role in this. She's done so much already. Although you know my first line of interest is the Palm Springs Department." I hoped that he'd sense my sincerity and allegiance, making him more comfortable in my follow-up questions, trying to pry some further information from him. He tossed me a comment I wasn't expecting.

"It's gone much further than that," he said, opening the front door and pulling up a strand of the yellow tape like a boxer being helped into the ring by his handler.

We entered Justin's house and there was a man in the living room. He said, "Mr. Anthony, allow me to introduce myself. I'm agent Patrick Henry of the FBI."

He stretched a black hand with light skinned palms in my direction for me to shake. It was attached to a man as black as the ace of spades, dressed in a blue gray suit; probably an Armani by the fit and not off the rack. It came snug at the hips without creating any wrinkles and gave him the wide shoulders of John Wayne, although Patrick Henry probably didn't need any padding. He looked as physically fit as a linebacker. He cast me a wide grin as his most fluent hello and kept his hand out until I shook it.

"Patrick," I said. "Patrick Henry, like the patriot?"

"Oh, you've heard of me," he continuing his grin and pumping my hand twice. Then, before I could speak again, "Mr. Anthony, I need your help. The case has taken on greater depth. That's why we've kept the home cordoned off and vacated the residents; to protect the integrity of the investigation and allow us to work more in private."

"It's taken on greater depth?" I repeated.

"Leonard Gaylon Beschloss," he emphasized, adding seriousness to the moment by using Leonard's full name, "has headed East." As Agent Henry said this, he turned away from me and walked to the middle of the living room and pointed to a map of North America on the coffee table. On it was several red circles in various cities. Agent Henry pointed to a black circle in the southern tip of Utah.

"Leonard's car was discovered here two days ago by a volunteer worker in Bryce National Park. It was cleverly hidden on a seldom used dead-end dirt road and pulled deeply into bushes to further complicate its discovery. It was sheer luck it was found at all." Henry had a captivating voice. Perry Mason would have no edge on him. I imagined Agent Henry on the Deck of a ship, Gregory Peck playing his captain at his side, and Henry stating in defiance of the English Armada, 'Give me liberty or give me death.'

The Author Murders

"Uh-huh," I said trying to add up the facts I was being shown and not be overwhelmed by Agent Henry's presence. The bulk of the pins were clustered in the Los Angeles area. There were a few in other states like Iowa and Oregon, plus one down south in Puerto Vallarta, Mexico."

Agent Henry waited for my mind to catch up to him and then continued, "As you can see, this is how we've determined he's heading east. He's abandoned his vehicle and is either hitch-hiking or has an accomplice driving him now, although personally I feel he's acting alone and it's more likely he's car-jacked some poor unfortunates who are either already dead or soon will be when he decides they're vehicle is of more use to him than their generosity."

I turned from the map to look Agent Henry in the eyes. They were crisp and dark with white pupils laced with a few red streaks and deep brown centers. He bore them full on into my face when he asked me his next question, drawing me deeper into his confidence. "We need your help Xanthe. We need to act before anyone else gets hurt. Can you look at his room and by assessing what's missing tell us where he's gone. Maybe he took something that can lead us. Maybe you can see something we'd miss. Maybe you can..."

I held up my hand to stop him. I understood what he wanted of me. If there was one item that might tell this tale, I knew where it would be. I walked into Leonard's room and stood in the center. I had to reorient myself to when I'd last looked into this denizen of demise. I spun only a quarter turn on my heel and reached for the shelf where I'd last seen a red leather bound book bearing the gold stamp of a dump truck on its spine. My fingers grasped air. It was gone.

"If I had to make a guess," I said. "I'd say he's on his way to Bangor, Maine."

35
The Favor

"THANKS CROWLEY. YOU'RE THE BEST." Donlagic snapped his phone shut. He liked technology. Least ways when it worked. Cell phones had to be the greatest invention going. He tapped the stubby antennae against his chin a few times as he thought about what he'd just learned, mixing it up with what he'd got from the kid in the hospital the other night it seemed to lead up to one conclusion. He flipped open his phone again and dialed long distance.

"Dah. Petre. Dis is Mikhail. Good. Good. I need favor." He slipped further into his accent when talking to one of his brethren from the old country. "I have friend I need you send someone to meet a few hours North of you tomorrow. Probably tomorrow. Maybe next day. But they should wait for him. Can you do me this?"

The voice on the other end asked a few questions and made a demand.

"Oh? Is high no? What would our mothers say if dey knew of so much. Would make dem cry. You're like family. What say we split da potatoe? Better not talk too much directly. You never knew who could listen in on these things.

The other end of the line made a small concession and agreed.

"OK. Dah. Have it your way. Is fair, yes?"

36
The Caravan

AGENT PATRICK HENRY WAS BREAKING ALL THE RULES, as seemed to be his standard operational excuse for his unusual work habits. He'd been up and down the ladder of promotions all the way to Special Agent, one step above Field Agent. But, that was before a series of compromising events spilled into a downward career spiral landing him back on the first base of duty, and earning him the lackluster title of Agent. It was like in that movie, Poltergeist 2, when the wife tried to convince the husband to return to the haunted house and the husband ranted, "Hey, I'm into downward mobility and I'm comfortable with that."

Only Agent Henry wasn't comfortable with it. Not really; not at all. After fourteen years with the Bureau he felt he deserved better. Sure, he'd messed up once or twice and maybe gotten what he deserved at the time. He couldn't honestly blame his superiors for the mistakes he'd made on the Jeffrey Dahmer case. Mistakes that cost two more Asian boys and one black boy their lives after a brutal act of barbaric cannibalism for a total of 17 murders. That was in 1991, and it hadn't been Henry's first mistake either.

His first mistake had been on the Richard Ramirez case in 1985 when he was stationed in Los Angeles as a junior agent, barely out of training. That mistake had been a whopper. He'd talked to a member of the media, thinking they were a witness and while questioning the reporter, who played along with the blunder, he'd used the phrase "Night Stalker" and the murderer was given a name. The spiral began.

Fomenting his frustrations, Henry let slip the possibilities of a racial discrimination claim against the Agency to a Human Resources department advisor. A note was placed in his file and the good cases never came his way again.

Until now that is.

Funny it should happen when he was once again stationed on the West coast. Palm Springs was a sleepy little hamlet when he was repositioned under the oldest district boss in the system. Many of his colleagues laughed that his superior was already retired and relaxing in God's Waiting Room for the retirement checks to come in. It was supposed to be a non-committal assignment with no action.

Then PSPD started investigating the Author Murders, scatterings of capital crimes culminating from this tired little cardiac pasture. But the real hit, the stinger that cemented Henry being on the team, was when the killers car was found in Utah on a National Park. Pow, Bang, Zippo, Bash. He was involved again. Now it was interstate crime; jurisdiction of the Department of Federal Bureau of Investigation and right in the lap of Agent Patrick Henry. These were the thoughts filling Henry's head as he skirted the skies in a Boeing DC-10 airliner towards his destination of Bangor, Maine, watching the blueness getting swallowed by a set of dark clouds on the horizon.

He was also skirting the proper request channels. No need to ask permission, because permission wouldn't be forthcoming. This was redemption time. This was his chance at the salvation of a career caught in the snags of outrageous misfortune. This was time to release the pangs of stagnation and move back into the good graces of his Uncle Sam.

If only he didn't have such a damn headache.

* * *

Leonard was wasting no time. His cuts and bruises from the Cowboy book dealer had mostly healed up but he still had a sore nose and his ribs hurt.

He'd driven across the country heading Northeast until reaching

Maine and then he slowed his pace, enjoying the scenery, acclimating himself to his new surroundings. He needed to act fast but wanted to be able to score his hit like a prize fighter with a winning one-two combination knock-out. He had to be careful not to over accelerate and draw unnecessary attention. Carefully, he pressed on.

Trees lined the sides of interstate like tent canopies at the circus. Leaves of green, yellow and brown filled the branches of more trees than Leonard could count. Early into the state he tried to name some of the trees. He could recognize Elm, Poplar, Oak and Maple, but soon he lost track. There were more than he could acknowledge. So he stopped at an Arco and picked up a local tourist pamphlet called Aboriginal Trees of Maine and passed some miles trying to recognize a few other species. He learned that Birch, Beech, Basswood and Butternut were also indigenous to the area and there were at least half a dozen types of Maple; a couple strands of Ash and a particular breed known as Witch Hazel. Wasn't that an arch enemy of Popeye? If there was this much color available now, then he could understand how people would be drawn to Maine in the fall. Green fields stretched between the forests. Lakes dotted the horizon and rivers connected the dots. Looking down one picturesque causeway, he spotted a covered bridge.

Eruptions of civilization parted the foliage. Towns were filed with postcard buildings tinted in Americana. Norman Rockwell and Alister Cooke could live an eternity here and not run out of material. The skies were turning gray. His blissful trip was coming to an end.

A green freeway sign welcomed him to Bangor and Leonard pulled off the freeway. The wind was picking up blowing him into town like a gunslinger in a spaghetti western.

He headed towards the city center and found a library. It was a colossal building of old world construction. It could easily have been transplanted from Westminster Abbey; a fine example of old England in the midst of New England.

Leonard parked the Hansen's Honda in the side lot and entered through a door on the same side. Inside, the main entrance was lit by a spectacular atrium illuminating row upon row of books. Hundreds of thousands of them at least. Off to the far side was a sign over a doorway leading to what Leonard wanted. Internet access.

He found what he was looking for in a matter of minutes. Knightly's home address:

57 West Broadmore
Bangor, Maine
04401

Then his work address:

49 Florida Drive
Bangor, Maine
04401

The internet was great, Leonard thought, stifling back a laugh. Where else could all the information needed to kill a man be so ready at hand.

But, not yet. He needed something first. Not much really, just a pen stroke on a piece of paper; a few swirly lines beginning with an S and ending with anything that looked like a G. And it had to be authentic because nothing less than an original would do.

After putting the addresses into Mapquest.com and receiving a detailed description of the routes, Leonard moved his car towards what he now called the vantage point.

* * *

At that same time another vehicle came into town after driving in from Boston. It was a white Yugo cube truck, miniature in size compared to American standards. A type of delivery truck more common in Europe but it filled the need for the men who drove it, trying to appear as if they had business in town delivering cargo. On its side read Zabik Farms – the Country's Best Sausage.

The two men inside were of healthy stock performing day jobs of feeding the hogs, lifting sacks of grain, manhandling the livestock and waking up early for other chores. Their names were of the old country: Nando and Stefan. They also had night jobs requiring less savory characteristics. Sausages were a great way to hide all sorts of things. No one knew exactly what they were made of. They were looking for a young man with blonde hair that looked out of place. They too knew how to use the internet and now that they'd arrived they needed to find a gas station in town to make sure they had enough gas for a quick getaway.

* * *

Leonard first drove by the King house, a vintage Victorian monolith complete with wrought iron gates and spires. It was a huge monstrosity looking remarkably similar to Disneyland's Haunted Mansion. How fitting that the Master of the Macabre, the King of Horror should dwell in his own creepy castle.

Then he drove past the work address, a typical 1970's office complex with straight edges and a flat roof, two stories tall and no flavor. All the doors were painted the same bland tan except one on the second floor at the top of the stairs. It was rustic hardwood with a polished brass nameplate upon it. Leonard didn't know it, but Knightly owned the whole building.

A vast field of tall grass stretched out to a set of railroad tracks, separating the office from a residential neighborhood. Knightly's haunted house was at the far end of that neighborhood, only a mile and a half away.

Confidence overtook Leonard's actions. He hid the car around the corner of Knightly's house and waited. The websites had revealed other information on the famous author, like the fact that he was currently trying to lose weight. This small bit of gossip made Leonard think of a plan. Sure enough, only a half hour later, at 9:38 am, Stephen Knightly came bouncing around the corner trying to gain momentum on what he called his Power Walk.

Leonard popped open the car door and chased down Knightly before he had a chance to hit his stride. Disappointed, but courteous, Knightly succumbed to the arm flagging and broke his pace to accept what appeared to be a gratuitous fan. With little convincing, he signed the 8 1/2 by 11 inch sheet of paper, with the new Sharpie pen, that Leonard claimed to just happen to have. "I wish I had something more appropriate for you," Leonard said.

As Knightly was signing, Leonard reached into his jacket vest pocket, grasped the handle of a carefully hidden large kitchen knife and...A door opened from another house on the block. A man in a single breasted blue blazer was yelling to someone inside, "I'll pick it up after work."

"Morning," said Knightly.

"Morning," said the man.

"Here you go," said Knightly, handing back the pen and conspicuously folding a corner of the signed page. It was his way of diminishing the value of what appeared to be an obvious autograph hound out for profit. Leonard was not pleased. Knightly was not aware of how close he'd come to own demise.

* * *

The plane was making its landing approach. Agent Patrick Henry peered out the small window of the 737. Below he could see the layout of Bangor. Several major highways overlapped an interlacing network of thoroughfares instigating from the banks of a blue thread which could only be the Kenduskeag River. As the plane lowered to only a few hundred feet he could sense the aroma of the town. The river was covered with brick bridges. The town was covered with brick buildings. The brick buildings were sparsed among narrow roads that at one time were filled with cobblestones. Timber yawned far into the distance, reaching up to grab Henry as he landed. The plane swaying slightly from the wind and then it touched tarmac.

Waiting in a white cruiser on the runway, was Federal Marshall Robert Carrier. Carrier and Henry had worked together many years ago on the Night Stalker case, back when Carrier had been on the LAPD. Carrier had wanted to take a different approach than Henry. But at the time, Henry was given the lead position on the case. Carrier understood. He could have reached the same conclusions, but had stuck to his hunch. Only Henry got to make the call. When the chips had fallen and Henry had taken a political and bureaucratic beating, Carrier had remained his friend. When Henry had called from the Palm Springs Airport and asked Carrier to help him, Carrier had considered it a personal favor he couldn't resist, like a friend calling from jail wanting bail; Carrier agreed to help.

After a handshake that included Henry grabbing Carrier's elbow and Carrier wrapping Henry's hand in both of his, the reunion done, it was down to business. Henry brought Carrier up to speed talking loud over the increasing wind. He wanted to remain in control of the case and not have it yanked away in transit by a local authority. So, Henry hadn't disclosed the whole situation. Stephen Knightly's house was only a few miles into town. After the briefing, Carrier swung his six foot bulk into the driver's seat of the cruiser, twitched his broad moustache back and forth as he set his mouth, and turned on the siren. Morning traffic through downtown could be thick.

* * *

Leonard watched Knightly walk away down the block and gain speed in his steps. At the end of the block, he took a narrow dirt path between a pair of three story wood frames with perennial gardens overfilling their white pickets. His bulk crammed the darkened pathway for only a few seconds, blotting out the sun at the far end, and then light burst back into the pathway as he cleared the plant made tunnel. Even with the restricted sightline, Leonard could see a field of tall green grass and the elevated dirt of a railway in the near distance. The wind was really starting to howl. Knightly was determined to finish his exercise even if he got soaked doing it. The skies were a dense gray and had began to drizzle.

Moving the Hansen's Honda for what Leonard hoped would be the last time before committing the act, he raced down Illinois Avenue, repositioning for the kill, and trying to think of another name. He didn't even notice the small white cube truck and the two men inside it staring at him as they passed by going the other direction.

He'd always been able to assume an identity close to his victims. Steffon Queen, Stephen Kink, Stevie Knight, Kingsley Steen. Yes, that

221

would work, Kinglsey Steen. He'd be a wealthy Englishman enroute to tour the Northeast. Cheerio, Good day Governor. Pleased to meet ya. A case of the Wogglies says ya. Well, we'll just have to take the nip off the morning for ya. Take away the warbles. Wouldn't want to ruin your day but I've got to run mind ya sir and you've me knicker in a bind. Nothing that another fifteen grand wouldn't cure though. Hate to hit and run...

Leonard laughed at how funny he could be. Another motorist, a pink haired lady on her way to morning coffee with her widowed girlfriends, pulled alongside him at a left hand turn and thought, What a nice looking young man, and so happy too.

After moving his car, he found a shaded overhang of bougainvillea creating a secluded spot up street from Knightly's entry point back onto the paved road by his business address. Knightly skipped over the railroad tracks and skimmed a stone along its metal rails like a ten year old passing the day. He stretched his arms above himself and then bent forward to touch his toes three times. Resuming his pace, he strode into the grass and seventy-five yards later reached the black top.

Leonard eased his foot from the brake pedal to the gas and let the car crawl forward. He had donned a black wig to conceal his identity. It wasn't even on straight, making him look like a petty criminal trying to get through customs.

At the far end of the block a battered Dodge Caravan backed out of a driveway and headed his way. It careened across the center line and then righted itself.

Success happens when opportunity meets preparation.

At the other end of the block a Yugo Cube truck came around the corner and spotting Leonard's Honda headed straight for him.

Leonard let his car creep a little further into the street but not enough to draw interest. He was only looking one direction and never even noticed the two men in the Yugo aiming for him.

The driver of the caravan wasn't noticing Leonard either. He had a brown mutt of a dog upright in the passenger seat drawing his attention away from where it should be concerned. His unshaven face was dipping over his right shoulder as he rubbed the dog's head and ears.

Leonard coasted further, till the nose of his car was in the intersection fully exposed and barely inched his tires to the left, expediting a speedy escape. Stephen Knightly was on the mark a mere fifty yards down the road pausing on the gravel shoulder to enact a few deep knee bends with his arms pointing straight out towards the grass field, the road at his back.

Byron Smythe drove the Caravan. He'd been drinking even though it was still early in the day. He usually drank. He'd drunk himself into three other Driving Under the Influence altercations and today was going to be no different. His dog, Sandy, a long haired golden collie whom Mrs. Smythe hated and therefore wouldn't spend the day alone with, was mischievously bouncing in the truck, jumping from the front passenger seat onto the rear bench and back, tossing a hacky sack to and fro, playing catch with himself.

The two Bosnians in the Yugo were barreling down on Leonard, their intent clear had he been watching. They were going to park in front of him preventing his escape and then they'd pounce. The oncoming Caravan was still far enough away and Leonard's car was on the pavement but they believed they could squeeze between the two and trap him.

But Leonard mistakenly popped his clutch and perilously jutted much farther forward into the oncoming traffic lane than the Bosnians expected and caught the front end of the truck, spinning it into traffic away from Leonard, creating a gap between the two vehicles. The Sausage Kings were thrown off guard and saw a new dilemma.

Smythe was driving in a less than perfect capacity. He was reaching back trying to get the hacky sack away from Sandy who continued on as if this was part of the same game. Nicking an edge of the hacky from the teeth of Sandy, Smythe raised his swill riddled head back to where his attention should have been all along.

It happened in a flash. Smythe raised his head and saw Leonard's car jutting into his path. And the front end of the Cube truck blocking his path. Swerving to the right, his van's tires left a rubber trail on the blacktop surface as he barely rubbed with Leonard's Honda but caught a thick section of the Cube trucks left fender, ripping off the bumper and causing one its tires to bust loose from its axle. The Bosnians were thrown against the far side of their cab and slowly it toppled onto its side.

The Caravan veered onto the dirt shoulder and sprayed rocks as Smythe tried to correct his course and over steered, shooting himself back across both lanes and onto the left hand shoulder. If he'd been sober, he probably could have stopped at this point. He would have thought to decelerate, remove his foot from the gas pedal, pump the brakes, anything besides accelerating, which is exactly what he did.

Later, he would tell the police he tried to stop. He even thought he'd stepped on the brake, perhaps there was something wrong with the van, a mechanical defect. Surely he didn't mean to do what he'd done.

What he did was over steer a second time while flooring the gas pedal. He sped up to full throttle velocity and slung himself out of his course correction like the Apollo 13 lunar module sling-shotting around the moon.

Stephen Knightly was deep in his third set of knee bends before he heard the approaching vehicle. He heard the crash and watched in disbelief, thinking he was safe when the van swerved to the right and caught the Meat Truck. Surely this would slow it down. When it swung over to the other side of the road and then headed towards him instead of stopping he briefly thought it was going to power slide into a row of weathered mailboxes. In its final track he realized there was no time to react. He froze like Bambi facing Godzilla.

It was Sandy who saved his life. The golden Collie took a retrieving snipe back at the hand of its owner in an attempt to regain the hacky sack, but in the entire misfiring Sandy bit the hand that fed her, catching Byron Smythe's hand across three fingers and causing him to yank the wheel away to the right as he pulled his hand away in pain.

Knightly was sideswiped instead of plowed under. He was thrown to the right as Sandy's door panel pushed him like a linebacker wearing a sheet metal uniform. He landed in not a single heap, but a series of skids and thuds.

Down the street, sitting in his borrowed blue car, Leonard watched the action unfold like a homemade movie. The swerving van tried to correct it once, twice as it hit the funny looking delivery truck, and then collided with the author whose works would soon be worth three to four times their normal amounts in bookstores and on websites everywhere. He saw Stephen Knightly fly in a haphazard fashion over the grassy field Knightly had just Power Walked across and then faced while doing his exercises. His body found the only tree in the nearly empty space, wrapped around it like a towel and stopped, shaking free the last remnants of the morning dew and a single leaf free. Three seconds later, while he was still lying there showing no signs of moving, Leonard slowly put his car in reverse and quietly fled the scene.

Dogs were feeding at the back of the white truck, its sausages spilled all over the road and the drivers cursing at the mutts in a language of Eastern origins.

* * *

Agent Patrick Henry and US Marshall Robert Carrier were crossing over the Kenduskeag River in the middle of downtown Bangor when the radio call sounded.

"Vehicular collision. Multiple vehicles. Pedestrian involved. Repeat. Pedestrian Struck by a vehicle on Texas Ave. Nearest Officer please respond." It was a woman's voice from the Bangor Police Dispatch. Crackle sounded and then was broken by a deep male response.

"Confirm Central. This is car 182. I am in the vicinity. Approximate time of arrival 2 minutes. Give address."

"Address confirmed" said the woman through a din of static, "57 Texas Ave. Enter from Florida Ave off Illinois. Over and Out."

"Roger."

Henry looked over at Carrier who set a crooked frown under his moustache as he stepped on the gas. Carrier flipped a switch on the dash to release a wail from the siren and the lights spun their blue and red splashes, pushing the traffic out of the way.

As they swam through the school of cars, ambulance lights blinked to life ahead, appearing from around a corner. They chased it to the scene arriving six minutes after car 182, in time to watch the paramedics take over from the officer delivering first aid. Waiting impatiently, as the officer drank from a bottle of water, his feet hanging sideways out the front door of his patrol car, Marshall Carrier showed his badge and asked the question.

"Is he still alive?"

"Ya, sure. He's alive don't you know," replied the officer in a thick New England brogue. "He's banged up pretty bad. Mayhap he might not make it through the night. But he'll not leave my watch without a breath in him." He poured a handful of water into the cup of his palm and splashed it across his brow."

The paramedics only applied the most immediate of attention to Knightly before loading him onto a gurney and sliding him into the back of the ambulance, while the officer talked to Carrier and Henry about the stamina of the man and commented on the girth of Knightly's frame cushioning his fall.

"Where are they taking him?" asked agent Henry.

"To County, ayuh."

"What about the other driver. The one who hit him?"

The officer took another swig of his water, polishing off the last drop and then used his sleeve to wipe his mouth. Regaining his breath, the officer said. "A drunkard. Man with so many moving violations it's a shame he could still buy gas."

Off to the left the overturned truck still lay on its side most of the dogs held back by Nando swinging a tire iron at them while Stefan talked into a cell phone explaining the situation to their boss in an apologetic tone. On the right the caravan was leaking fluid through its dented fenders, creating a puddle in the middle of the road.

"Are these the only cars involved? There wasn't anyone else?" Henry was incredulous. Leonard had to be involved. It was too big a coincidence for him not to be.

"Smythe, the drunk, claims there was another car that forced him to swerve and caused the accident. Not that I believed him much.

The man has a lie for every day of the week he drinks and that makes eight. But when those foreigners said the same thing I came to believe him, I did."

"Tell me about this other car," said Henry.

"All I've got is a color. Smythe wasn't too aware ya see and those immigrants over yonder say he came out of nowhere. Hard to understand them too if ya know what I mean, yah." The officer was standing up, putting his hat back on his head as he prepared to go help with the crowd control. "It was blue dey say." Then he walked toward the perimeter baying, "Move along," to the small crowd of onlookers who had waded into the street from their homes. "There's nothing to see here now. Move along."

Nothing to see and not much to go on.

37
From Milo's Lips

I WAS WATCHING GOOD MORNING AMERICA when Charlie Gibson broke off Diane Sawyer's in-depth reporting of the recent merging of High Tech companies with established media corporations; ABC joining Disney, Westinghouse with CBS, and AOL with Time Warner.

"Excuse me Diane," he said. "A special news bulletin just came in." The camera panned over to Gibson sitting at a desk with his fingers grasping a few assorted printouts which he kept referring to as he spoke. A picture of the famous author hung over his left shoulder. "The author Stephen Knightly has just been involved in a gruesome automobile accident while he was walking to work this morning. Knightly was on the side of the road when a van skidded into him, throwing him some thirty feet before his crumpled body slammed into a tree. Even as I speak, he is being rushed to the emergency room now of Bangor County Medical Center in Central Maine. His condition is considered serious. His spokesperson has said, Stephen is a fighter and if anyone can survive this, he will."

I drove to work in a trance; the thoughts swimming in my head splashing all about like kids playing at the YMCA pool, each one drowning the other.

Leonard had to be involved in this. There was no one else who had so much to gain. The Book was gone, headed east, fomenting a desecration on the literary world. The number one author in several lifetimes was now the victim of a heinous act. I had to call Detective

Daily. But, what would I say? I didn't know any more than what the news services had already told me. Plus, she had no obligation to share any knowledge she might have with me anyway, if she had any. Since she'd returned to her work, we'd drifted apart. Apparently our afternoon tryst had not been enough to cement a lasting relationship.

At CelebrityBooks.com, it was a morning where everyone worked. Jill was at the register, counting, so there'd be plenty of change for the day. Milo was in the backroom inputting inventory into the computers. We all talked of the same thing; the news would be rocking the foundations of literati everywhere. After we got the initial shock out of our systems, Jill and Milo asked me what I knew. They felt I had to be somehow included in the circle of informed persons because of my recent activity with Leonard, Daily and 'The Book'. To their disappointment, I was not in the know. I knew nothing more than what they did. Everything else was speculation.

It was Milo, almost two hours into the workday, who came up with the bit of information, conjecture really, nothing more than an educated guess, which moved me to pick up the phone and further my involvement in the case.

Milo began, "So what do you think Leonard will do now?"

"I told you I don't know" I repeated.

"He's got to do something doesn't he? He can't come back here. He's going to want to get out of the country. That's for sure. But where to go? And even if he's got enough money to do what he wants. You can't ever have enough money if you know for sure you're never coming back."

"He's probably got a hundred grand or more cash if he's been as smart saving what he's made as he was making it," I said. Milo's train of thought was intriguing me. I was on board wondering where this track would lead. "But maybe not. If he did want more money, where do you think he would he get it?"

"He could rob a couple Seven-Elevens on the way to the airport," stated Milo, leaning back in his computer chair and folding his hands behind his head, forgetting about his work.

"Too risky," I said playing along. "He wouldn't want to jeopardize his freedom for such a small reward. He'd have to get as much as possible in a single stop, with no danger of being spotted. He left here with just a few what he cold carry. He even left his car behind in Utah. The only thing he has, as far as I know, of any value is Stephen's Dump Truck and you can't sell that just anywhere."

"What about the high bidders?"

Milo and I looked at each other in silence for a standing three count, then he jerked his hands from behind his head and rifled through a drawer near the monitor at his desk. "Here it is," he exclaimed, locking onto the list.

I looked over his shoulder and we checked off the ones Leonard couldn't possibly conduct business with.

"He can't sell it to Stephen Knightly himself, because he's now incapacitated," I said.

"He can't sell it to Bert's Books in Bangor because there's too much chance they'd just as soon turn him in. I'm sure that Bert's is in good standing with the Knightly's and wouldn't jeopardize their friendship." Milo said this matter of fact, as if he'd had to choose between friends and money before in the past.

"The individual bidders aren't geographically convenient," I said. "That leaves..."

We said it together, "Baughmann's."

I got my little black book and called Detective Susan Daily on her cell phone. Presently, she was back in the City of Commerce.

"Daily here," she said on the second ring.

"Detective Daily," I opened in a rush, "this is Xanthe Anthony, from Celebrity Books in Palm Springs."

"I know who you are Xanthe," she stopped me, "but before you ask, let me say that I can't say anything. I honestly don't know anything. I just heard myself on the news a few hours ago and I know it's gotta be our boy. But I don't know more than that."

I hurried on. "I know too. He's the only one who could or would do this. It'd be too convenient for there to be two book psychos." I paused to gather breath. "But I think I know where he's going now."

"I'm listening."

The Author Murders

I told her what Milo and I had surmised. Walked her down the tracks of our thoughts, not only where we thought he was going now, but why none of the other high bidders would do.

Daily agreed with our speculation on Leonard's choice of fence. He'd need someone who could conduct a large book transaction in cash or have accessibility to a bank. He could generate enough identification to cash a check of any size.

"There's one more thing Detective," I said.

"Yes."

I gathered my wits. This was a bold move but I had to take a chance. Women like Susan Daily didn't just walk into my life every day. "I know you're the great detective and all. I'm sure you'll figure this one out just like you did the (memory hook) Hooded Bandit, but I have to ask you something. I want to go out with you. I'd like to take you out with nothing to do with this case. Can we go to dinner, share a coffee, work out sometime?"

Silence. She didn't respond. More silence. This wasn't good.

"Xanthe," she said. "I like you. I like you a lot. But," and this is when I knew she'd sink my boat. This is when I knew she was only being polite in all her prior remarks. "I don't want to go out with you. You want a Police Commission and I see that as citizen micro-management. In your heart, you think all police are corrupt and I'm a second generation cop. You want protection, security and safety but you also want neatness, efficiency and lawfulness. But the truth is sometimes you have to break the law to protect it and that'll always be a problem for you."

"Then why'd you sleep with me?"

"You're cute and I was on vacation."

"I was a suspect."

"You were cleared and a lot of good cops vouched for you. I believed them. But we'll never work as a couple, not in the long run."

"No you got me wrong," I protested. She didn't know me.

"I don't think so Xanthe," she finalized. "I've got to go. You did good work coming up with this destination. But that's all. I'll pass the information onto Agent Henry. It's his case now," and she hung up.

38
New York, New York

AGENT PATRICK HENRY HUNG UP HIS CELL PHONE with renewed determination. He was sitting in the passenger seat of Marshall Robert Carrier's patrol car watching him eat an early chicken burger lunch in the parking lot of a Wendy's.

"Can you drive me to New York?" Henry asked.

"It's not really my jurisdiction," replied Carrier, his cheeks bulging with processed poultry.

"I thought the entire U.S. was your jurisdiction?"

Carrier swallowed, thumping on his chest to help the food down, "I guess if we were in hot pursuit, we wouldn't want to give up chase."

As they backed out of their parking space and screeched out onto the street Agent Henry flicked the lights and siren on.

* * *

While I was back in Palm Springs licking my wounds from Detective Daily's rejection, Leonard was doing his best to maintain a steady southbound trek towards the Big Apple. His goal: to make the drive in as close to seven hours as he could. That meant no more than one stop for gas and limiting himself on food and bathroom breaks. Not an impossible task. He reminded himself that P.O.W.'s often were denied relief for far greater periods of time and in the very near future he'd be on a beach in Costa Rica, enjoying the warm comforts of a young waiter delivering colored drinks in tall glasses dotted with small umbrella's.

How strange that only a few years back he'd dreamed of a young waitress. Life, she is a changing again. Maybe it was time to revisit his former gender preference.

In Manhattan, he'd meet the dealer willing to pay his price for the now infamous book of Stephen Knightly's early writings. A book Knightly sought himself, but of course you can't sell a book to the man you just attempted to kill. He thought he had killed him, but on the drive he'd heard a radio newsman report that Stephen Knightly was still alive although in serious condition in a Bangor Hospital. The lack of demise was a bit of a disappointment, but still an event capable of sky-rocketing speculation on Knightly manuscripts.

He let his mind drift back to the road, a ribbon of asphalt unwinding to a new horizon at the crest of every hill. It was a gallant day; one of sunshine and soft breezes, tall trees and blue skies. The radio filled the car with loud music. Wanting to keep the adrenaline rushing, Leonard was blasting the rock and roll of a new girl to hit the charts, Alanis Morissette. To Leonard's ears she was blasting her lungs out with the sounds of his conscience:

By the second refrain he'd switch the lyrics to satisfy his own cause:

> *I'm sane but I'm overworked*
> *I'm lost and I'm hopeless, baby*
> *I don't care and I want a rest*
> *I'm free with a passport*
> *I can cheat and I can fight*
> *And what it all comes down to*
> *Is that no one's got me figured out just yet*
> *Well I've got one book in my backpack*
> *And in my hand is a Ruger*

Leonard continued his solo performance, chuckling at his own humor, as he calmly drove down the Eastern seaboard on I-95 heading towards the biggest deal of his life.

* * *

On the same interstate, a hundred and fifty miles behind, Agent Patrick Henry and Federal Marshall Robert Carrier pushed the engine of their Plymouth Gran Fury beyond all reasonable means. It was a dated vehicle for police work, having lived longer than for the purpose it was originally created. The speedometer had spun the hundred thousand mark three times over. It was the last of a breed of American iron and holding strong. The wailing of its siren was already grating on the ears of Agent Henry, who wasn't used to hearing a siren at all. His normal modus operandi was to be undercover until he so desired to alert the populace to his presence. But speed was of the essence. He figured Leonard would not want to drive too fast, so it came down to a fifth grade math problem:

If a car leaves Bangor, Maine traveling at 60 miles an hour and takes seven hours to reach its destination, how fast does a second car have to travel to arrive at the same location in two hours less time before the first car? Agent Henry posed this question to Carrier.

Carrier responded," That's easy. It's about 80 miles an hour. We got to increase our speed by about 25 per cent. See, you take the total distance and subtract by an equivalent for the amount of time lost. Then we're equal. So we have to go at least 80 miles an hour."

While Carrier worked the mathematics out, Henry was studying a map. "But that still just makes us arrive at the same time. We have to get there before him and what if there's traffic?"

Carrier pondered this for a moment then said, "You're right," and the Plymouth spat more fury as they fed it more road. They hastened their quest for a dozen miles more and then Henry made a request.

"Bobby," he said, growing more reacquainted with Marshall Carrier, "I need to make a phone call, two actually, and I need to turn off the siren so I can hear. You mind?"

"No," carrier didn't mind. "But I don't want to slow down. We'll just have to take that chance."

39
Baughmann's Books

Geoff Greggory was happy in his job as a rare book dealer. As chief appraiser and purchaser for the number one procurer of rare tomes in the country he had an auspicious position. He was capable of walking into any home or library and spotting a rarity with the blink of an eye. It was a far cry from his hearts endeavor of being the literary master he'd dreamed of when graduating from Leicester University, in England, back in 1965 whilst he'd tried to write several novels only to be turned down in due course. At the time, he credited it to the fact most of the agents and publicists were grads of Cambridge and Oxford, and therefore he was unworthy of their praise. Years later, after moving to the states, he'd succeeded in publishing a treaty on the subject of binding materials in 18th century books. It was dry work. But he'd developed an expertise in the subject after earning a living working in the New York Public Library rare works department.

His publication had caught the attention of a Mr. Fenickle at Baughmann's books, who maintained the stores reference library. He'd asked Greggory to come and have a chat, remarking on his interest in similar fields. The conversation ended with a job offer as one of Mr. Fenickle's assistants and the rest as they say, is history.

Today was to be one of Greggory's rare days of seeing a truly remarkable artifact. It would end with the procuring of a rarity of modern literature, a one of a kind binding bearing witness to the early works of America's favorite living versifier. Many dealers would begin that sentence with 'Hopefully.' But Mr. Greggory was one to never put his faith in hope. Instead he absolutely believed in the divine provenance of his acute procurity; a word he'd made up himself.

The item and its bearer were due to arrive in just a few short hours. Greggory had prepared a room called the Lounge, on the third floor of the building. It was a replica of times gone past; red hewn oak swirled upwards from the foot claws of couches and chairs to meet crushed velvet and paisley set adrift on frilled edges hanging down from the cross beamed ceiling. Carpets floated on the glossy polished wood floor surface resembling islands and paintings of renowned masters hung on the walls like windows to another time. Between two high backed leather chairs was a table made by the brother of Paul Revere. Here would be where Greggory would entertain Mr. Leonard Beschloss, who had learned long ago negotiations for the rarities he trafficked in were often best handled in a setting which implied the coveted item would be even more dearly treated in this home than it was in its last.

He was in the room now, polishing the silver tea set he would serve from to its highest luster when a middle aged secretary peeped her head into the room.

"Mr. Gregory," she said, "There's a phone call for you."

"I'll take it in here," he said motioning towards what appeared to be a museum piece from the Smithsonian made of black metal, resting on a nickel hook. He spoke into the dark microphone cone mounted on the wall and lifted the earpiece to the side of his head.

"Hello."

The instructions Mr. Greggory were given changed his mood demonstrably. There would be no pot of gold at the end of today's rainbow. It wasn't that he disbelieved Agent Henry. When it came to rare art or books, it was common for pieces to have a certain criminal provenance. It was just that, well, he didn't want to accept the situation lightly.

* * *

For the longest time, Marshall Robert Carrier kept his mouth shut about how they should approach the suspect once he was identified in New York. But as the duo saw the road signs become proliferated with landmark names, the impending need forced the issue. He told agent Henry they needed to seek help. But agent Henry needed to satisfy his own apprehensions.

"I want the bust. I need it Bobby," said Henry.

"I know Pat. But I want some back-up. This isn't the best way to get the job done right." Carrier's concern was justified. Their suspect was a nationally known homicidal celebrity in his own right. He'd killed at least four people they could prove and put another in the hospital and it wasn't a big leap of the imagination to assume he'd do it again to prevent his incarceration.

"You're right. The Bureau will take over everything though and I'll be delegated to fill the paperwork out with somebody else's name on top." Henry didn't want any interference he couldn't control.

"How about some of my buddies? You know, we're all Federal officers and I can call in a favor or two." Carrier reached for the shortwave. "I don't want an accident to happen. You know these things don't always go by the book."

"Wait a little while still and then use my cell if you don't mind. I'd like to keep this out of the airwaves to minimize any one trying to hone in too early. You know what I mean."

"All right then," said Carrier as he put the shortwave mike back in its cradle.

40
Best and Worst of Times

AS AGENT PATRICK HENRY AND FEDERAL MAR-
SHALL ROBERT CARRIER were getting caught in traffic on the Tri-
borough bridge crossing from Harlem into Manhattan, Leonard was
putting coins into a parking meter on Madison Avenue, only a block
down from Baughmann's.

Baughmann's Books was what would be considered a historical
site in any other city, a five story red brick building with a 19th century
tan stucco finished bell tower on the very top. Narrow in scope, only
four windows to a floor, it was the remnants of Catholic architecture,
having once been called a Priory in its former life. Today its bottom
floor was renovated with massive display windows outlined in painted
wood and a large sarcophagus style door admitting entrants.

It was squeezed between two of New York's finest examples
of post modern architecture. On the one side was the Sony building,
named for its main tenant and housing many of the burgeoning companies of the new economy like Intel and several wireless networks. It
stood 37 stories tall. On the other side was a building of less reputation,
because it had no significant tenant - it housed mortgage brokers, banks,
import/export traders and even a Penguin's Yogurt, although architec-
turally speaking it was of slightly greater prominence being 42 stories
tall. Both of these buildings were show pieces as far as their architects
were concerned but in New York they were relatively average.

Leonard waded through the crowded sidewalks till he stood in
front of the crypt like door leading into Baughmann's. He checked his

backpack one more time to make sure his book was still with him. He'd checked it five times since leaving the Honda, but once more wouldn't hurt.

* * *

Marshall Robert Carrier was getting anxious. The traffic was thick in the city.

"I think we better hurry," he said trying to spot a way through traffic.

Agent Henry turned left and right in his seat to confirm their predicament. "Do you think it's time to try this?" he said as he flicked on the siren and lights.

"That might help," said Carrier as some of the traffic began to edge towards the curb allowing him to bob and weave through the snarl.

* * *

Stepping through the large wooden portal, more fit for a dungeon than a New York bookstore, Leonard took a deep breath. It was enthralling. Two floors of hard wood shelving filled with books as old as the Bill of Rights greeted him, crying his name from afar of the past. Leather-bound volumes bound so long ago their crisp hide covers shined their glow upon the bare polished floor.

This was in the right place. It felt right. The temperature was cool, as a measure to help protect the longevity of the manuscripts but his blood ran hot with appreciation for the works within. He'd visited Baughmann's website many times in the past year, but it paled in comparison to being here in person. Here stood the original masterworks of the greatest minds of civilization and each was for sale for the right price. Where a sign read FICTION, he knew were books that lesser stores would call Classics. The writings of Dumas, Poe, Dickens, Fielding, Faulkner, Hemingway, and Fenimore Cooper could be found. Somewhere on that shelf was a signed copy of John Steinbeck's The Red Pony, if last week's New York Times Book Review ad was to be believed.

Another book case had the title WORLD AFFAIRS across the top of its highly sculpted head board. On its shelves were the authentic works of Jefferson, Gandhi, Mao, Lincoln, Roosevelt, Marx, Lenin and others. The same advertisement last week offered a signed copy of John F. Kennedy's Profiles in Courage - a book that if Leonard had had an extra $8,000 to spend he'd gladly like to fondle. He briefly wondered if he could manage a trade, plus some cash, of course.

The shelves drawing his eye the strongest were labeled FAN-TASIA and it held the most beloved novels of a genre predating the invention of most modern marvels. The creations of such minds as Verne, Shelley, Stoker, Clarke, Heinlein, Doyle, and somewhere, lost in this case was a rare copy of Tarzan of the Apes signed by Edgar Rice Burroughs. But then again, all the books on these shelves may very well be autographed.

Leonard was interrupted from his gazing by the approach of a tall man in his mid-fifties, the hair at his temples gone the color of Moby Dick. The man extended his hand and placed a smile upon his lips.

"Hello and welcome," he said in a distant sort of British accent, "I'm Geoff Greggory. You must be Mr. Beschloss."

"Yes," said Leonard, trying to remain calm, trying not to give himself away. Best not to belie his anxiousness both for the transaction about to commence and his wantonness to bury his head in the stacks surrounding him. This deal would be his salvation and his escape.

"I've been expecting you," Greggory said, ignoring the young man's obvious fascination with the books in the store and stepping aside to lead Leonard further into the glorious depths of prose. "I gather you brought the item with you?"

A glance was stolen to the backpack slung over Leonard's shoulder. "You could say that." Leonard did not want to play all his cards yet. He had to match his counterpart's patience with his own pacing. "I was wondering if you'd let me peruse some of your books in the Fantasia section?"

"Of course," replied Greggory. The prospect of a trade was always more inviting than a straight on cash transaction. Although compliance with the police would be inevitable, one did not always know how the end of the day would arrive and to what laws one must obey. "Would you like to browse? Did you have something special in mind? Or would you like me to have one of our staff prepare an assortment for you?"

Intriguing, thought Leonard. "That'd be fine," he said, playing the part of the dealer in rare antiquities. "Just four or five of your best would be excellent."

Seizing the moment, Greggory waved his hand over his head and snapped his fingers like a headwaiter calling for a busboy. A young man, barely in his twenties, wearing a shirt style last seen worn in the 1800's by bank tellers with a stiff short collar and darkened sleeves, jumped to attention and listened to his orders. Finished, turning away from the young man, Greggory said, "Please follow me," and he directed Leonard towards an elevator more appropriately called a Lift. Once inside, he slid the Iron Gate closed and ratcheted the brass handle that miraculously instructed UP.

After lurching to a stop on the third floor, Leonard found himself sitting in an amazingly comfortable high-backed leather chair and sipping tea from a china glass, poured from a silver pot. Elegance fit for royalty. The young man in banker's sleeves followed them up less than a minute after they sat. To Leonard's right was placed a short stack of aged, yet mint books. Even the ones that did not have a dust jacket were covered by formed plasticine, as if merely the air would devalue their currency.

"Comfortable Sir?" Greggory asked.

"Yes." Leonard hadn't felt as comfortable in weeks. It seemed all the adventures of his malicious juggernaut were but a well rehearsed performance and this afternoon a much merited reward.

* * *

"I can't put off calling in any longer Pat," stated Marshall Carrier. "We need to get some support over here."

"Make the call Bob. We're almost there." Agent Henry could see the bookstore in its former religious house up the street and he flicked off the siren for a quieter approach. He eyed the area as they approached the front of the store. The building was about five stories tall and squeezed between to taller ones. There was a narrow alley that ran between the building and the one on the left. That meant a minimum of two and maybe three exits, plus there were windows in the front and on the upper floors in the alley. Nearby were a bus station and two subway entrances. Both pedestrian and vehicular traffic was heavy. He should've realized it would be like this and threw himself a silent curse at his ego allowing him to be behind the eight ball. He'd have been better off to call sooner.

As the car skidded to a stop in front of the store he sprang into action, jumping out on his side and shouting back at carrier in the vehicle. "I'm going in before the rest of the badges show up. Unless he's already panicked I should be able to enter as just another customer. Come in as soon as you can." He slammed his door and ran into the store before Carrier could respond.

Inside the store, Agent Henry could not find who he was looking for. In under a minute he'd checked all the corners and peeked into a back room. He felt his wits slipping away from him when a rackety old elevator clattered to a halt and a young man in century old duds stepped out. Henry stepped up to question the man and pulled a picture of Leonard out of his pocket.

"Have you seen this man?"

"Yes, he's up on the top floor."

* * *

"Then let us proceed," instructed Greggory. "May I see the object?" He did not hold out his hand. That would be too presumptive. Although he gathered it was already in the room.

"Certainly." Leonard reached into his bag and pulled out the red leather-bound volume with both hands. He held it outright, like a Supreme Court Justice preparing for a swearing in ceremony.

The Author Murders

Greggory took it with both of his, handling it as gingerly as he would a kitten. His eyes widened in anticipation. He held it at last; the primitive work of a heralded monarch of the intelligentsia. Its recent personal chronicles adding to its import. "I have to ask. How did you come by this?"

Leonard had wanted to tell the tale for some time. From the stacks laid for his amusement on his left, he picked up the book on top. It was a copy of Dagon by H.P. Lovecraft. He casually flipped open the cover and saw the price of $6500 penciled on the inside of the frontispiece. Carefully he thumbed past a few more pages until he found the copyright - 1917. The book was immaculate; unlike anything he'd ever held before. The print within was from a hard press, made of inks no longer in use, from such sources as lead and earthy substances, not the chemicals of modern publishing. It emanated a musty smell, like something that had been buried and dug back up decades later. To him it was as rare as one of the Dead Sea Scrolls were to the Vatican. Priceless, yet it had a price. It was available if he wanted it. Before he let his desire overtake him he returned it to the stack and pulled the one out from beneath it.

"I made the book myself," Leonard lied. It was easier to lie if he only ventured a little from the truth. So he inserted himself into the story where Tracey belonged. Besides, if he admitted it was stolen, then this shark of an Englishman would offer considerably less money for it. "I was a library assistant at Knightly's University, where he later taught. He was already becoming famous and I realized the value of his college writings. It was easy. He was teaching at his own Alma Mater. The materials were readily available. Funny, later that year, I was asked to help clear out the very same material and archive it at the Friends of the Library headquarters. I'm thankful I acted when I did."

Greggory inspected Stephen's Dump Truck as Leonard spun his web. He thumbed the pages hoping for the slightest crack of the pages, a spot where a reader pried it a little too wide trying to read the words in the gutter. No marks on the margins. Not even a breadth near the title page, where there's usually the most wear. In the front, just as promised was the page with Stephen Knightly's signature boldly slashed across the wide middle in dark black script, legible and stark. But a flaw caught Greggory's eye. There was but one flaw to diminish the value: the signed page where Knightly himself creased a corner on the signature page.

"This page is bent." He held it out from himself as if looking at it more would magnify the blasphemy of such a magnificent piece.

"By the hand of the creator himself," Leonard said as he read the title of the next book in his short stack; the Strange Case of Dr. Jekyll and Mr. Hyde by Robert Louis Stevenson - old enough to be an original copy from the 1800's.

"Mr. Knightly himself bent this?" The provenance just raised a notch. Leonard could tell by the inflection in Greggory's voice.

"Of course he did."

"When?"

"This morning," Leonard acted unconcerned, "before the accident."

Aah, and that is why the police are involved. The elevator clanked into operation. It was coming up.

"Are you expecting someone?" asked Leonard, his heartbeat ticking faster.

"Probably just one of the staff," replied Greggory, standing and carrying the book to the window, letting the daylight help him inspect its quality and forcing Leonard to look away from the elevator towards the back of the room. Then to redirect Leonard's concentration Greggory asked, "Do you like the items we selected for you?"

Leonard looked down the spines, "They're very nice," running his finger over their titles: Dagon, Jekyll and Hyde, Dracula, Dune, and Conan the Invincible. While Dune was most likely a First Edition, it was also the least valuable of the bunch - a shill thrown in to see if Leonard knew his salt.

The elevator door creaked open.

"I would like to make you an offer on this," declared Greggory.

"My price has already been stated," asserted Leonard, "and it's final."

"I'm afraid you'll have to take that up with my friend," said

244

Greggory, allowing his eyes to shift over Leonard's shoulder.

Following Greggory's gaze, Leonard spun around and saw a black man wearing a fine Italian suit. He was a dark messiah and looked as out of place in this room as a flood. He had one hand stretched out in front of himself like a blocker approaching the offensive line and with the other hand he was stiffly pointing a revolver towards the floor.

"Mr. Beschloss," he said, "I've been looking for you. I'm Agent Patrick Henry of the FBI."

Reacting with the alacrity of a juggler, Leonard stood just long enough to gain his footing. Then he wiped his stack of perusals into the air towards Greggory who was so taken aback he tried to catch them all. An impossible task if there ever was one. He grabbed at the spraying bunch catching, one, two three of them, but Greggory lost his hold on the Knightly book which Leonard leaped at and was quick enough to snag after a single bounce on one of its corners.

Leonard ducked around his leather high-backed chair and kicked it in Henry's direction, catching the agent in the shin while snatching up his backpack and repositioned himself behind the kneeling Greggory. The purchaser of rare commodities had splayed himself like an idiotic abbot kneeling on Sunday, while trying to save his wares. He'd missed one, the Conan hardback, which landed hard enough to jar several of the pages loose from their fastening.

Leonard's hand quickly shook off the backpack and withdrew a pistol He gripped it forcibly while aiming at the man in front of himself. He'd used it many times before. "Get up," he said to Greggory, the nonchalance gone from his voice. When the book dealer was slow to respond, he kneed him in the ribs and repeated himself. "I said get up."

Geoffrey Greggory stood slowly not wanting to let go of his hold on the volumes he'd rescued. When he was halfway up, Leonard grabbed him around the throat and tugged him backwards, pulling him off balance and causing the books to slide from his grasp. Dagon landed wide open and face down, its front and rear covers spread wide.

Henry still had one hand in front of himself. He'd tried to rush Leonard during the mayhem but was unable to make up for the glitch of connecting his shin with the chair. Now, he held his gun at eye level.

"Don't make this worse Leonard," said Henry, not backing down.

Leonard laughed. "Worse. How could this be worse?"

"You could be dead. You might not walk out of this room."

"Hey, if you haven't noticed Nelson Mandela, I've got a gun too." Leonard waved it in the air for emphasis and then poked it into the temple of his hostage Greggory.

"Don't shoot," pleaded Greggory. "Not in this room. The art in here alone is worth more than any of your life insurances. Plus you might hit a book."

Great, thought Henry. The man's life is in danger and he's more interested in protecting his library. What kind of nuts am I dealing with?

"You heard the man," said Leonard. "Don't make me shoot. We might mistakenly take whole chapters out of history. Literally." He backed up Greggory who was kept on the rear of his heels to prevent any gaining of leverage. In this position Greggory's height was a disadvantage to Leonard's shorter stature.

Reaching the window, Leonard looked outside. He saw a segment of New York's skyline and only a fragment of the street below, but nothing directly under the window except a rusting metal fire escape balcony. That was all he needed. "Perhaps we should take this outside," he suggested. "But first, I want you to do something for me Agent Henry." He said the name with disdain.

"What?"

"I want you to put down your gun. It makes me nervous."

"I can't do that Leonard," Agent Henry moved a step closer.

"Oh, I think you can," Leonard proffered and then pointed the pistol at Agent Henry and then back at Geoff Greggory. "Or do I have to remind you who has the hostage?"

Mexican standoff.

"OK, OK," said Henry laying his pistol on the ground.

"Kick it to me."

Henry did.

"Now, I want you to get back into that elevator again." He nodded his head towards the capsule at the far end of the room.

Leonard backed him up one step at a time. When Henry was finally within its confines Leonard gave instructions, "Grab the handle and bend it out of shape. Pull it sideways so it won't work."

Henry put a hand on the lever.

"I warn you. Don't make me shoot up this room. Although it won't be books I'll be hurting in here." Leonard pointed the gun at Henry's head. Greggory struggled futilely, merely trying to keep from choking. Henry did as he was told.

"Now pull the gate shut."

Henry pulled the gate shut with a scrape and a clang. His suspect was outside his reach again. Another victim would suffer for his mistake of judgment. He should have had Carrier in here with him. Maybe he'd still make it in time. "You'll never make it. The exits are covered. I didn't come alone."

"I'll take that chance." Leonard raised the gun and fired a shot into the box holding Agent Henry. He caught Henry in the chest, the force of the bullet pushing him around face first into the back wall of the elevator. Slowly, he slid down the polished framework, darkening the bright wood and polished brass with a red stain.

"Dear God," said Greggory, his face shading a lighter hue of pale. He was tugged backwards again, towards the window. Leonard directed him to open it.

"I can't," said Greggory.

"I said open it," shouted Leonard.

"I can't. It's painted and nailed shut," insisted Greggory, noncompliance exacerbating his fear. He'd never seen a person shot or killed, except on television. And he was pleading for his life, "This is a rectory of literature man. We have to take some precautions."

Leonard seemed to ponder this. On a table near the window was what appeared to be a copy of the Maltese Falcon encased in glass? But why would a copy be encased in glass? He threw Greggory on the floor. "Rip down those curtain cords," he said pointing at the drapes alongside the window, "and tie yourself up." He slid the glass casing off the Falcon and lifted it by the neck, preparing to swing it like a bat.

Greggory went into shock. He'd been taken hostage and witnessed a shooting. He'd held a treasure in his grasp that shouldn't even exist and seen some of his own best books tossed around like playing cards. He was frightened and he was furious. He stood up to his full height and grabbed the curtains in both hands, pulling fiercely, trying to make them strike Leonard as they fell. They came down hard in Leonard's face but he backed up quickly, regaining his composure before Greggory could strike. From his new position he missed what Greggory saw in the window.

"You piece of..." In his anger, Leonard couldn't even finish his sentence. "I oughtta." He lifted his gun, taking aim at Greggory's face.

With a crash the window burst inward, glass spouted forth like a fountain, temporarily blinding Leonard who fired a shot. Federal Marshall Robert Carrier threw himself into the book dealer, pushing him out of the way as a bullet whizzed past Greggory's head.

Carrier was a trained professional. His weapon already drawn, he returned fire and caught Leonard in the hip, knocking him around as if kicked by a bull.

But Leonard wasn't through. He raised himself on one arm, lifting the other which held his pistol. He got off a shot catching Carrier in the ass. It was like a bee sting, from the grand daddy of all bees.

Carrier was down but not yet out either. The shot in the rump threw him forward while he was rolling Greggory out of the way. Continuing his roll, he reeled onto his side and fired a second shot narrowly missing Leonard and shattering tanother window into toothy glass shards behind him.

Biting his curled lip in anger, Leonard dove behind the classical chair where only moments ago he thought he'd been onto his greatest sale. Sticking his gun between the legs of the chair he fired the rest of his bullets in a spat of fury catching Carrier in the hand, the gut and twice in the chest. He kept pulling the trigger for three more dry clicks before completing his spasmodic raid.

The room fell silent as the smoke cleared. Leonard stayed ducked behind the chair in a ball. He was shot and hurt but he couldn't stay. He had to get up. Mustering all the wits he could find he slowly stood enough to peer over the top of the chair. Sirens were blaring in the distance.

Geoff Greggory was hiding behind the second chair which he had pulled up against the far wall. Henry was hurt but alive and he began shouting.

"Greggory are you alright."

"Yes, Yes. I'm fine," scared up Greggory.

"Check on Carrier," ordered Henry. "See if he's OK."

Leonard was reloading his pistol and challenged Greggory with a stare.

"I think not," appraised Greggory.

Leonard saw the books on the floor in a mish mashed pile, the short stack of great works he'd wanted to trade for and on top of the pile was his book Stephen's Dump Truck. It's bright red cover matching the tide of blood he'd brought upon his hobby. He'd spilled more in his wake across the continent than he'd ever intended and on the floor of this very room was the culmination of his efforts. But the past was over. His moment had come. He reached for it with a shaky hand, it was his chalice, his one ring, his mantra and he had to leave with it, now.

Agent Henry saw Leonard reaching for the book and was ready. He'd had a second gun hidden in an ankle holster. This time he took a steadier aim and clipped Leonard in the shoulder, making the book fly across the room and Leonard to spill wildly backwards.

Geoff Greggory took action and dove for the book, catching it before it smashed onto the floor.

Leonard was hurt badly, he'd been shot twice and in more pain than he'd ever felt. His body throbbed as if parts of him were fish hooks attached to anchors. Still he staggered to his feet and rushed to the window. Grabbing the corner of the paisley curtains, he swung himself through the glass using the curtains as a shield and landed hard on the fire escape as Henry sent another shot pounding into the window frame after him. Leonard staggered doggedly down the escape with the metal clanging as he ran down its rusty steps. One flight down he gathered his strength and drove himself to jump across the alley. The ground was half a football field below. He cleared the cement chasm to another buildings fire escape, broke through a second window and climbed inside.

Agent Henry heard the window break followed by the Whee-oo of sirens. The cavalry had arrived to Baughmann's books and Henry started yelling, "He's on the escape. Check the next building." It was no use. The NYPD and the Federal Marshall's had to take an inside staircase up to the top floor to find the crime scene. By the time they'd arrived Leonard had got away, Geoffrey Greggory was frantic about the state of his books, Marshall Robert Carrier was dead and Agent Patrick Henry's career was in once again in ruins.

Since they'd been kids the game had been played.

     First man, "Oh you want something."
     Second man, "Just what you've always promised."
     First man, "You always were such a baby."
     Second man, "Are you going to give it to me?"
     First man, "Baby, baby, baby."

PART III

41
Festival of Books

MONTHS PASSED AND WINTER ROLLED INTO SPRING.

I made plans to maximize several different issues at one time. For the longest time I had wanted to retain a stable of high caliber authors to make Celebrity Books a real celebrity bookstore. I also wanted to take my Villagefest book booth to the next level. And third, I wanted my store to become at least regionally recognizable amongst the ranks of famous bookstores.

Even before I got involved in the Author Murders I'd been hearing about a premier book fair to be held at the UCLA campus. The Los Angeles Times Festival of Books was being promoted as the greatest book spectacle on the west coast and it hadn't even been held yet. A tide of enthusiasm enveloped me as I thought about what it could be and the impact it could make on my little storefront coming of age. The greatest publishing houses in the country gathering on the west coast at an event to rival all events; my head swam at the possibilities.

I went for broke and spent every dime I had. The booth was $1000 per ten feet of space and I wanted two spaces. It hurt me financially to cough up the dough for it but I figured what the heck – you only go around once. So I had to live on top ramen and macaroni and cheese for a few weeks and not date anyone that wanted me to spend more than five bucks on dollar beer night down at the Village Pub. I told myself it'd be worth it all in the end and if I was wrong it'd make one great sob story about the big one that got away. And if all else failed, in another two months it'd be fire season in the desert. A poor joke if there ever was one. Fire season was what I called the end of June. It seemed there was always some business going up in flames just at the tail end of season and before we hit what I call deep summer. Truth was, I could never light a match to my books. It just wasn't my style.

So instead, I tightened my britches, battened down the hatches, flew the Jolly Roger at full mast and headed to Westwood in a rented Uhaul filled with my best stock.

Milo rode with me and Jill was driving herself, set to show up Saturday morning by 10 am. I had hired on some temporary help who promised to be there about the same time. I closed the store for the two day event planning to go for broke. It was make it or break it time. Even Thom was scheduled to attend and sign his books. The whole team had pitched in to make a go of it. I was proud and scared and thrilled to be doing something, anything to reach for a higher rung on the ladder of success. I had a few aces up my sleeve too.

We went directly to the University of California Los Angeles campus, arriving just before sundown to get the lay of the land. I had never gone to University myself, either to UCLA or any other and if this was to be typical of the quality of surroundings we as a society surround our young minds of tomorrow with I have to admit I was impressed.

The campus buildings were immense structures of stone and brick. They towered above like hallmarks to the men whose minds they'd shaped. I didn't know the entire registry of past graduates, but I thought George Lucas, Albert Einstein, Charles Darwin – OK maybe none of those people went to school here. I chuckled to myself but they were the level of individuals flying through my mind. Actually the only person I knew who'd attended from UCLA was Jim Morrison of the Doors and I wasn't even sure he'd graduated.

I mentioned my thoughts to Milo about Morrison and all he said was, "Cool."

He was taken aback by the layout also.

The Author Murders

We drove the car around the perimeter until we saw a long stretch of blacktop leading up a tree lined drive deep into the heart of the property. The buildings welcomed us in with a cold shoulder. We were on unfamiliar territory. As self-educated as I thought I was, here I felt like an elementary student. One building after another edificed my lack of standing until we finally came to a grassy clearing crossed from corner to corner with wide sidewalks and cornered with large trees, the thickest of which looked like a hundred years ago it had been knocked down and still wouldn't give up growing. It had grown sideways until it had the strength to reach upward a second time. It was an inspirational feat of nature, one which obviously captivated the spirit of the University: Beat us, berate us, call us names – we will not quit in our desire for achievement - even a sapling can become a mighty oak in the face of great opposition.

Once I tore my eyes off the tree I saw our destination. At the far end of the grassy square, between the heralds of architecture was a wide promenade filled with white canopies as far as the eye could see. It was as if the fairs of Arthur had sprung upon a plain. We only needed their colorful pennants to mark which knight owned each tent.

We parked the truck. It looked filthy and stained next to the buildings and tents. We got out and walked around marveling at the largess of where we were about to participate. We walked past row upon row of selling spaces. At each corner we looked down a path of greater immensity, more rows leading between another elliptical of booths stretching far enough that the opposing sides seemed to join together in the distance.

People were setting up. Laborers, tradesmen, dealers, their staff and families were roving about with a purpose that left me lost. Dollies stacked with boxes five high were wheeled about and around corners faster than I could imagine. After walking another dozen stalls I could take it no more.

"I wonder which one is ours," I said aloud more to myself than anyone else.

"Let's see," said Milo. He stopped the next dolly that came by. It was being wheeled about by a young gal, probably a student here, in coveralls wearing her long brown hair in pig tails as a way of keeping herself free to work. "Pardon me. Where do we find which booth is ours?"

She stopped the dolly as if its half dozen boxes were loaded with feathers instead of books, catching the top one from sliding off with a touch of her finger. Then, in a single motion she turned about and pointed back down a side row we'd not noticed and said, "I saw him down there a minute ago, a short round guy with a baseball cap on and carrying a clipboard. If you hurry he won't disappear."

And then disappear she did. We craned our neck to see where she was pointing, a long row like all the others we'd seen, bustling with activity and when we turned around to thank her all we caught was the pant leg of her jeans and the heel of her tennis shoes rounding a corner the other way.

We looked at each other, shrugged and quickstepped it in the direction she'd pointed. Four or five pallets of books later we found our man.

"Celebrity Books…,Celebrity Books..," he mumbled while searching his clipboard of papers for our information. "Ah, here it is." He pulled a piece of paper from the bottom of his stack. It was a photocopied map he'd obviously handed out dozens of times already today. Without waiting for us to ask directions, he quickly circled a spot and said, "You are here," and then with the hesitation of a hummingbird he circled a second spot and said, "This one's yours. Any questions?"

"No. I think I got it," and off we went.

Having paid for two, our booth was ten by twenty with a wide front for display advantages. It had good placement. Not on the main promenade but attached by a significant side street; an artery leading to several of the signing areas and lecture halls. We'd have plenty of traffic once the day got going. At the moment though the sky was darkening fast and there was still much to do.

42
The Help

WE STAYED THE NIGHT AT A HOLIDAY INN just off Hollywood boulevard. It was a bit distant from UCLA but I like Hollywood with all the grit and grime that sticks to the glitter during the day. At night it's bright lights and fame. But when the sun rises, it's just a bunch of people in black leather jackets that need a shave or rehab or worse.

At first light, we grabbed a cup of coffee from the lobby and drove back to the booth and began setting up. Lifting books is hard work. Books are heavy. But I like it and we were having more fun than humans should be allowed. Milo understood retail with a natural inclination and he took little direction to complete our tasks. By the time the sun had cut through the morning dew we were ready for the initial waves of customers and they were right on cue.

The early birds wanted first peek at the stock. They were the dealers, book scouts and most habitual of collectors, a strange breed of human. I had caught the bug myself at an early age and had quite the affixation for books but some people seemed to let all else in their lives go to pot for the written word.

I was talking to a man who had taped his glasses together and tied his dirty slacks together with a belt worn out three notches past his belt loop when Jill arrived. The crowd was bustling all around us. I was taking money in hand over fist on both sides of me and handling a serious conversation with my scrappily dressed five dollar customer who was bestowing upon me all the knowledge I never wanted to know on J.A. Jance and how she writes in both Arizona and the Northwest because she lives in both locations and sometimes she stops in Palm Springs, didn't I know, and perhaps could I contact her and have her stop by and sign a bunch of books during her overnight stay, or if that's not possible could I get her address so I could, on this man's behalf, mail her a couple of dozen books for him to get signed by her, or perhaps she had some bookplates already signed, or perhaps,...

Jill saw my dilemma and rolled her eyes at me in a He's one of them glance as she stowed her purse in the bottom box of a short stack of boxes under one of the tables and then she started helping customers. Right to work, that's her way. Jill was great.

I cut him off. "I don't know Miss Jance, nor am I making any inquiries to her on your behalf," I finally snorted.

He huffed back at me like a monkey being refused his banana and then, as if we'd never sparred with words, asked, "Do you have any signed Tony Hillerman?"

"Over there on the right," I pointed and he trundled off.

With Jill and Milo now handling the customers I gave myself a break to scout a few stalls for my own treasures. Most of the stalls were really of no interest to me personally. The one where a new author set up his or her own booth to market a metaphysical book or a children's tale or a travel guide I'm sure would find its customers. It just wasn't going to be me. What I liked was hardcover, older and usually had a fanciful cover showing either dragons or spaceships. I found a booth with a neat section in the back and perused. Fifteen minutes and $85 dollars later I left with a signed Brian Lumley, Necroscope; and a Joe Haldeman, The Hemingway Hoax. I turned to the left to seek another used book booth and got a glimpse. Fifty yards a way I saw a man in his early thirties of average height, slight build, wearing a red ballcap who looked like a murderer I knew. Then he was gone. I doubted myself; a coincidence. No he wouldn't; would he? I lunged forward trying to slip through the crowd like a jogger trying to go up the down escalator. By the time I got to where I'd seen him he was gone. I twisted my head this way and that way trying to recapture a sighting. No use. I settled for thinking I had to have been mistaken.

I headed back to the booth.

When I got there I found even more going on than when I'd left only a little while before. Thom Racina had arrived and taken his vigil at the front of the booth. He half-stood half-sat on a tall stool in front a table laden with all his paperbacks and was talking to a handful of onlookers explaining which book was more of a mystery and which one was more of a thriller and why each person should buy this one or that one. The he said, "Why don't you each just get three of them and I'll make you a deal for $20 even." Heads started bobbing in concentration and Thom saw me, "Is that OK?"

"Sounds good to me," I confirmed.

Twenty dollar bills flashed out of pockets and Thom said, "Oh no I just sign'em. Pay the gal on your right. Now how do you spell your name?" He was a pig in his own mud, wallowing in self-glory. He made it look so easy.

I spotted a friend of mine talking to a stranger and wandered up to their sides. My friend was a black man of incredible masculinity and fitness and he was talking to a tall gray haired man of rugged comeliness bearing a knowing confidence.

"Agent Henry," I intruded. "I see you made it."

He turned to me and grinned. "I wanted to be here."

"I'm glad," I said and extended my hand. "Welcome aboard. Just remember your promise."

He held up his right hand in a mock oath. "If I should open a store of my own I swear I won't do it within 75 miles of Palm Springs."

"One hundred," I corrected. "Did you see Detective Daily? She's working crowd control here today. I saw her earlier."

"No, not yet."

"She said she picked up some easy overtime working the book fair. I'm sure we'll run into her." In my exuberance I was ignoring the man Patrick was talking to when I'd walked up. I noticed him now and Patrick began introductions.

"Now, have you met our esteemed friend here?" Henry continued, "You may have heard of him. He tried to help us out on the case. Xanthe Anthony meet Larry McMurphy."

43
Returning to the Scene

THOM RACINA WAS IN THE MIDST OF A HAY DAY. He was having one of those rare magical moments when the sun just keeps shining and shining like unto an angel in a heavenly spotlight. He was radiant.. He could do no wrong. His readers were finding him. His books were being enjoyed, read, devoured and they wanted more. From where Thom sat there was an endless sea of milling heads floating down the arteries of the fair and they were coagulating in front of his table.

"Thank you, Thank you. I'm glad you enjoyed it. Is this your wife? Which was your favorite? Me too. Thank you for coming. Are you sure one is enough? I have a special three for $20 deal today. You would? How would you like it signed? Thank you."

His stockpiles were running low. Soon he would have to go fetch more. He had had no idea that today would be such a success.

When there were only two people in front of him he signed the last few books, laid a placard on the table saying he'd return in 30 minutes and excused himself. Jill said she'd watch the table and tell any fans he'd be back shortly.

Walking through the fair was a wonderful feeling. He was like a newly crowned Prince in a bazaar of paupers and Kings. He had arrived and was enjoying his moment. He walked slowly to savor the flavor. No other authors table was more engaged than his. Oh sure, some had longer lines but the buzz, the electricity of the admirers was no more alive than his were. He relished the warmth of admiration he'd received.

The Author Murders

The only thing that could be better than this was more of the same. He briefly wondered how an author could grow tired of this life. He knew it happened. It was common knowledge that many authors, actors, celebrities after seeking the spotlight and attaining it would become a recluse and hide from their fans almost as if their admiration could somehow become stifling, constricting, smothering. But that would be another day after a lifetime of letting the light fall on him. For now, he would bask in all the fame and glory he could draw.

His car was parked in a garage near the entrance to the fair. He still drove the old BMW 325i rusting around the edges but that would soon change. He'd been driving them since he was a kid and they looked like refrigerators. A new one would look nice on him, definitely another rag top. His next novel was already in the works and it seemed to be the best work he'd done so far. All it needed was a climactic ending. He even had a title for it: Deadly Games.

He'd parked one level down in the basement because finding a spot was easier. Most attendees went up the ramp to find a space rather than down. Here the spaces were plentiful, not all of them taken. He slid his key into the trunk lock and gave it a turn. The locks of the car clicked open as the trunk popped.

"Could I have your autograph?" A Startled Thom turned to meet his fan.

"You?"

* * *

Agent Henry, Larry McMurphy and I returned to the Celebrity books booth each loaded down with several volumes of our favorites, laughing and joking like old friends which we were already well on our way to becoming. The booth was busy and I saw Thom's placard on the table. Milo was standing in the far back corner answering questions in rapid fire and Jill was speed checking the register up front like a grocery clerk on the first Monday of the month. The clientele was shifting positions like an overstuffed kennel of kittens; commerce in motion. I called to her over the tops of everyone's head to catch Jill's attention.

"Where's Thom?"

She wiped her brow with a hand clutching a twenty dollar bill. "He went to his car to get some more stock."

I waved thanks and turned back to my friends. "You wanna come with me to help him out. I think he's going to need everything he's got."

"If you don't mind. I'd like to get something to drink," said Patrick. It was still hard not to think of him as Agent Henry."

"I'll go with you," offered Mr. McMurphy.

* * *

Back at Thom's car, Leonard was confronting Thom like the dearly departed loved ones reunited they were.

"You've really grown in your craft."

"I've worked hard at it."

"My help didn't hurt you either."

"I'm not sure what you mean."

"Oh, come on. Are you saying I did nothing?"

"What did you do?"

"It was your idea."

"Are you afraid to admit it? Or are you just afraid of being open about our love?"

"You're scaring me. What are you talking about?"

"I did it all for you. Just like you wanted. So we could be together."

"I like you…I mean I loved you…briefly. But it was never meant to be permanent."

"But you promised!"

"Promises are made to be broken."

* * *

We came down the stairs of the parking garage and found Thom talking to someone hidden behind the open trunk lid of his car.

The Author Murders

They were engaged in an intimately emotional conversation that included big hand gestures. The guy he was talking to was muscular in a lean sort of way. He had a great tan, black hair and stubble growth for a beard. He looked a little familiar. I stopped in my tracks and Thom saw me and McMurphy. The guy poked Thom in the chest and Thom grabbed his hand.

"NO!" Thom yelled as he was pushed backwards half falling into the bed of his trunk. The guy saw Thom looking in our direction and he turned towards us with one hand grasping Thom's shirt.

The antennae directing my life picked things up in slow motion. Time dropped to 1/33rd speed.

Larry McMurphy reached into the back of his jeans and pulled out a snub nosed derringer. He saw the surprised look on my face at the fact he carried a gun and replied with a simple, "Texas is a big state," and then to Thom's friend he said, "Leonard, you aren't going to get a way a second time."

Leonard reeled Thom out of the trunk and propped him as a shield while pulling out his own gun, something with a square barrel. He fired a shot that zinged off the cement near my feet.

"I've got fifteen more of those Mr. McMurphy," he yelled. "And you've only got six, if that."

"All I need is one," said the author. He held his gun like a pro, with one elbow slightly cocked and gripping it in both hands at eye level. McMurphy danced to the left. Putting some distance between us, forcing Leonard to bounce his attention back and forth between us but mostly focused on aiming at Thom's head.

My equilibrium caught up with the world. "Wait a second! Wait a second! Leonard I know you. This isn't you." I was holding each hand palms out toward McMurphy and Leonard, trying to direct them each to halt like a traffic cop in a nasty intersection.

"He doesn't love me," Leonard cried. He pulled the gun away from Thom's head long enough to wipe his eyes. Not long enough to gain an edge.

"He's crazy," Thom shouted. He was struggling to keep his balance. He was being drug backwards on his feet.

"I did it all for him. So he could be a star."

"Shoot him," yelled Thom. He was pleading with McMurphy. "He's done it before. He'll do it again."

"No. No. NO. You're a liar. That's all you do."

"But I'm not a liar Leonard," stated McMurphy taking baby steps forward. "I'm telling you the God's honest truth when I say that I'll put a bullet in you if you don't stop this right now. Let Mr. Racina go and put down your gun."

"Don't you see," the waterworks were on. "I was clearing a path for him. Eliminating the competition and he knew it."

"You did nothing for me. I did it myself." Thom had regained his legs under him. He tried to step away but Leonard gave him a hard shove towards the bookman blocking Mcmurphy's view long enough for the shooting to start. Thom slumped forward as his abdomen exploded outward in a scarlet spray. A second shot sizzled off the ceiling and started a car alarm whooping.

The cowboy author got off a round that clipped Leonard's foot and then he took one into the shoulder himself that spun him to the floor. Leonard fired again in my direction and with nowhere nearby to hide I covered myself with my hands and prayed.

When only the car alarm was sounding a few seconds later I lowered my hands, expecting to see the gun inches from my face and instead saw Thom bleeding on the garage floor, holding his hands under McMurphy's as they both applied pressure to Thoms wound. Mcurphy failed to acknowledge the fact that his shoulder had a bleeding hole of its own.

You'll be alright," McMurphy said. "Keep the pressure on it. But I have to go. Help will be here soon." He stood and stalked off the way we'd come, seemingly more machine than man, as if he couldn't rest until the job was finished. There was a trail of bloody footprints fumbling down a tunnel leading out under the road. A security guard was coming down the steps as we passed him.

"Get on the radio," instructed McMurphy. "That man needs an ambulance."

The tunnel was dimly lit with wire covered bulbs and it only ran about fifty yards, ending in a flight of stairs granting entrance to one of the buildings. I stayed a few feet behind the bookman but followed dutifully. He had a gun and I didn't. A metal door with a narrow window opened into a marble hallway. The footprints smeared to the left and we followed. Coeds stepped in and out of the rooms, looking surprised at the state of us and instantly acknowledged that one of us had a gun. They pinned themselves up against the wall. The third one we saw, a girl in a short skirt sporting a glittery top on that read 'Pepsi' pointed to another door that also had a sign on it reading 'NO ADMITTANCE.'

We pushed forward. It was a large room filled with a crowd of men wearing sports coats with padded elbows. The women all had business suits. They all wanted out, there were plenty of exits but at the far end of the room, near the buffet table, Leonard had one of the men adorned with a stylishly groomed beard in a choke hold. This was the green room. This was where all the authors went to hide from their fans before going to their next lecture or signing. This was supposed to be their safe haven and it had been invaded.

I recognized the man Leonard now held. His name was Sandy Ford Johnson and he was a legend of the Mystery trade, always writing books with the word Prayer in them; A Prayer for Darkness, Winter Prayer, Secret Prayer. Whatever. Right now I guess he was saying his prayers. I hoped for his sake someone was listening.

Larry McMurphy, relentless as the black and white vintage cowboy Sheriff's he wrote about recomposed his earlier gun gripping stance and began creeping forward again, restating his claims.

"Leonard, how many times are we going to do this?"

"I've still got 12 bullets left. I can make you rich Mr. Texas book man. Whose books do you have the most of?"

"My own. But you only have ten bullets left and you don't want to kill anymore. Let's go outside and talk." McMurphy was halfway through the room. As we passed people I started directing them towards the back of the room. I looked over my shoulder and saw some of them were leaving. A policeman swam through the throng and helped people out. Turning back to Leonard I could see two other doors creep open. Through one of them stepped FBI Agent Patrick Henry, his training confidently in place with his gun drawn and through the other came a blonde policewoman, wearing a bicycle cop's uniform and brandishing her weapon: Detective Susan Daily.

"It's time this all came to stop Leonard," McMurphy continued.

"But I can clear him a path to the top of the charts. He will love me. I know it." Leonard was convulsing. He was starting to quake. It's a symptom of a man going through a breakdown. The fear of where he was and what he'd done was overtaking him. He was losing his reality. His fears had come home to roost. "I can make things right. I did it for him. I owed a lot of money. I was pushed. I can fix this," and he went to place his gun at Sandy Ford Johnson's temple. Before it touched his scalp several shots rang out and Leonard danced away from his captive like a puppet on strings. He flipped onto the buffet table, landing on his back and knocking over a waterfall of champagne glasses, a fountain pouring bubbly onto his chest.

The last of the authors fled from the room. Mystery writers are more bluff than the stuff they adore. The press flooded in and started taking pictures. Every agency of the greater Los Angeles area had sent their best third rate reporter to cover celebrities writing children's book and today they got the break they'd always been waiting for. The Biblio-killer, the Author Murderer, or whatever other name some rag scribe or tube jockey had given the case got to see the final result of nearly six months investigations ending in a blazing shootout. It took a phalanx of security guards and LAPD to clear the room again but not before the feeding frenzy of publicity had been gorged. Within minutes there'd be images all over the news.

44
Wrapping the Case

I HAD OTHER COMMITTMENTS. The case would be finished by the professionals. Detective Daily rode with Leonard to Los Angeles County General Hospital. Agent Patrick Henry rode with Larry McMurphy to Cedars Sinai. Mr. McMurphy made a remarkable recovery. The bullet had missed every major artery and organ. He was treated as an outpatient and made it back the book fair on the second day and although he was quite stiff he said it'd take more than a punk with a gun to keep him away.

Leonard wasn't so lucky. He died before he made it to a doctor. He was pronounced D.O.A. – Dead on Arrival. Detective Daily tried to get him to talk but he was in a delirious state, only repeating Thom's name over and over again and saying "I loved you. I loved you." It gave her an eery feeling. One she followed up later with questions to Thom who'd came to the same hospital an hour earlier. Thom denied ever having met Leonard before and there was nothing else linking the two. Leonard was painted a crazed fan overcome with celebro-felicity. All the evidence supported this conclusion and the case was closed within a few days. After he died, Susan made a search of his personal belongings. He had a backpack with him and inside was the leather bound token with the gold stamp of a dump truck embossed on its cover.

Back at the book fair, delivery trucks began arriving as my own plan came to fruition. Men in uniforms began ferrying vases full of flowers to and fro up and down aisles of book dealers, delivering the bouquets to the major publisher's booths. I followed a brightly dressed young man carrying a bunch of yellow daisies set around three large sunflower blossoms and humbly stood nearby as he presented them to the women of Simon and Schuster. The women cooed over the flowers. They were thrilled and mystified as to who had sent them. They gave the uniformed man a tip and then pleasantly forgot him, enthralled with their gift. The eldest and coincidentally best dressed lady with an impeccable gray coiffure of hair plucked the card from its plastic stem and read it. As she finished reading, I stepped forward and introduced myself.

"Hello ladies, may I ask who's in charge here?"

"Why I am," said the lady with the card.

"My name is Xanthe, Xanthe Anthony. I was wondering if I could have a moment of your time?"

"Oh my," she said, placing the card over her heart and extending her other hand which I took gently and kissed even softer. Flustered but at the same time a woman of substance, she regained composure quickly. "You sent these. They're beautiful. Thank you. What can I do for you?"

"I was wondering if I could talk to you about sending some authors out to my store for some book signings."

"I might be able to help you. That's what I do. Who do you like?"

We talked and she was polite. She made no promises, but she was genuine and promised to check the author's schedules. She did offer two or three mid-level up and comers and I graciously accepted. I was straight forward, curt and persistent. In the course of a few minutes she gave me her direct number and when she said, "I'll let you know about the others, perhaps we could do something mid-week with the others you want…they do both San Diego and Los Angeles on the weekends mostly," I told her that Thursdays were my best day. She said we'd work it out and I thanked her and left.

There was another delivery man heading down a far aisle and I honed in on his direction. He stopped at the Random House booth and I did my introductions again. I couldn't have planned a better way to make a first impression on the pit bosses of literature. To those who were swooned by sweet talked I flattered with pure granulated chi-canery. To those who were more impressed with knowledge I talked of my specialties of the trade and to those who'd heard the sirens I spilled the beans from inside information that I'm sure Detective Daily would've preferred I'd kept zipped in my pie hole. I had a motive. I had the opportunity and I made the most of my fifteen minutes of fame. In the course of two hours I made more connections than I had in two years of phone work.

I got back to the booth near closing time. Jill had made a pile of Thom's books and they'd been picked over like cattle bones in the desert. The news had been to the booth more than a half dozen times and Thom's star was rising faster than a thermometer in August. He was going to be very famous very quick. In the near future he was going to get more exposure than he ever dreamed. We all were.

The news included a showpiece of a story for the detectives involved. For a few weeks it grabbed headlines and broadcasts throughout the country. The case was dubbed The Biblio-Murders by the press and it retained high ratings for weeks. Charlie Gibson even did a piece on Good Morning America by interviewing Thom from his hospital bed. He not only lived but achieved a full recovery from his wound. The bullet had punctured a lung and narrowly missed his heart. He was told that if he'd not been close to a major medical center he most definitely would have drowned in his own juices. As it was, three weeks later he was back to regular duty at Villagefest. Before that though, he made a gift of sending Larry McMurphy back to the Festival of Books with a dolly full of signed paperbacks for our second day of sales. McMurphy even shared one bit of news from Thom that made us all quaver in anticipation, "Oprah called."

* * *

Accolades were awarded to all the Detectives who participated. Detective Daily went up a grade; Palm Springs Detective Donald Craft did also. Brian Andrews went all the way to Lieutenant only a month after the case. Apparently, he'd been engaged in several other stings and therefore more amply rewarded; of course, in the local papers, the Chief over stated Andrew's and Craft's participation in the Author Murders. As the Chief told it, they'd been a key factor in the investigation for months before Daily even came to Palm Springs, through a special cooperative multi-jurisdictional task force. Without their help, Leonard may never have been caught. I'm just glad Detective Daily wasn't in town when this press release was revealed.

Agent Patrick Henry redeemed his good name due to his involvement in the case but he'd had it with trying to climb the ladders within the bureau. He wanted to try other things and had found a real love for literature. He followed Mr. McMurphy back to Texas and the two of them became best of friends. I still see them from time to time when they winter in Palm Springs. They've become my favorite snow birds.

* * *

Milo had his own adventures over the balance of summer.

First off, as a reward for his sleuthing, I offered him a more substantial job. I told him he could either work full-time for me at $10 an hour or he could earn 15% of gross online sales if he would take on the position of Internet Sales Manager. I explained to him that I thought the commission was a better deal even though it didn't come with any guarantees. He stopped me in mid-sentence and said, "I got it. I'll take the commission." He never regretted it, nor did I. In less than two months he'd tripled online sales and was making a healthy income.

He started calling his mom again and after a couple of frantic phone calls from her, he went back to Baltimore and brought her and his little sister out west. He came back with a fresh shiner over his eye and I didn't even ask. I knew there had to be an altercation with his step-dad but Milo didn't seem to want to talk about it and I let it go. He must have been happy with his outcome. He started putting on weight shortly thereafter. "Didn't I tell you," he said one day when I commented on it, "Mom bakes like Betty Crocker. She's the best." She must have been. Milo was no longer rooster boy. He was turning into more of an Ostrich.

$$* \quad * \quad *$$

The Stephen Knightly Book turned a new chapter.

Stephen's Dump Truck ended up at a police auction due to new drug property search and seizure laws. A situation I heartily disagree with. Because of Leonard's involvement with drugs coinciding with his murder spree, all of his possessions were confiscated and put up for sale on the grounds they were attained due to his drug dealings. A farce if there ever was one. The bulk of his property had been acquired through theft, divorce and murder. Drugs were a co-factor, but where does the law draw the line? The police drew it on the narrow side of confiscation. Possession is nine-tenths of the law and when the police hold the possessions and the law then they get to draw the line.

Detective Craft told me of what was going on with the book. I'd asked him to keep me informed and he did. The book was set to sell at an auction of seized property in Chula Vista that sold everything from automobiles to computers to jewelry to Zoot suits and anything else gathered by Police departments all over southern California.

I had my own reason for keeping an eye on the book and it wasn't just the prospect of selling it for a profit. I wanted to talk to Tracey. I hadn't forgotten about her. Perhaps the book would give us a better chance to introduce ourselves.

Pulling out my black book, I called her on the phone, "Tracey?" I said when she picked up. "I have some good news for you."

"Who is this?" she asked.

"Xanthe."

"Oh."

I admit, her response was deflating, yet I persisted. "I know more on your book. Would you like to know where it is?"

"Surely. I've watched the papers for news of it since the event." Her voice pitched upwards. "But, the killings seemed to get all the focus."

"The book will be put up for auction. It's not fair that it should go this way. But there is time to act if you want." I figured it would take the influence of a creative attorney to redirect the book's future. Property seizure laws were a new thing in the country and while some courts wanted to establish new law, others would act with judicial restraint, letting the police behave as they wished. Popular opinion was that anyone who ended up in this situation deserved what he or she got and fact was judges were elected to their benches. A judge who was soft on drug dealers held little chance of getting re-elected.

Considering the costs of hiring an attorney and combining the likelihood that his services would not be on a short term, even if an injunction could be issued to prevent the auction of the item, Tracey decided instead to attend the auction and be a bidder.

Her decision may have been the wisest choice when balanced against the injustices of a system leaning on the probability of guilt without a conviction. Leonard did have and sell drugs. They had been married when he took the book. It was taken in the course of an official investigation from a vital crime scene. Her chances were slim at pre-empting the sale. I agreed with her decision.

Furthermore, I wanted to see her and told her so. "Would you like to go out sometime?"

"Xanthe," she began. It's always a bad sign when a girl begins a sentence with your name after you ask her out. "I admit I found you interesting..."

"But," I inserted.

"But," she continued, "I met you in the arena of my ex-husband. You are both book dealers and the similarities between the two of you are more than physical. I admit, you are a handsome man and I do like blondes but I simply can't at this time."

"At this time?" I thought this might be my opening.

"Maybe at some other point in my life; if we didn't have the connection we do now, if the timing was better and the circumstances different. Then maybe."

"I understand," I lied. I made notes in black book for another day.

The Author Murders

* * *

The day of the auction came and I found myself wandering around, perusing the display cases, looking at the Rolex's trying to tell the difference between the fakes and the real things. The people who knew how to spot real gold and gems really had the rest of the world by the balls. It made me wonder why there are so few books on the subject. I guessed that those with the knowledge were not too eager to share it.

I was tapped on the shoulder as I stared into a glass case with at least fifty time pieces crammed into it. Bumped would be a better word for it. "Excuse me," I said as I looked up.

"Excuse yourself," said the man with his arm in a cast. He wore a Tommy Bahamas shirt and had a Bosnian accent.

"Michael Donlagic," I exclaimed, letting my mouth grow into a smile and spreading my arms wide to mimic his usual gesture. "You look like crap. And it couldn't have happened to a nicer guy." He did look like crap. His face was swollen and he looked a little softer, a little older. His hair a little grayer and badly cut.

"My new girlfriend has a new boyfriend. We had a disagreement." He was still mean as hell and not worth underestimating. "Been in any public restrooms lately," he laughed as he walked off.

His appearance here told me he still had a buyer for the book. The auction could go higher than I anticipated. At the beginning of the day, I had thought the book to be an obscure item, demanding little notice amongst a large audience in attendance.

Worried, I did one last check throughout the room. Most of the buyers were of poor taste in both clothing and haircuts; your typical fire sale bidders looking for an undersale. But there were a few people scattered about wearing nice suits and sport coats. One man looked a little like the Hermitage Books seller I'd seen around at some of the Book fairs in Las Vegas and Glendale. There was another man too well dressed to be missed in the back of the room and he had a cell phone welded to his ear. I had new insight into how the day might transpire.

I took my seat to wait for the item to come up. Minutes before the auctioneer began his ramblings, Tracey took a seat in the front row. As I remembered, she was a vision: stylish clothes cutting her soft figure with class and hair that set the world on fire. Then I looked over at Donlagic and my anger boiled. If no one else, he could not get this book.

The bidding began at $50 and Tracey raised her paddle. Donlagic immediately raised his too. The bids escalated quickly 50-60-70-80-100-110.

I was about to jump into the fray when Tracey did a bold move. "One thousand dollars," she said raising her paddle.

"One thousand dollars to the lady up front," the auctioneer chimed. Patrons not already involved turned their heads to see what was selling. "The bid is to you sir." The auctioneer motioned to Donlagic,

"Fifteen hundred," Donlagic returned.

"Fifteen hundred. Mam the gentleman says fifteen hundred. What shall you bid?"

"Twenty Five hundred," Tracey returned.

The crowd gave murmurs of "Ohhh" and "Oooh" and "Ahh." People began to disregard the displays scattered about to watch.

"The bid is twenty five hundred to you sir." The auctioneer saw no need to jibber jabber like a man with rubber lips. He stated the amounts in clear crisp tones.

Before Donlagic could speak the man with the cellphone shouted, "Three thousand."

Another man in nice clothes in the middle of the crowd held up a paddle, "Four thousand."

Donlagic's head spun like an owl and he joined the fray, "Five thousand," demanded Donlagic.

"Five thousand," the auctioneer repeated.

Without even being asked, Tracey said, "Ten thousand."

A crowd had gathered. If the people hadn't pulled up close to the seats, they were in them. Each bid was bringing sounds of "Wow."

"Eleven thousand," shouted Donlagic. It seemed his dander

was up. He was getting mad.

"Fifteen thousand," said the man with the cellphone.

The auctioneer was a mere spectator at this point. He would look at each of the participating bidders. He needn't make a comment. They heard each other just fine without his interruptions.

"Twenty thousand," came from Donlagic, he popped a couple of pills into his mouth and chased them with a Dr. Pepper.

And then Tracey did a strange thing. She'd been going up in Five thousand dollar increments but she increased her bid substantially.

"Thirty thousand dollars," she hollered.

Donlagic began cussing at his friend he'd brought with him and threw down his paddle. He was out.

The room was quiet; on pins and needles. Other than some of the cars, nothing had gone for this much money at auction all day and it was on an item few people in the room would have even paid attention to, let alone a sum such as this.

"Fifty thousand dollars," shouted the man in the middle.

"Seventy-five thousand," shot the man on the cell phone.

Tracey looked a little weathered; like a ship captain caught in a storm. I saw her set her lip and then she held up her paddle, "Ninety-five thousand."

People watched. It took the auctioneer a second to gather his wits. "The book is ninety-five thousand." The room took a breath.

Tracey still didn't respond. The book was nearly five times more than it was when it was yanked off eBay. I was sure she was evaluating how badly she wanted it.

"The auctioneer looked at the two men, one of them shook his head no. He too was out of the auction. The man on the cell phone held up a finger to prolong the moment.

"Ninety-five thousand going once."

The man in the back lowered the phone from his ear and shouted at the top of his lungs, "One hundred and twenty-five thousand."

"One hundred and fifty thousand." Tracey shouted instantly and quieted the auctioneer who once again had to gather his senses.

"One hundred and fifty…" the auctioneer lost his track.

So, Tracey repeated herself, "One hundred and fifty thousand dollars if you please."

The auctioneer repeated her bid. He said it even louder than she had.

Donlagic pulled at his collar and flung his arms about in wild confusion. The man in the middle kept looking over his shoulder towards the man in the back. The man in the back spoke only a second more into his cell phone and then clapped it shut. He waved his hands in a show of non-compliance.

The auctioneer repeated the bid again. "One hundred and fifty thousand. Going once, going twice.".

No one breathed. No one moved. The thought of where she'd take the bid next if he stayed in must have been too much. Would she go another $25,000? Or would she go more? In the end all her opponents threw in the towel. They did nothing.

"Sold," the auctioneer roared, banging his gavel down hard.

The room let out a collective cheer. Hoorah. Hands applauded and everyone stood.

Tracey left with demure elegance. She walked to her left, across the length of the front row towards the payment booth. Everyone she passed either shook her hand or patted her on the back. "Well done" or "Good job" was said to her over and over.

I waited a couple minutes and then caught her as she was leaving the payment booth. I asked her, "Twenty five hundred was an odd amount to go for in an increase. Why'd you pick that number?"

"It felt right," she replied. "If I'd done less I believe that other man would have kept bidding. It had to be a significant increase to urge him to stop and it worked."

"It worked," I repeated.

"So it did."

"Well, good day," I said, wanting to leave before I made a mistake.

She surprised me. "Till we meet again," and then walked away.

The Author Murders

* * *

It was scarcely less than a week until I heard from her again. Eight days to be exact. She walked into Celebritybooks.com and told me she wanted to sell the book.

"It's not the same," she told me. "There are too many memories with it that I don't want anymore. Will you do this for me?"

"Of course I will." I'd have done even more had she asked. "How much should I sell it for?"

"You're the professional. Just make sure and make me a profit," and she placed the book in my hands.

At first I wasn't positive how I would do what she asked. She'd paid more for the book than any party I knew of so far in its history; more than any book I'd ever seen sell for. How was I to get more for her?

I was tossing the idea around with Milo of how we should do this. We could put it back for sale on eBay with a reserve amount setting the minimum we'd accept for a sale. The idea didn't feel right although it would be fun to watch the bids climb.

"We could just contact Baughmann's," injected Milo. "They wanted to buy it once. I'm sure they'd want it again."

"Yeah, but that'd still be a wholesale deal no matter what they paid, because they'd only buy it to resale it anyways. With the notoriety this book and Leonard's spree has developed, I'd like to get top dollar."

Then it hit me. Months ago, when the case first started and I needed information on Stephen Kinightly, I'd ordered a biography on him. The Stephen Knightly Story by Barry Green. In it, he wrote about why Knightly didn't ever publish a book of his early writings for mass consumption. It'd be a natural best seller. See the development of his style and creativity from the beginnings of his desire to become the great writer he is today. His fans would crave copies as a way of gaining an understanding of the boy their hero author had become as a man.

He didn't do it because he didn't think his first writings were worthy of publication. He felt that publishing lesser quality even at this

279

point in his life would diminish the perception of his life work; an insane concept. His fans would never leave him. They would only appreciate him more. But Stephen Knightly is the 800 pound gorilla of modern day lit and what he says goes.

So who better than he to buy Knightly's Dump Truck?

Milo got his email off the list of bids from the original eBay auction and we sent him an email telling him of the book owner's desire. He responded within a day stating his willingness to purchase. Now it was time to set a price.

$250,000.

He didn't even blink. The phone rang within an hour after I sent the proposal. It was Stephen Knightly himself wanting to pay me with a credit card. I told him I preferred a check because, and I hoped I didn't offend him; I'd been burned once on a large credit card purchase by an individual who later reported the card stolen. Not that I think he'd do that. But also I had to pay 2.5% of the price to the credit card company. Of course he'd increase the price to cover any costs, he said.

"Well, there's one more thing I want Mr. Knightly. Well two really."

"What's that?"

"I was wondering why? Why would you pay so much for your own work? I mean you don't have to answer this I guess. But, I just don't understand. Why do you want this so much? It can't just be what I'd read, that you didn't want your writings as a young man published because you thought it beneath your standards. So why?"

"When I am ready to have these writings printed I will do so. And one day I will do just that. When I do, this will all seem like small potatoes. And your second thing?"

Oh yeah, I almost forgot.

"I'd like a letter from you, on your personal stationary, thanking me for selling you this book so I can have a memento of my own for all the trouble I've had with this whole scenario from its inception."

"No problem," he said. "I'll put the letter and the check in the mail today."

The Author Murders

He held to his word and I got the check and letter two days later via Federal Express. My bank had never seen a check so large deposited into my account and put a hold on it for a week. That was fine by me. I needed a couple of days and I'll tell you why. But first I want to tell you another little happenstance in the course of this whole adventure.

The following week, after the book was mailed off to Stephen Knightly, but before I'd driven Tracey her money up to her, minus my 20% commission, of course. The largest single profit I'd ever made on a book or anything else in my life. I liked the woman. She fascinated me. But, I was still a businessman and $50,000 would pay the rent for a long time. That and the prospect of many improvements to the store filled my head like dancing sugarplums.

In the interim of her getting her money and Stephen Knightly getting his book, I was visited by a repo-man.

He came into my store wearing cover-alls and dangling a tooth-pick from his lip. He looked like a wide body reject from Hee-Haw, perhaps the younger brother-in-law who undeservedly got to marry the pretty cousin. He shuffled into my clustered world of books and showed me a key.

"I'm looking for where this might fit," he said. "I've been sent to repossess a Chrysler Le Baron convertible from one Leonard Beschloss. I hear you knew him?" This last was more of a statement than a question.

"Yeah, but I don't know where his car is. Have you tried his house?"

"Yeah-huh But it aint there and his roomie, or whatever he is, don't know nuthin about it. Or so he says. There's a hundred dollars in it for ya. If you can tell me where this key fits. I got it from his key ring out of the Police evidence locker." He said it Poh-leese.

A hundred dollars, I thought. My big commission hadn't slowed me down from making even a modest profit for little effort. "Show me the key again."

It was a standard Schlage key. Brass, with teeth down one edge and the other left straight. It belonged to a padlock. This much the repo-man had to know already. He probably surmised it went to a garage or a storage shed somewhere also. It must have been worth a hundred bucks to him just to see if I could narrow down his search to a single trip. Leonard had bought the car up in Orange County while he and Tracey were still married. The repo-man just wanted to get back home before dark.

The key was stamped with a code on it that read E-41. I figured the repo-man would have checked the storage facilities in the Palm Springs area. If he hadn't he wasn't worth his salt in the first place. I knew of three storage shed places around Joshua Tree that used letters. This man wouldn't know this, but I did. Because, I'd been to enough shed sales to learn this over the years. Most used strictly numbers. This cut the search down demonstrably.

He followed me in his truck and found what we were looking for at the second lot we scouted: All American Storage. There was a unit E-41 and it had a matching brass Schlage padlock on its roll up door. We parked the repo-man's tow truck just past the entrance to the unit and slid the key in the lock. It clicked. I was as excited as the first time a girl said yes to a dance.

The door slid upwards revealing a white Chrysler LeBaron convertible with a clean white roof. There was a dresser with clothes piled on top of it, a bed that looked like at one time it had been slept in and half a dozen book shelves filled with mostly leather bound books with gold gilded edges to the pages.

It was Tracey's Easton Press collection. I knew it as soon as I saw them. It had to be. There was no other explanation. I walked up to the shelves and pulled one. It was a signed copy of Robert Heinlein's Stranger in a Strange Land.

"There any money in those things?" the repo-man asked.

"Sometimes, if you find the right one," I said nonchalantly. "But, you usually have to dig through a lot of lard before you find the oil. If you know what I mean."

"Don't I know it," he said, putting the Chrysler in neutral and pushing it out into the alley between the storage units.

"What's going to happen to this unit?" I asked.

"Nothing. Police don't care about it. They already got their man. This Chrysler owner aint gonna come back for it. That's for sure. Why don't you go through it and see if you find anything. It'll all just end up being sold at auction if you don't." He chained the Le Baron up to his tow truck and let the winch drag it onto the bed. "Here's your hunskey," he said and thrust a 100 dollar bill into my hand. He flashed me a toothy grin and asked, "You want a ride back to your store?"

"No thanks," I said. "I think I'll stay here for a while."

"You're gonna need this then," and he added the key to my hand with the bill.

* * *

Tracey was thrilled to have made so much on the sale of the book. Apparently that kind of money was more substantial to her than I'd first realized. She was nearly equally overjoyed to learn I'd found her missing Easton Press Science Fiction collection. She wanted to go out immediately and get them. I told her I was hungry and asked if we could get dinner first. She bought me a fantastic meal at a place where the cost of a steak was more than what the repo-man gave me for finding the car. It was a quaint place called the Arches on Pacific Coast Highway that, even with my windfall, I will most likely never be willing to afford to eat at again. It was the best meal of my life; not only for the food, but the company. The second most intimate thing I know is sharing a meal. I had a great time getting to know Tracey and she must have had a great time too. Because she said she'd do it again.

I felt a little guilty about the whole affair though. I'd mentioned earlier I needed the time it took Stephen Knightly to mail me his letter and the check to clear. In that week I went to see a friend of mine. Her name is Martha.

See, the book and letter knightly sent me had a couple things in common. They were both by and about Stephen Knightly for one thing. For the other, they were both 8 1/2 by 11 inches; the size of a normal sheet of paper. The book had been made on photocopied sheets of paper and then privately bound, which made me think. If this could be done once, why couldn't it be done again?

Martha is a bookbinder by trade and does excellent work. She's also a Board member for the Palm Springs Library and has access to top quality photocopiers. In those eight days, she was able to disassemble Leonard's book, photocopy the pages and reassemble the book, leaving no trace this had ever been done.

One week after my mailing off Stephen Knightly's copy, Martha finished building me another book, just like the first in all ways but one. This book is also red leather, with marble end boards and gold gilded edges with gold print and a dump truck on its cover and spine. The only difference is in the front of my copy, bound into the book itself, and is a signed letter from Stephen Knightly on his own stationary. I don't keep it at the store; it's in my own library, at home, where I can pull it out every now and then and enjoy it personally.

* * *

A few days later, I thought I was done with the whole affair of the Author Murders when I got invited to Leonard's funeral. I was more than a little uncomfortable about the idea at first. I had played a significant role in his death. But all my Palm Springs book friends were there, Sal Moor, Gary Craig, Justin Blake and Brad Connifer and they begged me to come. Besides I had known Leonard before his fall from grace.

I ended up standing next to Leonard's mom, a little old lady wearing her Aunt Bea outfit and a pillbox hat with a short veil. After the ceremony I made my condolences to her and she said, "At least he was happy in his relationship finally at the end."

"Oh yes, Justin is a nice man." I didn't want her to know about their troubles.

"Justin?" She declared. "His boyfriend wasn't named Justin. He had a Mexican boyfriend Tomas. I never got to meet him but apparently he was an old friend from one of his earlier homes."

"What do you mean?"

"Leonard was adopted. But please don't judge him or me by that. He had a hard life before I got him and even after I raised him.

All one can do is try their best."

Her words kept ringing in my ears. I'd missed something important. "He'd been adopted. He'd run into an old friend." As the days passed, it was making sleep difficult for me. Her words filled me with more questions than answers. I thought about my earlier assumptions that the killings were never about money. There simply wasn't enough to be made to justify all that bloodshed. This was further proved by all the booty discovered at the All American Storage facility.

I called the storage sheds main office and told a white lie. "I'm sorry but I'm settling the debts for the estate of my deceased brother. I believe he had a unit rented there and if you wouldn't mind could you tell me the balance owed on unit E-41? I'd like to send you a check."

"There's really no point," I saw a feller empty it out of anything worth anything a short while back."

I knew he'd seen me even if he couldn't remember me exactly. "If you don't mind checking please, just so I can close the book on his finances."

"Let me check my accounts due log. No. It looks like we're the ones who should be sorry."

"I'm not sure what you mean," I asked.

"Well, we're going to owe you a check sir. There's still nearly two months left on the lease and it's paid in full. I'm sorry to hear about your brother. He was such a sweet man. Where can I send the refund to Mr. Racina?"

* * *

I called Detective Daily to tell her of my finds. She wasn't interested.

"Xanthe," she said in a school teachers tone. "The case has been closed for a month, besides there's no one to corroborate. Even if Thom Racina did play a part, we'll never prove just how much. The storage shed doesn't prove he had anything to do with the murders."

I argued my case but the new found evidence was a Pyrrhic victory. I knew. I knew. But I couldn't prove. I pondered my situation for days until I was at the point of having an aneurism. Then an epiphany hit me. I grabbed my blue notebook and called Justin Blake, I needed his help. And after Justin there was always Tracey. This story would make a fabulous book. The only thing I didn't know was, would it be fictional or true crime?

The End

An excerpt of another great Eric G. Meeks thriller:

Witch of Tahquitz

WHEN I WAS YOUNG, my mother would to tell me a ghost story to get me home before dark. It was about a witch-shadow in Tahquitz canyon that would swoop down on bad children, taking them away from their parents, never to be seen again. I thought it just a campfire tale used by adults to scare kids – at least, I thought so until Papa passed away.

Papa, my great-grandfather, died in 1992. In his will he left me a tattered old leather saddlebag that contained four items: an old Rochester camera, an undeveloped roll of film, a relic of a flintlock pistol which still works, and his constables log. In the log, he revealed a secret history of my family that had been kept from me my whole life. He was the second constable in the Village of Palm Springs.

The following story was the greatest case he ever cracked.

To fully tell it, I had to research many books, interview some of the oldest Indians in Palm Springs and investigate some areas of the city that are typically off limits to the general public.